The Hope of Her Heart

SHILOH RIDGE RANCH IN THREE RIVERS, BOOK 12

LIZ ISAACSON

ISBN-13: 978-1638760252

The Glover Family

Welcome to Shiloh Ridge Ranch! The Glover family is BIG, and sometimes it can be hard to keep track of everyone.

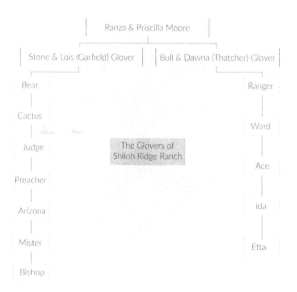

Ranza & Priscilla Moore

Stone & Lois (Garfield) Glover   Bull & Dawna (Thatcher) Glover

Bear	Ranger
Cactus	
	Ward
Judge	
	Ace
Preacher	
	Ida
Arizona	
Mister	Etta
Bishop	

The Glovers of
Shiloh Ridge Ranch

There is a more detailed graphic on my website. (But it has spoilers! I made it as the family started to get really big, which happens fairly quickly, actually. It has all the couples (some you won't see for many more books), as well as a lot of the children they have or will have, through about Book 6. It might be easier for you to visualize, though.)

Here's how things are right now:

Lois & Stone (deceased) Glover, 7 children, in age-order:

1. Bear (Sammy, wife / Lincoln (9), step-son, Stetson (newborn), son)

2. Cactus (Allison, ex-wife / Bryce, son (deceased))

3. Judge

4. Preacher

5. Arizona (dating Duke Rhinehart)

6. Mister

7. Bishop (Montana, fiancée / Aurora (16), step-daughter once they marry)

Dawna & Bull (deceased) Glover, 5 children, in age-order:

1. Ranger (Oakley, wife)
2. Ward
3. Ace (Holly Ann, fiancée)
4. Etta
5. Ida (Brady Burton, fiancé)

Bull and Stone Glover were brothers, so their children are cousins. Ranger and Bear, for example, are cousins, and each the oldest sibling in their families.

The Glovers know and interact with the Walkers of Seven Sons Ranch. There's a lot of them too! Here's a little cheat sheet for you for the Walkers.

Momma & Daddy: Penny and Gideon Walker

1. RHETT & EVELYN WALKER
   Son: Conrad
   Triplets: Austin, Elaine, and Easton

2. JEREMIAH & WHITNEY WALKER
   Son: Jonah Jeremiah (JJ)
   Daughter: Clara Jean
   Son: Jason

3. LIAM & CALLIE WALKER
   Daughter: Denise
   Daughter: Ginger

4. TRIPP & IVORY WALKER
   Son: Oliver
   Son: Isaac

5. WYATT & MARCY WALKER
   Son: Warren

Son: Cole
Son: Harrison

6. SKYLER & MALLERY WALKER
   Daughter: Camila

7. MICAH & SIMONE WALKER
   Son: Travis (Trap)

The Glovers know and interact with the several of the cowboys and their families at Three Rivers Ranch too... There's a lot going on in Three Rivers!

You'll see:

1. Squire and Kelly Ackerman

Mother / Father: Heidi (owns Ackermans bakery) / Frank

Son: Finn

Daughter: Libby

Son: Michael

Son: Samuel

2. Pete and Chelsea Marshall (Chelsea is Squire's sister)

4 sons: Paul, Henry, John, Rich

3. Reese and Carly Sanders: They're the admins for Courage Reins, Pete and Chelsea's equine therapy unit at Three Rivers Ranch.

Chapter One

Etta Glover bent to put baby Betty in her stroller, noting the closed door on Charlie's office. She'd picked up another sponsorship for the holidays, but Etta didn't mind coming down to take Betty and Preacher for their walk.

"Ready?" she asked once the six-month-old was all buckled in. Preacher Glover, her cousin, stood right behind the stroller, both hands on the handlebars, his big, black lab waiting patiently at his side.

"I get to push Betty." She raised her eyebrows, clearly telling him to move aside.

"I can push my own daughter in a stroller," he said, his voice like a drought in Texas.

"Of course you can," she said. "But it's my turn."

"It's been your turn every day this week." He shuffled out of the way, reaching for the sideboard to steady himself.

"If we don't hurry, it'll start to rain on us while we're out there."

"I checked the weather," he said, reaching for his cane. He hated it, but Etta had been given about ten talks from Ward, her brother, about how Preacher would try to take the easy way out of his physical therapy. He went to a facility three times each week, but it was important he walk every single day. Only by forcing him to use the muscles in his back, core, and legs would they heal.

"It'll be fine through lunchtime," he said, turning toward the side door without twisting his hips. "C'mon, Biscuit." He stepped outside onto a long, narrow porch that ran toward the back corner of the house and held the door for his pup. They went right instead of left, where Ward and Bear had built a ramp for Preacher.

Etta took an extra moment to tuck a blanket around Betty all the same, because the darling girl wouldn't like the wind should it gust up. And if anything was predictable about winter in Three Rivers, it was the wind.

"Two months," Preacher grumbled, loud enough for Etta to hear. She watched him go by the window in his slow, somewhat stilted gait. "How much longer, Lord? I'm workin' hard here."

Etta's heart bled for her cousin. He'd been in a terrible car accident over two years ago now. He'd had several surgeries, and just when it seemed like he was doing so well, something would happen. This last time, Preacher had fallen and reinjured his hip and lower back. He'd been experiencing sciatica pain since, and he'd had to relearn how to walk with the new limitations on his right leg.

He hadn't endured any more surgeries, and Etta thanked

the Lord for that each day. "Come on, baby Betty," she said. "You come with Auntie Etta, and let's go walk with your daddy." She aimed the stroller through the doorway and followed Preacher down the ramp, where he and Biscuit waited at the bottom.

He flashed her a tight smile. "Thank you for coming," he said. "I'm sorry I'm in a foul mood."

"You're allowed," she said. "Now." She took a deep breath of the cool air, felt it infuse her lungs and life with energy, and blew it all out. "Yesterday, we walked the full circuit—down around all the cowboy cabins, back up here, across the road, along Mister's new homesite, and back—in thirty-two minutes and twelve seconds."

It could only be maybe a half-mile to do all of that, so Preacher's pace wasn't anything to write home about. Still, he improved every single day, and Etta could go slow, listen to Betty babble about nothing, and enjoy time outside without having to say much.

"I'm going to set my timer for that, and our goal is to be right here, on this spot, before it goes off." She tapped on her phone, Preacher's eyes boring into the side of her head. She didn't care, not really.

Some in her family had called her *stuffy* in the past. *Stuck-up* had entered her ears a time or two. Mother had called her Miss Priss as a teen. Ida, her twin sister, used to say Etta was the sophisticated one while Ida the country girl. Etta could admit to liking nice things, fancy food at even fancier parties, and getting dressed up in pumps, pearls, and perfume just to go to church.

But in a lot of ways, she'd calmed down immensely in recent years. Since Noah Johnson, if she were being honest. He'd been one of her high-brow cowboy boyfriends. Rich, classy, mature—and a lot older than her.

Because of that, he hadn't wanted more children, and Etta had been unable to walk down the aisle and meet him at the altar. A stab of guilt poked right into her chest, though she'd come to terms with what she'd done, and she'd done her very best to make it right.

"Ready?" She looked up and away from her thoughts.

"A timer, Etta?"

"Let's go, baby," she said, pushing *start* on her timer. She put the phone in the cupholder on top of the stroller and took the first step. Preacher came with her while Biscuit trotted ahead, and she knew her cousin wouldn't talk. If she had something to say, she said it, but more often than not, they just walked together. Then she'd go inside and make fresh coffee and make sure Preacher got settled on the couch with his canine friend. By then, Charlie had been coming out of her office, and Etta had been going back up to the homestead.

It worked out that this morning walk got her back home about time to put together lunch, and since she didn't do field trips up to Shiloh Ridge in the winter, she'd been feeding anyone who wanted to come to the homestead for a week or so now.

After the successful Thanksgiving dinner a couple of weeks ago, where she'd invited August Winters and things had gone well with her core family of four siblings, their spouses, children, and Mother, Etta had considered asking him to come to the ranch for lunch. Or offering to meet him in town, as he had a very busy construction job.

He used to have a very busy construction job, she corrected herself. August had just taken a new job, and he was starting on Monday. He was moving into a new place today, as Etta had learned a few days ago when she'd texted him to see if he could get together this weekend.

They didn't see one another in person all that often, because he had a nine-year-old daughter he wanted to protect. Dating was new for him, he'd said, and Etta understood the complexities of having children and trying to fit a new love interest into the situation.

She was fine going slow and being cautious. It gave her time to make sure the man she'd started seeing was being honest with her. So many in the recent past hadn't been, and perhaps Etta wore jade-colored lenses in her dating glasses.

"You're lifting your leg well," she said.

"It feels good today," Preacher said.

Betty screeched and threw her plastic keys on the ground. Etta kept right on moving, bending to swoop them into her hand as she passed. The baby started to fuss, but Etta didn't give her the keys. She set them in the cup holder with her phone and kept a steady pace.

When Betty really got herself worked up, which only happened after a few more steps, Etta reached for the sippy cup in the other part of the cup holder. "Okay, Betty Boop," she said. "Enough of that." She stepped next to the stroller and extended the two-handled cup toward the girl. She had fat tears clinging to her lashes, which made Etta's whole soul light up. "Oh, you poor thing. Here's your milk. No more crying now." She made sure the girl had a good grip on the cup before she moved back behind the stroller.

The road snaked right and into the small cowboy community, and Biscuit, Preacher, and Etta went with it. "Looks like someone's moving in," she said, noticing two cabins down at the end, both with trucks backed up to them.

"Yeah, new hires," Preacher said. "I can't really do anything with birthing season, and I hired a couple of new men."

"Two people for what you do alone," she said with a smile. Preacher did not return it, and a sigh moved silently through Etta's body. "Preacher."

"I don't need praise, Etta. Not right now."

"I'm sorry," she murmured.

"I don't even know why I'm still foreman. I've told Bear and Ranger and Ward to get Judge to do it a hundred times. They won't let me resign."

"No one wants you to do that."

"What about what I want?" he asked, sliding her a glare out of the corner of her eye. "Instead, I have to hold a bogus title and then hire people to do what I can't. It's ludicrous."

"They wouldn't be foreman."

"Judge could do it."

"Judge doesn't want to do it."

"Then Mister."

"As soon as you're better, it's—"

"I'm not going to *get* better," Preacher said. "Why am I the only one who can see that?" He looked up into the sky. "Dear Lord, open their eyes to the reality of the situation I'm in."

"You *are* going to get better," Etta said, surprised by his out-loud prayer. "You're stronger and faster every single day. Why do you do the exercises if you don't believe you're going to get better?"

"So my wife won't leave me?" It sounded like a question, and Etta turned her full attention to him while she usually looked for rocks and potholes in the dirt road.

"Preacher," she chastised. "Charlie loves you just how you are. Sickness, health, fall, no fall. It doesn't matter to her."

Preacher looked away, his jaw tight. He finally said, "I know."

"Are you seeing anyone?" she asked.

"It's required to see a counselor when you do the level of physical therapy I do," he said.

"Good," Etta said. "After Noah, I—" She swallowed. "It helped me to talk to someone."

He looked at her. "I didn't know you went to a therapist after Noah."

"I did."

"You don't still feel guilty about that, do you?"

"Here and there, it jabs at me," she said. "But it doesn't hold me back the way it used to. In fact, I started seeing—" She cut off as she saw the man she'd started seeing. She and August hadn't kissed yet, but they'd held hands. They'd flirted *a lot* through text messages. They'd been out a few times.

"Etta?"

"He's right there," she said, her brain misfiring at her. What in the world was August Winters doing here? Taking a lamp and a frilly pink suitcase from the back of his truck? Her step slowed to the point where Preacher was moving faster than her, her eyes scanning for Hailey, August's daughter.

If he was moving in here—and it sure seemed like he was —then he'd have his daughter with him. Etta had met her, of course. Hailey had come to Shiloh Ridge on a field trip with her third-grade class a couple of months ago. August had come along to help chaperone, and that was how Etta had met him.

The handsome cowboy had asked for her number before the bus had left, and they'd been talking and seeing one another since.

"That's August Winters," she said as he disappeared into the last cabin on the right side of the road. "Did you hire August Winters?"

"Yeah," Preacher said slowly. He whistled for Biscuit to come back, as the dog had been trotting merrily along. As the black lab turned and started to return, Preacher looked at Etta. "Why? Should I not have?"

Etta suddenly wanted to come face-to-face with August. He knew she lived here at Shiloh Ridge. He knew her family —the Glovers—owned and operated it.

"No," she said, a bit of fire lighting inside her. "He's a great guy."

"Why do you look like you're going to rip his face off then?"

She got moving again, causing Preacher to hobble to keep up with her. August came out the front door, laughing about something. His fair daughter followed, and Etta quenched part of the flames burning through her.

August looked toward the road, and she knew the moment he'd seen her. His smile fell right off his face, and he dang near tripped over his own feet. She lifted one hand and both eyebrows, a silent demand to know what in the world was going on.

"Etta," he said smoothly, continuing toward her in a normal gait now. "Good mornin', Preacher." He bent down and patted Biscuit, bringing a doggy smile to the canine's face.

"Yeah, I don't know about that," Preacher said, his gaze volleying from August to Etta and back.

"What are you doing here?" Etta asked as Hailey arrived at his side.

"Miss Etta!" she said, throwing herself into Etta's arms. She softened, because she loved children, and she'd helped this one once upon a time. "Daddy got a job here as a cowboy. A real, live cowboy. We're gonna live in this cabin, and have all these fields to roam in, and there are horses *right there.*"

She looked like she'd harnessed the world in a single throw, and Etta couldn't help absorbing some of her enthusiasm. "That's amazing, Hailey. Has your daddy ever been a cowboy before?"

"Yeah, once," Hailey said, reaching up to push her wayward hair back out of her eyes. "We each get our own room here too. It's awesome."

"Hailey," August said, his voice definitely made of several emotions woven together. Etta wasn't sure how to pull them apart and analyze them fast enough. "Grab your laundry basket of dolls and take it into your new room, okay?"

"Okay, Daddy." She skipped over to the tailgate of the truck and did what her father asked.

He watched her until she went up the steps and then he turned back to Preacher and Etta. She put one hand on the stroller handlebars and cocked her hip, clearly female-speak for *Well?*

"Surprise," he said with that devilish smile that made her stomach turn to heated marshmallow and made her mind conjure up such fantasies as tasting his mouth with hers.

"Surprise?" she repeated. "That's what you have to say for yourself?"

Chapter Two

August Winters swallowed and looked at his new boss. He shook his head, far too much glee on his face. Preacher Glover wasn't going to help August, that much was clear.

"I told you I got a new job," he said. "This is it."

"You know I'm a Glover."

"Yes," he said with a smile. "As you've told me a million times now."

"I have not, you rascal," Etta said, stepping out from behind that stroller to swat at his chest. He laughed as he warded off her hands, managing to wrap one of his around her wrist.

Sparks and fireworks and entire forest fires moved through August's bloodstream. He hadn't felt anything like this with a woman since he'd met his wife, about fifteen years ago now.

Josie had been the sun to him, and he'd been willing to

be her satellite, revolving around anything and everything she did.

Etta Glover possessed the same magnetic, centrally strong pull on him that Josie had, and August had no idea what to do about it.

Etta finally stopped struggling, her own smile decorating her pretty face. She huffed out her breath and tugged on the bottom of her jacket. Her fingers slipped through his as they faced Preacher, and she said, "I was just telling Preach about this man I'd started seeing. And then, like fate, there you were. Here you are. Here he is."

August grinned at Etta, because it was rare to see her flustered. A slight pinkish hue had crept into her cheeks, and that only made August's desire for her shoot toward the stratosphere. He'd met her siblings and mother a couple of weeks ago, but not her cousins.

Well, Preacher he had, obviously.

"August Winters," she said. "I'm seeing August Winters."

Preacher lifted his right eyebrow. "Is this going to be a problem for me?"

"No, sir," August said quickly.

His boss's face melted into a smile as Etta started swatting at him, saying, "You—walk—yourself—around—Mister," with every playful whap against his shoulder and chest. August noted that she stayed on his left side, as Preacher walked with a cane on the right. He didn't know the whole story there, and he didn't need to.

He understood how some things weren't fun to talk

about—a fact that stared him in the face every single day that he continued to text and talk to Etta and he didn't bring up his late wife. She hadn't asked yet, but August suspected she would soon enough.

"We're never going to beat the timer now," Preacher said, laughing the same way August had at Etta's pretty pathetic attempts to punish him.

"Yes, we will," she insisted. "I'm just going to have to push you harder." She resumed her spot behind the stroller, the cutest, chubbiest baby girl sitting up in the front seat. "Lovely to see you, Mister Winters," Etta said, her chin aiming for the stars. "Let's go Betty Boop. Your daddy has walking to do."

She continued by him, and August watched her go, stunned that was really going to be the end of their interaction. No other questions? No invitation to the homestead for lunch? She'd been texting him pictures of all the delicious food she was feeding other cowboys this week, and it had taken a great deal of willpower to stay at his construction site and eat his sad peanut butter and honey sandwich.

They rounded the corner, Preacher tossing a look over his shoulder at August. Etta, however, did not. The woman was like a rock. A steel rock, and August wasn't sure if he liked that or if it intimidated him.

He turned back to his truck, plenty left to unpack. He got busy doing that, because he only had today and tomorrow to get himself and Hailey settled in this house before he had to start the job here at Shiloh Ridge.

Everything about this job was better than where he'd

been for the past seven months. He hated the construction job, because he had to be clocked in by six a.m., and that made life really hard with Hailey. He had to get her up really early and completely ready for school. Then his next-door neighbor watched her until the bus came at eight-twenty, and he had to rely on his nine-year-old to text him and let him know she'd made it to school.

It had been very difficult to get time off, and he'd barely made enough to keep him and Hailey in a one-bedroom apartment. He'd slept on the couch, his long legs hanging over the end of it and the sound of the refrigerator coming on to refill the ice-maker waking him without fail near two a.m. every night.

Here, this cabin stood tall and proud, brand-new and brilliantly white against the stormy sky threatening to drop rain at any moment. He had a front porch and a back one. No garage, but that was fine. Two bedrooms. Two bathrooms. A living room with really nice furniture—brand-new. Everything here on this part of Shiloh Ridge was new, and everything broadcasted dollar signs.

August picked up the pace with bringing in boxes when the first rumble of thunder shook the sky. He'd just managed to get everything on the covered porch when the raindrops fell, and he and Hailey could get it all in from there.

By the time he thought to check his phone, he had four messages from Etta. *Lunch at the homestead will be at noon.*

You're welcome to come.

Don't think just because you live here now that you can just come up and see me whenever you want.

Or maybe you can.

They'd all come within seconds of each other, because they had the same timestamp on them, and she must've only been around the corner from him when she sent them, because they were a good forty-five minutes old.

If you can handle two extra mouths for lunch today, Hailey and I will be there.

I suppose that's fine, Etta sent back, and August smiled at his device, at her ruse to make him think she wasn't as interested in him as she was. He could see the interest light up her dark blue eyes every time he looked at her. He wondered if he put off the same feelings, and he suspected he did. Josie had told him he wore everything right on the surface, and while he'd tried to shelve things and hide them after her death, he wasn't great at it.

Were you surprised to see me? He didn't need to ask to know. She'd worn her shock as evidently as he did.

Yes, she said, and he hated texting when he couldn't see her face. He'd spent some time with her in the past couple of months, and Etta had a quirky sense of humor buried beneath her more proper exterior.

I told you it was a good job and good move for me.

I'm glad, she said. *I really hope that's true.*

I do too, he sent, and he looked up, only getting an eyeful of the ceiling. But it was a brand-new ceiling, with pristine, white paint and the canister lights only found in the nicest, newest homes.

"Daddy," Hailey said, skipping into the kitchen from the hallway which led down toward the bedrooms and bathrooms. He even had a laundry room right here to do their wash. He'd taken so much for granted in Dripping Springs, and while he'd wanted to move to Three Rivers to give himself and Hailey a chance at a fresh start, he hadn't realized how much it would cost.

Monetarily, emotionally, spiritually, physically, mentally, it had cost him so much.

He once again paused and waited for the weight to come into his heart. When he thought of the farmhouse he'd left behind in the past, a load of bricks would settle on his chest. When he thought of how far away his wife's grave was and that he couldn't go see her whenever he wanted, someone pumped hot steel into his veins and his whole system turned to metal.

Today, however...it didn't. None of that happened, and August's heart kept beating blood through his body.

"I'm ready," he whispered. Josie had died four years ago, and he'd lived long enough in the darkness hanging over the farm they'd run together in the Hill Country.

"Daddy," Hailey said again, and he blinked himself back to the situation at hand.

"Yeah, sweets?"

"What do we have for lunch? I'm getting hungry."

"You know what?" August asked, grinning at his daughter. Sometimes he swore he could see Josie when he looked at Hailey, and right now was no exception. "Miss Etta invited us up to the homestead, thinking we might not have any food."

Hailey's face lit up, making his next question unnecessary. He asked it anyway. "Do you want to go?"

"Can we?"

"I know the way," he said with a smile. "She said it would be at noon." He looked down at his phone. "We've got about a half-hour. Let's make sure our beds are set up for tonight, and after lunch, we'll go get some groceries, and then we won't have to do anything else if we don't want to."

"Okay," Hailey said, and she started a joyous skip back down the hallway. Her room was still a jumble of boxes, clothes, dolls, and a bare mattress, so despite the exhaustion in August's soul, and the fact that he had to do everything himself, he dug in and started getting his daughter's bedroom put together.

No matter what, he would not let her down. Not again.

His phone buzzed in his pocket, and he suspected it would be Etta again. After finishing with the purple pony comforter his mother had bought for Hailey, he said, "Start hanging up your shirts, little lady," and he stepped out into the hallway.

He made it into his bedroom, which needed as much work as his daughter's, but he chose his phone over making up his bed.

Etta had texted: *What are you going to tell Hailey? Do I need to be prepared to say anything? Should I tell my family to play it cool? I don't want to put you in a difficult position, and I'm really fine to follow your lead on this.*

August looked up, the curtain-less window showing him

the wide world of Shiloh Ridge Ranch beyond the glass. He liked this woman. He liked Etta Glover a whole lot.

He'd never told Hailey about his feelings for anyone but her mother, and he didn't know how to get these new words about Etta to align in his throat.

Two things, he typed out, his thumbs flying to keep up with his brain. *Let's go to dinner one night next week. You tell me when you can, and I'll get a babysitter for Hailey. Two, I'd like a little more time before I tell Hailey about us. If that means you've got to tell your family something, I'm sorry. Can I have a little more time?*

He read over the text, the question in his mind—and surely the one that would be in Etta's—was, *Time for what, August?*

You can have as much time as you need, Etta responded quickly. *I'll just send them a text to let them know to keep things cool at lunch today. Not everyone comes, and most of my cousins don't know about us anyway. So this will open that can of worms...*

Sorry, he said. *Maybe just tell your siblings?*

No, Etta said. *I once hid a boyfriend for a long time from my family, and I don't want to do that. I'll just tell them about us quickly and ask them to please, please be reasonable and respectful. They can do it.*

August wanted to hear more about this other boyfriend. August wanted to know everything about Etta, absolutely everything, and that alone made him swallow hard.

"Help me," he whispered to the stark walls around him. He wasn't sure if he was speaking to God or Josie, but he knew he'd need help from one of them to protect his daughter...and his heart.

He couldn't believe he was going to take his heart out of the box where he'd stored it years ago, but he was. As he stood in his bedroom and read over Etta's texts from the past week, he realized he already had.

It beat in a new way, and it seemed to say *Et-ta, Et-Et-ta* with every thumping sound.

"Daddy," Hailey said, causing him to jump and guilt to gut him.

"Yeah."

"It's time to go," she said. "Can we go?"

"Sure, sweets," he said, shoving his phone in his pocket. Now, he just had to figure out how to hide all of his soft feelings for the lovely Miss Etta in the time it took to drive a mile up the hill to the homestead.

.

Chapter Three

Etta set a second pitcher of apple cider on the counter, trying not to flinch toward the front door when it opened. Tried, but failed.

She glanced over to Oakley, who sat at the counter with her daughter, Fawn, on her lap. She didn't look up from her phone, because people came and went from the homestead the way normal people turned on and off lights. It was a constant activity.

"These cookies are still warm," Holly Ann said. "There should be enough."

"You didn't have to bring them," Etta said, checking behind her sister-in-law to see if August had come in with her. "You might need them for your party."

Holly Ann gave her a smile and a half-hug, the sheet tray of dessert between them. "They bought five dozen cookies, and I'm taking six. Someone has to eat the dough, because these aren't gluten-free." She continued on toward the counter and slid the tray onto it.

A groan came out of her mouth as she sat on a barstool next to Oakley. "Did you ask her?"

Etta looked out the arched doorway, expecting her brother, Ace, to enter with his and Holly Ann's son, but no one stood in the foyer.

She took a moment to admire the angel tree and think of her father, then her grandmother and grandfather, while Oakley said, "No, I didn't ask her."

Etta took a deep breath and told herself to calm down. August said he'd come to lunch, and Etta had gotten confirmation from almost everyone in the family that they wouldn't embarrass her. She wasn't sure if that was truly possible, but she'd prayed for help, sent the text, and she supposed whatever happened during the meal would have to be what happened.

Her nerves trembled, and she turned back to her sisters-in-law. "Go ahead and ask me," she said.

Holly Ann exchanged a glance with Oakley, who nodded for her to go ahead. "We know you don't get to see August very often," Holly Ann said, blinking her long lashes like she was actually nervous. "And we wanted to ask him—or let him know—that we'll take Hailey anytime he wants. Or needs."

"So you two can go out alone," Oakley said. "It won't be weird, because they live here now."

"I asked Charlie, and she said she'd of course take Hailey anytime."

Etta hadn't expected such an offer, though now that it had been vocalized, she should've. The women who'd joined the Glover family over the past five years were some of the best Etta had ever met. Her heart expanded, and she turned back to the slow cooker which held the baked beans she'd put together.

"We won't ask him or offer if you don't want us to," Holly Ann said. "That's what we wanted to ask you. If we could talk to him about that while he's here."

Etta started to nod, the motion slow and somewhat deliberate. "I think that would be fine," she said, lifting the crock from the heating element of the slow cooker. She turned toward the counter and set the baked beans on a hot pad she'd laid out. "As long as Hailey isn't nearby. He is not ready to tell his daughter about...us. Dating. Going out." She met Holly Ann's eyes, then Oakley's, hoping they understood. Hoping they didn't find her naïve or weak for going along with August. "I've never had a child," she whispered. "I don't know what it would be like to have to talk to them about dating."

"No judgment here," Oakley said. "We'll respect his wishes."

Holly Ann nodded, and they all looked toward the side door as it opened, and Willa's voice filled the air. "Hold it, Cam. Lynn, hurry up...No, Chazzy, leave the ladybug outside."

A dog barked, and Willa told Tank to hurry up too.

They all spilled into the house—Willa with her four youngest kids and two dogs. She seemed frazzled and yet put together at the same time. "Mitch is here, isn't he?" A glance into the living room told her that no, her son was not there.

"Haven't seen him," Oakley said, getting up to go help her with the kids. "He's probably with Link, and Ranger was going to meet him, Bear, and Sammy in the equipment shed." She balanced Fawn on her hip and took Lynn by the hand. "Come get a cookie, sweetheart."

Chaz ran everywhere he went, and he barreled toward Etta, saying, "Etty, Etty, Auntie Etty," and she scooped him into her arms, laughing.

"Chazzy, look at your new shoes."

"He left his other ones outside," Willa said dryly. "One of the ranch dogs chewed holes in them."

"Meat," Chaz said, grinning down at Etta.

She burst out laughing. "Chazzy, did you leave meat in your shoes for the ranch dogs?"

He nodded, clearly pleased with himself, while Willa bobbed her head too, obviously *not* pleased with him. He turned his head and caught sight of Holly Ann, his face brightening. "Gun," he said, squirming to get down. "Gun, Gun, Gun."

He fired off the name as if he were the firearm, and Holly Ann picked him up saying, "His daddy's bringing him. They're not here yet." She reached for a cookie. "Willa?"

"He can have one."

Holly Ann gave him a cookie, and Etta turned toward the oven as the timer went off. She pulled out the tray of tin foil miniature meat loaves she'd made, then a second one. The other oven held two more trays, and she started piling the packets from one tray onto the first, deftly sliding in two more trays a few moments later.

The homestead filled with voices as she did that, and when she turned to face the group again, she found Bear had come in with Ranger and their little boys, Sammy and the rest of her kids now flowed toward the big picnic table, and a handful of Shiloh Ridge's cowboys stood in the arched doorway.

She needed to get some of these people eating. She pulled the step-stool out from beside the fridge and stepped up so she stood taller than everyone in the huge room. "Everyone," she called. "There's hot food ready, and we can start eating."

August appeared in the doorway, and Etta nearly fell off the stool. Her voice definitely went mute as August smiled at her. She could only stare at him, because he was just so handsome, and she'd enjoyed her time with him so much.

She felt all the eyes shift toward him, and he lifted his hand, his gaze sliding away from her and across everyone else. Etta cleared her throat and managed to say, "Ranger? Will you call on someone to pray?"

She got down from the stool and fell back against the sink, her heart pounding in her throat, ears, and stomach. *Get it together,* she told herself.

Ranger said grace himself, and then everyone waited. Etta realized she usually went over the food, welcomed everyone, and then faded into the background while she took a baby for someone who needed twenty minutes to eat without another human being on their lap.

"I made tin foil meatloaves," she said. "They'll have a little hash brown casserole in them, and there are more coming out of the oven soon, so don't be shy."

She got back on the stool, more in control of her emotions now. "Baked beans are here. Apple cider and sweet tea. If you want lemonade, you'll have to go to the outside fridge or next door to Bull House, where Ward and Dot have a secret stash." She grinned at her brother, who hovered not two feet from his very pregnant wife.

Dot was due three days ago, and still there had been no sign of the baby. She looked miserable, despite the smile on her face.

"Holly Ann brought cookies, and they're limited, so please just take one to begin with." Etta reached for one right now, actually. "Let's eat."

She got down off the stool and slipped into the background as people started to queue up and take the aluminum foil packets, baked beans, chips, and drinks.

She took a bite of the cookie, instant happiness filling her mouth with the sugar and chocolate. She had skills in the kitchen, but Holly Ann existed in another league. She caught Sammy's eye, and she chin-nodded toward the arched doorway.

Instead of running straight to August's side, Etta moved toward Sammy and reached for Heather. "I'll take her. I ate a bowl of baked beans before they came off the heat."

"Okay," Sammy said. "I'd love to meet August, if you aren't opposed."

"I'm not," Etta said. "Come with me." She finally faced

him, and he'd come inside the kitchen now. "Heya, Heather," she cooed at the baby. "This is August Winters."

The smile on her face felt genuine and real, and she moved her gaze from the baby to the man she would call her boyfriend.

"Hi, August." She leaned up and kissed his cheek.

"It smells great in here, Etta," he said, one hand landing on her hip and drawing her closer even as he kept the distance between them.

"Meat and potatoes," she said as if she hadn't put any effort into the meal. "Where's Hailey?"

"She saw a couple of boys out front with a dog, and that was that." He beamed at her. "I can grab her when it dies down a little bit."

Etta nodded and shifted her weight so Sammy could step forward. "This is Sammy Glover," she said. "She's been in the crazy the longest as the first in-law that joined us five years ago."

"Not true," Sammy said. "Oakley married Ranger on the same day I married Bear." She smiled at August in a way only Sammy could. She welcomed everyone to the ranch and the family with unfailing enthusiasm. "It's nice to meet you, August."

"And you," he said, shaking her hand and then giving her a kiss on the cheek. "Bear's the oldest, right?"

"That's right," Etta said, twisting to find him. "He was around here...."

"He went to get the boys off the front lawn," Sammy said. "So Hailey will probably be in momentarily. That was my son and Willa's son out there. A pale cocker spaniel? Doing tricks?"

August nodded, his eyes widening as if Sammy was clairvoyant. "That's right."

"Etta," someone said, and she turned toward Kyle.

"You've only been married to Bear for five years?" August asked.

"That's right," Sammy said.

Etta wanted to stay and listen, but Kyle gestured at her to come help him. She glanced at August, and said, "Excuse me," just as he said, "And you were the first."

"Yes," Sammy said as Etta took the first step away.

"Those boys on the lawn were at least twelve or thirteen," August said.

"Yes," Sammy said. "Lincoln's my son. Mitch is Willa's. She married Cactus, the second oldest in the family. So they're our kids, now Glovers by marriage."

Etta smiled to herself as she hurried to put a plate under the dripping tin foil packet Kyle was trying to take. "Thank you, Auntie," he said. "This is for my dad."

"Where is he?" Etta asked, handing him the plate. Cactus didn't generally enjoy large group gatherings, and Etta could admit she enjoyed going out to the Edge Cabin to eat with him and his family and no one else.

"He's on the deck," Kyle said. "He said I could eat out there with him."

"That's great," Etta said. "Have him text me if he wants a drink."

Kyle beamed up at her, and Etta watched as he took the

plate with two tin foil dinners, two cookies, and a lot of chips out the side door to the deck.

Though the December weather sometimes kept that door closed, today the rain had moved quickly on, and the sun shone over the Texas Panhandle.

She replenished the paper plates and helped Smiles get up in a chair at the table next to his uncle Ace, who had arrived with Gun without Etta noticing.

She ran her hand down her brother's shoulder, and he looked up at her, tenderness and love in his expression that she rarely saw. "Thank you, Etta."

"You got the one without the breadcrumbs? I should've pulled it for you."

"You did," he said. "It was on a plate by the sink, marked."

Etta looked at Holly Ann across from him, and some-thing unspoken passed between them. "Okay," she said. "Thanks for coming, Ace."

It wasn't easy for him, as he'd told her that it felt like everyone watched every bite he put in his mouth, and he hated being under the microscope.

"August needs you," Ace said, nodding back toward the doorway.

Etta turned that way, noting that Lincoln, Mitch, and his daughter had arrived, along with Frost, Mitch's hearing dog. Hands flew, and the kids laughed, and August looked like he'd been hit with a baseball bat.

Etta had made it a point to learn sign language, and she watched Link and Mitch as she approached. "Mitch said

Hailey should come watch *The Grinch* tonight. They're starting it out at the Edge at seven."

She signed to the boys and spoke aloud too. "This is August and his daughter. Link, you have to talk out loud for them."

"Sorry," Link said out loud. "I forget sometimes."

"Can I go, Daddy?" Hailey asked.

"Oh, I don't know," August said, putting his arm around his daughter's shoulders. "We just moved in today."

"We should definitely ask your mom," Etta said, signing to Mitch. "It's at your house, and she might not want anyone but your family."

She said Link could come, Mitch argued back.

"Okay," Etta said. "But Mitch, you still have to ask if *Hailey* can come." She faced August. "Willa is great. She's Cactus's wife."

"Yeah, Sammy told me," August said, smiling though he was obviously overwhelmed. "She pointed her out, but she was busy with her toddler."

"I can introduce you later," Etta said just as her timer went off.

"Timer," no less than four cowboys yelled, though no one moved a muscle to actually get up and get it.

Etta rolled her eyes. "That's my cue," she said.

"I'll get it, Etta," Bishop said, passing her with a grin. "Anything else going in?"

"No," Etta said. "Thanks, Bish." She hadn't seen him arrive either, but Etta felt like her vision had tunneled. "Did you get something to eat?"

August shook his head, and he made no move to wade into the kitchen. Etta handed him the baby and said, "I'll get us one of the hot ones and meet you on the front porch. Deal?"

He hipped the girl like he'd held many babies before, and Etta would lie to herself forever if that didn't make her blood boil and her attraction for the man double. Maybe triple.

"Okay," he said. "What's your name, baby?"

The nine-month-old simply gaped at him.

"She's Heather," Etta said. "Chips? Beans?"

"All of it," he said. "Thank you, Etta." He turned and went back toward the front door, glancing at the Christmas tree in the lobby.

Etta prayed that the Lord would bless the rest of the family to leave her alone, and she plucked a couple of packets from the fresh sheet pan and put them on the same plate.

"Thank you, Bishop."

"I've got things in here," he said, leaning his palms into the kitchen counter. "Want me to bring out some tea or cider?"

"I'll ask him," Etta said. "Cider for me, please." She put baked beans on another plate and stacked nacho cheese corn chips on the other half of it. She normally adored spending time with her siblings, in-laws, and cousins, but when compared to talking to August, he definitely won her attention.

She used her elbow to get the door open, and she toed it closed. Cactus pointed his plastic fork past her to the left, and said, "Hailey can come to the movie tonight. That's no problem."

"I'll tell him," Etta said. "Thanks, Cactus." He nodded and fed a bit of meatloaf to one of his dogs.

She went left and found August around the corner, sitting on the porch with his legs dangling off the front of it and Heather facing him.

"There she is," August said. "It's okay."

"Is she crying?" Etta asked. Heather didn't make a lot of noise, but she did get some anxiety getting passed around. She set the plates on the deck between her and August and exhaled as she sat down. "I hope I can get up again."

"I'll help you." August offered her a smile and passed her Heather.

"Tea or cider?" she asked.

"Tea, please," he said. "I can go get it."

"Nope," she said. "I'll text my cousin. He offered to bring it out to us."

"Your cousins are helpful," he said.

"Most of them, yes." She picked up the plate with the tin foil lunch and texted Bishop to bring out more plates, the drinks, and forks, which she'd forgotten.

"Sammy and Oakley said they'd babysit Hailey anytime I needed them too."

Etta nodded, her chest pinching. "They asked me first. I said it would be fine to talk to you about it."

"You want to go out with me more often, is that it?" he teased.

Etta didn't see what she needed to hide. She was

attracted to August, and he'd asked for her number on a field trip he'd chaperoned with his daughter.

So she said, "Yes. I'd love to see you more often," and looked up as Bishop's boots sounded on the deck. "Ah, thanks, Bish. This is August Winters. August, this is Bishop, my youngest cousin."

"Great to meet you," Bishop said, handing August the plates, and then bending to put the sweet tea and cider on the ground. "I'll take Heather. Russ just dumped beans everywhere, and Sammy said they're leaving."

He picked up the little girl and made his exit, Etta's words still hanging between her and August.

Chapter Four

"We can definitely go out," August said once Bishop Glover's footsteps had receded completely. He took the plate with a single dinner on it now and looked out past the railings on the porch. Seeing Etta among her family over Thanksgiving had reminded him so much of what he'd lost in Dripping Springs.

Or rather, what he'd driven away from. He reminded himself over and over that *he* was the one who'd chosen to leave the farm. *He* was the one who'd packed up everything he owned—including his daughter—and *he* was the one who'd put his past in the rearview mirror.

He hadn't seen any other way around it.

"I didn't mean to put pressure on you," Etta said. "I know that's not Oakley, or Sammy, or Holly Ann's intention either. They're just being nice. Supportive."

"You guys seem to definitely be that," he said.

"Does that bother you?" Etta paused with her forkful of beans in midair, her expression honest and open.

He thought about her question, and in only a few seconds' time, he saw a future here at Shiloh Ridge. People everywhere. No privacy. Babies moving from person to person to person.

"I have two brothers," he said, as if that answered her question at all. "You have three. Just immediate brothers. And a sister. And like, fifteen hundred cousins." He couldn't look at her, and instead, he let his eyes follow the land as it swelled up a dirt road toward that blue barn where the field trip had started, and then down the road to where he now lived.

"Fifteen hundred." Etta giggled, the sound driving right into August's heart. He didn't want to discuss serious things today, but he knew those conversations wouldn't be put off forever. Etta wasn't the type of person to allow that.

"When I came here to interview," he said. "I could feel something different about this place. I didn't know what it was." He still didn't, but he didn't say that.

"Probably the fifteen hundred cousins," Etta said, plenty of dryness in her tone.

He let a smile touch his face, but it wasn't the cousins. "Maybe the people," he said. "You Glovers do possess a certain...energy the regular person can't duplicate."

"I'm not sure if that's a compliment or not."

August thought it was, but he opened his tin foil packet instead of insisting it was. A perfectly shaped meatloaf sat there, about as long as his fingers, and with steam rising from the foil and the cheesy potatoes making his mouth water, he finally relaxed.

He looked over for a fork and found Etta holding it toward him. "Thank you." Their eyes met, and dang if August didn't get electrocuted way down inside his lungs. They seemed to ignite at the very bottom and burn upward, and no matter how hard he tried, he could not look away from her deep, dark blue eyes.

"It was a compliment," he said. "I've never met anyone like you. Or your family."

"Nice save, tacking that there on the end." A smile graced her face, and August could watch her smile softly at him like that all day and all night. With difficulty, he pulled his attention back to his food, the embers of his attraction to her still glowing throughout his whole body.

He'd told her precious little about his life pre-Three Rivers. She hadn't asked a whole lot of those questions either. He wondered if now was a good time, if she needed to know something soon, or if he should hope she'd never ask.

"I'm not doing any more school visits or field trips until January," she said. "We wouldn't even need to go out. You could just come up to the homestead for dinner. Or Hailey could, and I could sneak down to your cabin for dinner."

"We don't need to sneak," he said.

"Oh, I thought—"

She cut off, and August found he'd really like to know what she thought. He took a bite of his barbecued meatloaf and the creamy hash brown casserole and looked out at the ranch where he'd be working. They'd only been out a few times, but Etta sometimes needed time and space to answer a question, like when she'd told him she'd been burned by a few men on the dating app most people around Three Rivers used.

She hadn't gone into specifics, and they'd been interrupted by the choice of raspberry tuxedo pie or New York cheesecake.

Etta had chosen the chocolate, and she'd told him there were few desserts better without it. August had noted that, just like he'd noted how she'd introduced her family at the Thanksgiving dinner they'd shared. She was definitely close to her sister, which made sense, as they were twins and worked the ranch's community outreach program.

Of her three older brothers, she was closest with Ranger, which again, made sense to August. They lived together in the same house. A huge, hulking yet homey house, but together nonetheless. He had not been surprised by Oakley's offer to watch his daughter.

Nor had Holly Ann right at her side provided any shock to his system. She was Ace's wife, and Etta got along well with Ace. He had some dietary restrictions, and Etta had been perfecting gluten-free pizza dough for months now, at least according to one of their texting conversations.

She loved Ward and Dot too, because it seemed Etta had a good relationship with nearly everyone, and August actually wondered what it would be like to see her get upset. Even when she'd tripped in the equipment shed weeks ago, on the field trip, she hadn't really gotten too rattled.

"What did you think?" he asked, finally turning to look at her.

"I thought you didn't want to tell Hailey about us."

"It's not that I don't want to," he said, a sigh filling his whole soul. "It's just that there's been so much changing in our lives recently. I'd like to give the dust some time to settle."

"Mm."

He didn't like the sound of that, and he looked away from his food to focus on the woman. "What does that mean?"

Etta had no problem meeting his gaze, steadiness and confidence in hers. She reminded him so much of Josie that he blinked, and his late wife's image superimposed over Etta's.

"Tell me what you're thinking," she said. "So I don't make any erroneous assumptions."

"What would those be?" he asked.

"That you're not really interested in me," she said, looking away as her eyes dropped to her lap. When she looked up again, it was with a deep breath. "That you liked what you saw in the beginning, but you're not sure now. That you're embarrassed to be seen with me. That my family is too big for you, what with your two brothers and all."

August could not form a response to all she'd said. "Etta," he said, liking the shape of her name in his mouth. Before he could continue, the door behind him slammed open, and many voices came out onto the front porch.

"Just back up," a man said.

"You are all not coming," another said.

"Good luck with that," a woman said.

"Hold my hand, Dot."

"She's my wife. I've got her."

"Go get the truck, Ward."

More clamoring, and August leaned forward and peered around the corner while Etta got to her feet. She strode away from him, a sense of surety in her step that once again fanned the sparks of desire into flames.

"What's going on?" she asked.

"Dot's water broke."

"Ward's taking her to the hospital."

"Take Bear's truck," someone called.

August felt like the best place to be was right where he currently was, and he stayed out of the way. He quietly gathered up the plates, noting Etta had eaten some of the beans and left most of the chips. He popped a couple of them—his favorite ridged kind—into his mouth as he moved to the corner of the house to take in the complete scene.

No less than the fifteen hundred cousins had come out onto the porch, and most were following the very pregnant Dot Glover down the steps, still rattling off advice and calling for Bear to get his keys already.

August smiled at their camaraderie, and a powerful sense of missing out on something he hadn't even known he wanted moved through him.

Etta turned back toward him, a panicked look on her face.

"Go," he said, because he knew she'd want to go down to

the hospital to meet her new niece. The children in the Glover family seemed to have carved a place in Etta's heart, and she loved each and every one of them in a way August had never seen before.

Could she love Hailey like that too?

The thought perched in his mind, and it would not fly away. He wasn't sure he wanted it to. He needed more time to examine it from every angle, and he wanted more time with this family to see how they treated Mitch, Lincoln, and the three foster children Cactus and Willa had brought to the family recently.

He had never once thought that he'd be able to find a woman who would love Hailey as their own. But he'd watched Etta with Lincoln and Mitch, neither of whom shared any blood with her whatsoever, and it had been clear to him that she loved them.

Everyone in the house had loved them. Sammy had brought Lincoln to her marriage with Bear and Willa had brought Mitch.

If they can make it work, maybe you can too.

The thought started out as a whisper, hardly there at all. But every moment since August had asked Sammy about the two teen boys, it had gotten louder and more prevalent in his mind.

Can I, Lord? he asked. *Can I actually find someone to love who will love me for me, and love my daughter too? Be a real mother to her?*

As Etta came back toward him, he had the very strong feeling that if anyone could easily step into the role of

Hailey's mother with absolute authenticity, it would be Etta Glover.

You can't like her for that, he told himself even as she opened her arms and then stepped into his. As they embraced, she said, "I'm going to go, if that's okay."

"Of course it's okay," he said, leaning down almost against his will and taking a deep breath of the scent of her skin, her hair, her very being. In that regard, she was not like Josie at all, who smelled like hay and horses ninety percent of the time.

Etta smelled like brown sugar and lemons, and together, those two scents suddenly became his very favorite.

"He's your brother," he said. "Text me what they name her." Apparently, Ward and Dot had been having a small feud over the name of their baby girl, and Etta had started a secret pool where every family member had put in five bucks on one name or the other.

"Oh, I better get down there and push Ward toward Patty. I can't lose to Glory." She stepped back, shaking her head. "Glory Glover. Can you imagine?"

"I think it's cute," August said, tucking his hands in his pockets and smiling at Etta. "You'll love that baby with everything in you, no matter what they name her."

"Yeah, but I want the hundred bucks." She grinned and turned back, the last of the group heading either down the steps or inside. "I should stay and clean up."

"Nope," August said, giving her a little nudge. "I might need a minute of your time to help me find my daughter, and then you're going down to the hospital."

"Okay, fine," she said, clearly teasing him. "I'm pretty sure I know where Hailey will be." She led the way inside, where August threw their paper plates in the oversized garbage can in the kitchen while Etta leaned over the back of the couch and said, "Hailey, your daddy is leaving."

He peered over the back of it too, where Hailey sat right next to one of Cactus and Willa's boys, the two of them peering at something in a book. A legitimate book. August thought he needed to let Hailey come hang out with these kids more often, because she already had a phone she spent too much time on.

"Let's go, Hay," he said.

She looked up at him and then back at the book. "Okay." But she didn't get up right away.

"Cam," Cactus said from the side door. "Right now, son. We've got to get back to the Edge quickly."

The boy got to his feet, closed the book, and handed it to Hailey. "You can take it."

"Really?" She stood too, clearly wanting to take the book but unsure if she should.

"I've read it before," he said. "Really, take it."

"Okay." Hailey took the book, and August caught sight of a big, purple dragon on the front. "I'll bring it back."

"Cam," Cactus said.

"Okay," Cam said, turning and hurrying toward his dad. "Sorry, she wanted to borrow—" His voice got cut off as he left the house and closed the door behind him.

Hailey turned toward him, her face aglow. "Look, Daddy," she said. "It's that dragon book Miss Pfeiffer gave me last year. I had to give it back before we moved, remember?"

So many memories choked in his throat, and all he could do was nod.

"I'm coming," Etta said. "I'll swing by and get you, how does that sound?"

He glanced at her to find her on the phone, and then she hurried around the couch and toward the fireplace. She tapped on the wall about two-thirds of the way up and to his surprise, a door opened right out of the wall. She paused, looked over to him and lowered the phone, "You're okay to go? I'm sorry."

"Of course," he said. "We're fine." He motioned Hailey around the couch, and she came to his side.

Etta went through the door and it swung silently closed behind her as she said something else to whoever was on the other end of the line. He turned around and saw the enormous mess in the kitchen, on the bar, and littering the whole dining room table—which easily sat fifteen hundred.

He instinctively knew who would be tasked with cleaning up, and he wanted to alleviate that for Etta. "Come on," he said to Hailey. "Let's get back to the cabin. You can read your book and I'll come back up here and get this place cleaned up for them."

"I can help," Hailey said, and his heart reminded him of what a great daughter he had.

"Okay," he said. "But I want it to be a surprise for the Glovers, so let's go wait in the truck until Etta leaves."

"Good idea." Hailey beamed at him, and August led the

way out of the large kitchen, past the pretty flocked Christmas tree with all the crocheted ornaments, and toward their truck. He stewed about how to tell Hailey he wanted to take Etta to dinner, just the two of them, on a date. He'd done that a few times now, but each time, he hadn't told his daughter the real reason why she'd needed to go next door while he went out alone.

They ducked down, Hailey giggling, when Etta came dashing out of the house. A couple of vehicles away, her truck's engine roared to life, and August peeked up over the dashboard to watch her make the turn and head down the hill toward the highway.

"Okay," he said once the dust had settled. "Let's go." Maybe while he did dishes and straightened pillows, he could come up with a good explanation or to order such delicate words about his feelings for Etta in any sort of rational fashion.

Maybe.

Chapter Five

Etta had fast fingers, and when her phone went off about the same time as the half-dozen people in the near vicinity, she was one of the first to open the message.

She swiped and read the text from Ward, the picture of his darling new baby coming up only a moment later. Etta sucked in a breath at the sheer perfection of the infant, who had her eyes closed and plenty of dark, wispy hair on her head. "Oh," came out of her mouth, and Ace said, "He sent a picture," as if everyone in the waiting area outside of maternity hadn't gotten the text.

Etta couldn't look away from her new niece. Great longing pulled through her, but this time, it was more like a yank. A hefty, harrowing yank that brought her heart down to her stomach and her hope plummeting toward the ground.

Another message popped up. *Bathed and ready for snuggles. Out in ten probably.*

She wanted to ask him what they'd named the baby, but she forced her fingers to stay still. If he didn't send something soon though, Etta might lose her mind.

A message popped up just as her phone started to darken, and she practically lunged at it. *I know there was a pool of money going around for the name.*

"Come on," she muttered. "Tell us what it is."

"If they went with Patty, I'm going to seriously question his sanity," Zona said from down the couch.

"No," Etta said, grinning down to her. "Patty is *so* cute."

We named her Glory Rose, Ward said, and a cheer went up by those who'd voted for that name. Etta groaned as loud as those celebrating, and she immediately started thinking of nicknames for the girl.

"Glory Rose is adorable," Charlie said. "It's cute together, don't you think, Etta?"

"Do you think we can just hyphenate it?" She looked at Charlie, who held Betty on her lap. She'd won the battle on the old-fashioned name for her daughter, and Etta should've known better than to bet against Dot.

Ward loved her with everything he had, and he'd do anything she asked—including name their baby Glory.

"I think you can call her whatever you want," Ida said. "And they won't even know. The amount of kids we have around? Call her Glory-Rose if you want."

Etta reached over and took Ida's hand in hers. "The twins will be two soon. Are you and Brady going to have more kids?"

"Not for a while," Ida said, leaning her head back while

she was toddler-free. "Brady just works so much, you know?"

"And now you're dealing with Mother too," Etta said, keeping her voice low. She prayed for her mother morning and night, and she looked away from Ida and across the lobby toward where she sat. Lois, Etta's aunt, never got very far from Mother, and an outpouring of love for the older generation in her family filled Etta.

Aunt Lois lived in town, so it was easier for her to get over to the assisted living facility where Mother had been for a while now. Etta went as often as she could, which had been a lot since Thanksgiving. Every time, Ida had gone with. Someone would take the twins, usually Oakley or Sammy, and they'd entertain them while Etta and Ida went into Nestled Oaks and attended appointments with their mother or just sat with her.

Then Oakley and Sammy would take a turn to visit with Mother, and Etta wondered if there was anything sweeter than to see women coming together to love one another through hard things. She didn't think so, and she squeezed her sister's hand.

"There are plenty of us to help with Mother," she said. "You don't have to do it alone."

"I know," Ida said. "But I'm the closest, and my life is fairly stable."

"Judy is my favorite baby of all the Glovers."

Ida scoffed, her eyes coming open. "You're such a liar."

"She sleeps through the night when you leave her with me." Etta shook her hair over her shoulders as if she alone had tamed Ida's almost-two-year-old. "Let me take her tonight."

"You can have her any time you want her."

"Done."

The doors opening across from her caught her attention, and she jumped to her feet. "He's here." She hurried forward to help Mother stand, and she led her over to Ward and that baby with all that hair. Etta loved babies more than anything in the world, and while she'd imagined over and over what it would be like to have her own, wonder still filled her from top to bottom at the sight of this new human being who'd just come to the earth.

Ward gazed at the infant with pure love in his expression, and when he looked up, Etta thought for sure her tough, cowboy brother had been crying. "Dot did great," he said. "They're moving her to a room right now, and then people will be able to come back. Who wants her?"

"Etta," Mother said. "Let Etta have her, and she'll sit by me."

Etta reached for the baby, no complaints about being nominated to hold the precious baby first. Ward slipped Glory Rose into her arms, and it suddenly didn't matter what the baby's name was. She smelled like soap and powder and cotton, and Etta fell in love with her instantly.

"You come with me, baby girl," she whispered, leaning down to press a feather-light kiss to the soft spot right on top of Glory's head. "Let's meet your gramma."

* * *

A couple of hours later, Etta pulled up to the homestead. Oakley and Ranger had left the hospital before her, but they'd gone with Sammy and Bear to visit Sammy's parents. She wasn't surprised to see they hadn't returned to the homestead yet.

Mister lived here too, and he had one of his former rodeo buddies staying in his suite right now. They worked at a Christmas event down the hill from Shiloh Ridge, and Etta had heard them come in a couple of nights ago, when she couldn't sleep. Other than that, Mister and Dave were quiet and respectful. She didn't see either of their trucks either, and they'd probably already gone to Golden Hour Ranch, where the Country Christmas had live music on the weekends.

Relief moved through Etta at the thought of having the house to herself, which didn't happen very often, but a heaviness entered her heart when she thought of how the homestead had been left. Food on the counter. Had she even turned off the oven? Had Bishop? The garbage can had been nearly full when she'd strode past it on her way out.

She opened the front door and paused at the angel tree. She hung an actual angel every year for her grandmother. She'd crocheted it so the lady had an open, O-shaped mouth, as if singing God's praises every day of her life.

Etta wanted to live like that, her heart open enough to praise the Lord. Open enough that the songs would come pouring out of her mouth. She hung a cowboy hat for Noah Johnson. She'd contemplated not hanging it for him this year, but in the end, she'd done it. She did want him to be happy, and if she could feel good about herself by hanging an ornament, she would.

Other than that, Etta usually hung an ivory heart with red thread woven through it for herself. Every year for the past few, she'd closed her eyes and said a single-sentence prayer for herself.

Bless me to be the type of woman that is worthy of love, both divine and from friends, family, and perhaps a man.

Could August be that man? Etta wasn't sure, and the holidays hadn't even hit yet. She had plenty of time to find out. She could admit—only to herself—that she'd hung that heart this year with his face in her mind.

She breathed out and continued past the angel tree, and the moment she stepped into the kitchen, she froze. "What in the world?" she murmured to herself. And the sparkling clean surfaces glinting back at her.

Someone had been here and cleaned up. Relief and gratitude combined into a perfect cyclone of emotion, and tears touched Etta's heart and eyes. She took a step further toward the bar, almost expecting it all to wink away and the dirty plates, half-drunk plastic cups of tea or cider, and the slow cooker crock full of cold, crusty baked beans to reappear.

They didn't, and she turned in a full circle, finding the pillows back on the couches. "This is crazy," she said. Those pillows never stayed on the couch for longer than ten seconds, especially if Smiles came over to play with Wilder.

She pulled out her phone and texted Holly Ann. *Did you come clean up the homestead? Thank you so much!*

Holly Ann hadn't been at the hospital long, because she

had a holiday party tonight, and she'd come back to the ranch to finish the prep and get the food where it belonged. She was probably either in transit to the party right now or setting up, so she probably wouldn't answer.

Etta stepped over to the fridge and opened it, immediately realizing Holly Ann hadn't been the one to clean up. The crock itself sat in the fridge, a piece of plastic wrap pressed around it. That was fine with Etta, but Holly Ann would have never done that.

Etta backed out of the fridge. The garbage can sat there, a new bag in it, but she didn't see the full trash bag. Holly Ann wouldn't have taken that out to the big barrel, because she'd have to come back up the stairs, and with only two and a half months until she delivered, she would've just put it on the deck.

Etta stepped outside and saw no trash bag. *It wasn't me*, Holly Ann said as she moved back inside. She texted Willa, who'd also taken longer to come down to the hospital, because she and Cactus had a lot of children to wrangle now. Not only that, but it had been afternoon, and she'd stayed to babysit several of the younger babies who needed naps. Only then had she loaded up as many car seats as her minivan would hold and come down to the hospital.

I didn't do it, Willa said. *I've barely had time to think past my nose.*

Etta frowned. Everyone else had come down to the hospital about the time she had. Cleaning up the homestead had likely taken at least thirty minutes. Etta knew, because Etta did it all the time. People came over, made a mess, and left. They never really thought about the fact that people actually lived in this house, and they had to clean up after company. Or if they did, they still left their cups on the table and didn't replace the toilet paper when it ran out in the main floor bathroom.

Etta sent a text out to the family, determined to know who'd cleaned up for her so she could thank them properly. *Thanks to whoever cleaned up after lunch. Speak now, and I'll bring you your favorite dinner one night next week.*

She loved cooking, and it was one of the major ways she'd been able to serve others throughout the years.

It was me, Preacher said quickly. *I love those chicken taquitos you make.*

It was not, Charlie said. *Don't listen to him, Etta.*

Judge tried to claim credit, but Cactus said they'd driven down together, and there was no way it could've been Judge. The ribbing went back and forth for several minutes, but the result was the same: No one in the Glover family had cleaned the homestead.

"So who did it?" Etta took in the spotless kitchen, and all at once, like a lightning strike from thunderclouds, she knew. She dialed and lifted the phone to her ear.

"Etta," August said pleasantly. "How's Ward and Dot? You never texted me what they named the baby."

"Did you clean the homestead?" she asked, completely ignoring his question.

He didn't answer for a moment, which was all the answer she needed. "August," she said, her voice soft and overflowing with emotion. "Thank you. Thank you so much. What a blessing to come home to a clean house."

"I'm glad it was a blessing," he said.

Etta went into the living room and sank onto the nearest couch. "I texted the family, asking them who'd done it and promising them their favorite dinner one night next week." She let the sentence sit there, hoping he'd volunteer his favorite thing to eat for dinner.

"How about Tuesday night?" he asked. "Monday's my first day, and I think I'll be okay. But by Tuesday night? I'll be thrashed." He gave her a light chuckle, which tickled her eardrums and made her smile.

"Tuesday night is perfect," she said. "What would be your favorite dinner?"

"That would be ribs and mashed potatoes, sweet pea salad, and whole wheat rolls."

Surprise kept Etta's laugh contained for a couple of seconds, and then she let it fly. "Wow," she said between giggles. "That's surprisingly specific."

He chuckled with her. "Yeah, I suppose so. My in-laws used to make a meal like that for my wife's birthday, and it was my favorite." He sucked in an audible breath, as if he'd just now realized what he'd said.

Etta's curiosity skyrocketed, but she'd rather be sitting across the table from him when she learned more about his in-laws and his wife. She noted that he didn't say "ex-wife," nor "late wife," but simply "my wife."

Her chest stormed at her, just as it had done earlier on the front deck when she'd asked him to tell her what he was thinking. She'd then given him some options—none of which were good—and he hadn't said anything but her name.

He had said it with kindness and a bit of reproach, but they'd been interrupted by Dot's labor, and the conversation had never concluded.

"I'll see you Tuesday," she said. "With all of those things you just listed. Six? Six-thirty? Sweet barbecue, or spicy?"

"Let's do six-thirty," he said. "And I like some sweet with heat."

"Ooh, I see how you are," Etta said, flirting with him and hoping she'd pulled it off. "Sweet with heat. That about sums up the entire state of Texas."

He laughed again, and Etta's satisfaction knew no bounds. "Maybe we'll see you at church tomorrow too," he said. "So, what did they name the baby? Are you buying the groceries for our meal together with your winnings?"

"I wish," Etta said, sighing as she sank further into the couch. She didn't need the money, and she wondered how to bring that up with August. They'd talked a lot, but Etta felt like they'd only been skating along the surface.

He'd blown that wide open with the mention of his in-laws and wife, and she said, "They named her Glory Rose, which I can admit is growing on me."

"I'll bet it is," he said, teasing her. "I've seen you with babies, and I don't think their name matters much to you."

She grinned up at the ceiling, unable to argue with him. "Thank you, August," she said again. "Really."

"Anything for you, Etta," he said, and she could close her

eyes and sail softly into sleep with those words in her head. She had a date with him on the horizon, and she really didn't think he didn't like her or was embarrassed to be with her.

His reluctance to talk to his daughter probably has something to do with that wife, she thought, and she decided then and there to dig deeper than the surface on Tuesday night.

Chapter Six

August hunkered into his jacket collar on Monday morning, part of his attention down the lane at his cabin, part of it up the road at the main homestead at Shiloh Ridge, and the last part focused on Preacher Glover.

He was not the only new-hire from that weekend, and August currently stood with three other men. Walter Renchild now lived right next door to August and Hailey, and he'd arrived about the same time as they had on Saturday. He had blond hair, a big, reddish beard, and bright blue eyes that seemed to laugh before the sound came out of his mouth.

Walt had invited August and Hailey over for a hot dog roast last night, and they'd gone. August figured the more stuff he did, the less obvious it would be when Hailey went up to the ranch so he could go out with Etta.

Walt's cabinmate, Jess Cochran, had arrived Sunday afternoon, and he was probably a decade younger than both

Walter and August. He had dark, curly hair that he obviously had no intention of taming, and it spilled out from underneath his cowboy hat in damp ringlets. August had no idea how the man could survive the itching from all that hair, but he didn't have to live with it, so he didn't much care.

Bill Miller had moved in during the hot dog roast, which Walt had done in a portable firepit right on his front lawn. After Bill had taken in his few belongings, he'd joined them. He had to be close to August's age, or perhaps nearer to forty, and he hadn't said a whole lot. He possessed wisdom in his dark green eyes, and he kept his medium brown hair shaved close to the scalp. No itching under his hat.

"There will be times when I need you all," Preacher said. "I can't predict when the cows will go into labor, and sometimes we need more hands than we have."

August nodded, because he'd lived through plenty of birthing seasons. On the ranch in Dripping Springs, they only had about five hundred cattle, which was a drop in the bucket compared to Shiloh Ridge, but he'd been out at two a.m. helping a calf come into the world, and he'd been in birthing sheds trying to save a calf who'd endured a difficult breech birth.

"Phones have to stay on all the time, unfortunately," Preacher said, and August sure did like him. He was serious, but he didn't take himself seriously. This morning, he leaned on a crutch and not the cane he'd seen him use on his walk with Etta over the weekend.

"Even mine is on all the time." He gave them a rueful smile. "When the boss calls, I answer."

August smiled back at him, hoping Preacher remembered that he'd asked for mornings off so he could get Hailey to school. In truth, anything would be better than the situation at the apartment where they'd been living.

"So." Preacher lifted up his phone and adjusted where he held it so he could see it. "I've got Bill taking the early morning shift. He said he likes getting up while it's still dark, and that suits me great." He smiled at the man, who returned it easily. "So he'll go out first thing in the morning and check the herd. We've got four ATVs down here to do that."

He cleared his throat, obviously uncomfortable about something, though August didn't know what. "He'll go out at five. My goal is to have him break for breakfast and our morning meeting, about this time each day, then he'll be done by two in the afternoon." Preacher switched his gaze to Walter.

"Walt is going to be our afternoon and evening man. So he'll go on when Bill goes off. I want the two of you to check-in every day at the switch, so Walt knows how the morning went and he can take us into the evening. He'll work until eleven. At that time, if there's obviously going to be a birth between eleven at night and five in the morning, he'll let us all know, and we'll take turns going out. I don't want anyone out in the middle of the night alone. So that'll happen in pairs."

August nodded, because things could happen quickly in

an emergency situation. He knew more than most, and his throat suddenly felt stuffed full of cotton. He tried to swallow it all away, but memories didn't go as easily as he'd like.

"That leaves August and Jess for our day shifts. August has a daughter who might be coming to our morning meetings, and then he'll be gone for about an hour right after this to get her to school." Preacher glanced at August, who nodded though no one else seemed to care about his personal life.

He knew who did, however, and he had a suspicion that Etta wouldn't let too much more time go by without asking some questions August didn't want to answer. He straightened and told himself that he *did* want to answer them. Maybe everything would be easier if he could just get his secret things out in the open. Then he didn't have to censor what he said—like the slip about his wife's favorite meal last night. Then he didn't have to wonder when she'd find out, what her family would think, and why explaining things to Hailey would be difficult for him.

"When he gets back, he'll work with Bill and Jess until about six. Jess, I want you to start around noon and go through nine."

"Sounds good, boss," Jess said.

"My family is loud and crazy," Preacher said next, and August hadn't expected that. He looked up, surprise lifting his eyebrows, especially when Preacher ducked his head and shook it. "Sometimes my wife will make a meal—breakfast, lunch, or dinner—right here at the farmhouse.

But usually, we're gettin' fed out of the homestead at the top of the road. All of you came up to the main ranch to interview, and I'm sure you saw the homestead. It's the huge, hulking building you can see from here. The ranch wives sometimes get together to cook there, sometimes it's my cousin, sometimes my sister. Whoever it is will send out a text on the ranch group text, which I added all of you to about twenty minutes ago. I'm going to text out a welcome for you to everyone, and you should get it. So let's see."

He started tapping on his phone, and a few seconds later, he said, "There. Keep in mind that there are probably forty or fifty people on this group text. It's for ranch business only. And important ranch business at that." He indicated the group of them. "We have a text string for the five of us too. I put my wife and my admin team on it—that's Bear, Ward, and Ranger—so they can help me manage things while I'm going through my physical therapy and healing. Okay?"

"Yes, sir," August said while the others gave similar words of assent.

"Just be mindful of what you send to the big group," he said. "It includes all of my brothers and sister, all of my cousins, and all of their wives. All of our cowboys and cowgirls on the upper ranch as well."

August's phone chimed, and his was the first among them. Within seconds, various sounds and signals filled the air, and he chuckled. Preacher's name sat on the text, but August knew it was a group message from the four little heads in the icon. He quickly named it "Whole Ranch Text" and looked back toward his cabin.

Hailey sat on the top step, her backpack on her shoulders, and he whipped his attention back to his phone. They didn't have to leave for another ten minutes, and his adrenaline sank back into his stomach.

"All right," Preacher said. "I'm going to take Walt and Bill with me. Jess and August, I'd like you back here in a couple of hours, and we'll go through the same thing I'm going to do with them right now." He met August's eye first, and much more was said between them.

August appreciated the silence and the understanding, and he nodded. The meeting broke up, and he headed back down the road to the cabin in the corner. "Ready, my sweets?" he asked his daughter.

Hailey wore a sunny smile as she came down the rest of the steps. "I'm glad you get to take me to school now, Daddy."

"Me too," he said, distracted by another chime on his phone. Etta had texted, causing his heart to burst and bump and beat with more enthusiasm.

Do you need any help getting Hailey home in the afternoons? Remember how I'm not doing anything with the outreach programs right now?

August's first instinct was to decline the help. He'd been planning to have Hailey ride the same bus she'd been riding back to the apartment building where they used to live. Then, she could stay with Ruth, the next-door neighbor that had been kind enough to take her in the mornings.

My mother isn't doing well right now, Etta continued while August fought with himself. *I'll be down in town anyway, and she can come up to the ranch with Mitch, Lincoln, Cameron, and Kyle. They're all coming to a pudding cup afternoon at the homestead anyway. I'd love to have her too.*

August felt the world tip. Would he rather send his daughter back to a stuffy, cat-riddled apartment with a seventy-three-year-old woman? Or up to a vibrant, beautiful homestead with a vivacious, gorgeous woman and four other children his daughter's age?

The pudding cups really pushed him over the edge, and he typed quickly. *That would be fantastic, Etta. Thank you.*

You've seen my truck, she sent back. *Let her know I'll be in the parent pick-up zone.*

Just the fact that Etta knew there was a parent pick-up zone at the elementary school told August a lot. He'd never dropped off or picked up his daughter from school, and a new sense of failure came over him. He'd been trying so hard to be both mother and father to Hailey, but with bills to pay and difficult schedules to manage, he hadn't been doing a very good job.

He'd been praying for a solution to the things he struggled with, and as he sent another *thank you* to Etta, he wondered if the woman had been placed in his life as an answer to some of those prayers.

"Daddy," Hailey said, and he looked up, realizing she'd already gotten in the truck. "We're going to be late."

"Right." August hurried around to the driver's side and

got behind the wheel. "Now, listen, sweets. I just talked to Etta, and she said she can pick you up after school." He glanced at her, Hailey's big, wide, blue eyes feeding his bravery. "She's hosting a pudding cup...something at the homestead for the older kids—Mitch, Lincoln, Cameron, and Kyle—and she invited you to go."

He didn't need to ask if she wanted to go. The desire to do so sat right there on her face, the hope in her eyes flinging straight up into the sky.

"Do you want to go?"

"Can I, Daddy?"

He smiled and nodded. "Yes, you can. But you have to promise me you'll be good for Etta. She doesn't have to do this for you."

"I will be so good." Hailey promised, actually making a criss-cross motion over her heart.

"All right," August said. "I'm done at six, but I'll tell her she can send you back to the cabin any time. You don't need a babysitter after school. You can lay in bed and read your dragon book or put cartoons on, right?"

"I can," she said. "But pudding cups sound *so* fun, Daddy. Do you think there will be chocolate pudding?"

August thought about Etta's dessert choices on the few dates they'd been on, and a secret smile filled his whole soul. "Yes," he said with confidence. "I think there will be chocolate pudding." And banana and pistachio, if he knew anything about Etta's skills in the kitchen, which he did.

"Can I read to you, Daddy?" Hailey lifted her purple dragon book, and August couldn't tell her no. He nodded, and then they spent the drive to school with Hailey spinning a tale about a dragon with the biggest wings in all the land… who was afraid to fly.

"Bye, Daddy!" Hailey called the next evening. She launched herself away from the front window, where she'd been sitting for the past twenty minutes. He hurried after her, catching the front door before it could bang into the wall and put a dent in the brand new paint and plaster.

"You listen to Sammy!" he called after his daughter, whose white-blonde hair streamed down her back as she scampered down the steps.

Sammy Glover got out of the oversized SUV and came around the front of the hood. She smiled at Hailey as if she truly enjoyed seeing her, and once she said something to her and Hailey started for the back door, she looked up to the porch.

August lifted his hand in acknowledgement and gratitude, wondering if a wave could convey such a thing. Perhaps he should go down to the sidewalk and pour his heart out to her. But Sammy waved back and returned to the vehicle. Just like that, she drove away, circling around the cabin community until she got back on the road that led past the farmhouse and out of this part of the developed land.

Dust kicked up behind the SUV, and August went back inside. From the back porch, he could watch the progress of the big, black vehicle as it went up the lane toward the ranch, and he watched it until it turned off on the side road before the arch and went north.

He'd been up that road today, and he'd found another house with a yard laden with Christmas decorations, and then further down the road, Sammy and Bear's place, and then way out on the edge of the ranch, the Edge Cabin, where Cactus lived with his family.

August sighed at all the new names and faces in his life, though all of them were welcome. Hailey had talked non-stop about her pudding cup afternoon, and August had listened vaguely while he baked frozen pizza and opened a bagged salad for dinner.

Then he'd texted non-stop with Etta about the pudding cup afternoon, as well as a little bit about his new job here at Shiloh Ridge, their date for tonight, and his schedule.

She'd offered to get Hailey every day after school, and August had told her no. He couldn't ask her to do that. She'd then told him that Sammy had a son going to preschool, and one in junior high. Willa had three going to school in town, one at the junior high and two in elementary school. Someone was always going to town to pick up the kids—usually Cactus or Sammy—and that they would have no problem fitting Hailey in their car.

He'd relented, and Hailey had come home with Cactus that afternoon. He'd dropped her at the cabin and then texted August that he had no problem taking the girl out to the Edge if she wanted to come with his boys.

I'll put her to work, mind you, Cactus said. *But it's easy stuff like cleaning tack or exercising a horse. My dogs always*

*need someone to play with, or my toddler needs someone to lay
by him so he can sleep. That kind of stuff.*

August hadn't answered him yet. He didn't know how
he felt about allowing the Glovers to help so much.

What's the big deal? he asked himself as he went back
inside. He'd had to rely on Josie's parents in Dripping
Springs. Here, he didn't have family to rely on...at least not
any he was biologically related to. But the Glover family
certainly seemed inclined to help him if they could.

Why shouldn't he let them?

His doorbell rang, and he nearly jumped out of his
skin. "Get yourself together," he muttered as he went to
answer it. Of course it would be Etta, as she was bringing
dinner that night. He could smell the barbecue sauce
already.

He opened the door, and sure enough, she stood there.
Stunningly beautiful in the evening sunlight. The smile on
her face broadcasted her happiness, and she extended the
sheet pan toward him. "You take this, please. I'll get the
rest."

He took the pan, wanting to say so much. But she was
gone in a flash, and August took the ribs into the kitchen.
He returned to the porch just as she arrived at the top with
another tray carrying two big bowls, with another tray
balanced on the top of it. He lifted that away and gave her
the brightest smile he could.

He had no idea what that looked like on his face, but he
followed Etta inside and closed the door with his cowboy
boot. She set about uncovering the food, all while August's

mouth watered and his chest tightened and tightened and tightened.

He needed more time to get a speech prepared. He prayed the Lord would give him the right words when the time was right.

When Etta looked up at him, he didn't have the words ordered right. He didn't even know what he was going to say. He simply opened his mouth and said, "I was married once. My wife's name was Josie, and she died in an accident on our ranch four years ago." He cleared his throat, surprised he hadn't choked on Josie's name. He'd said it so little in the past few years. He also experienced no tears and no hitch in his chest any longer.

"This was what she ordered at this little barbecue dive in the Hill Country for our first anniversary," he said, half-laughing and half-something else as he took in the food. "Yours looks much better, I have to admit."

He wasn't sure he could look at Etta and see the sympathy in her expression. He hated seeing that edge in people's eyes once they found out about Josie, and he really didn't want it to sour his feelings about Etta.

So he kept his gaze down, easily seeing Etta out of his peripheral vision as she entered his personal space and wrapped him in a hug. She didn't say the typical things people said when they found out about a death. She didn't say anything.

She simply held him tight, and everything inside August that had been spring-loaded and clenched released. Just like that. With one touch from a woman who August had not believed he would ever find.

Not again, at least.

He let himself put his arms around Etta and hold her too, and as they stood there in his silent kitchen, August felt the weeping, wailing part of him heal completely.

Chapter Seven

Etta had not experienced the loss of a spouse, but she had been through several debilitating losses in her life. Her father had passed away very early. Almost too early for Etta to truly know him.

She'd lost a man she loved, a man she was going to marry. In her mind, she'd never categorized her break-up with Noah Johnson as a loss, but standing with August after he'd told her about the death of his wife, Etta truly felt like she'd lost him.

Perhaps she'd *chosen* that loss, which was a major difference between hers and August's experiences, but she had lost Noah all the same.

Time came roaring back to full speed again, and Etta stepped back. August released her, and she lifted her eyes to meet his. The moment caught again, and Etta said, "Thank you for sharing her with me."

She turned toward the food, her own pulse thundering

like wild horses's hooves through her chest, her bones, her vital organs. "I have never been married, but I have been in love, and it is a terrible thing to lose." She reached for the plastic wrap over the rolls. "I just need the oven at four hundred and fifteen minutes, and these will be hot."

She hadn't made it back to the homestead in time that afternoon to get the dough made and through two rise cycles before she'd needed to load everything into her truck and come down the road to August's cabin.

Dot had brought Glory home today, and Etta had not left Bull House until she absolutely had to. Dot had seemed grateful for the opportunity to shower and brew coffee while Etta tended to Glory, and Etta had told her she'd be over every day if necessary.

She had relinquished the baby to the other ranch wives who'd stopped by, but that had only been Sammy for a few minutes right before naptime for her baby, and she'd brought diabetic-friendly brownies as Dot had to watch her blood sugar fairly closely.

Beeping sounded, and Etta turned to find August setting the temperature on the oven. When he faced her again, Etta offered him a smile she hoped was kind, flirty, and sexy all at the same time.

"Did you sell your ranch in Dripping Springs?" She opened the fridge and put the bowl of pea salad inside. She liked hers cold as ice, and even fifteen minutes out while the rolls cooked was too long.

"No," he said. "It was my wife's, and after she died, I couldn't, well." He swallowed. 'I couldn't keep working the ranch. It was too painful. I saw her everywhere, and I couldn't help reliving the last time I'd seen her." He closed his eyes and shook his head, as if living through all of it again.

"I moved Hailey out to a house in town, and I worked another ranch. Josie's parents took over the ranch. They still have it."

Etta nodded, trying to imagine what it would be like to go through a traumatic experience like that. "I'm sorry, August. That must've been hard."

"She fell from a roof," he said, his back to her. "It's a terrible way to die, and she was alone. Josie was so headstrong. She never needed help from anyone, you know?" He gave a light laugh that sounded more bitter than nostalgic. "We don't know how long she was there. I was mowing that day, and that can steal hours from a man. Her father and I went out to find her when she didn't come in for dinner."

Etta didn't know what to say. How could a husband and a father happen upon their deceased loved one and not be changed forever? She wanted to comfort August, but she didn't know how. She knew that when she was right in the thick of her own hardships, she didn't want sympathy. She didn't want someone to tell her it would all be okay one day. She didn't want someone to quote some meaningless platitudes.

She just wanted to feel like she wasn't alone. The oven beeped, indicating it had come to temperature, and Etta bent to open it and slide the unbaked rolls inside. *Please help him to know he's not alone*, she prayed.

Straightening, she said, "I'm right here. You can tell me anything about her, and I won't judge you."

August nodded as he fiddled with the aluminum foil over the bowl of mashed potatoes. "Strange as it seems, Etta, I actually believe you."

"Why is that strange?"

"Most people judge," he said. "Even when they say they won't." He tilted his head, barely looking at her out of the corner of his eye. "But you...like I said the other day. You're not like anyone I've ever met. When you say you won't judge me, I actually believe you."

Etta nodded, her throat thick with unsaid words. "I was in love with a man named Noah Johnson," she said, her voice warbling, almost like she'd swallowed a music box that needed new batteries. "We were engaged to be married. He was several years older than me." She shook her head, frowning. "No, he was a lot older than me. Twelve years. Fourteen years. Something like that. He had three teenage children, and he didn't want any more."

August lifted his head fully, his eyes widening. He knew what that meant for Etta, and she hated that it had taken her so long to be brave enough to admit it and do something about it.

"I thought I would be okay without having any children of my own," she whispered, all of her loneliness, her longing, and her self-loathing rearing up and washing through her. Wave after wave of it kept her from speaking again, and this time, August gathered her close and held her right against his heartbeat.

It wasn't frantic or flopping, and Etta took comfort in the slow, steady pace of it against her cheek.

"I couldn't go through with the wedding," she said, strong enough to admit it now. "I did a horrible, terrible thing to him, because I couldn't tell him until the day of the wedding. I just kept praying and praying that it would be okay. I loved him. It was enough. *He* was enough."

She shook her head and stepped away from August. She couldn't breathe in here. Retreating from the kitchen quickly, Etta sucked at the air. Her mind whirred, and she suddenly stood in the bride's room in True Blue, the restored barn where many of her family members had managed to walk down the aisle and say I-do.

Failure rained upon Etta, and while she hadn't cried over this particular situation in her life in quite a while, the tears came now.

"It wasn't enough," August said from somewhere behind her.

She shook her head. "I really wanted it to be. I apologized to him a thousand times. Some days, I feel at-peace and I know he's okay. Some days, I really hate myself for what I did." She turned back to him, a hot, angry feeling licking up through her core now. "I'm better now, August. I won't do that again. I'm more open, and more honest, and I listen to God better than ever. And no, I don't judge people quite the way I used to."

He stood on the other side of the island, leaning into both hands. Heaven knew Etta had plenty to be judged for, and now August did too.

"I don't judge you," he said. "I wasn't there. I don't know the situation."

"I'm just saying, I won't do that to you. If we keep dating, and things aren't going well, and I'm not feeling good about us, I'll just tell you. I won't wait until the wedding day."

A ghost of a smile touched his mouth. "Sounds like a deal." He glanced down at the counter and turned to open a cupboard. He got down a couple of plates and set them beside the bowl of mashed potatoes.

"I never did say why it's hard for me to tell Hailey about us," he said. "You asked, on Saturday, before Dot went into labor. Remember?"

Etta had definitely not forgotten. She nodded, glad when he turned his attention back to the silverware drawer and she could wipe her eyes quickly. She'd done a fast job on her makeup, because Etta didn't wear much makeup, especially when she didn't have to go to schools or host people at the ranch.

"I'm not sure how anyone could be embarrassed of you," he said, laying out two knives and two forks. "I'm one-hundred percent interested in you. I liked you from the moment you crouched down in front of my daughter with that baggie of Band-aids, and every time I talk to you, I learn something new and fascinating about you that makes you more of a whole person to me."

Etta shook her head. "You can stop."

August came around the island, shaking his head. "I'm not going to stop." He didn't speak loudly, and Etta liked this more subdued, quiet nature. At the same time, power flowed from his eyes, from the set of his shoulders, and from his mouth when he did choose to say something.

"I'm glad you're not perfect, because I would feel so inadequate beside you, and I don't think your family is too big." He offered her a smile but stopped several feet away. "Your family is great. Hailey loves them to bits and pieces, and I've decided to swallow my pride and let y'all help me with her after school."

Etta's soul lit up. "That's wonderful, August."

"The truth is, Etta." He took slow steps toward her. "I'm scared." He reached her and took both of her hands in both of his. He looked down at their fingers, the moment tender and real between them. "I'm scared of what might happen to my heart if I let someone as amazing as you into my life. I'm scared of letting Hailey get too close to you, only to have you abandon her."

Etta didn't think that would ever happen, but she couldn't say so for sure. Not right now. She had dozens of dating horror stories, and she wanted more time with August to make sure she knew him, understood him, and that they had similar goals for the future before anything lasting was said or done.

"I don't mind waiting," she said.

"As long as you know it's not because of you," he said. "It's a weakness inside of *me*. It's a fear *I'm* working through." He looked up and into her eyes, and time stutter-stopped again. He released one of her hands, reaching up, and brushed her hair back from her face. "Okay?"

She nodded. "Okay."

They breathed in together, and that made Etta laugh. The sober moment and time for confessionals ended, and she held his hand as they went back into the kitchen. "All right," she said. "Butter and jam with your bread? Or are you making barbecue rib sandwiches tonight?"

"Guess," he said, teasing her. Flirting with her.

She cocked one hip and pretended to study him. "Butter and jam," she said. "I know a man with a sweet-savory tooth when I meet one." Not only that, but she'd seen no less than four jars of jam in his fridge when she'd slid the pea salad inside.

"I've got apricot, raspberry, peach, or strawberry-rhubarb," he said, pulling open the fridge, looking at her with questions in his eyes. "I'll just get out all of them."

Chapter Eight

Montana Glover knew her daughter would come around the corner in her husband's truck at any moment. She may or may not have been following Aurora and Oliver's journey since they'd crossed the Arkansas state line and entered Oklahoma.

They'd finished their semester at the Savannah College of Art and Design, and they'd be on the ranch for the next three weeks. Montana missed them so much, and tears pressed against the backs of her eyes.

"Stop it," she told herself. "You will not cry when you see them." Aurora and Ollie had been married for almost a year now, and they'd come back to Three Rivers a few times. This wasn't the first, only, or last time Montana would see them.

Aurora loved her design and fashion classes at the SCAD, and Ollie had been taking more and more technology and animation classes instead of the equine studies he'd started with last January.

The big truck Ollie drove came around the corner, and Montana burst to her feet. "They're here," she said to Robbie, her little boy, and he looked up from the toy cars he'd spread out across the porch. She stepped over him and the toys and opened the front door. "Bishop, they're here."

She laughed as she turned and went down the front steps just as Ollie brought the truck to a complete stop in front of the house. "Mama," Aurora said, spilling from the passenger seat.

"Hey, baby," she said, her voice cracking as the emotion took over. She reached Aurora and gripped her tightly in a hug. "You've been driving forever. How are you?"

"So good," Aurora said, her grip on Montana just as tight as her mother's. Bishop came down the steps, Robbie in his arms, and Aurora squealed as she went to greet them. She loved Bishop as if he were her biological father, because he'd always acted like he was.

They laughed together, and Robbie kept saying, "Rowa, Rowa, Rowa," as if no one but him knew who she was.

Montana grinned at Ollie and opened her arms to the boy. He was a man now, but Montana still struggled to think of him that way. He took good care of Aurora in Savannah, while managing his own studies, their household money, and all the lawn care.

"How are you, my boy?" she asked in a whisper. "You tell me straight. What can I do to make your life easier?" She knew she couldn't do much. Ollie had plenty of resources should he need them, and he possessed a cheerful, optimistic outlook on life.

"I would kill for one of your cannoli cupcakes right now," he said, his voice full of a grin. "And Aurora said if you don't have Mexican corn in the house, she's going to go stay with Etta." He pulled away and grinned at Montana.

"Food," she said. "I should've known." She laughed and shook her head. "Lucky for you both, I have everything I thought you could want."

"She's not kidding," Bishop said, joining them and hugging Oliver too. "I've been up to my elbows in pastry dough all morning. The kids want croissants, Bish. Can you get started on the croissants? They'll be here before eleven, and we can have brunch." His voice pitched up in a poor imitation of Montana, who folded her arms.

"And are the croissants done?" she challenged.

"No," Bishop said with a laugh. He passed Robbie to Oliver. "I guess I better go get that done. I can't have my wife mad at me."

"No, sir," Ollie said, smiling. He glanced at Montana as Aurora came to his side. He put one arm around her, and with Robbie in his arms, it sure looked like they could be a family. A young family, just starting out with their first child.

Montana didn't hate the idea, though she'd spent the first six months of this year praying that Aurora and Ollie would just wait a little longer to start their family. They had so many years ahead of them, and she wanted them both to have the educational opportunities they'd worked for in Georgia.

A wave of unrest hit her, and Montana turned toward the house. "The cupcakes are done, at least. I made those last night. Come on." She led the way up the steps to the front porch, because now wasn't the time to obsess over the fact that she hadn't been able to get pregnant again, or worry that maybe Aurora wouldn't be able to either.

Then her prayers would've been wasted, just like they had been for the past nine months as she'd begged the Lord to give her and Bishop another baby. Her husband loved kids, and he had a heart as big as the moon and as wide as the sky. He was younger than her, and she still had several years where she could bear children. They hadn't had any problem conceiving Robbie, and Montana had started to wonder what she was supposed to learn from this experience.

Bishop always played music while he baked, and the rock song on the Internet radio filled the house. Aurora and Ollie started dancing with Robbie, and Montana simply stood back and allowed herself to feel the joy that came from these people, from this small family she'd managed to build.

Bishop stepped to her side, one arm slipping around her waist easily. "They sure seem happy."

"They do," she said.

"Are you okay?" he asked, his voice nowhere near loud enough to be heard over the music.

She wasn't sure if she should nod or shake her head no. She gave a half-hearted shrug, a smile touching her mouth, her eyes, and her soul as Robbie started to giggle and giggle. The boy had been a blessing to her, but he could also be a devil. He loved getting into the pantry and climbing up on the buckets and then the shelves to get to the yogurt-covered raisins. He could slip away from her in the blink of an eye, and she'd find him covered in mud, flour, or grass clippings, none of which were that fun to clean off an almost-two-year-old boy.

She loved him fiercely though, and Robbie reminded her so much of Bishop. Full of life, full of mischief, full of faith. He had a heart of gold, and plenty of charisma, and she couldn't wait to watch him grow into a fine young man.

The song ended, and Ollie set Robbie on the floor.

"When are you going to see your parents?" she asked.

"Tonight," he said. "They're having a big dinner at Seven Sons." He wore a smile, but he seemed nervous. "They act like they haven't seen us in years."

"They just miss you," Montana said. "I'm sure Jeremiah does too. You worked hard around that ranch."

"I think it's actually Uncle Skyler and Uncle Micah," Aurora said, wrapping her arms around Ollie and beaming up at him. "He babysat for them a lot, and when he left...no babysitter."

Ollie shook his head, but he didn't contradict her. "We are watching the kids this weekend, so my aunts and uncles can go to the Country Christmas. I guess there's a big concert there?"

"Yeah," Bishop said. "Mister might be able to get you some tickets. Libby puts on the Country Christmas."

"We'll see," Ollie said. "I think my family just wants us to watch the kids so we'll see how much work they are and not have any for a while." He and Aurora laughed, but Montana just looked back and forth between them.

"Are you going to have any soon?" she asked.

"I doubt it," Aurora said easily. "We're doing great in school, Mom, and I don't know." She stepped away from Oliver and linked her arm through Montana's. She'd never quite known the exact right thing to say to her daughter, and she didn't now either.

"When we're ready, we'll have a baby."

If only it was that easy. Montana nodded like it was, and she pasted a smile on her face. She caught the way Bishop watched her, and she wished she didn't wear her emotions so obviously. "You'll know when the time is right," she said with confidence. "Not only that, but whenever you start your family, it will be a blessing. Babies are a gift from the Lord."

She truly believed that, but it did leave her wondering one thing: Why didn't the Lord want to bless her? Was she not worthy of getting a gift from Him? And if not, how could she change?

A week later, Montana had no more answers for her questions. Aurora and Ollie had left the previous evening to go spend a couple of nights at Wolf Mountain Lodge, and they'd be back in time for Christmas Eve dinner, which Judge and June were hosting at the Ranch House this year.

They'd stay in Three Rivers through the New Year, and

then start their journey back to Savannah. Montana missed her daughter already, and she couldn't put off taking the pregnancy test for another day.

She'd missed her period four days ago, and she'd been resisting the hope that she might be pregnant. After nine months of unsuccessful attempts to have another baby, hope was a terrible, frightening thing. It ate at her and ate at her, and she hadn't even told Bishop that she was late.

Drawing a deep breath, she got out the pregnancy test. "No matter what," she told herself. "This isn't going to define me. Even if I can only have Robbie and Aurora in my life, I will be happy. There are lots of other children here at the ranch." She had plenty of opportunities to help others with their children, and lots of ways to serve her own family members.

She wasn't so worried about herself. She worried about Bishop. He had six siblings and five cousins, and he adored his big family. She wanted him to be happy, and she didn't want him to have to field questions from his brothers, sister, or cousins.

Several of them had a lot of kids already, and none of them waited very long to start their families. Montana told herself it was because they hadn't gotten married when they were twenty, with plenty of years to bear children and raise a family. Bear hadn't even started dating until he was forty-five. He didn't have time to waste when it came to expanding his family.

Montana *knew* all of these things intellectually. She *knew* it wasn't a race. She *knew* no one judged her or

Bishop based on how many children they had or how close together those children were. But in the corner of her heart that really wanted another child, it felt like everyone in the family was gossiping about when Bishop and Montana would stop building houses and start building their family.

Her stomach lurched and tightened, and Montana turned away from her reflection. She sat down, and everything inside her went numb. She didn't need the pregnancy test.

She'd started her period.

She could only stare at the wall across from the toilet, and she had no idea how long she sat there. Eventually, she remembered how to take care of herself, and she managed to do that and leave the bathroom.

Another month, she thought. Another text she'd have to send to Bishop. Another vase of flowers he'd bring home after work, another night he'd reassure her that he was okay with just the one son, another week of tears every time she saw Holly Ann or Dot or anyone in the family.

"You just won't leave the house for a week," she told herself as she moved on wooden legs down the hall. "It'll be fine. No one missed you at that luncheon last week." No one had asked where she was on Sunday after church when she'd sent Bishop, Robbie, Aurora, and Ollie over to the homestead alone.

She should be reattaching her tool belt to her waist and getting back to work. She'd only come home for a quick snack—and to take the pregnancy test without Bishop around—and he was likely waiting for her down near Preacher's place.

Mister had asked for a house at Shiloh Ridge, and the administrative board had met with Bishop and Montana. A site had been chosen across the main road that led up to the ranch, almost parallel to Preacher and Charlie's farmhouse. That would give Libby easy access to the highway that led out to Golden Hour, where she would continue to work on her family's ranch.

She and Mister had set a date for their wedding in February, which was the shortest engagement of all the Glovers. Well, besides Preacher and Charlie, who'd decided to get married spontaneously once they'd been trapped on the ranch together.

Montana sank onto the couch, tears threatening to over-flow down her face. She couldn't go back out onto the ranch to work. She couldn't even see straight. She couldn't think.

The doorbell rang, and she didn't move. Why would someone come here in the middle of the day? While Holly Ann, Sammy, Oakley, Willa, Zona, and Dot got together in the middle of the day, Montana didn't join them very often. She still had a very busy job to do around Shiloh Ridge, and Bishop usually took Robbie with him or he dropped him off at Ace's, Bear's, or Cactus's for the day.

The ranch wives have been nothing but good to Montana. She shouldn't have such negative and bitter thoughts about them and how easy their lives were. But the truth was, she did.

"Maybe that's why you can't get pregnant," she

murmured to herself, and that only made the tears too heavy for her to contain. They flowed down her face, and she wished they would take all the bad feelings with them.

"She's here," someone said, and Montana looked toward the door as Willa and June entered the house. What in the world was June doing here? She ran a busy networking company, and she didn't have time to come back to the ranch for mid-morning snacks, lunch, or even dinner sometimes.

She couldn't stop crying, even when Willa sat right beside her and drew her into a tight embrace, saying, "What's wrong, Montana? Please, tell us what's wrong so we can help."

Chapter Nine

Willa Glover's heart hurt at the pain and devastation pouring from one of her dearest friends. She'd been standing in her kitchen with Chaz on a chair beside her, the two of them pushing chocolate candy kisses into peanut butter cookie dough when she'd had the overwhelming thought to *leave now! Go to Montana's.*

She'd paused while her son continued to mash candy into dough. "Momma," he'd said, and all Willa could hear was *Go now, Willa. Go.*

So she'd scooped Chaz into her arms, and she'd left the Edge Cabin. She'd left the cookies. She'd left the oven on. She'd loaded up Chaz and Lynn, who didn't have preschool on Thursdays, and she'd started the journey in from the Edge. June had flagged her down from the backyard as she'd started to pass the Ranch House, and she'd said, "I have a terrible feeling inside. Do you need something?"

"Not me," Willa said. "It's Montana."

"Did she call you?"

"No," Willa said. The Lord had called her. "Let's stop at the homestead and see if Etta will take the kids."

She had, of course. Etta always wanted the kids, and she'd said she'd pray for Montana. June and Willa had continued down the road and behind the barn. She'd rung the doorbell three times, as Montana's truck sat out front. Willa had known she was inside, and June had finally reached for the doorknob and opened the door without being invited inside.

Willa met June's eyes over the top of Montana's head. Seeing her sobbing on the couch had wrenched her heart into the wrong position inside her chest, because Willa knew devastation like this. She'd once lost her son to her ex-husband, and she'd once had to spend hours, days, months, and years on her knees and working hard in her life to fix the things she'd done wrong.

She stopped asking Montana to talk to her and instead just held her. June stroked her nearly white-blonde hair and murmured things like, "We're right here, Montana," and "We can help you."

Willa wasn't sure if that was true or not, but she'd like to believe it was. Sometimes just being with a person helped them, and eventually June fell silent too.

Montana quieted very soon after that, and Willa once again met June's eye. June was new to the family, but Willa had spent a great deal of time with her. Cactus and Judge were close, and that had allowed the two women to become close too.

June nodded once, and Willa straightened and removed her arm from around Montana's shoulders. Her back ached, the remnants of an old car accident still coming forward sometimes. "We...." Willa didn't know how to continue. "I'll just be honest, Montana. I was making cookies with the kids when God yelled at me to get over here." She knew that sounded crazy, but she was one of the pastors in Three Rivers, and she could sound crazy if she wanted to. "I think June got the same message, because she flagged me down from the backyard, and she's wearing her pajamas."

"I wasn't feeling well this morning," June said. "So I didn't go to work. I'd gotten up to use the bathroom and get a drink when I felt like I better get outside. There was something wrong, and I needed to...go."

"Go where?" Montana asked.

"I didn't know," June said. "Not ten seconds later, Willa came by. I asked her if she had something wrong. She said it was...you." Her voice trailed off, and her eyes stayed so wide.

Montana's face crumpled again, and she shook her head. "Bishop and I have been trying to have another baby," she said. "I was late, and I was so hopeful, and I was going to take a test this morning. Then I saw I'd started my period, and I don't know, I guess I just sort of...lost it."

Willa reached over and took her hand. She didn't say she was sorry, because that was such a poor thing to say to someone in such obvious distress. Instead, she squeezed

Montana's hand and prayed that the Lord would allow some of her sadness and hurt to flow through Willa.

She'd shoulder it for Montana if she could. Tears pricked her eyes, and her emotion kept her silent.

"I'm so sorry," June whispered. "I would do anything, so you didn't have to feel like this."

Montana actually smiled through her tears and leaned her head against June's chest. She cradled her there, the two of them crying together. "I know you would," she said. "When are you going to tell everyone you're pregnant?"

Willa's eyes widened as June looked at her through her tears. She hadn't known June was pregnant, and she almost felt like asking God why He'd send a pregnant woman to minister to someone who desperately wanted to be pregnant.

It sure didn't seem fair or kind, both things Willa knew the Lord to be.

"Christmas Eve," she said. "But that doesn't mean you can't come. I know you've been staying away from the family gatherings. Please, you can't do that on Christmas Eve. I need you there."

"We'll see," Montana said. "It's just so...merry." She sounded disgusted by such a concept, and her sobs turned to laughs in the next moment. June's did too, and Willa giggled and smiled with them. They all fell into sighs and silence then, and finally Montana said, "Holly Ann brought over that chicken gumbo last night. Should I heat it up, or will the smell of it make you sick?"

She looked from June to Willa. "I have cornbread and

beef stew too. Aurora and Bishop made that." Her face fell and she studied her hands. "I can't cook very well. Maybe that's why I can't have another baby."

"Nonsense," Willa said. "Cooking ability doesn't matter."

A desperate, caged look filled Montana's eyes as she looked at Willa. "Maybe it's because I'm so jealous of Dot, and Holly Ann, and you, and June."

"No," Willa said gently. "No, Montana. Being jealous doesn't make it so you can't get pregnant."

Tears splashed her cheeks when she nodded. "I'm trying not to be. I love you guys. Of course I do. I love Holly Ann, but even just now, I had to work really hard not to say something disparaging about her. It's not her fault. It's *my* problem."

"It's not a problem to want a baby," June said. "You're a human being, Montana. We have this huge range of emotions, and no, life isn't fair. I think—and Pastor Glover here can correct me if I'm wrong—but I think that everyone views God as this almighty being who's pulling strings in our lives. I don't think that's who He is at all."

Willa waited, because June was such an interesting person. She had big ideas and most of the time, Willa agreed with her.

"I think God allows us to go through pain and sorrow sometimes. He's not going to swoop in and rescue us from every hurt, every heartache, every harrowing hour. He's just not. He sent His son to feel those pains, those hurts, and those heartaches, and He expects us to turn to Him when we have them."

Willa found herself nodding by the end of the first sentence. "And He can't be everywhere," she added. "So he sends people who can help us. That's why June and I are here. To help you." She got to her feet. "So I'll heat up the beef stew, because gumbo makes my tongue happy but my stomach mad." She gave a light laugh. "June? What do you want?"

"Stew for me too," she said. "The baby doesn't like spicy things." She smiled at Montana as Willa walked in front of them. "Honey, I love you." She hugged Montana, who gripped her back.

"I love you too, June," she whispered.

Willa set about heating up lunch, though it wasn't terribly close to lunchtime yet. She ignored her phone when it chimed, because she wanted all of her focus right here, on Montana and June and building the relationship she wanted to have with them.

As the three of them sat down to eat, she reached over and covered Montana's hand with hers. "Do you know why Cactus and I decided to foster?"

"No."

Willa's chest heaved, but she pushed through the shallow breaths and took deeper ones. "I know exactly why you want a baby so badly. I'm willing to bet everything I have that it's not for you."

Montana's eyes filled with tears, and she ducked her head.

"These Glover men—some of them—have the biggest hearts in the world," Willa said. "I know Bishop, and I know he wants a half-dozen kids, preferably all boys." She laughed lightly, though there wasn't much light about this morning. "And you love him." Her voice broke, and June's eyes filled with tears too.

"You love him, and you want him to be happy, and having a big family will make him happy. But Montana, it won't make him love you any more. He loves you already."

"I know."

"Because of my accident, I have physical limitations," Willa said. "My pregnancy with Chaz was very hard on me, and I told Cactus I couldn't do it again. I *know* the disappointment, Montana. I felt it and saw it and lived it."

She nodded and dipped her spoon into her stew.

"Maybe you just have some physical limitations," Willa said. "Maybe there's another way for you and Bishop to grow your family, *if* that's what you think you should do."

"How do you know what to do?" she asked, her voice small and childlike.

Willa didn't believe for a moment that she didn't already know. "You do the exact same things you've been doing for so long." Montana looked up and met her eyes, and Willa smiled at her, feeling strong and sure about what she should say. "The Lord loves you, Montana. He is not upset with you or anything you've chosen to do. He understands human jealousy, and he does not fault you for it. He has put good men and women in your life for you to love and lean on, and that's it. That's what you need to do.

Keep doing what you've been doing. He'll keep guiding you."

"But He doesn't pull strings," Montana said, shooting a look at June.

"I don't think so," June said. "Otherwise, everything feels so very...wrong. Like, why would He step in and intervene to save Lucy Mae in that car accident last year, but not the man who was driving? Does that mean God loves my daughter more than him? No." She shook her head, her resolve firm. "No, I don't believe that. I think God allows the good and the bad into our lives, and it's up to us to show Him what we'll do when things don't go our way."

Willa grinned at her, finally lifting her first bite of stew to her mouth too. "She's smart," she said, and June smiled on back. "It can be easy to feel like God is punishing us when we don't have things go our way. Sometimes that's true—and sometimes it's not. In this case, Montana, I don't think it's true."

"It's just an experience," June said after she finished her bite of stew. "One you will find your way through, as long as Bishop keeps making this stew."

The three of them laughed, and Willa's heart warmed at the joy and happiness she could now feel in Montana. No, everything wasn't magically fixed by a few minutes of conversation and a bowl of soup. But it certainly didn't feel like the world was about to end anymore either.

"Thank you," Montana said, sobering again. "Really, I mean it. Thank you for coming."

"Anytime," Willa and June said together, and Willa knew

she'd be there for anyone who needed her, and that June would be too. She loved having such good examples in her life, and as June loaded their dishes into the dishwasher, Willa sent a quick text to all the ranch wives.

I love you ladies. Thank you for including me in your lives.

Chapter Ten

June Glover took off the blue sweater with the big, bold star on the front of it. It was festive, sure, but she didn't like how the bottom two arms of the star curved around her belly. "You're pregnant," she told herself as she tossed the garment on the bed. It joined three other tried-and-rejected items, and June paused to look at the red and white striped blouse.

She'd pulled it off at first, hating the way the red made her skin look even more blotchy than it already did. Now, she picked it up again and tugged it over her head.

"Oh, that's cute," Judge said, coming out of the master bathroom. He wore a towel around his waist and nothing on his torso, and June grinned at him. He ran his electric razor along his neck, getting a close shave there. "It's like a candy cane."

"That's why I rejected it in the first place," she said, looking down at the flowing fabric. "But it hides the baby."

Judge grinned, his free hand reaching for her. He cupped

their unborn baby, the look of adoration on his face price-less. "It's not going to be hidden much longer," he said. He lifted his eyes to hers. "Right? We're telling everyone tonight?"

"Yes," June said. "Lucy Mae knows now. Your mother, and Montana." She'd taken her daughter to lunch the day she'd returned from her semester of college in California, and she'd be there that night. In fact, Lucy Mae had volunteered to do a lot of the set-up for that evening's Christmas Eve feast, which Judge and June were hosting at the Ranch House.

June could cook, if all it involved was opening packaging and setting a temperature on the oven. Then a timer. Other than that, she let Judge dominate in the kitchen. Or she went down the lane to Bull House, where Ward always seemed to have something delicious on the stove, or to the homestead, where everyone knew Etta could whip up gourmet goodies in less time than it took to report on how everyone in the family was doing.

The vast size of the Glover family helped in that, and if Etta wasn't home, June could continue past True Blue, turn left and end up at Holly Ann's, and the woman was a professional caterer. No, June did not have to hunt very hard to find something to eat.

June put her hands on her husband's bare chest and leaned into his strength. "What do you think of Ashley for a girl? We could call her Ash."

"That's very tree," he said with a smile. He lowered his razor and then his head to kiss her, and June could get lost inside his slow, sensual touch. She had, many times, but they didn't have the luxury right now.

"Your whole family will be here within an hour," she murmured against his lips.

"Yeah, you're right." He kissed her again, one hand slipping around to her back to hold her in place. June had done her best to resist this man, and in the end, she'd been very bad at it.

The doorbell rang, and Lucy Mae yelled, "Mom!" from somewhere beyond the closed door.

Judge groaned, but June giggled as she danced away from him. "You get dressed. I need you to fold all the napkins. Lucy Mae better have those tables up and set."

"She will," he said, but June went to check anyway.

Her daughter stood at the front door, holding it open while a team of people carried in trays of food. Judge had ordered a traditional Christmas feast from a new restaurant that had come to Three Rivers—Bears and Bison.

They served untraditional meats alongside more normal fare too. June met them in the kitchen, where a man wearing a very chef-like coat started going through the list. "Mashed potatoes," he said. "Three." He peeled back one of the lids and looked at her with a question in his eyes.

The scent of salt, butter, and starch hit her nose, and June smiled. "Looks great."

The chef smiled too. "Roast turkey, twenty-five pounds. We've got candied ham, ten pounds. And roast beef, fifteen pounds." He nodded at his people, and they all lifted the lids to show June.

"Fantastic," she said, knowing Judge had ordered way too much roast beef so he could enjoy sandwiches through the rest of birthing season.

"Creamed corn and creamed peas," the chef continued. "Twelve dozen rolls. Three pecan pies, two apple, one key lime, one chocolate mousse, and one lemon chiffon." The food kept piling up and piling up, and June started to get overwhelmed.

She reminded herself that Judge had eleven siblings and cousins, and they all had a significant other coming tonight. That alone was twenty-four people. Then she had to add on children. Then some of the in-laws' loved ones—for example, when Holly Ann had RSVP'ed, she'd done so for seven, not just three.

Her father, her sister and her husband, and their baby were all coming. June and Judge had been praying for good weather for three weeks, and it sure seemed like the Lord had listened. They'd told everyone they would provide all the food, but June didn't think for even a moment that Bishop wouldn't bring a cake or a pie. Holly Ann too. Etta and Ida would definitely have some food item in tow when they walked in.

June didn't mind. She loved all of the Glovers in their own way, even the ones who talked really loud and had more bark than she personally liked. She liked the quiet ones, like Judge, and she liked the ones who came forward on special occasions, like Zona did when the family decorated the angel tree every year.

Judge's mother and her husband would be there. Aunt

Dawna was staying at Bull House for a couple of weeks, so she'd be there too. Judge had made sure anyone on the big ranch text knew that if they didn't have anywhere to go for the holidays, they were welcome at the Ranch House.

Only three of the ranch workers had taken him up on his offer—Jed, Royce, and one of the new men Preacher had hired down at the Kinder Ranch, Jess. August Winters and his daughter would be there, as Etta's guests. Mister had his fiancée now, and all of the rodeo cowboys who'd come to help Libby with her Country Christmas.

June had stopped keeping track at forty people. Judge had said he'd handle it, and she'd let him. The holidays were extremely busy for her, as everyone wanted Internet connections that worked in a blink of an eye. Businesses thrived when their networks worked properly. Families wanted to do video calls and chats without issues.

She'd once again put Judge's show online, and he'd been in the top three on the voting for the Christmas light show since it had started the day after Thanksgiving. He didn't seem concerned about winning this year, but June had been adding him and his show to her prayers for the duration of the show.

The theme this year was deer, and Judge had only used reindeer or deer in his decoration. He'd hoped to get across that Christmas was the time to remember all those that were *dear* to a person, but June wasn't sure people understood. Not only that, but parents usually voted for the show that their children liked, and the kids in Three Rivers definitely weren't enthralled with his deer.

"Ma'am," the chef said, and June blinked her way out of wires and code and Wi-Fi connections. "I just need you to sign if everything looks good."

"It sure smells good," Judge said, entering the kitchen, now dressed in a pair of jeans, the cowboy boots he wore to church, and the ugliest Christmas sweater she'd ever seen. She gaped at it, wondering where in the world he'd gotten it. "Howdy, Blaine."

"Judge." The two men shook hands and exchanged smiles, and Judge took the clipboard and signed it.

"Thanks for bringing all of this."

"Anytime," Blaine said, and he and his team vacated the house.

"Wow, you're really off your game," Judge said.

June blinked away from the sweater, which actually had lights sewn into it. Blinking lights. "Where did you get *that*?"

Judge chuckled and snuck another bite of roast beef. She swatted at his hand, and he backed up, laughing fully now. "It's hideous, right? I'm totally going to win the ugliest sweater contest tonight."

"I didn't even know there was a contest."

"That's because I only told the men," he said, grinning at her.

"So for our first Christmas together, you thought it would be a good idea to hold a contest you didn't tell everyone about." She folded her arms and gave him her best *are-you-serious?* look.

"There will be a few games," he said. "And June-Bug, this is not our first Christmas together."

"Where we're married, it is." She tried very hard not to melt into his arms, but she failed. "Sure seems like you don't want to stay that way."

"Oh, but I do," he said, sliding his lips down her throat.

"Games? Why didn't you say anything?"

"Because I didn't want it to be more work for you." He stepped back and turned away from her. She'd seen this tactic before. "You stress about stuff you don't need to stress about."

"He's right, Mom," Lucy Mae said, and June twisted toward her, having forgotten she was even there.

"Don't gang up on me," she said.

"I'm doing a game with the kids," Lucy Mae said, putting her arm around June's waist. "Did you ask him about Ash?"

"I did," June said. "He has no opinion."

"We don't even know if it's a boy or a girl," Judge said, turning back to the two of them with a bottle of lemonade in his hand.

"For a boy, you have to do Birch," Lucy Mae said, smiling for all she was worth.

Judge growled—actually growled at her.

"Come on, Judge," she said with a giggle. "In this family? It's perfect. Birch Glover."

"I don't hate Birch...." June knew Judge didn't really care what they named their baby. He didn't care if it was a boy or a girl. He sure was fun to tease about some of the more earthy names out there.

"I thought you were the outcast," Judge said, giving her a sharp look. "Why can't we just go with something like Emma or Adam? My name's John, for crying out loud."

"That's why we need a little color in our baby's name," June said.

"We have nicknames for that," Judge said, lifting the lid on the roast beef again.

June flattened it, almost catching his fingers in the process. "So we name the baby Adam, and then call him what?"

"Acorn," Lucy Mae said, and only two beats of silence filled the house before all three of them burst out laughing.

"No," June said. "No, no, no. No baby of mine is going to be called *Acorn*."

The back door opened, and Bishop, Montana, Aurora, and Oliver entered. "We're early, I know," Bishop said, holding the door with his foot for his family to enter. "I wanted to put this to finish in the oven here, and Montana said you wouldn't care."

"We don't care," June said. "Come in."

Bishop carried a partially-baked cherry cobbler past them and into the kitchen, where he slid it into the oven and set the temperature. "I heard you and June are expecting." He grinned at Judge and drew him into a hug. June wanted to flick a look at Montana to see how she reacted, but she couldn't look away from the two brothers.

"Yeah," Judge said, his eyes closing. "Due at the end of April."

"That's so great," Bishop said, and his voice pinched along every letter. June did look at Montana then, and she saw the glassy quality of the woman's eyes. She reached for her hand, and with one squeeze Montana took a deep breath and nodded.

From there, people continued to arrive. June had to play hostess, but she kept an eye on Montana, glad when Willa never seemed to get too far from her. Yes, Montana stayed on the outskirts of the crowd, but June usually did too. It wasn't uncommon for a lot of people to want to be two or three deep instead of on the frontlines of this family.

Thankfully, there were a lot of children, and they seemed to steal the spotlight whether they wanted it or not. Aurora and Oliver, who didn't live here full-time, always had people around them, and Lucy Mae had been folded right into the Glovers as well.

Montana had brought her Aunt Jackie and Uncle Bob, and she stayed close to them too. Holly Ann, who June loved and who Montana did too, seemed super-busy with her sister's baby and her father, and that brought some relief to June.

She hugged Lois, who put one hand on June's baby bump too. "I can't wait to meet them."

June smiled at her fondly, since her own mother lived so far away. "We can find out next week if it's a boy or a girl. Do you think we should?"

Her eyebrows went up. "I'm not going to answer that."

"My mother is smart," Judge said, joining June in front of her. "Hello, Mother."

"Hello, baby."

"I want to find out," June said.

"I said I'd do what you want," Judge said.

She didn't want him to do what she wanted. She wanted him to say what *he* wanted, so she didn't have to feel guilty all the time. "Judge—"

"I want to find out too," he said, turning back to the house. "Is everyone here?"

"I haven't seen Ida or Brady," June said.

"Yes, they just came in the back," Etta said from nearby. "I think they parked down at Ward's and took the twins out onto the ranch for a little bit." She smiled at June, her eyes falling to her torso though the blouse did a good job of hiding the baby. "Congratulations," she whispered.

"Thank you," June said, stepping over to hug Etta. The woman loved children with everything she had, and June wanted to ask her about August. He'd arrived with her, as had his daughter, but they didn't stand too close, and August had not reached for her once. He currently stood over by Mister and the rodeo cowboys, laughing and talking.

Hailey, his daughter, had sought out Cam and Kyle, and the three of them crowded on the couch around a magazine the little girl held for all of them to see.

"Nothing yet?" she asked.

"Things are going *so* well," Etta said into her shoulder. "I hate to jinx it, actually."

June pulled away but didn't let go of Etta's shoulders. "*So* well?"

"I see him several times a week now," she said, her gaze going to August's and back in a blink. "I get to see Hailey almost every day. It's far better than texting and maybe going out once a week."

"I'm glad," June said. "You seem to really like him."

"Again, not jinxing anything." Etta's eyes sparkled like stars in all that navy darkness of night. "But June, I *really* like him." She laughed lightly, and the two of them turned toward Ida in tandem. "Hello, my sister." Etta hugged her first, and then June took her turn.

Ida's eyes were round as beach balls when she jerked away from June. "You're pregnant." She wasn't even asking.

"They haven't told everyone," Etta hissed, but several people in the vicinity had heard Ida. She hadn't exactly whispered.

"Judge," June said, and her husband somehow heard her from clear across the house. He turned away from Preacher and Charlie, must've seen something on her face, and started toward her just as Arizona asked, "Are you pregnant?"

Judge had seriously long legs, and he knew when to use them. He arrived at June's side and tucked her into his as they faced the family.

"I'm sorry," Ida said in a much quieter voice, but June gave her a small smile.

"Welcome, everyone," Judge said. "We're so glad to be hosting at the Ranch House this year." He beamed out stars and rainbows from his face, and June's heart warmed at his obvious happiness.

"Just a friendly reminder for anyone who hasn't voted yet—the Christmas light show ends tomorrow night." He looked down at June. "I didn't ask anyone if they had announcements, so we'll go first, and if anyone else has something to say, they can say it."

He paused, a hint of anxiety entering those beautiful eyes. "June and I are expecting a baby in April."

"April?" Bear bellowed loud enough to be heard above the shrieks and gasps and congratulations coming from others.

"I never want to be accused of keeping to myself again," Cactus said, once again loud enough for everyone to hear. Most people laughed, June and Judge included, and June let herself get swept up into the crowd, as the Glovers were a huggy bunch, even the men.

Thankfully, Judge didn't let dinner be delayed too much, and he said, "All right, all right. We're not running out. We'll be here for all of dinner and the evening activities." He looked around as the family settled down again. "Anyone else?"

June wasn't sure who to look at. She didn't want to put any pressure on Montana, and she was sure this was the part of the night she hated the very most. Ida's kids were older than Robbie, and Zona's daughter was coming up on her second birthday too.

Neither of them said anything, and it was Sammy who said, "Bear and I have decided to sell the mechanic shop."

"*She* decided to sell the shop." Bear frowned at his wife. "I have no say about that."

Sammy rolled her eyes, though she and Bear got along real well. "Fine, *I* decided to sell the shop," she said. "The kids keep me busy, and the boss around here is a real grump when his tractors break down." She cocked her head at Bear, obviously challenging him to contradict her again.

"Yeah, he's a real *bear* when things don't go his way," Cactus said, eliciting another round of laughter.

"A grizzly," Preacher said.

"Roars at everyone and everything," Ranger chimed in.

"Okay, okay," Bear said, plenty of fire shooting from his eyes. "I *ask* Sammy to come to the equipment shed when the ranch needs help."

"Sure," Ward says. "Like you *asked* me to make sure there would be gravy for days at this dinner."

"I just—"

"Those exact words," Ward said, chuckling. "Gravy for days."

"I like gravy," Bear bellowed. "Judge hasn't—"

"Papa Bear," Smiles said, his clear, high voice cutting through the house. Bear looked down at his son. "Too loud. Indoor voice, okay?"

June started to laugh, but she didn't dare let any sound come out of her mouth. Her chest shook, and beside her, Judge's did the same thing. Etta's near-silent laughter nearby reached June's ears, and there was going to be a swell of sound any second now.

Bear bent and scooped his son into his arms. "Yes," he said. "Sorry, buddy. Indoor voices at Christmas Eve dinner."

"Merry Christmas, everyone," Judge said, his laughter infecting his voice. "I guess you'll have to elbow Bear away from the gravy, which should last for days."

The room exploded then, with every single person smiling or laughing. June had never felt anything like it, and she sure did love this family who had welcomed her in, made her feel like one of their own, and forgave each other when they didn't use an indoor voice.

Chapter Eleven

August went down the hall in his cabin and into the bedroom, ignoring the wailing coming from Hailey's room. Such a feat didn't actually happen, but he pretended that he hadn't heard her. On the outside, he'd given no indication that he cared about her alligator tears and that she'd said he was unfair and that their house was lame.

"Lame," he said with a scoff. He couldn't help it that Cactus had five children, about ten dogs, a brand-new swing set, and a trampoline out on the Edge. He had no reason— and no resources—to have those things.

Hailey and Cameron were in the same grade in school, and while they didn't have the same teacher, they'd become fast friends. All the third graders ate lunch at the same time, and they had recess together, and Cam and Hailey were actually in the same reading group.

Great. August wasn't upset that Hailey had found

friends. He was upset that she didn't even seem to notice how hard he'd tried to make her life as easy as possible.

He sighed in frustration as he paced over to the window. This one in the corner looked south, and all August could see was a dormant field. Then another, and another. The land here could bleed into one great big square, making a man feel small and insignificant—the way August always felt.

Not always, he thought. When Etta looked at him, he felt like he held the world in the palm of his hand. Not only that, but he felt like he could actually harness it and give it to Etta, along with his heart.

He was kidding himself, of course. All he had to offer was a cabin he actually got as part of his job for *her* ranch, and...yeah, that was all. A half-heart? A few hundred dollars in the bank? A nine-year-old daughter who sometimes came across as so selfish?

A knock sounded on his bedroom door that sent his pulse up into his ears. That was not a child's knock. "Hello?" he called as he stepped toward the door. Someone had just come inside his house. Who?

He yanked open the door, his patience for the day gone. He had no idea who he expected to see there—maybe Walt from next door, or maybe Jess—but he found Etta.

She flinched backward. "Sorry," she said. "It's just me." She gestured over her shoulder. "Hailey let me in."

The girl stood in her doorway, sniffling, and August dang near rolled his eyes. He wasn't about to invite Etta into his bedroom so they could have a private chat, so he stepped out into the hallway too. She shrank back out of the way, and then she tore her eyes—wide, worried eyes—from his and marched down the hall.

August glared at Hailey as he approached. "What did I tell you about answering the door?"

"It was Etta," she said, lifting her chin. "I asked, and she answered."

"If she invites us up to the ranch to do something, *I* will decide if we go," he hissed out of the corner of his mouth. Etta invited him and Hailey to plenty of meals and parties up at the main ranch. August sure did like that, and he'd enjoyed attending. Hailey had too.

"*I'm* the dad, not you. You don't get to decide what we do, and throwing a fit doesn't help anything." He paused in front of her, her eyes filling with tears again. His heart softened, but he told himself to be strong. Be firm. She needed a father not a friend.

"In fact, because of your fit this morning, you might have jeopardized any chance of leaving the cabin today at all."

"Daddy," she said.

"No," he said. "Don't beg me. *You* chose to throw a tantrum. There are consequences of that." He walked away while he still could, and the moment he entered the larger half of the cabin, with more open space, his shoulders sagged. Parenting was such hard work, especially alone.

"Hey," he said, wanting to step over to Etta and gather her close. At this point, he wasn't sure if he cared what Hailey thought. At the same time, he did. He still strode toward where Etta stood in the kitchen and brought her close to his chest. "How are you?"

"Good," she said. "I came down to walk with Preacher, so I was here. Otherwise, I'd have called or something." She stepped back, concern in her eyes. "Is everything all right?"

August rolled his neck, trying to get the tension out. "Not really, but it's fine." He offered her a small smile. "Cactus invited Hailey out to the Edge to play the games their family got for Christmas, and I said she couldn't go." Frustration filled him again, and he nodded toward the back door.

Etta went through it first, with August following, and he sighed as he sat beside her on the top step. If this woman was his girlfriend or wife, he'd reach over and take her hand in his. They'd spent most of their time together either in the homestead or his cabin, with an occasional restaurant thrown in. He hadn't touched her a whole lot, even in private, but he found himself craving her fingers tightly woven between his.

He touched her hand, and she turned hers over and laced those fingers through his. He stared at them as heat licked its way through him. As his vision popped with white stars. As his heart pulsed out a half-warning and a half-hallelujah.

"Why didn't you want her to go?" Etta asked.

"Because," August said. "It's...I know your family is open and they don't care if we come and crash their parties or encroach on their family activities. But today, *I* cared. She got a bunch of stuff for Christmas she can play with right here."

Etta nodded, her gaze moving out into the fields beyond the cabin. "Cactus wouldn't have invited her if he didn't want her to come."

"I know that." August didn't want to talk about this, but he thought about what Etta had told him about her fiancé. Sometimes, hard things had to be said. "In truth, Etta, it made me feel inadequate as a father. Like, I can't provide this amazingly fun time for my own daughter, so I'll drive her out to the Edge, where Cactus can do it." His chest heaved, and he just wanted to go back to his bedroom. Be left alone. Anything to not be drowning in these debilitating feelings of inadequacy.

Her hand tightened in his, and she said nothing. That only drove nails into August's nerves, and he said, "Did you want to stay for lunch? June sent us home with a ton of food, and I still have plenty." He'd made the holiday breakfast casserole Josie had while she'd been alive, and August and Hailey had enjoyed their Christmas morning together.

Preacher had said there would be desserts at the farmhouse, and August had gone over there in the afternoon to get a couple of sweets for him and Hailey. They'd ended up staying for an hour, as had several other cowboys. He hadn't felt bad about it, and whoever had baked up the raspberry tarts and the chocolate walnut brownies had some skill in the kitchen.

Etta hadn't been there, but he'd texted with her a lot yesterday. "I can stay for lunch," she said now. "And I hate to bring it up, but I'm going to bring it up. Judge won the Christmas light show for the second year in a row, and we're having a big party-slash-dance at True Blue tonight." She faced him, her beauty striking him right behind his breastbone, right where his heart beat against his desire for her. "I'd love it if you and Hailey came."

"Ah, I see," he said, feeling better and better by the moment. "You want to see if I live up to my texts."

"That's right," she said, plenty of playfulness in her voice. "You've been boasting about your dancing skills for weeks now."

August chuckled as Etta moved her hand out of his and up his arm. She curled her hand just above his elbow and leaned into him, making him feel strong and powerful. He loved that about her, and the next time he breathed, all of the unrest of the morning vanished.

"We'll come," he said. "What time does the party start?"

"Well, Bear and Ranger are hanging the disco ball right now," Etta said. "Could be any moment."

"Mm." He didn't move, and Etta didn't either. Sitting with her in the country stillness made a part of his heart that had felt dead for the past four years flood with blood, and it started living again.

He reached over and took her far hand with his, rubbing his thumb along her fingers slowly. "I'm working tomorrow," he said. "As usual. Can Hailey come up to the homestead? I don't know what you're doing, but...."

"I'm doing a brunch for my nieces and nephews," she said. "A few of them are sleeping over after the party tonight. I'd love to have her come."

August smiled into the sunshine pouring over the fields.

"Etta, you are a remarkable woman." He leaned down and pressed his lips to her forehead. He couldn't believe it, but he had the desire to kiss her, and not on her forehead. She turned toward him, a smile on her face. It slipped away at whatever she saw in his expression, and he wanted to ask her what that was.

Instead, he leaned down a little further, and Etta's eyes fluttered closed. He could definitely kiss her, and all of his muscles tightened in anticipation of doing exactly that.

"Daddy," Hailey said behind him, and August jumped away from Etta and to his feet in the same motion.

"Yeah," he said. "Yep? What's up?" He herded her back into the house without looking over his shoulder to the woman who had turned his whole world upside down with a bag of Band-aids and her insane kindness.

And how beautiful she is, he thought as his daughter started to apologize for her tantrum that morning.

And her amazing family. And her past experiences. Though they didn't entirely echo August's, Etta had been through some hard things, and she'd grown and changed from them.

"It's okay, sweets," he said, folding his daughter into a hug. "Etta just invited us up to a dance and a party, and I told her we'd go."

Hailey pulled away and looked at August, pure hope in her eyes. "Really, Daddy?"

"Really." He smiled at her and booped her nose with his. "Not only that, but she's doing a big brunch with all of her nieces and nephews tomorrow, and she invited you."

Hailey's eyes rounded further, and she searched August's face. "Can I go?"

"You better talk to her about it," August said. "Find out if you even want to go."

Hailey immediately turned her attention to the back door, and August turned that way too, watching Etta come inside and close the door behind her. "Etta," Hailey said, skipping a couple of times to get to her. "Daddy says you're doing a brunch tomorrow, and I might be able to come."

Etta reached out and stroked the hair off Hailey's face and around the back of her head. "I am," she said. "It's all the nieces and nephews," she said. "Even the little babies. Well, not Glory Rose, but everyone else. Even Heather, and she's only seven months old." Etta smiled at Hailey and then August. "You could help in the kitchen or with the littles. My sister is coming, and I recruited Libby and Holly Ann's sister, Bethany Rose, to come. Well." She shrugged and August thought he saw a bit of apprehension in her expression. At least for a moment.

"Bethany Rose wanted me to teach her how to make a specific dish, so she's coming for that. She has an adorable baby girl named Mary Ann, and she sits right on the counter while her mama cooks." Etta put her arm around Hailey, and together, they faced August.

"I could help with the littles," Hailey said. "Or help in the kitchen. I don't know a lot about cooking."

"I learned from my mother and grandmother," Etta said. "You can learn a lot from watching, but we're doing easy things even four-year-old Lynn can help with. You could definitely help in the kitchen."

"What time?" August asked, his voice a little rough coming out of his throat. Maybe because of the way Etta's desire sparked across the space between them. He couldn't believe his daughter had interrupted his first kiss with this woman. He couldn't even fathom that he *wanted* to kiss her.

But he did.

"Some of them are sleeping over," she said. "But it's a brunch, so the cooking will start about eight-thirty?" She sounded like she was guessing, which she probably was. "Anytime after that, and there will be people up and things happening."

"I can get you up there any time before nine-thirty, sweets," he said. "And afterward, you stay and help Etta clean up, and then you do whatever is easiest for her." He switched his gaze to Etta, silently begging her to understand what he said next. "She can come back here alone just fine. She has plenty to keep her busy, and she has my number and Charlie's right next to the phone."

"Can we put Etta's number by the phone?" Hailey asked, looking from August to Etta, that undeniable hope flaming in her eyes. "She could come help me if I needed it." She moved toward the wall-mounted phone that sat between the fridge and the back door. "What is it, Etta?"

Etta smiled at August as she recited her number for Hailey to write on the wall. "Okay, got it," she said, turning back to them both. Anxiety flowed from her, and he could probably say what came out of her mouth next. "I will help clean up. I won't cry about anything. I can come back here or stay up at the ranch with Etta, or someone else. Whatever is fine with me."

August nodded, trying to conceal his smile. Etta let hers shine through, and she stepped toward Hailey and drew her into a hug. "How very mature of you," she said. "We'll see how tomorrow morning unfolds. It might be chaotic, and I'll need a nap afterward. It might be awesome, and we can put on movies and spend the afternoon resting instead."

August wanted to spend his afternoon "resting" with Etta, but he kept his mouth shut. "Lunch," he said, lurching forward. "Are you hungry, sweets?"

Etta's phone rang, and she plucked it from her pocket and said, "Oh, this is Mother. Excuse me for a minute."

"I want some of that ham," Hailey said. "Do we have any of that left?"

"Sure," August said, his attention divided, and he didn't have the contents of his fridge memorized.

"Daddy?" Hailey asked, and he blinked as the front door closed behind Etta.

"Mm, yeah?"

"You like Etta, right?"

August's gaze flew to his daughter's. "Yeah," he said, his voice full of falseness. "I like Etta." In fact, truer words had never been spoken, and August's brain screamed at him to tell Hailey about his relationship with Etta. "Do you like Etta?"

"Yeah," Hailey said, climbing up on the barstool as August set a container next to her of what he hoped contained some of that ham she wanted. "I like her. You should ask her to dinner."

August's eyebrows flew toward the ceiling. "I should?"

"Yeah, if you like her, you should take her out. That's what Miss Grimes says. She says she doesn't get why men don't just ask a woman to dinner. It's just dinner."

August wasn't sure what he should address first—going to dinner with Etta or what her reading teacher was actually teaching the children in her class. "Do you think I need a girlfriend?" He didn't bother to pretend to do anything else.

"Sure," Hailey said. "If you want one. You haven't had a girlfriend since Mom."

August appreciated the innocence of nine-year-olds. "Mom was my wife," he said. "That's totally different than a girlfriend."

"Etta isn't married," Hailey said. "She could be your new wife."

"Wow," he said, chuckling. "What is Miss Grimes teaching you?"

Chapter Twelve

Etta sighed as she passed under the arch signaling her return to Shiloh Ridge. The party in True Blue had started at least an hour ago, but she told herself she didn't care. She didn't have to be there the moment the event started—and she hadn't been.

Her sister had been helping their mother a lot, and Etta's guilt gnawed at her in bits and pieces. So when her mother had called about lunchtime and said she needed to run a few errands, and could Etta help, she'd apologized profusely to August and Hailey and gone to town.

"A few errands" had turned into grocery shopping, a trip to the pharmacy, a hair appointment, and then helping Mother make dinner. They served meals at the assisted living facility where she lived, but tonight was fish and chips, and Mother didn't like fried food.

Etta had offered to bring her up to the ranch for the

party, which would have plenty of non-fried food. Mother had been too tired. Heck, Etta was too tired, and she pulled up to the homestead with half a mind to go inside and go straight to bed.

Only the thought of dancing with August had her going inside, where the house sat in warm silence, and into her suite off the living room. She changed out of the clothes she'd been wearing all day and that felt too heavy and into a fun maxi dress that she usually wore to summer parties.

Once she made it inside the barn, she could take off her shoes, but for now, she slipped on a pair of sandals no one would be able to see anyway. She'd kept August up-to-date about her progress with getting back to the ranch, and once again, the thought of seeing him and being touched by him drove her outside to her vehicle.

She normally walked down the road to True Blue, but tonight, she decided to drive. Several cars and trucks had been parked near the entrance, and Etta took the closest spot she could find. The dark night around her radiated a sense of serenity, despite the music coming from the barn and the light spilling from the windows.

Judge had won the light show by a margin of forty-seven votes, and he'd been stunned once the list had been published that morning. As Etta approached, her feet crunching over the gravel in the parking area, she heard a woman laugh and a man say something in his deep voice. She couldn't make out the words, but she didn't want to happen upon anyone kissing, married, not married, engaged, or otherwise.

"I'm walking here," she said, and the giggling stopped.

"Etta," Libby said, stepping out of the shadows. "Just the woman I wanted to see." She towed Mister with her, and neither of them seemed embarrassed that she'd nearly caught them making out.

"Don't tell me you can't come tomorrow," she said.

"I can," Libby said. "I was telling Mildred about it, and she asked if she could come too. She'll help with the kids and the food."

"Sure," Etta said. "I think we'll need all the help we can get. I'm planning to put a gate from the couch to the piano and putting everyone two and under in the living room, except to eat."

"We can throw toys in there. Put on a movie," Libby said, smiling at Etta.

"Yes," she said. "This is a done deal."

"There's no crying at parties," a man said in a cross voice. "If you don't knock it off and leave your momma alone, you won't be able to sleep with Auntie Etta tonight." Ranger put his eldest son on the ground, one of them still sniffling quite violently.

Etta wanted to run to Wilder and scoop him into her arms and tell him he could come to her suite any time he wanted, no matter what his daddy said. But she'd learned that as the aunt, she couldn't undermine the parents.

"I'm sorry, Daddy," Wilder said through his tears.

"Your mother is tired of the whining," Ranger said. "I am too. You're a big boy, Wild. Big boys who get to come to parties don't cry over nothing."

Wilder clung to Ranger's leg, and Ranger softened visibly as he reached down and patted his son's back. "Tell me what happened."

"Chazzy got cake," Wilder said. "I want some. He no share."

"It's his cake, bud," Ranger said, crouching down now. "Plus, you had cake when we got here. Momma said you couldn't have very many sweets tonight, because you didn't eat much dinner." He pushed his son's hair off his forehead, so tender and so caring despite his initial irritation with his son. "Remember when you don't eat real food and then eat a lot of cake? You get sick. Do you think Auntie Etta wants a sick boy in her bed?"

August arrived right at the end of Ranger's question, and Etta caught the look of shock on his face. She stepped into the light coming from the entrance of the barn and said, "Hey, everyone."

"Auntie Etta!" Wilder flung himself into her arms, and she laughed as she picked him up. "I no sick, Auntie."

"I hope not," she said. "We're making that tater tot casserole tomorrow morning, and you won't want to miss that."

Wilder looked at her collar and put his hands on her face and in her hair. He was a tactile child, and Etta was used to his touch. "I sleep with you?"

"Not if you're sick," she said, glancing at her brother. He nodded his appreciation at her. "How much cake have you had?"

"A little." Wilder looked at her, tears in those dark-as-tar eyes. "I not sick."

"Okay," she said, bending to set the boy back on his feet. "You go find the other cousins and have fun. When I'm ready to leave, I'll come find you, okay?"

"Okay." He started back for the doors of the barn, and Ranger looked from August to Etta.

"Thanks, Etta," he said. "Howdy, August." He shook August's hand, though he'd obviously been inside True Blue already. "Mister, what are you and Libby doin' out here?"

"Just talkin' to Etta," Mister said, which so wasn't true. He grinned at her as he passed, and then Etta and August stood alone in the lamplight outside True Blue.

He wore his cowboy hat, which threw his face into shadow, but plenty of flirtatiousness came out in his voice when he said, "Do you just let anyone come sleep with you?"

Etta wasn't sure if she should be horrified or laugh right out loud. "Most people under age five," she said. "As long as they're not sick, clearly."

He laughed, and Etta moved toward him, sliding her hand into his without hesitation. "How was your day with your mother?" he asked, dropping his head and taking a deep breath of her. Etta loved it when men did that, as it made her feel so good about herself, like they couldn't get close enough to her or couldn't truly experience her without their sense of smell.

"Tiring," she said. "I think she's losing quite a bit of her hearing, and I have to yell everything at her."

"Mm, I'm sorry."

Etta sure could hear the sexy, husky quality of August's voice, and she closed her eyes and let him hold her, breathe with her, move with her. "I think we should go inside to dance," she said. "This is just swaying."

August chuckled, but he didn't move or let go of her. "Hailey said I should take you out to dinner," he said.

Etta jerked away from him as if he'd emitted a painful shockwave that would gel her blood if she stayed too close for too long. "She did?"

August wore the brightest smile Etta had ever seen, and she didn't know what to make of it. "She said that you could be my new wife."

"My word." Etta pressed her palm to her pounding heart. "What were you talking about?"

"I asked her if she liked you, and she said yes. She asked me if I liked you, and apparently, she has a single reading teacher who's really been working hard to find a boyfriend and husband."

"Sheri Grimes," Etta said. Everyone knew Sheri Grimes had been out with a lot of men. Etta had started to gain on her in the past year or so, as much as she didn't want to admit that.

"Apparently," August said again. "So Hailey said if I liked you, I should take you out. You could be my girlfriend, like her mom."

"Oh." Etta's breath flowed out of her body. "And you said something like there's a difference between a girlfriend and a wife."

"Something like that, yes."

Etta reached for his hand again, feeling a bit outside her body as she watched her skin touch his. "Did you tell her we were seeing each other?"

"I hadn't quite made it there yet," he said. "But the door is open now, Etta. I'm going to talk to her really soon."

"Or just tell her you're taking me to dinner the next time we go."

He grinned at her, and once again, Etta had the distinct feeling that August possessed a new brand of happiness she hadn't seen or felt before. "Are you asking me to dinner?"

Etta shook her head, a laugh right behind her vocal cords. "No, sir," she said. "I agree with Hailey and Sheri Grimes. If a cowboy is interested, he should ask a woman to dinner." She tugged on his hand to get him to turn back toward the barn. "Come on, I'm starving, and then I want to see some real dancing."

August didn't immediately go with her, and she turned back to him. "What's your schedule like this weekend?" he said. "Dinner on Friday night? Me and you. I'll tell Hailey."

Her heart boomed like multiple bombs dropping one right after the other. A spark moved through her, lighting all of her nerves and attraction to August Winters on fire. "Friday night works," she said.

"I don't get done until six-thirty," he said. "I could pick you up at seven? We'll head down to town for a late dinner."

"That sounds fine," she said, and August stepped with her this time. Etta felt like she'd grown an additional five feet, and she paused in the doorway leading into the hall where her family lingered, danced, talked, and ate.

She and August surely had a bright spotlight on them, and everyone would turn and look. Hardly anyone did, however, and Etta only met Ward's eye before she stepped into the hall.

"You made it," her brother said, stepping over to her and giving her a quick hug and kiss on the cheek. "Did August tell you he won the line dancing dance-off?"

Etta rounded on August, her eyebrows flying sky-high. "No," she said in a burst of air. "He did not."

"It was me and a bunch of kids," August said, but his smile gave away how he really felt about the victory.

"Hey, Bishop hung in there through several rounds," Ward said.

"Duke too," Ida added as she joined their little huddle. "Zona said he did quite a bit of dancing while he was away from his ranch." She turned toward Etta, her eyes and the set of her shoulders asking dozens of questions, most of them about Mother, but some about August too. "Hey, Sissy. How was the afternoon?"

"Good enough," she said, silently telling Ida she'd tell her more later. "I'm starved. Tell me those ham-and-pineapple pockets aren't gone."

"I saved you one," Ida said, linking her elbow through Etta's. "I'm going to steal her for a few minutes, August."

"That's fine," he drawled, and Etta felt his gaze on her back as she and Ida moved further into the hall and the crowd.

"Auntie Etta," a child said, and Etta turned toward Smiles. She crouched down and reached out to cup his face, a smile already in her heart for this boy. He held up a chocolate moon pie. "I saved this for you."

"You sweet boy," Etta said, taking the treat. "Thank you." She drew him into a hug, and a hug from a happy, optimistic, four-year-old was the best thing in the world. Of course, Etta hoped that once she kissed August, that would take the top spot from Smiles and his hugs.

"Momma brought my bag," he said. "I can sleepover tonight, right?"

"Yes," Etta said, straightening and taking his hand. "I'm counting on it. You and Wilder and Lynn." They were the oldest of the young kids, and Etta had room for all of them in her suite. The younger children—all those born almost two years ago now—would come in the morning. The older teens and pre-teens who'd joined the Glover family would come then too.

She ate her ham-and-pineapple pocket and her moon pie, and then she stepped back onto the dance floor to find her dance-off-winning cowboy. It didn't take long for her eyes to meet August's, and he bowed at the waist though he stood several paces from her.

She curtsied and did her best not to run to him. She approached at a normal speed, and he took her into his arms effortlessly. The music was an upbeat ballad, and he rocked and stepped to the beat without missing a single one.

Within the strong circle of his arms, Etta forgot about her worries about her mother, her busy day tomorrow, and what the future might hold for her. There was only August, and while Etta had been telling herself not to fall too fast, she felt herself doing exactly that.

Chapter Thirteen

August braced his boots against the pillars of the fence and pushed with his legs as he pulled with his arms. "Come on, Mama," he said, his voice full of the same tension as that which ran through his muscles.

"Almost there," Jess said, and in the next moment, the calf slid all the way out, and August fell back. "There she is." Jess jumped to work, wiping the birth off the calf's face so it could breathe. "Come on." He rubbed its face and neck, and then down the chest.

The mother cow lowed and tried to turn in the birthing chute, and August hurried to get to his feet to keep her there. The last thing they needed on this last day of the year was to get kicked or otherwise injured.

"Hey, shh." He patted the cow's back while keeping one eye on the calf. The worst part about birthing season was the fact that not every calf made it. He and Jess had been working for hours with this mother, and he really wanted this calf to survive.

Jess knew what to do, and August didn't need to get in the way. He tugged the mother a bit further down the chute and unlatched a gate to put her in the recovery area. It had plenty of clean straw and water, but she came right over to the fence where her baby lay. A distressed mother cow could make a lot of noise, and she certainly didn't hold back.

"Come on," Jess said, clearly frustrated. He rubbed the calf's ears roughly, and then wiped his face again. The calf's eyes opened, and a pitiful bleat came from its mouth. It tried to stand, and August grinned at the same time Jess did.

"There you go," he said, standing with the calf. "Yeah, let's get you over there with your mama." He led the calf into the same pen as his mother, and August sighed. He loved the work here at Shiloh Ridge, because the operation was set up the way August would've done for his own ranch. The men and women here loved the animals, and they respected them. Preacher and Ward, the other foreman, expected good, hard work, and they gave the same. The owners of the ranch, Bear and Ranger Glover, got dressed and dirty every single day alongside their hired help. It felt like a real family operation, and since August had come from that, he really connected to it.

Shiloh Ridge was simply many times bigger than the ranch he'd worked in Dripping Springs with Josie. He waited for the overwhelming, almost debilitating sadness to punch him in the gut, but today, it didn't.

"Final rounds?" Jess asked. "Then you're off, and I'll know what I'm dealing with."

"Yeah," August said. "Let me wash up first." They both stepped over to the industrial sink and started getting sudsy, washing off anything and everything on their hands and arms.

Outside, they each swung their leg over their own ATV, and Jess led the way out onto the ranch. They kept their pregnant cattle in three pastures, and they'd learned quickly to check on the way out and the way back in for any problems. August couldn't see everything from the road, and he followed Jess down the barely-there trail alongside the first field.

A chill rode in the air with them, the sky overhead of the threatening type with dark clouds and the promise of precipitation at some point. August didn't mind the cooler weather—they certainly hadn't gotten much of it in the Hill Country.

The Texas Panhandle was a lot different than what he was used to, and he loved it here. He could see himself staying here, raising Hailey here, and being happy here.

With Etta? he wondered. Everything had gotten a bit convoluted for their date on Friday night, and he'd ended up sitting with a stubborn mother when he should've been dining with his girlfriend.

Yes, he'd started thinking of Etta as his girlfriend, though they hadn't defined themselves with labels yet. He also hadn't spoken to Hailey about taking Etta out, because he hadn't actually done that yet.

Tonight, however, if all the fields looked good and none of their cattle would be delivering in the next few hours, August had a real, going-out date with Etta. He'd have to tell Hailey then.

"You want to tell her," he muttered to himself, the growl of the ATV swallowing his words the moment they left his mouth. He'd spoken true. He did want to tell his daughter about his relationship with Etta.

Three fields later, August waved to Jess, who still had a couple of hours on his shift, and headed down the hill to his cabin. Preacher had told them to do the basics that day, as it was New Year's Eve. The Glovers were having a party, of course, at True Blue. August had said he and Etta could attend that, but she'd said she'd rather go out if that was an option.

To August, it was definitely an option, and he'd called to get a reservation at The Cattleman's Dairy, a newer restaurant in town that served a variety of beef-based dishes that boasted plenty of cheese. Just the pictures of the French onion soup had set his mouth to watering.

He showered and texted Etta to say he just needed about ten more minutes and then he'd be leaving to come get her. Oakley had accepted his request to watch Hailey that night, and she'd get to go to the New Year's Eve party at the barn, just without him.

"Hay," he called as he left his bedroom. He adjusted his tie, wondering if it was overkill. He'd not necessarily dressed up so much when he'd gone out with Etta before. Would she think he was trying too hard?

"Yeah, Daddy," she said from inside her bedroom. "I'm almost done with my chapter."

August stood in the doorway and smiled at his daughter. "Can you pause for a second? I wanted to talk to you about something." He cleared his throat and tried to swallow down the suddenly-narrow passageway.

Hailey stuck her bookmark in the pages and sat up. Her room looked like she'd been living out of it exclusively for the duration of the holiday break, which admittedly, she had been. An empty bowl even sat on her nightstand. August stepped over to it and picked it up.

"I was going to get that," she said. "It's just from my Cheerios this morning."

"It's fine, sweets," he said, sitting down on the bed. "Listen, I'm going out with Etta tonight."

Hailey said nothing, and August looked at her to make sure she hadn't started reading again.

"You like Etta, right?" he asked.

"Yes," Hailey said.

"You said I should ask her to dinner," he said. "So I did. She said yes. We're going tonight."

Hailey's face expanded slowly into a smile. "Really, Daddy?"

"Really." He chuckled. "I like her, and who knows? Maybe we'll be...maybe it'll be a good thing. Me and her. You and her. Her and us." He didn't know how to use words like *wife* and *mother*, not in this initial conversation. Hailey didn't need such specific terms anyway.

"Miss Grimes would be so proud of you," Hailey said,

leaning forward and hugging August with her skinny arms. "Where do I get to go?"

"Oakley and Ranger said you could stay at the homestead with them until the party."

Hailey's eyes lit up like the ball that would drop in New York City in a few hours. "The New Year's Eve party? You said we couldn't go to that."

"Well, that's because I wasn't going to go," he said. "Because Etta wanted to go out to dinner and not to the barn with her whole family."

"Yeah, the barn with her whole family isn't a date, Daddy."

He chuckled at the supposed wisdom of his nine-year-old. "You don't think so?"

"No." She shook her head. "Are you going somewhere nice? Etta seems like she'd like nice places."

"We're going to a nice place," August said, though he wasn't sure if that was true or not. He didn't have the opportunity to eat at a lot of restaurants, as he didn't exactly have a lot of spare time. "Now, listen. I don't know if Oakley is going to let you sleep over or anything. We'll talk to her when we get there, okay? *I'll* talk to her."

"Yes, Daddy."

"Okay, get up and get dressed. We're goin' now."

"Right now?" Hailey got out of bed, and she was wearing a pair of fuzzy white pants with brightly colored kittens splashed across them. "I need to get dressed and at least brush my hair. It's a *party*."

August headed for the door. "You get dressed. I'll help

you with your hair." He smiled to himself as he went into the kitchen. He'd had to learn how to do his daughter's hair after Josie's death. In some ways, he'd risen to the occasion and been able to be both Mom and Dad for Hailey. In other ways, he was sure he was still failing.

He sent another quick text to Etta, telling her he and Hailey were running a little bit behind, and she responded that they could take their time. With her, he didn't want to take his time. He found himself wanting to accelerate the relationship, and his mind drifted along the road that led him and Etta to his back porch, under the moonlight, sharing a kiss.

Twenty minutes later, he crouched down in front of Hailey. "I'll be back before midnight, probably. Oakley says they're not staying the whole time. You do whatever she says, ya'hear?"

"Yes, Daddy."

He glanced at Etta, who smiled at him. "Etta says you can sleep in her bed until we get back. You got your pj's?"

"Mm hm." Hailey put her arms around August's neck and hugged him. "I'll be okay. Go have a good dinner."

He pressed his eyes closed and smiled. "Okay, sweets. Love you."

"Love you too, Daddy."

With her cute Texas twang in his ears, he straightened and reached for Etta's hand. It was the first time he'd shown any affection toward her in front of anyone, his daughter included, and a blip of nerves pounced through him.

Her grip was firm in his, and that gave him strength and

courage to head for the front door. "Bye, Range," she said, pausing briefly to give her brother a quick kiss on the cheek. "Tell Oak thanks too."

"Will do. Have fun," he said, and with that, August and Etta spilled out of the homestead. Alone. Hand-in-hand. Free.

August felt more free in that moment than he had in four, long years, and a sigh of contentment and gratitude streamed from him.

"Okay?" Etta asked, and August nodded.

"Yeah," he said. "I'm okay." They went down the steps together, and August went right over to the passenger door of his truck, telling himself not to be embarrassed by it. Etta had ridden in the old thing before. She hadn't commented on it at all, and it was a good, reliable vehicle.

He opened the door and stepped back. Etta crowded right into his chest, one palm flat against his pulse and the other hand curling up and around the back of his neck. "Thank you for telling her about us. I'm excited for what this new year will bring."

August wanted to say something sweet and romantic. Maybe something teasing and playful. He had no idea what, on either front, and all he could think about was kissing this gorgeous woman who'd come into his life and thrown him a lifeline. A way back to real living. A chance to love again.

"Etta," he whispered, and because it was wintertime, the sun had already set, casting them in near-darkness. The next thing he knew, he'd leaned down far enough to meet her mouth with his, and entire waves of heat rolled through him, over him, and around him.

His hands came up to cup her face, holding her where he could kiss her, and kiss her, and kiss her. In fact, kissing Etta Glover was the only thing August wanted to do for a good, long time. Thankfully, she seemed to like the idea, and she kissed him back with as much energy as he gave.

Chapter Fourteen

Etta had never been kissed the way August kissed her. His large hands held her face so lovingly, and while they'd only met about three months ago, it felt like she'd been waiting her entire life for a kiss like this.

She breathed in through her nose, trying to commit every moment of this intimate moment to memory. She enjoyed the scent of him—clean, crisp, and cowboy. She pulled on his warmth. She could not stop herself from kissing him again and again.

He finally had the willpower to break the kiss, and they breathed in together. In the past, Etta had giggled and smiled shyly after a first kiss. She'd ducked her head, too embarrassed to look the man she'd just kissed in the eyes. She'd pulled away and stepped away when it had been bad.

This had been the opposite of bad, and she wasn't embarrassed or shy. She raised her eyes to August's to find him watching her, and the moment between them lengthened. A charge hung in the air, and Etta hoped it would never leave.

"I really wasn't going to do that," August whispered, his eyes drifting closed as he leaned close and pressed his lips right against the corner of her eye.

"I'm glad you did," she whispered back. "I've been thinking about kissing you."

His chest rumbled with a slight laugh. "Is that so?"

"You've thought about kissing me too," she said. "I know you have."

"Guilty," he said, pressing her door open further and stepping back. "Your chariot awaits."

She gave him a smile then and climbed up into the truck, being careful to gather the skirt on her dress and tuck it under her leg so it wouldn't get caught in the door. He closed it and went around to the driver's side. He didn't have much to say on the way to town, and that left Etta to relive the kiss again and again, which she gladly did.

He pulled into the parking lot at The Cattleman's Dairy, as had dozens and dozens of other people. "Wow, this place is popular," he said. "Good thing I got a reservation."

Etta only smiled at him, and she tucked her hand in his as they made their way toward the entrance of the restaurant. A woman greeted them there, with a tray of cheese-stuffed beef bites. Etta wasn't sure what that was, or if she would like it, but the moment she popped the crispy, fried ball into her mouth, she moaned. "I need this recipe," she said around the tender beef and salty cheese.

"Mm, yes, you do," August said. He stepped away to talk

to the hostess, and when he returned, he didn't look happy. "Ten minutes."

"That's fine," Etta said, not wanting anything to disrupt their evening together. She found a corner for them to sit in, and she held August's hand with both of hers. "Did you know that a person's hands can tell you a lot about them?"

"Is this some sort of palm reading?" he asked, grinning at her.

"No," Etta said, her smile on the small side. "Yours are a little rough, for example. So your skin says you work outside. You've got a scar here." She ran her fingertip along the line on the back of his palm. "How'd you get it?"

"Stringing fence," he said. "That roll of wire, near the end, can really whip back if you don't have a firm grip on it."

"Did you have to get stitches?"

"Five," he said. "I was thirteen. I started wearing gloves after that."

"I'll bet you did." She liked talking to him about anything and nothing. "Tell me about your two brothers. You've only mentioned them once."

"Ah, okay, let's see. Lawson's the oldest. Christian is a couple years younger than him. I'm the youngest at four years younger than Christian." He grinned, his eyes focused somewhere else in the waiting area. "My momma used to say she had to wait longer in between kids, because Christian gave her so much grief."

Etta smiled too, the way he spoke of his family telling her how he really felt about them. He loved them, and he likely missed them. "Where do they all live?"

155

"San Antonio area," he said. "My granddaddy had a ranch on the northwest side. We all worked it. Lawson runs it now, and Christian runs a small law firm on the outskirts of the city. He mostly represents farmers and ranchers with disputes over water rights."

"Interesting," Etta said.

"Water is blood for a ranch or farm," August said.

"That it is." Etta didn't mean to sound disagreeable. "Are they married?"

"Yep," he said. "All married—my momma and daddy are even still together. I have five nieces and nephews. It's a far cry from what you've got, but they're fun." He finally tore his gaze from whatever ran through his mind and looked at her. "Good people."

"I'm sure they are," she said. She refrained from saying she'd like to meet them, because she and August had a long way to go before serious things like him taking her home to meet his folks happened.

"Sometimes I feel like I gave up a lot when I left the Hill Country," he said. "If I think too hard about it, I start to question my decision."

"August," a woman called. "For two?"

They got up and followed the hostess back to their booth. It sat in front of a huge window that looked right out toward one of the rivers that made up Three Rivers. "This is great," Etta said, feeling like all the bad dinners, all the blind dates, and all the bold moves she'd made were finally paying off.

"Great view," August agreed. A waiter came over and

told them of the night's specials and asked for their drink orders.

Etta had been out with him once in the far distant past, and since Harmon didn't act like he recognized or knew her, she didn't say anything either. Once he'd gone, Etta focused on the man across from her in the booth.

"Do you regret leaving the Hill Country?"

"No," he said firmly. "Only if I think too much about it. But no. Every morning when I wake up and look out over those fields surrounding my house, I know I'm in the right place."

"Three Rivers, specifically?" she asked. "Or Shiloh Ridge?"

"Both," he said, removing his cowboy hat and hanging it on a hook beside the window. "What about you? Ever thought about leaving Three Rivers?"

"No," she said truthfully.

"Have you traveled much?" he asked.

"No."

"Interesting," he said, and Etta reached for her water glass.

"What's interesting about it?" she asked, evenly setting the glass back on the table.

"I don't know," August said, and he seemed perfectly at-ease. "It just seems like...." Something entered his gaze, and his voice trailed into silence. "Nothing."

"It's something," Etta said, though she didn't want this conversation to ruin their evening.

August ran his hand down his face and shook his head. "It's nothing."

Etta wanted to take him at face-value. She wanted to believe what he said. In the back of her mind, she knew what he was thinking, and forcing him to say it would leave a dark mark on their New Year's Eve date.

Let it go, she thought, and she decided to do just that. "If you're sure," she said.

"I'm sure," he said, and he sounded it. He reached for the menu. "Have you looked at this yet? What do you think you want?"

"I'm going to get that pork chop special," she said. "The creamy risotto with peas sounds divine."

"Is this a nice enough place?" August asked, looking at her over the top of his menu.

"Of course," Etta said, frowning. "I don't care where we go."

He smiled and said, "Good. Hailey said to make sure I took you someplace nice, and I wasn't sure if this would be it or not."

Etta relaxed, not sure why she had so many defenses up right now. "You can tell Hailey that you did a spectacular job of choosing a nice restaurant."

August laughed, and Etta joined him. She told herself not to get too wrapped up inside her own head. She'd been out with August before. She'd known him for almost three months. He wasn't a liar or a con man. He didn't have another girlfriend she didn't know about. He didn't use an alternate name. He wasn't fresh out of a relationship.

In short, he wasn't anything like any of the men Etta had been dating over the past few years. She needed to stop expecting him to mess up and start believing that the Lord had put him specifically in her path so their lives could intersect.

* * *

Etta put the last piece of white wedding cake in her mouth. "Mm," she said, letting her eyes roll back in her head.

"That one?" Libby asked.

Etta nodded without opening her eyes. The white cake and the white frosting had been baked by heaven itself, and Etta could die happy with this dessert as the last thing she'd eaten. "This one."

"Not chocolate?"

Etta opened her eyes and looked at Libby. "Chocolate is for children's birthday parties and family functions," she said. "Weddings are upscale. They're pure. You need the white cake." Plus, it tasted like sugar and clouds, with just the right hint of vanilla in the frosting. No lemon crème in the middle. Nothing extraneous. Just pure deliciousness in every bite.

"You could have chocolate cake for the reception," Mildred suggested, and Etta nodded at her.

"That's an idea," Etta said. "Or for the bridal shower. The formal dinner the night before. Any of those other occasions. But for the actual wedding cake?" She smiled fondly at the white cake in the middle of the table. "I say white all the way."

Libby forked up another bite of it and slid it in her mouth. "It *is* good," she said around the cake and frosting.

Etta nodded her approval, not that Libby needed it. She could do whatever she wanted for her marriage to Mister, Etta's cousin. She'd been somewhat surprised to be invited along on this cake tasting in the first place, but Libby and Mildred had come to Etta's brunch day with all her nieces and nephews, and they'd been trying her recipes since.

The three of them had been texting about cooking and baking, and Etta found she'd really enjoyed broadening her friendship with the two of them. Mildred had gotten married only a few months ago, and Libby's wedding would take place in only one more month.

"I think I'll go with the white," Libby said to the baker once she returned to the table, and she started filling out the forms she needed to get the wedding cake ordered.

Before August, Etta would've returned to her place at the back of the homestead after an occasion like this. She'd change into sweatpants and watch sappy romantic movies all night, letting whoever came to the homestead fend for themselves.

She'd known for a while now that she'd be the last single Glover standing, and the thought had irritated her and brought her to her knees many times. As Libby finished paying for the deposit on her cake, and the three of them stood, Etta didn't feel like that.

She felt like the Lord knew her and had been mindful of

her situation. She would never go so far as to say that August's wife had died so that Etta could have him in her life, but she absolutely believed the Lord had guided August to Three Rivers at this time, so they could find one another.

He fixed something inside her that had been broken when she couldn't walk down the aisle. She liked to hope that she healed something inside him that had been damaged upon his wife's death. They got along well, and since the New Year's Eve kiss, a day hadn't passed where she hadn't seen him and kissed him.

So things were going *really* well, at least in Etta's mind and in her All Things Dating Book. She'd even told him about a few of the dating disasters from her book, and they'd laid together on his couch, laughing while Hailey slept down the hall in her bedroom.

As she hugged Libby and Mildred and they went their separate ways, a new kind of hope filled Etta's heart. Hope that she could gather those she loved around her to help her pick out wedding cake, the perfect dress, and the precise paper for the invitations. Hope that she could have the happily-ever-after she'd always dreamed of.

Hope that she and August could build a relationship with one another and then a family together, even after so much heartache and so many disappointments.

She drove toward Shiloh Ridge, saying, "Whatever Thy will, Lord, I'll do."

A distinct thought entered her mind—*don't plan for anything, Etta*—and she kneaded the steering wheel in her truck. Etta sure did love making plans, and she had fantasies about her partner and what her wedding would be like that dated back three decades.

"I'll try," she whispered to herself, and to the Lord. After all, she didn't need an elaborate wedding cake, the most fashionable gown, or a shiny announcement in order to get what she'd always wanted. Sometimes fantasies were exactly that—fantasies—and Etta wanted real, lasting love in her life.

Now, whether that was with August or not, she could only hope; she didn't know yet, but she was excited to keep exploring the relationship and see where it led her.

Chapter Fifteen

Sammy Glover hurried her children up the steps at Bull House, glad there were only a few. Russ could get distracted by a piece of debris floating in the air, for crying out loud.

She knocked on the door and then opened it so Dot wouldn't have to get up and come answer it. "It's just me," Sammy said. "Come on, Smiles. Hold the door for Momma."

Smiles stepped in front of her and did what she asked, and Sammy gave him a smile as she moved past him. "Hold it for Russ. Come on, son."

Dot rose from the couch, and she looked like she hadn't slept much the previous night. Sammy stalled. "I'll call Etta," she said.

"I already did," Dot said, offering Sammy a weary smile. "Glory just had a rough night, that's all."

"Auntie Dot," Smiles said. "Look at my toof." He ran toward her, and Dot grinned as she crouched down to look at Smiles's front tooth, which had started to wiggle a couple of days ago.

"Oh, you're going to lose that so soon." Dot straightened and patted Smiles's head. Behind Sammy, the door opened again, and Etta said, "I brought lunch."

Sammy got out of the way so Etta could move past her with a pot of what smelled like her famous curry chicken soup. A plastic grocery sack swung from her arm, and Sammy spied a bag of pumpkin seeds and a container of sour cream.

"I can reschedule the meeting," Sammy said.

"Nonsense," Etta said as she bustled into the kitchen. "I'm not doing anything today, and there's no reason I can't be here with my favorite boys." She set the pot of soup on the stove and turned toward Smiles as he ran toward her.

"Auntie Etta, look at my toof!" He grinned at her and used his finger to move it back and forth.

"Holy moly," Etta said with just the right amount of drama. "Your first tooth. I've heard the Tooth Fairy brings chocolate chunk brownies for a front, first tooth." She glanced up at Sammy, who wouldn't deny Etta anything to do with her nieces and nephews.

She didn't need to bring brownies for a loose tooth, but Sammy knew she would. Etta stood and reached for Heather. "Go. We're fine here. Just so you know, as soon as Glory Rose wakes up, I'm abandoning your children for her." She giggled and took the baby into the living room with Dot, saying, "Come on, Smiles. Russ, climb up here beside me with that book. I'll read it to you."

So it was that Sammy left Bull House with all three of her young children gathered around Etta, her even voice reading about a puppy who gets lost and meets a chicken on his quest to get home.

She went down the road to her house, because her husband, Bear was meeting her there. She went through the front door, the silence that greeted her absolutely foreign and unwelcome. When she'd first gotten Lincoln after her sister's death, she'd craved a few moments of silence. He'd grown so much in the past seven years, and so had she.

She closed the door behind her and breathed in deeply, wondering what she should do with her few minutes of free time. *Nothing*, she decided, and she went into the living room and dropped onto the comfortable couches she and Bear had picked out when this house had been finished.

As Sammy exhaled, she had the very distinct feeling that she needed to have another baby. Bear had said several months ago that he thought he wanted to be done having kids. They had four now, three of them under the age of four. He'd wanted a big family, and as he was quite a bit older than her, they'd gotten started right after their marriage.

Most days, Sammy ran on empty starting about three p.m., but as she sat in the silence, she didn't want a different life. She loved living on this ranch. She loved her husband with her whole heart and soul. She adored her children. She wanted to be here at Shiloh Ridge to help the other ranch wives, their husbands, and their children.

The back door opened, and Bear walked in. "Heya, hon. I just need to wash my hands, and I'll be ready."

Sammy rose to her feet to meet him in the kitchen. He grinned at her and bent down to kiss her quickly. "I got into some moldy alfalfa, and wow, I'm so itchy." He continued toward the sink.

"Bear," she said, following him. "I think we should have another baby."

Bear flipped on the water and twisted to look at her. "We talked about this."

Sammy nodded, pressing her palms together. He'd be fifty-one this year, and he still worked a lot around the ranch. Being involved in the lives of the men and women who lived here or worked here was important to him. So was being a present, loving father.

"I know," Sammy said. "I just got home a few minutes ago from dropping off the kids, and it was so quiet here."

Bear scrubbed and scrubbed and said nothing.

"And I just had this overwhelming feeling that there's one more child for us."

Bear shut off the water and sighed as he reached for the towel hanging from the oven door. He faced her as he wiped his hands, that calculated look in his eye. He'd watched her like this before, when he was trying to figure out what she'd meant or how she really felt. When he was confused and trying to riddle through things in his mind.

"Really?" he asked.

Sammy stepped into him and ran her hands up the front of his shirt. "Take a little while to think about it," she said. "I feel like we should, but if you really don't want to, then we won't."

"Don't do that to me," he said, replacing the towel. "It's fine."

"No," Sammy said. "We've always talked through our family decisions, and this one's no different." She moved away from him and toward her purse on the counter. "Come on. If we don't have to be late, I don't want to be."

The folder where she'd tucked the sample contract poked out the top of her bag, and she led the way out to Bear's truck in the back driveway.

Sometimes the drive down to Three Rivers seemed to take forever, and sometimes it passed in the blink of an eye. Today, Bear pulled up to the mechanic shop before Sammy had even realized they'd left the ranch.

"Ready, baby?" he asked, and Sammy blinked.

"Yes," she said.

"You don't have to do this."

Sammy looked up at the big, swooping S on the sign that bore her name. It had hung on the roof of the mechanic shop since the day she'd opened, over a decade ago.

Well, except for when the trio of tornadoes had come through town. It had been blown down then, but Bear had recovered it, fixed it, and put it back up for her.

"There's a lot of good memories here," she said, surprised at the emotion racing through her. She barely came down to the mechanic shop anymore. About once a week, she came and did a few hours of office work. She hadn't been under a car here for months.

"There sure are," Bear said. Neither of them got out of the truck, and Sammy knew she needed to pull the door handle first.

She drew a deep breath way down into her lungs and held it. As she exhaled, she cleared her mind. "I want to do this. I love this place, and it'll go to someone who loves it the same way I do."

As if on cue, the glass door opened and Jason Essex walked out, wiping his hands on a dark gray cloth. He wore a smile and the dirtiest jeans on the planet.

Sammy smiled at him through the windshield and said, "We should've bought lunch."

"I'll order something during the meeting," Bear said.

Sammy opened the door, and Bear followed suit a moment later. She got out of the truck and reached back inside for her purse. Then she faced Jason and moved to embrace him. "Hey, you."

They laughed together, and Sammy stepped back so Bear could shake his hand. Jason looked from him to Sammy. "This is serious business."

"I told you I wanted to go over contracts," Sammy said. "Is everyone here?"

"It's Drew's day off." Jason nodded toward the shop. "It's just me and Logan today."

"I wanted to talk to you first anyway." Sammy exchanged a glance with Bear, and he opened the door so they could all go inside.

The whole place smelled like metal and grease, and Sammy pulled in a glorious breath of it. She told herself she could still get her oily fix under the cars, trucks, and ranch equipment which needed to be fixed around Shiloh Ridge.

She wouldn't have to deal with customers who didn't pay, or those who called upset their car wasn't done when they wanted it to be.

She wouldn't have to process payroll, or deal with texts about time off from her guys. She wouldn't have to spend hours on the phone trying to find rare parts.

She moved behind the desk and sat down as Jason did too.

"Bear's not coming in?" he asked, glancing at the open office door.

"I think he's going to order lunch." Sammy grinned at Jason. "So you better tell your wife she won't need to cook for a couple of weeks."

"I'm within earshot," Bear said, appearing in the doorway, looking at his phone and not Sammy.

"Did I speak untrue?"

"Just for that, I'm ordering the thirty-piece nugget." Bear grinned at her and stepped away. "I'll ask Logan what he wants from Chicken Fry."

Sammy laughed as he left, and Jason grinned mightily as well. She sobered, not sure how to start this conversation though she'd practiced at the kitchen table with Ranger, Mister, Bishop, and Bear.

She pulled the folder out of her purse, clearing her throat. "Jason," she said. "I'm going to...I don't want the mechanic shop anymore."

Jason leaned forward, his eyes full of anxiety. "Okay."

"I'm not going to list it for sale."

"Good," he said. "I'd love to have a chance to buy it."

Sammy opened the folder, her heartbeat pulsing and pouncing through her whole body. "You can't buy it," she said.

"Sammy," Jason started, a touch of frustration in his tone.

"Because I'm not listing it for sale." She pushed the sample document to the edge of the desk, which needed a serious cleaning. "I'd like to gift it to you."

Jason stared at her, his mouth opening. He reached for the paper.

"It's a sample Bear and I came up with," Sammy said easily now that the hard part was out of the way. "It's not set in stone. The bottom line is, I can't keep this place anymore, and I want it to go to someone who loves it as much as I do. That's you, Jason."

"My name isn't on this," he said, looking up with wonder in his expression.

"I wasn't sure if you'd want it," Sammy said, reaching for the mouse to wake the computer. "I emailed it to myself so I could make some adjustments here. I wasn't sure if you'd want it in your name or under yours and Gina's. And if you didn't want it, I thought I'd talk to Logan. You and him came on at the same time, and you've been with me for ten years."

Tears filled her eyes, and she cleared her throat and focused on the screen. "I think I emailed it to myself."

"Sammy," Jason said. "You can't do this."

"Yes, I can." Sammy looked at him. "Surely you know Shiloh Ridge does just fine."

"It doesn't matter if you don't need the money," he said. "This is your place."

"It's time for it to become someone else's," she said. "I want to gift it to you, and I won't accept a single penny for it. Those are my terms."

Jason looked at the paper again, and when he looked up this time, he wore a wide smile. "Just a second." He stood and strode out of the room.

"Jason," she called after him, but he didn't respond or come back. The door leading out to the garage slammed, and several seconds later, Jason said, "Just come on. The Four-Runner can wait."

He came back into the office with a frowning Logan right behind him. He saw Sammy, and his expression changed. "Hey, boss."

Jason picked up the paper. "Not for long." He handed it to Logan, who looked at him and then the paper.

"What is this?" Logan studied it, and Jason grinned at Sammy, gesturing between the two of them.

Sammy stood up, Jason's idea somehow moving from his mind and into hers. "I'm ready to give up the mechanic shop," she said. "And I'd love to offer it to the two of you as a partnership."

Jason started to laugh, and Logan looked the same way Jason had a few minutes ago. "A partnership?"

"We should form a company," Jason said. "Me and you, Logan. We've been talking about it for months. Sammy transfers ownership of the shop to us, and we hold it jointly in the name of our company."

Sammy wanted to ask them what they'd been planning to do with their joint company, but she kept her mouth shut. Logan looked up from the paper, met Jason's eyes, and then looked at Sammy.

"There's no price on this paper."

"I'm not selling the shop." Sammy folded her arms, her smile filling her whole face. "I'll gift it to one of you or both of you. If neither of you want it, I'll figure out something from there."

"I want it," Jason said. "If you'll give Logan and I some time to work out our company, so we can put that on the top line there."

Sammy looked at Logan. "Logan?"

"I bet we can talk to my sister and get it done quickly." He wore hope in every pore of his body. "Her husband is a lawyer."

"I'm willing to wait until you're ready," Sammy said. She walked around the desk and hugged Jason and Logan. "You guys have been my best friends for so long, and there's no one else I'd want running the shop."

They wrapped their arms around her too, and Sammy stood there and let her joy roll through her.

"Oh, it looks like it went well," Bear said. "The food is ten minutes out."

Sammy laughed and stepped back. "They're going to form a partnership and we'll give the shop to them." She joined Bear in the doorway. "So they need a little time to get that put together."

"That's okay," Bear said. "Right?"

"Yes," Sammy said. "It's okay. You got me the popcorn chicken sandwich, right?"

"Who do you think you're dealing with?" Bear asked. "Did I get you the popcorn chicken sandwich." He shook his head and left the office, muttering about how he'd gotten three of them, just in case.

Sammy looked at Jason and Logan, and the three of them burst out laughing.

Chapter Sixteen

Liberty Bellamore woke on the morning her wedding would take place, the scent of coffee in the air. Instead of getting up to go tell Mildred *good morning* and *thank you*, Libby snuggled down into her comforter.

She and Mister would live right here in this house until the one at Shiloh Ridge was finished, and he'd brought a few boxes over in the past couple of days. His personal effects and some of his summer clothes. One whole box of cowboy boots, and one with all of his rodeo memorabilia.

Libby wasn't sure if she'd fallen asleep or just imagined it when Mister said, "Libs, baby, it's time to get up."

She sat straight up, her nerves firing at her as she looked toward the doorway. Her cowboy about-to-be-husband stood there, wearing what she saw him in every other day of the year—jeans, cowboy boots, and a deliciously black and white plaid shirt.

They weren't getting married until five o'clock that evening, but Libby hadn't expected to see him that morning.

"What are you doing here?"

"I made breakfast, but you just keep snoring away." He did not step into her bedroom, though by tonight, it would be theirs. She'd bought new sheets and new blankets, and part of what Mildred and Mama were coming to help her with that day was a bedroom redesign.

"I'm coming," she said, sliding out of bed.

Mister's gaze slipped down to her bare feet and back to her eyes. "I like those pajamas."

Libby giggled as she stepped into his personal space and he refused to back up and let her go by. His hands moved effortlessly along her waist, and Libby melted into the touch of this handsome, good man. Every time he beamed at her, kissed her, or said he loved her, she needed a moment to bask in the wonder and glory of it.

"Isn't breakfast getting cold?" she teased as Mister kissed her ear and then down her neck.

"Oh, long ago," he said. "I thought you got up at the start of dawn."

"I usually do," she said. "It's my wedding day, Mister. I'm allowed to sleep in."

"Can we sleep in tomorrow too?" he murmured, his lips like magic along her collarbone.

"Mm hm, yes," she said. "Where will that be?"

"San Antonio." His voice stayed low and husky, and Libby burst out laughing.

"I got you," she said, pushing against his chest. "San Antonio? What are we doing there?"

Mister blinked, obvious regret in his eyes. "You sneak," he said, reaching to tickle her. "We're not staying in San Antonio. We're flying there after the wedding, just for one night. Then we're moving on."

Libby held onto his shoulders as they walked backward. "Moving on to where?"

"Nowhere," he said. "I want it to be a surprise. I told you what to pack." He turned around, his smile playful, so she knew he wasn't mad.

Giddiness spread through her as she entered the kitchen behind him, the scent of salty sausage and crisp toast hanging in the air. "What did you make?"

"Breakfast pizza," he said. "Scrambled eggs, sausage, bacon, cheese, with a salsa sauce on the dough." He bent and pulled the tray out of the oven, the delicious-looking pizza making her mouth water.

"I love you," she said as he set the pizza down. "Thank you."

"Yeah," he said. "Let me tell you, getting Mildred to give me an hour this morning almost caused World War Three. She'll be here at eight-forty-five sharp, so we better get eating."

The clock on the stove read just past eight, and Libby wished he'd come to wake her up earlier.

"Sorry," Libby said. "She just has a lot of plans for today. My hair, my makeup, my clothes. Then we have to get my elderly aunt, and all the women in the family have to get everything done too."

"I thought your mama ordered the food."

"She did."

"Then what do they have to get ready?"

Libby knew how stressful it was to put on a wedding, because she'd helped a ton with Mildred's. Of course, her sister had moved up her date by two months, and that had caused a lot of stress.

"The wedding planner is handling the decorations," Mister said, pulling out the pizza cutter from the large utensil drawer. "So everything will be set up. The caterer will have the food here and ready. Lord knows there will be enough people to eat it. You ordered two cakes, and the band, and Mildred can give me an hour."

Libby stepped away from him, surprised at the level of stress in his voice. "Mister."

"Sorry." He served her a piece of pizza and moved around the island. "It's just that we're not getting married until five, and I've got an alarm set for three-thirty so I can shower and get dressed and get here by four-thirty. That's what time your mama told me to be here, and I need an hour."

Libby followed him to the bar and sat beside him. She put one hand on his thigh, which made them both tense, and said, "I have way more hair than you."

"I know," he said. "I'm sorry. Forget it. It's just that Mildred literally put me through the wringer for wanting an hour for breakfast today."

"It takes thirty minutes to lace me into my dress," she said.

"I can't wait to see it," Mister said.

Libby grinned at him. "After we get married, I have a party dress for the dinner and dance, and guess who's going to *unlace* the dress?"

"Mildred," Mister said in a deadpan and stuffed half his pizza in his mouth.

"I was going to ask my husband to help me." Libby lifted her pizza to her lips and took a bite. Mister choked on his pizza and coughed while she calmly chewed and swallowed.

He gulped a glass of orange juice and looked at her, that mischievous glint in his eyes. She'd seen that look before, and excitement bounced through her system.

"I bet I can get it unlaced faster than thirty minutes."

"I'm counting on it," Libby said. "You obviously know how Mildred is going to be about today's schedule. I believe she gave me forty-five minutes to change and be ready for dinner."

* * *

That evening, Libby stood with her hair done, her nails freshly painted, her dress laced, her makeup flawless, and her father's arm through hers. "Ready, baby?" he asked.

"Yes," she said. She'd been waiting to marry Mister Glover for years, and she could hardly believe today was happening. She'd asked Judge, his brother, to marry them, as he'd married quite a few of the Glovers. He hadn't wanted to in the beginning, but Mister had talked to him, and Judge had come on board after that.

They hadn't done a rehearsal dinner or anything like that, because Libby didn't see the point. The Glovers knew a lot of people around Three Rivers, and so did her family. They both ran and worked generational family ranches that had been in the area for decades, and Libby had tried to pare down the guest list.

In the end, Mister had said he had enough money to feed the whole town. So they were doing exactly that. After the ceremony.

The music in the barn where they usually served dinner for the Country Christmas faded and her dad said, "We're up, Libby. I'll go slow."

"Thank you, Daddy." The doors in front of her opened slowly, and it felt like she was about to step into her future. The future she'd been waiting to arrive.

The crowd stood in a wave from back to front, and a new brand of music came through the speaker system. A more upbeat, wordless type of music, and Daddy stepped left with Libby right behind him.

Step-tap, move right. Step-tap, move left.

She grinned and laughed as she and her father danced down the aisle—which seemed to go on forever—toward Mister.

He moved with them, his smile genuine and full of joy as he snapped along with the tune as well. Libby took the last couple of steps toward him quickly, and they laughed together.

"I love you so much," he said among the chuckles. He shook her father's hand, and the music ended. A pause filled the barn as the guests took their seats and Judge came out of the woodwork to stand behind the altar.

Libby had asked Mildred to make it, and her sister had put together a stunning piece that she'd made from one of the water tubs they used here on the ranch.

She'd painted it in bold, bright colors, put Libby's and Mister's names on it, and filled it with grasses, ferns, and flowers. Right in the middle of it, she'd mounded up dirt and covered it with a piece of leather that had been embossed with a G for Glover.

Libby teared up at the sight of it. She'd known the Glovers for so long—since she was a little girl. Her father texted with Mister's oldest brother all the time about ranch business. He attended ranch owner's meetings with Bear.

Libby had been invited to do things with the other Shiloh Ridge Ranch wives, and she'd started attending their mid-week luncheons in the past month or so.

"Welcome everyone," Judge said, his voice loud and projecting through the mic without an issue. "It's so good to gather together as friends and family for the occasion of finally making my only single sibling into an honest man."

Judge grinned at Mister, who shook his head, his own smile permanently stuck to his face.

"I've had the rare opportunity to know Mister for his entire life, and for those of you who haven't, let me assure you that he has always wanted to live life to the fullest. When Dad asked for boys to go out to the Edge with him, Mister volunteered instantly. See, he thought there'd be cliffs, and he fully planned to jump off of them."

Libby smiled at the man she loved, looking back over the altar as Bear came forward and took the mic from Judge. "Imagine his disappointment when it was just our land edged with a fence and then more Texas prairie beyond that. Needless to say, Mister wasn't so quick to volunteer to go out there with Dad again."

A few people in the crowd laughed, and Libby looked at Mister. He'd said Judge would give them a beautiful ceremony, and she did like hearing stories about him.

"Once, Mister came home from school with a rat for the weekend," Bear said. "He was so excited, and Mother —well, I'm sure you can imagine how Mother felt about having that rat in the house." He passed the mic to Ranger, one of Mister's cousins, who grinned out at the crowd.

"When our barn cats got a whiff of that rat, they wouldn't leave Mister alone. He wouldn't leave the house without the rat in his shirt. I don't know why he thought that could protect it from a mouser, but well, Mister's always had a unique mind."

His hand over hers tightened, and they exchanged a quick smile.

Cactus took the mic next. "The rat and Mister lost against the cats, obviously. Mother had to take Mister to school on Monday and explain to his teacher why sending a rat home with a farm boy was a bad idea. Then, much to Mister's annoyance, he had to buy his teacher a new classroom pet with his allowance." He chuckled right into the mic, and Libby did too.

"Then, Mister came home with a girl, and he told Mother and all of us that she was his absolute best friend and we better be nice to her." Cactus looked at Libby, and her whole chest constricted. "Mister has always been extremely protective of Libby, and while I'm not sure he tried very hard to save that rat, he sure has—and will—fight for Libby." He pressed one fist to his chest, right over his heart, as she'd seen the Glovers do for one another in the past, and looked between them.

"Mister knows how to fight for what's right, and for what he wants. He never has shied away from those hard conversations, and he inspired me to make changes in my life, even if I've never told him and he didn't know until this moment."

Mister fisted his right hand and put it over his heart too, and Cactus passed the mic to Jack, Libby's oldest brother.

Anxiety filled her, because her siblings had not spoken to her about this. She had no idea what was about to come out of her brother's mouth.

"Liberty is the youngest in our family," he said. "But she has never been the quietest or the meekest. While Mildred let me and Cord talk for her for months, Libby always made her voice known. She loves Texas, and she loves the land, and she loves a cowboy. She always has." He looked at Mister, his smile brotherly and kind. "She has a special spirit that can't be lassoed and brought to the earth, but I think she finally found the cowboy who'll let her be who she's meant to be."

He passed the mic to Cord, who stood behind the altar as if he'd marry them. "I think Libby's been in love with Mister for longer than any of us know. In high school, the two of them were inseparable, and when she didn't have a date to the prom one year, I asked her why Mister didn't take her. She rolled her eyes—actually rolled her eyes—at me, and said she and Mister were just best friends. I think it's such a blessing to be able to marry your best friend, and I'm glad Libby and Mister are finally getting that opportunity today."

Mister leaned down and touched his lips to Libby's temple while Cord passed the mic to Preacher. He'd walked to the altar without a crutch or a cane, which was a huge accomplishment for him. "When Mister got the phone call that he'd be roping in the professional rodeo, he threw the phone right up into the air and yelled *yeehaw!* at the top of his lungs." He grinned at Mister, who actually had a little water in his eyes. "The phone broke, and Mother made him pay to replace it. Mister breaks a lot of things, Libby, so fair warning if you don't know that about him."

She cocked her hip in mock disbelief, like that alone would be enough for her to call off the wedding.

"He's also extremely careful with the things he cares about." Preacher gave his brother a warm smile and pressed his fist over his heart. "He's come to help me every day since I re-injured myself, and I'm no picnic to be around most of the time. He knows what that's like too, as he had some pretty rough times where he was so unhappy with himself and his life." He nodded and handed the mic to Bishop.

He cleared his throat, and he couldn't seem to look at

Mister. "But one thing about Mister is that he's willing to change. Once he knows what it is he needs to do, he puts his head down, he closes his mouth, and he gets the job done. He's just older than me, and I've always been trying to keep up with him."

"Not true, brother," Mister murmured, but Bishop kept going.

"He's been a great example of hard work as I watched him go to school all day, then rodeo practice all night, then do his ranch chores, his homework, and his household chores. Mother and Dad never let him off the hook for any of it, and he never complained."

"I'm sure I did," Mister whispered.

Bishop pressed his fist to his chest and practically threw the mic to Ace, another cousin. Ace took his place at the top of the altar and smiled at Libby, then Mister. "Preach said Mister is very careful with what he cares about, and that's true. I've watched him pamper his mother and mine for years. I watched him leave Shiloh Ridge every day for the past eight months to drive over to Golden Hour to help Libby when she hurt her ankle, and then to get the Country Christmas up and going. He brought in his friends for the show. He made sure they were happy, healthy, and housed. He didn't do that for himself; he did it for Libby, because he cares about her and loves her. I've seen him come to my aid."

Ace cleared his throat, and Libby choked up at all these tough cowboys and their emotions. "Once, he showed up with this gluten-free bag of pretzels, and boy, let me tell you, they were so disgusting." He chuckled, and Mister did too.

"But we sat on my back deck, and we ate them. Every single one. He didn't say anything. He just sat with me, and sometimes that's all a man needs—a good friend and a good cousin like Mister to sit with them so they don't feel all alone."

Ace turned to pass the mic to his brother, Ward, then he twisted back with his fist over his heart. Mister reached up and touched his too, the moment tender and real.

Ward cleared his throat and said, "When Mister and Judge weren't gettin' along, he'd come stay at Bull House with me. I was always glad to have him, storms and all, because I understand the wind that blows in his soul sometimes. I have to say that I haven't seen it inside him in a good, long while. He learned how to cleanse himself when he went to Oklahoma. I missed him terribly, but I had the reassurance from the Lord that He was remaking and remolding Mister into the kind of man he needed to be, so he could be standing here with a good woman like Libby."

He lowered the mic and leaned right over the altar. "I love you two," he said out loud, and Libby reached up to pat him on the shoulder. He pressed his fist to Mister's chest, and handed off the mic to Zona.

She was joined by Etta and Ida, and the three of them made a little rainbow around the mic. Libby loved them so much already, and she looked up, blinking fast to keep her tears in check.

"Mister and I have been buddies for a while," Etta said. "Since we're the last two single Glovers. Well, I guess in about ten minutes, it'll just be me. But because of who

Mister is, I know I can still go to him, and he'll still listen to my woes and worries. I'll bring the triple chocolate fudge ice cream."

"I'm in," Mister said loudly, and the crowd twittered with laughter.

"I'm thrilled he managed to get Libby to give him a second or third chance," Etta said. "She is a person I really admire, not only for her work ethic, but for the size of her heart." She nodded at Libby, who didn't feel deserving of such praise.

"I've been badgering Libby, I'm afraid," Ida said, her smile glowing on her face. "I just want all the new ladies in the family to feel so welcome, and when I stand on this side of the altar, I get what Judge has been seeing all these years. I see pure love between the two of you, and it's wonderful and glorious. Thank you for sharing it with us." She looked at Zona, who wiped her eyes quickly.

"For those of you who don't know, I'm the only girl in my family," she said. "For years—decades maybe—I tried so hard to keep up with my brothers. I had good relationships with some of them. Strained times with others. Mother told me I was full of spit and fire, and I was determined to prove her right. The only person who was saltier than me was Mister, and I loved him all the more for it. He got into trouble with me; he rescued me when I got into something too big for me to handle on my own." She sniffled and looked down. "He showed me what it takes to overcome a massive challenge with grace and dignity. I've never seen anyone fight their way back from such a devastating injury—

well, besides Preacher now. But I know he thinks of Mister on his toughest days, and he's going, *Mister did this. I can do it too.*" Zona's tears slipped down her face. "I'm thrilled to have another true cowgirl in the family in Libby. She lets me talk about all the crazy things that happen on the ranch, and she actually gets it." She laughed, and Libby smiled through her own tears.

None of the other ranch wives were actually ranchers. Zona was; Libby was too.

The three women leaned over the mic. "We love you, Mister and Libby." Etta took the mic and gave it to Mildred.

Libby could not hold her tears in then. Her sister—her closest friend on the planet—was already crying, and seeing that was just too much for Libby.

"Libby has always been a good sister," Mildred said. "She adores dancing and festivals, and when she came to me and said we should put on a Christmas festival, I thought she was crazy. And she is." She laughed and swiped at her face.

Libby thanked the Lord for waterproof makeup, if only so her sister wouldn't have to be embarrassed if hers got smeared. "But she also has the biggest heart and the kindest spirit I've ever seen housed in a body. She has wanted to find a forever love for a long time, and I'm so glad she has."

She blew a kiss to Libby, who pressed her palm over her heart. She drew herself up with a big breath as Mildred passed the mic to Judge.

He retook his spot behind the altar and smiled. He'd been emotional at other weddings she'd been to, and Libby liked that about him. She also knew he and Mister had not always gotten along. Of course, neither had she and Mister....

"Mister's real name is Michael," he said. "Mother named him that because she wanted him to be a protector, an archangel, over the last part of the family. He's really been that for the whole family, whether he knows it or not. Our grandmother gave him the nickname Mister for how often he caused mischief."

Judge grinned at him and Libby and then out into the crowd. "He could empty a ten-pound bag of flour in under thirty seconds. He could climb a tree without shoes while Mother turned her back to get him a cup of lemonade. He could throw a football and hit a mark the size of a dime, so when he hit you in the back of the head or on the shoulder, you knew it was on purpose."

More laughing from the crowd.

"Mister can throw a rope like no one I've ever seen," Judge continued, his voice taking on a sober quality. "He's always been too big for this world, and my greatest regret is that I tried to tether him to it. When he left for Oklahoma, I was the last to know. He literally told me on his way out of town. I was devastated, thinking I'd driven him away from Shiloh Ridge, away from all he held dear. He's since assured me and reassured me that it wasn't my fault, that I was right, and that he's glad he went, but I endured many restless nights praying for him. I know he does the same for me, though we've not always been our best selves with each other."

He cleared his throat. "Mister is forgiving, thoughtful,

and talented," he said. "His determination is to be admired, and I'm lucky to count him—and Libby—as friends."

"Thank you," Mister said, and Judge lowered the mic and stepped right around the altar to hug his brother. They both came away with wet eyes, and Libby quickly wiped hers too.

"Can I say something?" Mister asked.

"It's your wedding," Judge said, handing him the mic. Mister stood on the wrong side of the altar and met Libby's eye, and then looked out at the vast crowd of people who'd gathered. When the dining barn was full, they could feed three hundred people. There were easily that many people here tonight.

"I was not always the easiest person to live with," he said. "I had a lot of growing up to do, and I'm sure I still do. Judge is usually the one who gives all the good advice at weddings, but I said something to him once that I think would be perfect for the theme of my wedding." He swallowed, and Libby saw every one of his nerves.

"When I left for Oklahoma, I apologized to Judge, not only for the things I'd done wrong, but for all the time I wasted by *not* apologizing. So if there's someone that needs to hear the words, *I'm sorry*, please say them. Don't let another minute, hour, or day go by with that between you. It's a waste. There's so much more to be had out there, and while my family has said kind things about me, they could've just as easily said the bad things too. But I don't like shying away from hard conversations. So I hope to be able to apologize to Libby when I do something wrong or bad, as I'm sure

I will. And I hope she'll forgive me. If you have someone in your life that needs an apology, go to them and freely give it."

He nodded and handed the mic back to Judge, saying, "That's all."

"That was perfect," Judge said. "And what I was going to say is now really lame." He chuckled. "So let's just get this marriage done, shall we?" He drew a deep breath and looked at Libby. "Unless Libby has something to say."

Libby absolutely did not have anything to say, and she shook her head.

"Okay," Judge said. "Liberty Denise Bellamore, do you give yourself to Michael Mister Ranza Glover, to be his lawfully wedded wife, with love, devotion, and fidelity?"

"Yes, I do," Libby said.

"Michael Mister Ranza Glover, do you take unto yourself, Liberty Denise Bellamore, to be your lawfully wedded wife, and pledge to her to be her lawfully wedded husband, with love, devotion, and fidelity?"

"Heck yes, I do," Mister said, all of his boyish charms shining through. He laughed next, along with several others, and as Judge pronounced them husband and wife, Mister reached up and tossed his cowboy hat high into the air, and shouted, "Yeehaw!" before he took her into his arms, dipped her, and kissed her.

His wife.

Libby was now Mister's wife, and she had never been happier.

Chapter Seventeen

Etta reached for another segment of Hailey's hair, the soft, fine quality of it slipping right through her fingers. Still, she managed to get it into the braid and tucked under the next piece. "What kind of cake do you want for your birthday?"

"Yellow," she said. "Daddy makes this one out of a box. I think it's just called yellow." Hailey looked up from the tablet Etta had put on the bathroom counter in front of her. "Is that a type of cake?"

"Yes," Etta said, though she would never make a cake from a box, and yellow cake was actually vanilla cake with plenty of egg yolks and butter. "What kind of frosting?"

"He puts chocolate on it," she said. "But they have these tubs with white frosting and lots of sprinkles." Her face lit up like the stars did at night. "I've always wanted that."

Etta smiled at her and reached for a piece of hair on the right side. "Have you ever had chocolate cake?"

"Yeah, sure," Hailey said.

"Pudding cake?"

"Pudding cake?" Hailey repeated, her eyebrows folding in. "What's that?"

"Lemon cake?" Etta asked.

"No, but Daddy would like that," she said. "He loves sour things."

"Yes, I've heard that," Etta mused, finishing up with the hair on the girl's head and continuing the braid down her back. "And pudding cake is just a cake with pudding mix in the batter. It makes it really spongy and moist."

"That sounds good," she said.

"Does your daddy decorate with balloons?" Etta asked, as all girls turning ten needed a lot of balloons for their birthday.

"I don't think so," Hailey said, her attention returning to the mermaid show on the tablet.

Etta finished her hair and said, "Hand me that mirror, Hay." She'd been spending more and more time with the girl, especially after school. Hailey knew Etta and August were dating, although if she knew what that actually meant, Etta didn't know.

Hailey handed her the mirror and Etta held it up for her. "That's a French braid. I could do that on your birthday."

"Oh, that's so pretty." Hailey reached back to lightly touch her hair. "Could you, Miss Etta?"

"Of course," she said, setting down the mirror and giving Hailey a squeeze around the shoulders. "Now, come on. It's time to put dinner in the oven, and then your daddy will be here."

"He won't let me stay," she said.

"Probably not," Etta said as she led the way out of the bathroom. "He likes a quiet evening, Hailey. He works hard around the ranch."

"I know, but I could stay, and you could take me home."

"You'll not ask him," Etta said firmly as she went into the kitchen. "He's your father, and he gets to decide." She opened the fridge and took out the casserole she'd made that morning. She'd then done three classes at the high school for the junior rodeo students, accompanied by Mister and Wyatt Walker, as they'd started some classes and demos last summer.

She'd picked up Hailey from school and they'd spent the afternoon feeding the ranch dogs and the chickens, then talking about her upcoming birthday, which was next Saturday. August had approved a birthday party for the girl here at the homestead, and Etta had volunteered to be the party planner and baker.

"But you'll invite him, won't you?" Hailey continued to needle, a slight whine entering her voice. "Our cabin is so boring."

"I'm sure that's—"

"It is?" August said, and Etta whipped her attention away from the oven she was reaching to set the temperature on.

"Daddy," Hailey said, her voice a cheer as she ran toward him. "Look at my hair. Etta did it in a French braid."

"I see that," he said, smiling. The action didn't reach his

eyes, however, and Etta sensed a storm inside him. "It's very pretty."

"She's going to do it for my birthday party," Hailey said.

A switch flipped on August's face, and Etta turned back to the oven so she could hide her reaction to whatever he was about to say. She'd seen him do this a couple of times before, usually when Cactus or Sammy invited Hailey to come do something that made him feel inadequate.

"About that," he said.

"What?" Hailey asked. She did have a short attention span, but so did most kids her age.

"I don't know if we can have a party here."

When Etta turned from the setting the temperature, she found August looking at her, not his daughter.

"Daddy," Hailey whined. "Why not?"

"I think we ought to go see Grams and Gramps," he said. "They love seeing you on your birthday, and this'll be the very first one they haven't spent with you."

Etta's pulse thrummed through her body the way electricity did through a high-voltage fence. So much so that she could feel and see it giving off energy waves. August probably could too, if the sympathetic look on his face meant anything.

She couldn't tell if he was pretending or not, and that really bothered her.

Hailey cheered and danced around. "Yes, yes!" she said. "Let's go see Grams and Gramps."

"And my mom and dad," August said. "We can leave after school next Friday. Stay for the weekend." He grinned at his daughter, but Etta felt like he was erecting a fence between them.

Hailey hugged her father, and he said, "Go get in the truck now. We don't need to be eatin' with Etta every night." He hadn't said one word directly to her yet, and she hadn't spoken at all. "Get over there and tell her thank you for pickin' you up and doin' your hair."

Hailey turned toward Etta, pure sunshine on her face. "Thank you, Miss Etta." She wrapped Etta in a tight hug, and Etta couldn't help letting her eyes close in bliss.

"You're welcome, my sweet girl," Etta whispered. Hailey grinned as she skipped out of the kitchen, and the moment the front door closed, the mood shifted again.

"We could have the party another day," she said. "The following weekend. Or on Wednesday night or something." She leaned back into the counter behind her, hoping she didn't come off as accusatory or demanding.

"Sorry about that," he said, almost ignoring what she'd said. "I've just had a feeling all day that we should go see everyone. My brothers. My folks. Josie's parents." He cleared his throat and couldn't seem to look at her.

"It's fine," Etta said. "I haven't bought groceries or anything yet."

"Good," he said. "You really don't need to do a party for her on another night."

"I know that, August," Etta said, too much bite in her voice. She sighed and ran her hand through her hair, feeling it stick up in odd places. "It's not about *need*. It's about *wanting* to."

"I know you *want* to," he said quietly. "You will always *want* to."

"You make that sound like it's a bad thing." Etta pulled open the oven and slid the glass casserole dish inside, though the appliance hadn't come up to temperature yet.

"It's not," he said. "But I don't *need* you to, and I don't *want* you to." His tone carried edges now too, and when Etta turned back to him, fire shone in the dark depths she'd come to love.

"What will her grandparents do?"

"Spoil her rotten."

"And your brothers?"

"Make cake and throw a party."

"Then why can't I?" Etta asked. There were plenty of opportunities for Etta to perfect her birthday-cake-making skills in the next few months. Smiles, Wilder, Robbie, and Kyle all had birthdays in March, which sat just around the corner. Holly Ann was due any day now. They'd already had a cake for Gun, and one for Chaz, and both Shiloh and Heather would celebrate birthdays before summer hit—and those were only the children in the Glover family.

For some reason, Etta wanted to throw a party for Hailey. She wanted a chance to bond with the girl, because deep down, she'd been hoping to become the girl's mother someday.

August didn't *want* that, nor did he *need* it. That was what Etta heard when he said things like that.

"Because, Etta," he said softly, the fire extinguishing as

quickly as it had flared up. "Everything you do is so wonderful."

"Is this because you'll feel inadequate?"

"I already feel inadequate with you." He put his hand on her waist and slid it around to her back.

"I wish you wouldn't."

"Maybe you shouldn't be so perfect."

"Stop it." She wanted to lean into him and take a deep breath of his shirt. She'd get the outdoors, hay, horse, and earth. The scent of his dryer sheets, and his skin, and his cologne. "I'm not perfect."

"But you have so many more resources than I do," he whispered, his lips dangerously close to her ear. "It makes me feel like a charity case."

Etta stood firm in his arms, refusing to give in to his deep, throaty voice or his delicious lips. "I need you to answer something for me," she said.

August finally got the hint that he couldn't sway her by kissing her. This problem wasn't going to simply vanish because they were physically attracted to one another. He sighed and backed up. "All right."

"Are you going to be able to move past this?" She folded her arms. "Because if not, I'm...." She couldn't bring herself to say that she didn't think they'd work out. She absolutely did not want to break-up with this man. She'd fallen too far already.

"Define 'this'," he said.

Etta gestured to the enormous, luxury kitchen. The long dining room table. The huge living room that seated all twenty-four adults who came here for family meetings, plus their children. "This," she said. "Who I am, and what I want to do to hopefully build a bond with your daughter. My money. My family and how 'helpful' we are. *This*."

Her emotions twisted the way opposing winds did, creating a tight tornado in her torso. She really didn't want him to say no. What would she do if he said he couldn't get past this? Tears pricked her eyes, but she wouldn't let him see them.

In fact, she turned away from him and set a timer on the stove. She had a feeling that after August left, she'd retreat to her bedroom and spend the evening alone. She was so tired of doing that, but she didn't see a way around it.

"I'd like to say of course," he said. "Of course I'm going to be able to move past this."

"I hope so," she whispered. She wanted to tell him that when he kissed her, the earth moved. When he held her hand, she could see the two of them walking down the aisle together. She had no living father, and she didn't want one of her brothers to give her to her husband. She wanted to step into their future together, hand-in-hand, and she wanted to be evenly at his side. Not ahead. Not behind.

"You just have so much," he said. "I have nothing to offer you. I can't tell you how many times I've laid awake at night, wondering why you like me."

Etta reached out and put her hand against his chest. "I like you because of what's in here. Not what you have out there." She gestured to the space around her. "I like you *so* much, August. It'd be cruel of you to not tell me the truth right now. If you can't get past all of this, just say so."

"I can," he whispered. "I'll work on it."

She took him into her arms then, her tears barely touching the outer edges of her eyelids. "Please, *please* let me have a small party for her here. I could even just do it with Cactus's older children. Or all of the littles, none of my siblings or cousins. No adults except me and you. They could all have the night off." She held onto his broad shoulders, silently begging him, silently begging God.

"I don't know how to say no to you," August whispered.

"Don't say no then," Etta said, pulling back and meeting his eye. "It's just a birthday party, but it could be so good for both me and Hailey." She backed up, a horrible thought striking her right between the ribs. "Unless you don't want me to have a relationship with your daughter."

"Etta," he said. "Of course I do."

Etta nodded, because she had to believe what he said. August had never lied to her, and she wasn't sure the cowboy could do so even if he wanted to. "Okay." She didn't know where to go from here. "I know you just sent Hailey out to the truck, but do you want to stay for dinner?" She pointed to the oven. "It's just chicken cordon bleu casserole, but it's pretty good."

"Again, I don't know how to say no to you." He smiled and cupped her face in one hand. He gazed down at her with such adoration that Etta didn't think he could fake. Not even the best con artist could replicate the love shining from his eyes. He lowered his head and kissed her, the sweetest kiss of her life. Slow and steady and strictly on the surface so she would know the promise of his passion to come at another time.

He held back, however, and Etta had the distinct feeling he was doing that in more ways than just this kiss. She sure did like a slow, sensual kiss that didn't go too deep, and August knew how to deliver one.

You don't have to have everything planned right now, she told herself, and that thought allowed her to simply enjoy the kiss, enjoy his presence, and enjoy the opportunity to keep getting to know him.

He pulled away and whispered, "We can have a party on Wednesday night, okay?" his lips catching on hers as he spoke.

"Thank you, August," she whispered, her eyes still closed from that weak-in-the-knees kiss.

Chapter Eighteen

August lifted his head as he heard the front door open. He wasn't finished with his prayer, but he honestly wasn't sure he'd ever be done asking the Lord to help him. Guide him. Clear his mind. Protect his daughter. Give him clarity with Etta Glover.

"Daddy," Hailey said, her footsteps coming closer.

August stayed on his knees as she came through the door. She stalled, her eyes wide. "Sorry," she said. "Are you done?"

"Come on in, sweets," he said, reaching for her. She stepped into his side, and he held her close, giving her a squeeze. "What's up?"

"Etta said as she dropped me off that I could come help her plant some flowers around the homestead tonight." She seemed a bit nervous, which only made August's guilt twist inside his stomach. He wasn't sure where the line was between accepting help and having friends—and he knew without a doubt he wanted to be more than friends with Etta.

"Can I go?" she asked.

"Yeah." He groaned as he got to his feet. "I'm on a break right now. Let's get you a snack, and you can come out to the fields with me."

"On the quad?"

"Yep." He smiled at his daughter, hoping he could show her the right way to find a solution to her troubles. "Did Etta say anything about dinner?"

"No," Hailey said. "There's always dinner there, Daddy. Maybe you could take her to dinner, and I could go to Cam's?" The hope in her voice reached the roof, and August didn't want to blame his daughter for wanting to spend time with her friends. It was certainly better than hanging out with him while he snoozed on the couch.

"We'll see," August said, hating the answer. "If it's okay with everyone, I'm sure it'll be fine." He knew that wouldn't happen tonight. Etta had planned a surprise birthday party for Hailey, and August had enjoyed her enthusiastic planning texts about the event. She'd said she'd invite Hailey up to the homestead at a specific time, and that all he needed to do was get her there. He could even leave during the party, which was a kid-only affair at the homestead.

With over ten children age four and under, he'd told her he'd stay. She said a couple of the ranch wives had volunteered to stay and help with the littles under two, and Etta had games and activities ready for the older children, all the way up to Mitch, who had turned fifteen recently.

August got down a box of chocolate chip cookies and handed it to Hailey. "What homework do you need to get done before you go plant flowers?" He reached for her backpack, noting that he needed to get back out to Jess soon.

"I did it in the car with Etta," Hailey said. "It was the math worksheet. She helped me with the division."

August waited for the annoyance to sing through him. He didn't need Etta to help his daughter with her homework. It didn't come right away, and he found that to be a great improvement. Perhaps the Lord had been listening to him and helping him reason through things before he let his natural instincts take over.

"Great," he said. He didn't have to do anything with her that night. "I talked to Preacher today. He said I can have Friday off too, so I'll call your teacher tomorrow and find out if there's anything you can do for that day before we go."

"Okay," Hailey said, clearly not caring about her third-grade curriculum. In truth, August didn't either, but he'd make the phone call anyway. He'd call the school and excuse his daughter for Friday and Monday. When he thought about making the drive to the Hill Country, he was excited. Then the dread would fill him, and he'd have to find a way through that darkness to see the good in taking Hailey to see everyone she'd grown up knowing.

It's the right thing to do, he thought. And it was. He knew it was. *Executing* the right thing wasn't always easy, however.

"Okay, well, let's go," he said, dropping her backpack

onto the couch again. "I left Jess out in the fields and promised him I wouldn't be long."

* * *

Hours later, and one more calf alive in the world, August had showered, changed into more casual clothes, and drove up the lane to the homestead in his truck instead of on the ATV. Hailey rode beside him instead of behind him, and she hummed along to the country music song on the radio.

Since it was almost March, the sun hung in the sky a little longer than usual, but dusk had definitely arrived over the Texas Panhandle. He didn't see how Hailey thought they'd be outside planting anything, but he said nothing.

There weren't dozens of vehicles parked in front of the homestead, and August relaxed a little bit further. He brought the truck to a stop and peered through the wind-shield. He knew a surprise waited beyond that big, heavy, wooden door, but Hailey didn't.

She jumped from the truck, and he followed, pulling his phone from his pocket. He wanted to get her reaction on video—or at least one photo he could send to his parents and Josie's.

He thought of Shannon and Daniel—Josie's parents—and how they'd tried to stay involved in August's and Hailey's lives. Moving to Three Rivers had definitely put a damper on that for everyone in August's life, but he didn't spend a moment worrying about it.

Moving here had absolutely been the right thing for him

and Hailey, and knowing that he'd already done something hard but necessary buoyed him up and made his step lighter as he preceded his daughter up to the porch.

He knocked and then opened the door, calling, "Howdy, Etta. We're here." She didn't respond, of course, but the heavy scent of frosting hung in the air. He went into the house first but held his palm out to keep Hailey back. She didn't come with him, and August's pulse picked up as he walked toward the kitchen.

He saw no one through the arch, but he could hear some childish giggling, then someone shushing that. "It's okay, Hay," he called. "You can come back." He went to the end of the island and held up his phone to record her reaction.

From there, he could see over the couch, and he saw Etta crouched down there with a little boy holding his forefinger to her lips as if she needed to be reminded to be quiet. Dot Glover and Montana Glover kept the children around them quiet too, and August grinned at Cam and Kyle, the two boys who had been such good friends to Hailey.

She came through the door, and he turned his attention back to her, nodding. "Where is she?" she asked. "It's getting dark, and—"

"Surprise!" a few people—mostly the older children and the adults—yelled at the same time, with various renditions of the word coming from the mouths of the babes over the next few seconds.

They all popped up from behind the couches, and the adults put the two-year-olds on the furniture. Every single person wore a smile made of joy, and August felt the emotion permeating the air. It touched his father-heart, and he watched the screen on his phone as his daughter realized what was happening.

She melted, positively melted, and then her face scrunched up, and she started to cry.

He lowered his phone, not expecting that. He had no idea what to do with a daughter who cried over good things, but he strode toward her. "Hey," he said, shielding her from the others in the room. "It's a birthday party. For you. A surprise birthday party."

She clung to him, her arms right around his middle, and she sniffled for only a couple of seconds before she released him. She wiped her eyes quickly and stepped past him. Cam and Kyle and Etta had led the way around the furniture, and pure anxiety lived in Etta's expression.

August didn't know what to do either, so he stepped out of the way as Hailey said, "You're so sneaky."

"Were you surprised?" Cam asked, glee on his face. Maybe he hadn't noticed the break-down.

"So surprised," Hailey said.

"Look, lookie," Kyle said, pointing to something on the counter. "We all helped Auntie Etta make you a cake." He hopped on the balls of his feet, his excitement unable to be contained within his body.

"Happy birthday a few days early, honey." Etta enveloped Hailey in a hug while the littles clapped from the other side of the couch.

"Thank you, Etta," Hailey said, and when she stepped

back, she was made from all-smiles too. She looked at August. "Did you know about this?"

"Yep." He held up his phone. "Do you want to see how surprised you were?" He could edit out the end of the video where she started to cry, but for now, his daughter, Cameron, Kyle, Etta, and Smiles all crowded around the phone and watched the few seconds of video.

Hailey laughed and pointed at her wide eyes. "You guys really surprised me."

"And we almost got everyone to say it at the same time," Etta said. She tipped up on her toes and kissed August's cheek. "I've decided that there's no better time to eat dessert first than a ten-year-old's surprise birthday party."

"Of course," he said, though he would literally never think to serve dessert to over a dozen kids without making sure they ate something healthy first. That was why all the children at Shiloh Ridge Ranch loved "Auntie Etta" so much.

"Everyone to the table," she called, and a scuffle happened as the older children helped the younger ones into highchairs and booster seats. "Hailey, you get the birthday throne today." Etta indicated a dining room chair that had been draped in a bright yellow cloth. Someone had then painted gems along the tops and sides of it, and a legitimate tiara hung from one side. Etta picked it up and placed it on Hailey's head, beamed at her with such love and adoration that August thought he'd entered an alternate reality.

No one would ever love his daughter the way he needed

them to—that was what he'd believed after Josie had died. That he might be able to find someone to love him, but Hailey would always be an afterthought. Hailey would always just "come with him." Hailey herself would be tolerated or overlooked.

But that so wasn't the case with Etta. She loved everyone who came in contact with her, and August felt himself falling, falling, falling in love with her as he watched her settle that tiara on his daughter's head and help her into the throne. She sat higher than the other children, and while Etta had been doing that, someone had lit the candles on the birthday cake.

Dot came forward slowly with it and she said, "All right, everyone. Remember the song we practiced?"

"Sing it with me," Etta said, and she started very slowly with, "Happy birthday to you...."

Everyone joined in, even the teenage boys, and Dot set the flaming cake in front of Hailey. Montana stood on the other side of the table, her phone up, and August experienced a profound moment of gratitude for these women who'd made his daughter—who'd made *him*—feel so worthwhile and cherished.

The song was sloppy, with everyone laughing at some point. But they made it to the end, and Hailey sat up straighter and blew out all ten candles with one breath. Cam, Mitch, and Link cheered like grown-up cowboys do at the rodeo, and that got all the younger kids riled up.

"Okay, okay," Etta said, holding up both hands. "Auntie Dot, Auntie Montana, and I will start serving the cake. But only to those boys and girls who are waiting patiently and quietly."

Instantly, all the noise died at the table, except for Chaz, who already held his fork in his hand. He banged it on the table and said, "Cake, cake, cake, cake," in his cute little-boy voice.

"Chazzy," Montana said, gently taking the fork from him. "Quietly."

"I so quiet," he said, looking up at her with pure innocence in his eyes.

"I quiet," Gun said.

"You just talked," Etta said.

"I'm the quietest," Smiles said, and August started laughing. These children certainly possessed big personalities, and he found himself loving them with every argument one of them made about how they were being the quietest.

"I guess I'll have to eat this cake myself," Etta said, her hands moving for Mitch, who sat down at the end. He stood up and waved his hands to get everyone's attention. Then he started signing, and Link, Cam, Montana, and Etta all started laughing. Hailey did too.

"What did he say?" he asked Hailey.

"He said he's obviously the quietest because he never talks, and his ears hurt with all the bickering over which little boy is being the quietest."

August grinned down to the teen, who grinned on back at everyone else.

Etta awarded Mitch with the first piece of yellow cake with white frosting practically bedazzled with colorful sprinkles. The second went to Hailey, his precious birthday girl, and then he started helping the other adults get cake out as fast as possible. He'd rather do that then have a two-year-old mutiny on his hands.

What he really wanted to do was take Etta outside and kiss her until he couldn't breathe. Their eyes met, and though he'd just put a piece of delicious, moist cake in his mouth, he nodded toward the foyer.

She set her cake down and murmured something to Montana, who leaned closer to hear and then nodded. She then took his hand, and he abandoned his cake in favor of the woman who'd made it.

He'd barely stepped outside before he said, "Thank you, Etta. I don't know how you do it, but thank you." He took her into his arms and kissed her, hoping with everything in him that she'd let him do that for the rest of the night.

Of course, she wouldn't. She couldn't. She had games to play with the children, and he'd spied a piñata on the corner counter beside the sink. This night was far from over, and the party was just getting started.

But she kissed him back as enthusiastically as he'd started the action, and right now, August focused on her, and only her.

* * *

An earthquake shook every organ inside August's torso. His heart hadn't been beating normally since he saw the "Welcome to Dripping Springs," sign, and his stomach had cinched tight and hadn't let go yet.

The houses and farms and ranches were spread out over the Hill Country, and he couldn't see the place where he'd used to live and work as he took another curve with trees on both sides of the two-lane highway. In the passenger seat, Hailey slept, and August almost wanted to keep driving so she wouldn't be disturbed.

To the untrained eye, every tree and driveway looked the same, with perhaps some differences in the gates or arches near the road. But to him, he knew he only had about five more minutes before he had to wake Hailey and face Shannon and Daniel Jones.

He swallowed, but his throat barely seemed wide enough to pass saliva. The miles and the minutes ticked away, and he made the turn at the dark red brick gate and passed through it. Daniel hardly ever closed the gate, and August couldn't even imagine having to phone him and ask him to let him in.

"Hailey," he said, reaching over to nudge the girl. "We're here. Wake up now."

She started to stir, and August took in the hay fields on either side of the road. The barn he knew so well stretched tall before him, and to the side of that, the house where he'd once lived with his wife and daughter.

"Do you think Gramps still has that dog?" Hailey asked, yawning.

"I haven't heard of him passing," August said quietly. He couldn't think of anything but *Josie, Josie, Josie*, and Hailey had asked about an old golden retriever? "There he is." He spied the dog on the front porch, panting though it wasn't hot yet, and in the next moment, Daniel stood from the chair.

He moved over to the front door and called inside. Not ten seconds later, about when August eased the truck to a stop in the driveway, Shannon came outside wearing a flowered apron he'd seen many times.

Everything here was so familiar, and yet so foreign. He'd been here countless times before, and he used to spend hours every day working alongside Daniel.

Hailey opened the door and tumbled from the truck while August took his time unbuckling his seatbelt and then reaching into the back to get out the lemon poppyseed bundt cake that Etta had made for his in-laws.

His mind rioted. How was he supposed to tell them about his new girlfriend? Were there words for that? Would they feel betrayed?

His feet and legs knew the way to the front porch and up the steps, and he arrived in front of Shannon and Daniel, who were both hugging Hailey and firing questions at her about Three Rivers, her school there, and the ranch where he now worked.

Daniel came up for air first, and he went straight to an embrace. August leaned into the comfort of it, feeling like he was hugging his own father after a long time away. All of the jitters and twitters inside him quieted, and he said, "Hello, Daniel. It's so good to see you."

"And you." The man's voice scraped his throat, and he cleared the emotion and stepped back. Shannon wiped her eyes as she finished smiling at Hailey, and everything trembled on her face when she looked at August.

Neither of them spoke as he took her into a hug too, and he clung as tightly to her as she did to him. Josie had sported the same light blonde hair as her mother, and that gene had passed right on to Hailey. Shannon's was going gray now, and he'd seen the lighter strands of it sparkle in the sun from time to time.

She eventually released him, and the four of them stood on the porch. August looked at Hailey, his bravery continuing to climb. He lifted the cake. "We brought you this. It's lemon-poppyseed."

"My, thank you," Shannon drawled. "Should we go have some right now? I've got a special cake for you too, Hailey." She grinned down at the girl, and it was clear that August taking their granddaughter from them had been difficult on them. He hadn't meant it to be. Again, it was another situation that had been hard to do but absolutely essential.

"Did you make this with your daddy?" Shannon asked, and August's muscles tensed instantly.

"No," Hailey said, going with her grandmother. "Etta let me help her make it."

Shannon had already turned around, but Daniel's gaze landed plenty heavy on August's face as his wife said, "Who's Etta?"

"She's my girlfriend," August said, clearing his throat. To Shannon's eternal credit, her step didn't so much as stutter. He met Daniel's gaze. "We've been going out for a few months."

Daniel blinked, his smile spreading slowly across his face. "That's great, August." He clapped his hand on his shoulder. "Come tell us about her. Do you have a picture?"

August once again felt like he'd entered some sort of alternate reality, or perhaps the Bermuda Triangle. He hadn't anticipated his former in-laws being *happy* for him that he was trying to find someone new to spend his life with.

At the same time, he wouldn't want someone he loved to suffer forever. They'd told him to get out there and date. He just hadn't known how, especially after his one failed attempt at putting himself into the dating pool after Josie's death.

"No pictures," he said. "Next time I see her, I'll get one and send it to you."

"We'd love that," Daniel said. "So her name is Etta...?" They arrived in the kitchen, where a three-tiered, bright pink, birthday cake stood on the counter. "Shannon, he's dating a woman named Etta."

"So Hailey said." Shannon flashed August a smile and continued poking candles into the cake. "Etta Glover, right?"

"That's right," August said, feeling a bit rumbly in his stomach again. "She runs the community outreach programs—for the people of Three Rivers, as well as classes and demonstrations at the junior high and high schools—for Shiloh Ridge Ranch. I work there now."

"Oh, is that how you met her?" Shannon asked.

August glanced at Hailey, who couldn't look away from

the pony perched on top of the cake. "I actually met her on the ranch, yes, but before I got the job. Hailey's class had taken a field trip to the ranch. We both met Etta then."

"She is so nice," Hailey said. "She is the best cook too, and she let me help her plant a bunch of flowers around the homestead."

"She is a good cook," August said.

"She lives in the homestead?" Daniel asked.

"With her brother and cousin," August said, suddenly tired of the explanations about the Glover family. "There are a lot of them, Daniel. She's one of the younger ones. The only one not married right now. There's like a million adults, and they all live there. Well, most of them. They have a lot of kids, specifically two-year-olds."

"Show them the video of my party, Daddy."

August dug in his pocket for his phone, almost dreading the idea of showing them the surprise party Etta had designed and pulled off. "I guess I do have a picture of her," he said. "She'll be the one right beside Hailey's birthday throne."

He showed them the video of Hailey's surprise, and then the video Montana had shot of all the Glover children singing *Happy Birthday* to his daughter.

Shannon sniffled as she stepped away from the phone. She opened the drawer and pulled out a book of matches. "That was wonderful. All those beautiful children."

Daniel looked up and handed the phone back. "She seems great."

"She is great," August murmured as he pocketed his

phone. He didn't quite know how to stand in this house anymore. He felt too tall and like he was taking up too much room. "I really like her."

"Do you think you might marry her?" Shannon asked.

August dang near choked. "I have...no idea," he said, his eyes glued to Hailey's. She wore her wide eyes, almost like she was as surprised as August was at the question. "I'm not trying to replace Josie."

"We know that," Daniel said. "But we hope you can get close. We want you to be happy, son."

August nodded, because he wanted that too. He thought about his level of happiness, and since he'd left Dripping Springs, the mercury in his meter had definitely risen. "I'm doing well in Three Rivers," he said. "Hailey is too. She's got some good friends at school and on the ranch, and...yeah. We're happy there."

"And that makes us happy," Daniel said while Shannon nodded.

"Should we sing first?" Shannon asked. "Then I have your favorite paninis ready to go on the grill."

"Bacon and egg?" Hailey asked, her eyebrows flying sky high.

Shannon laughed and hugged her granddaughter. "What else?"

August grinned at Shannon and Hailey, another part of his heart that had been mortally wounded suddenly healing in a way he hadn't anticipated.

Chapter Nineteen

Etta shrugged into her robe as she hurried out of her suite and through the living room. Ace had texted only thirty seconds ago, and she'd needed to use the restroom. Her bladder was why she was awake at this hour at all.

She didn't want him to knock or ring the doorbell, not that he would. She also didn't want to cause him and Holly Ann to be delayed in getting down to the hospital in any way, so she jogged under the arch and into the foyer, the nightlights stuck into the wall lighting up with her movement.

After yanking open the front door, Etta continued out onto the porch just as her brother reached the top step. His two-year-old son lay folded over his shoulder, clearly snoozing.

"I've got him," Etta whispered, taking Gunnison from his father. "Go."

"I obviously have no idea how long we'll be."

"I'm sure I can find someone to take him while I run to the high school today." She smiled at Ace, already rocking back and forth so Gun would settle back to sleep. She patted his back gently. "I won't say anything until you do via text."

"Thanks, Etta."

She lifted her hand, hoping Holly Ann could see her through the windshield. Ace ran back down the steps and to his truck, and Etta stayed on the porch as their headlights cut through the middle-of-the-night darkness and headed down the hill.

She drew in a deep breath and gazed out toward the cemetery. Gun bore his grandfather's name as his middle name, and he was a lovable, happy little boy who loved his cousins. He'd love his new sister too.

"Come on, baby," she murmured to the sleeping child. "Let's go back to bed."

Hours later, with Gun safe at Sammy's and Etta's presentation done at the high school, she drove toward the hospital. Ace had texted the family to let them know that Holly Ann had gone into labor, but that it was going very, very slow and they should all stay up at the ranch until they heard from him again.

It had been five hours since his last message, and Etta wasn't buying it. Holly Ann had already birthed one baby, and that one had come very, very quickly. If she hadn't had the little girl yet, there was a problem. Etta suspected that she had, and Ace and Holly Ann wanted a few hours to themselves.

She supposed she didn't fault them for that, but she was

already in town, and she figured she could just stop by. The moment she parked, her phone rang, and she glanced at the screen in her truck.

August's name sat there, and she smiled. She tapped the screen to answer the call and gave it a moment to connect. "Howdy, baby," she said, plenty of flirtatiousness in her voice. "Where are you right now?"

"My parents'," he said. "They wanted to take Hailey bowling for her birthday, and I begged out of going."

"You don't like bowling?"

"I don't like sleeping in hard beds and then driving for a couple of hours and *then* going bowling," he said.

"I think someone is an old man," Etta teased.

August laughed, and she leaned her head back against the rest in the driver's seat and basked in the sound of it playing through her speakers. "I am going to be thirty-eight this summer."

"Ooh, that's so old," she said.

"Where are you? Sounds like I'm on speaker."

"I'm in the car," she said. "I just finished my presentation in the animal health and safety class, and I decided to stop by the hospital and see what's going on with Ace and Holly Ann." She looked out the window to the three-story hospital. "I think they've had the baby and haven't told anyone."

"Oh, my stars and stripes," August said, plenty of teasing in his voice too. "How dare they want a moment to themselves?"

Etta burst out laughing, her voice mingling with

August's over the line. They quieted, and Etta said, "I miss you, August. I hope you're truly having fun."

"I am," he said, and he sounded sincere. "It's been different than I anticipated, and I'm not sure why I was so nervous."

"I'm glad," she said. "I've been praying for you and Hailey."

"I appreciate that," he said. "And I miss you too, Etta. You've been a very good friend and a very steady force in my life for the past several months."

Etta wasn't sure she liked the sound of that, but she didn't know how to call him on what he'd said.

"Of course," he said. "We're way more than friends."

"Mm," she said, smiling as her worries evaporated. "I would hope you don't kiss all your friends the way you did me before you left."

He chuckled, and she could just see him ducking his head and the redness creeping up his neck. "Definitely not."

Etta drew in a deep breath, wanting to take the conversation to the next level. "Where do you see us going, August?"

"I don't want to break-up."

"Well, my sister told me once that there's really only two roads a relationship is on."

"Oh?"

"Yeah," Etta said. "One that ends or one that never ends."

"I see."

"For me, a relationship that doesn't end will have a wedding in it," she said. "And then kids."

"Mm, yes, I know you want children."

Etta's chest clenched. "Do you, August? Want more children?"

"Yes." His voice reminded her of calm water and a wispy breeze.

"Well, good," she said. "I sense you're lying on the couch, because the bed at your mother's is just as hard at your in-law's. So I'll let you go get your afternoon nap, and I'll go find out what's going on with my new niece."

He yawned and combined that with a laugh. "Text me what they name her. I know that's important to you."

"Holly Ann is a bit of a free spirit," Etta said. "Last I heard, she had decided on Stormy, and Ace was trying desperately to offer her another alternative."

"Are you more of a free spirit when it comes to names? Or a traditionalist?"

"My name is Etta," she said. "How many people under ninety do you know with this name?"

He laughed, and Etta's hopes grew wings and flew. She'd tried to keep herself grounded, but with every passing day and week and month she got to spend with August, it had become harder and harder.

"So a traditionalist."

"I think so," Etta said.

"What's your favorite name for a girl baby?" he asked.

"Well, Charlie took Betty," she said. "I think Emma is too close to Etta."

"Wow, you've thought a lot about this."

"Did you expect anything less?"

"No." He chuckled, and more voices came through the line. "Hey, baby, I have to let you go. My brothers just walked in."

"Darn," she said. "No naptime for you."

Laughter came through the line, and then August said, "No, hey," amidst a ton of scuffles.

"Hello there, Etta," another male voice said. "This is Christian."

"Give him the phone back," another man said.

"Hello, Christian," Etta said, plenty of playfulness in her voice. "Tell me, are you as good-looking as your brother?"

"My word," Christian said. "I thought this was a normal person. Who did you call?" His voice faded as he moved further from the speaker.

"It's my girlfriend," August said, and then he added, "I'm sorry, Etta. Go find out about the baby. We'll talk later."

"Your girlfriend?" one of his brothers demanded.

"What in the world? Do Mom and Dad know?"

The line went dead, and Etta giggled to herself. Then she turned off the car and got out, facing the hospital with a new goal in mind: Find and hold her new niece.

Twenty minutes later, Etta had located the room where Holly Ann Glover was assigned. She knocked, her throat housing her heart, and then pushed into the room.

"I told you it would be Auntie Etta," Holly Ann said from the hospital bed. She sat up, wearing one of those awful gowns, and she held the most perfect infant in her arms.

"I was just in town," Etta whispered, slipping all the way inside and closing the door behind her. "Can I come over?"

"Of course." Holly Ann gave her a kind, sisterly smile, and Etta did her best not to run toward her.

"How did it go?" Etta pushed Holly Ann's dark hair off her forehead. "You look tired. And where's my brother?"

"He went to get something to eat." Holly Ann shifted so the pretty little girl faced Etta. She grunted with her eyes closed, and Etta fell in love with her instantly, with her darker skin that came from her mother, with the shape of her nose that matched all the Glovers, with the wispy hair the color of the dirt roads at the ranch.

"Better be that barbecue pizza you like." Etta grinned at her, her fingers itching to touch the baby.

"Right?" Holly Ann laughed and looked down at her daughter. "You must've left Gun with Sammy."

"Yeah, I had to do a class at the high school." Etta reached for the baby. "Can I? What did you name her?"

"Pearl Jo." Holly Ann moved the infant into Etta's arms, the quietness in the hospital room only adding to the reverence of the precious life she now held.

"That's cute," Etta said, stepping away and bouncing the little girl as her face started to scrunch up. "Are you going to keep both names like you and Bethany Rose?"

"Yes," Holly Ann said. "You should've seen Ace's face when I said we could call her PJ."

Etta grinned, but she couldn't tear her eyes from the baby. "August said he wanted more children."

"Etta, that's so great." Holly Ann's voice carried equal kindness and surprise. "Are you two getting pretty serious?"

"I mean, I think so." Etta managed to look up from Pearl Jo's face and meet Holly Ann's eyes. "It's not like I've told him I love him."

"But you do."

"No," Etta said slowly, taking a few moments to examine her feelings. "I don't think I'm in love with him yet. But I feel like the potential is there, and I don't know. It's exciting. *He* excites me. The thought of getting to spend my life with him is...an amazing thing."

"I'm so happy for you," Holly Ann said.

"Well, it's nothing yet," Etta said. "We're dating. But he is the most put-together, most down-to-earth, most honest man I've been out with in a long time. Since Noah." Her voice immediately hushed afterward, and she refocused on Pearl Jo. "When are you going to text out that she's here?"

"She was born around nine-thirty this morning," Holly Ann said with a sigh. "I suppose we better tell everyone. I'm surprised Ida hasn't barged in here with the twins."

"Oh, she won't bring the twins," Etta said, smiling at Pearl Jo as her eyes opened. They were made of all pupil, but Etta saw a thin, dark blue ring around that. "Johnny has started cutting a molar, and he's an absolute beast right now." She said the sentence in a coo, as if having a toddler with a slobbering issue and a two-second temper was a sweet thing.

She looked up as Pearl Jo closed her eyes. "I won't stay. I

know it's hard to have the family here, hovering." She moved back over to Holly Ann, who accepted the baby back.

"You don't have to go."

"Ace will be back soon. You guys enjoy your dinner, and then send out the text. I'll go grab Gun and bring him back down."

"That's an hour-long drive," she said. "And you'll have to go home again."

"I'll stay at Ida's," Etta said, the plan forming as she spoke. "Or with Mother."

"Ace did tell her. I think he's stopping to get her on his way back here. It's not like we're going to have a romantic dinner with a rolling hospital tray and a new baby between us."

Etta grinned at her. "Before August, I would've said that sounded about ten times better than any date I'd been on recently."

They laughed together, and Etta leaned down and hugged both Holly Ann and Pearl Jo. "Okay," she said. "I'll tell Sammy to bring down Gun, and I'll call Ida to make sure we can stay with her."

"Thank you, Etta," Holly Ann said. "For taking Gun. For being the perfect aunt."

Etta didn't know what to say, so she just smiled and headed for the door. By the time she stepped out, Holly Ann's eyes had drifted closed. Even Etta could admit not having thirty-plus people waiting in the lobby down the hall from maternity created a more peaceful entry into the world, for both baby and parents, and she determined to do what Holly Ann and Ace had done when she had her first baby.

Keep it to herself for a little while.

She imagined what a baby boy or girl would look like with her darker hair and eyes, and August's lighter ones, the thoughts a bit dangerous to be having so soon. Etta simply couldn't stop herself, and she told herself that Ranger and Oakley had fallen in love in a matter of weeks. She and August had been seeing each other for almost five months.

And she *really* liked him.

Chapter Twenty

August pulled out a set of eight cloth napkins and held them up for Etta. They were the color of the sky, and his mother had embroidered flowers and birds in the corners. "My mom sent these for you." He gave them to her. "They're napkins."

"I know what they are," she said, taking them. "They're beautiful. Does she make them herself?"

"Yes," August said. "She loves needlepoint. She even tried to teach us boys to do it."

Etta giggled and asked, "How did that go?"

"Not great," he said. "Have you ever tried to get an eight-year-old boy to sit down and use a needle and thread? I think I stabbed myself once just to get out of doing it." He laughed along with Etta, and as their voices came down, he slid his hand along her arm and then dropped it to her hip. "Hailey is on her way to the Edge cabin."

Etta took a tiny step closer to him. "Yes, she is."

"I sure did miss you, Etta."

"I could hear you say that a hundred times," she murmured, and as she came closer and his mouth met hers, August breathed in through his nose. He got sugar and sweetness, as well as sunshine and springtime.

She pulled away before he let himself get too out of control. "I'm glad your visit to your family went well. I know you were worried about it." She reached for his hand. "Do you want to go for a walk or something? I don't feel like staying inside this afternoon."

"Sure, okay," he said. "Where are you going to take me?"

"Up the road a little," she said with a smile. "There's a cottage up the hill about a half-mile. Can you go that far?"

"I've been driving for hours," he said. "I can go a mile."

"It might be a mile there," she said. "In a car, over the bumpy roads, it takes about ten or fifteen minutes to get down, but I know a path through the woods."

"Ooh, a path through the woods," he said, plenty of fun, flirty vibes in his voice. "Are we going to meet any big, bad wolves?"

"I don't think there are any wolves in this part of Texas, sir," she said, laying on her accent real thick. "Besides, I can protect you if we do run into one."

"Oh-ho," August said, going with her as she started for the front door. The Christmas tree was finally gone, and he paused. "Tell me what happened with the tree that was here."

"The angel tree?" Etta asked, and she gazed at the spot where it had been standing for so long.

"You guys left it up all the way through January," he

said. "And it was up the first time I came up here, before Thanksgiving."

"It's our way of remembering who we are," she said, her hand reaching out to fondle the dead air. "Our Glover heritage. We put it up on the last Sunday in October, and it stays up until someone who lives here gets sick of it and takes it down." She glanced at him, a soft, maternal smile on her mouth. August loved the different sides of Etta. She knew how to have fun. She could throw a party for anyone, of any age, and make them feel like the most special person in the whole world.

She could take control of a group of unruly school children or hold a crying child close to her chest and whisper to them until they calmed. She loved her family deeply, and she possessed mad skills in the kitchen. She definitely held a particular place within this family, and while she was the only single Glover left, she didn't cry about it.

"Who, let's be honest, is usually me." She shook her head. "Zona comes and helps, because she stores all the ornaments at her house."

"Where does she live?" he asked. "She's not here on the ranch, right?"

"Just across the southern border," Etta said. "We'll be able to see the fence line between us and the Rhinehart place up at the Top Cottage."

"Ah, it does have a name," he said, smiling at her. All of their houses here had names. The homestead. Bull House. Ranch House. Edge cabin. Only the newer ones didn't seem too, but he'd heard people refer to them by who lived in them.

"It has a name," Etta said, reaching for the doorknob and leading him outside. "Want to see the family graveyard?"

"Do I ever," he said, squeezing her hand so she'd know he was joking. "Your dad died young, right?"

"Yes," she said. "Only about oh, ten years ago now." She blew out her breath. "I was twenty-six. Both he and his brother had prostate cancer. Last year, when my brother was sick, he was scared he'd have it too."

"Did he?"

"No," Etta said, and walking beside her in the country evening sure did soothe a man's weary soul. She spoke in a sexy, Texas lilt, the pitch of her voice entering his ears in just the right way. "Ace has Celiac disease, and that was making him sick. But it was a good reminder for everyone in the family to get their scans done. Bear's been preaching it for years. His dad's been gone for a lot longer than mine."

"That's too bad," August said, wondering what life would be like without his father here on earth. He had suffered a massive loss, with conversations that had been started and never finished.

"I've lost someone really close to me like that. Someone I could talk to one day and then not be able to the next. I honestly know exactly how hard that is."

Etta remained quiet, the moment between them powerful. August took in the quaint cemetery right off the left side of the road. He'd seen it before, of course. He'd come up to the main part of the ranch plenty during birthing season.

Right now, he spent most of his time down in the flatter parts extending toward the highway, prepping acres and acres that had never been planted for their first crop.

"My daddy's right here," Etta said, pausing in front of a big, gray headstone. "Bull Dwayne Glover." She bent down, releasing his hand, and pulled up a tuft of weeds that had started to encroach on the gravesite. "I do miss him powerfully sometimes. He was a good man."

"I'm sure he was."

"He'd make a huge kettle of hot chocolate on Christmas Eve," Etta said, pure fondness in her voice. "Mother would give us the pajamas she'd spent the month of December sewing, and we'd gather around the Christmas tree with Daddy and his guitar." She stood, pure love streaming from her. The memory was so powerful that August could almost hear the strumming of a guitar and smell the chocolate hanging in the air.

"Daddy was a fantastic singer," she said. "My brother, Ward, got that from him." She hugged herself though the nights had started staying warm as spring arrived. "He was almost a famous country music star."

"Ward?"

"Mm hm." Etta moved over a couple of feet and stood in front of another grave, this one also well-tended. "This is Uncle Stone. He was older than Daddy, but they only had each other. I think they really had a competition to see who could have more kids." She bent down again, this time to trace her fingers along the letters in his name. "He died twenty years ago. I was still in high school."

August could barely hear her, but the energy pulsing from her had turned blue. "He was a good friend to my dad. They didn't do anything around here without consulting with one another. They made a ranch and family motto, and they stuck to it."

"What's that?" He reached for her as she stood again, tucking her into his side so she'd know she didn't have to live inside painful memories alone.

"Reuse, repair, and recycle. Daddy and Uncle Stone fixed things when they broke. They turned tires into bits and put them under our swing sets. They built a barn out of reclaimed wood from fences around the ranch." She nodded behind her to the glorious blue barn. "When it was deemed structurally unsound a few years ago, some of my cousins and brothers worked to fix it up and make it a new family centerpiece."

"True Blue."

"Daddy and Uncle Stone built it themselves. They hired out, at least while we were all still growing. Then they just relied on their boys and girls to work the ranch."

"Do you like what you do for your ranch?" he asked.

She nodded. "Yes. Ida and I came up with the school programs and community outreach arm of the ranch, because we both like people, and we wanted to be as important as our brothers."

"I'm sure you were," he said. "You are."

"Mm." Etta took a few seconds to gaze at the few other graves in the cemetery, all of which bore the last name of Glover. Grandparents, and even a set of great-grandparents.

"Sometimes I wonder." With that, she turned and went up the obviously new sidewalk and through the gate to the gravel road that led toward a slight incline.

August caught up to her, unsure of what to say next. "True Blue," she said. "If you look past the roof, you can see another one. That's where Bishop and Montana live."

"Ah, yes, I remember seeing it on the field trip. We went out the back door of this barn."

"Yes," she said, sliding her hand into his again. "If you go left here, that's Ace's place."

August looked as they walked by, and two vehicles sat in front of the house, which didn't have a poured driveway. Just pristine gravel that went to a white picket fence, a little patch of lawn, and then the front steps. "Did they bring Pearl Jo home?"

"Today, I think." Etta kept walking, which surprised August. Something wasn't quite right with her, and he thought about how to ask. Perhaps she simply needed some quiet, reflective time.

"We're going to deviate from the road right here," she said, angling their path right and giving him one last glance before she ducked into the trees. If he hadn't been mistaken, she'd been carrying coyness in her expression, and he couldn't quite make that match up with the way she'd been talking and the energy she'd been putting off.

He followed her between the trees, which would leaf up soon enough now that the sun was starting to warm everything again. "I expected it to be darker," he said, but he could still clearly see Etta only a few paces in front of him.

"When the trees have leaves, it is," she said.

August found a clear trail, which was only wide enough for one person, and he and Etta followed it in silence. His breathing increased, because they were moving uphill, and after a while, she said, "Here are our top cabins."

August stepped out of the trees and to her side, trying to catch his breath. Five cabins spread before him, and they looked one stiff wind away from complete collapse. One inspector short of being condemned.

"Bishop and Montana started a renovation on them a while ago," Etta said, her voice oddly eerie under all the trees. "But they quickly had other more pressing things to build."

August needed a human connection out here among so many billowing branches. He put his arm around Etta, who leaned into him as she put her arm around him too. "Is that what they do?" he asked. "Build houses for family members who need them?"

"They've been very busy with that for a while now, yes," she said. "The second half of the ranch was quite time-consuming too."

"Now they're working on Mister's house."

"Yes."

"What about you?" he asked. "Where will you live when you get married and start having all those kids you want?"

She looked up at him. "I imagine I could find a little patch of land here on the ranch and order myself a house too," she said. "But I wanted to show you the Top Cottage as a second choice. Come on." She continued past the cabins and back into the trees, and only about a minute later, another house appeared in the woods.

It definitely looked like a cottage straight from a fairy tale, complete with all the frosting dripping from the eaves. Not really, but it was quaint and what August would describe as "cute," with white shutters around the windows, a big, long porch along the back, and neat trim along the roof.

The house itself was made of logs, which made it seem rustic. August knew, however, that nothing the Glovers did was really all that rustic, and he expected to find stainless steel appliances inside, along with hardwood floors and granite countertops.

"It's a two-bedroom house," she said. "Arizona used to live in it with her mother. It's seen a lot of occupants, and even a couple of tornadoes. Most recently, Preacher and Charlie lived here before their place was finished."

Etta went up the back steps and right through the unlocked door. "It would be nice to be removed from everyone a little bit."

"Really?" he asked. "I thought you thrived on having the family at the homestead."

"I do." She sighed. "But I think everyone needs a break sometimes." She offered him a small smile, and he found he couldn't quite return it.

"Tell me what's in your head," he said. "Straight up. Point blank. Just lay it out."

Etta drew in a breath, and those shoulders, usually a bit slight and oh-so-feminine came up and formed a powerful box. "I'm wondering if you can see us living here while our dream house is built. Me, you, and Hailey. Because I can see it, August. I can feel it. I can almost taste it."

He wasn't sure what she was saying. It wasn't exactly *I love you, August*, but that was implied inside the fact that she could see the three of them living in this house together, as a family.

"For a long time," he started, speaking slowly and in measures. He'd told his brothers and parents about Etta. He'd shown them the same videos he'd shown Josie's parents. In usual fashion, his mother had tried to give him a ton of stuff he didn't want, some of it for Etta. He'd compromised by taking the napkins, and he'd taken a picture of Etta with them and sent it to his mother, so she'd know he'd given them to Etta.

They'd asked him just as many questions as the Jones' had, and August had given them the same answers.

How serious is it?

I'm not sure. I like her. We're dating.

Are you thinking about marrying her?

Yes, Mom. I'm thinking about it.

Wow, Christian had said. *This is a huge step for you.*

Yes, I know.

Will you stay in Three Rivers?

Yes, her family is there, and her ranch. I have nothing to offer her to draw her away from that.

Does she like Hailey?

She loves Hailey.

August knew he'd told everyone the truth this past

weekend as he'd been down in the Hill Country and San Antonio to visit everyone he'd left behind.

He cleared his throat and started again. "For a long time, I wasn't sure I could even fathom finding someone else to love." He dang near swallowed the last word. "Certainly not someone who could understand what I've been through, or how to love my daughter as much as they might love me. I've seen people get remarried after death or divorce, and the child is always forgotten. I vowed I wouldn't let my daughter go through that."

Etta didn't move, didn't speak, didn't even blink.

He stepped forward, the house around him forgotten. The whole world stood right in front of him, and his throat turned to sandpaper. "I don't think it was an accident that we met, Etta." He swallowed, the walls of his throat sticking together.

August gathered her into his arms. "I hold everything I want when you're in my arms," he whispered. "I'm falling in love with you. So yes, I can see us living here, or in the homestead, or even that cabin down the hill. It doesn't really matter much to me, as long as it's me and you."

Etta's shoulders started to shake, and August wanted to ask her why that made her cry. Something told him to simply hold her and let the silence echo back to him—and to her— what he'd said. So he did that.

After a few seconds, or maybe a whole minute, she stepped back and cupped his face in her hands. "I'm falling in love with you too," she whispered, her eyes drifting closed as she kissed him. "And I love that little girl who belongs to you. I would never forget her or treat her as less than anyone."

August believed her unconditionally. He'd seen her with her nieces and nephews, some of whom didn't share a single drop of Glover blood with her. Heck, he'd seen her with Hailey, and if anything, the two of them would be the ones leaving him in the dust.

As he kissed her, another of his mother's questions filled his mind.

Do you love her?

Not yet, but I think I could.

The answer shifted in that moment, and he only had one word for the question now.

Yes.

Chapter Twenty-One

Duke Rhinehart turned the corner and saw his father's truck ahead of him. Relief flowed through him, because his father arrived first to every meeting, which meant that Dawson wasn't there yet.

Duke loved Dawson with his whole heart. He really did, despite him being sixteen years younger than him and from a different mother. His thoughts immediately flowed back to the time when his own mother had passed away, and how heartbroken he'd been.

Daddy was too, Duke reminded himself. He'd been thirteen, and the next few years had been some of the hardest of his life. Not the absolute hardest, but difficult enough. He'd already been working the family ranch with his father, so that hadn't changed.

The way his dad spoke to him had, however. Wade Rhinehart had dealt with his grief in his own way, and that included harsh commands when he chose to speak at all.

He'd come out of that when he'd met Abby, and they'd been married a few days after Duke's fifteenth birthday.

Dawson, their first son and Duke's first half-brother, had come along about fifteen months after that. The years between them had prevented Duke from knowing Dawson all that well. With all the changes in his life, Duke had started searching for something to give his life meaning.

He'd fallen away from his religion, and he'd spent some years blaming God for the extreme loneliness that still sometimes plagued him.

An image of his beautiful wife filled his mind, and along with Arizona came his daughter, Shiloh. They loved him beyond measure, and most of the time, Duke had no idea why. He'd done terrible things to Zona's family, and as he pulled in next to Daddy's truck, he expected his shame and guilt to punch at him as it had in the past.

Today, it didn't. It hadn't for a while now, and Duke took a deep breath and closed his eyes. He'd already spent a half-hour on his knees that morning, rising extra-early to pour his heart out to the Lord. He'd been in private and group therapy sessions before he'd returned to Three Rivers, and he'd met with Pastor Corning several times since coming home.

Duke asked the Lord the same question he'd pondered this morning. *Am I really forgiven?*

The answer now, sitting in his truck with the spring sun barely rising behind him, was the same as it had been beside his bed, with his wife breathing softly into the darkness as she slept.

I remember them no more.

Duke wished he could forget. He'd prayed his father would too. Out of anyone, the people Duke had stolen money from had been the most forgiving. He thanked the Lord for Bear and Cactus Glover every single day. Cactus had definitely been spiny, but he'd still come when Bear had sat down with Duke, listened to him talk, accepted the apology, and watched as Bear engulfed Duke in the biggest, best hug of his life.

Cactus had shaken his hand, his eyes still full of wariness. Duke had seen that same emotion in plenty of other glances, especially when he and Zona had first started dating. They'd disappeared quickly, another thing for which Duke was grateful.

His dad knocked on the passenger window, and Duke opened his eyes. He rolled down the glass and smiled at his father. "Morning, Daddy."

"Morning, son. You're here early."

"Yeah." Duke didn't say why. He simply hadn't wanted to be last. Dawson still lived at the homestead, and as they'd been meeting over the past several months, Duke hated walking in last. "Where's Dawson this morning?"

"Oh, Momma had some trouble with the chickens this morning. He was helping her round them up." He looked back down the road, as if he'd be able to see the fenced-off area where the fowl were supposed to stay. Chickens had a knack for getting out at the worst times, and that alone had kept Duke from getting his own.

Zona wanted some, because she wanted Shiloh to experience true farm life. He'd told her she could take their daughter to either ranch, and Shiloh would get the same experience.

"It's not the same as standing on the back porch and throwing oats for the chickens in your own backyard," Zona had said.

Duke would relent to her one day; he always did, because he wanted his wife to be happy. He'd prayed her into his life, and he was the luckiest man alive to have her.

He'd also spent a moment that morning praying the Lord would soften his father's heart. As his father smiled at him and opened the passenger door to get in the truck, Duke wondered if something had changed since the last meeting.

Duke worked like a dog around Rhinehart Ranch, one of the only ranches surrounding Three Rivers that bore the family name. He did anything and everything his father asked, at any time of day or night. As his dad had started getting older in the past couple of years, Duke had entertained the idea of becoming foreman of his family ranch.

When he'd finally found the courage to bring it up with Daddy, he'd been shocked to learn that Wade Rhinehart's will listed Dawson as the heir to Rhinehart Ranch. He hadn't been happy about that, and the revelation had led to a lot of discussions and these meetings.

The conversations had been good, if painful. They'd been necessary, in Duke's opinion, and his relationship with his father, Abby, Dawson, and Brandon—his other half-brother—had changed dramatically in the past six months.

"How are you feeling, Daddy?" Duke didn't look at his

father as he asked. If there was one thing his dad didn't like, it was being stared at. Evaluated. Judged. Duke had never thought he'd ever done those things, but he'd become more mindful of it now.

"Abby wants me to go to the doctor."

"Maybe you should." Duke didn't know all of his father's health issues, though he probably should. "What's the problem?"

"I'm pretty sure I have some prostrate issues," he said, sighing.

"Daddy," Duke said, trying to keep his voice as kind as possible. His mind zipped around, trying to land on the right thing to say. "I could go with you."

His father swung his attention toward Duke, who turned and looked at him too. Something passed between them, and his father nodded. "You're a good man, Duke."

"So we'll call the doctor today," he said. "There's no reason to suffer if you don't have to."

The growl of an ATV sounded behind them as his dad agreed. "I'd like it if you came with me," he said. "And Duke, we're talking about a foreman today."

Duke stalled in his movement to turn off the truck. "We are?"

"It's time, and I'm ready." His dad groaned again just twisting as he opened the door. As he got out of the truck, something Duke had seen him do thousands of times, something new happened. He saw his father with different eyes.

He saw the pain in the movement. He saw the paleness in his dad's normally tough, tanned skin. He saw how...

elderly his father had gotten. Funny how he'd seen his father every day for the past five years, but he hadn't *seen* him clearly until now.

Perhaps he'd needed to have his mind softened, not the other way around. His heart bobbed painfully in his chest too, because he didn't want to go through losing another parent. Doing that once in a lifetime was enough for Duke. In a lot of ways, he'd lost his dad when he'd stolen from his own family farm, the Glovers at Shiloh Ridge, and fled Three Rivers.

He'd repented. He'd come home. He'd tried everything in his worldly power to make things right. He'd been repaying Bear every month for years, from his own salary here at the Rhinehart Ranch, before Zona saw the checks. She didn't know about that, and Duke didn't want her to.

She had a ton of money from her inheritance—all the Glovers did. Having her pay for the plot of land where they'd built their house, and the house, and a lot of other things too had been incredibly difficult and humbling for Duke. He'd worked through most of his inferiority issues with a counselor and the pastor, and as he got out of the truck, he was once again reminded of how very much the Lord loved him.

"Mornin'," Dawson said as he dismounted from the ATV. "Getting hot already."

The Ides of March had definitely hit Texas, and a muggy, moist feeling had settled over the Panhandle a couple of days ago. "Yeah," Duke said, lifting his cowboy hat and wiping his forehead. "Should be good for getting the gardens in though."

Dawson smiled at his older sibling and asked, "How's Zona doing?"

"Good," Duke said with a smile. "She thinks the morning sickness will be gone in a couple of weeks." A chuckle spilled from his mouth. "She's convinced this baby is a boy, because she wasn't this sick with Shiloh."

"I'll keep praying for that." Dawson grinned too. "I think she might die if she has two girls in a row."

Duke simply agreed, because Zona had not been happy with the prospect of raising a girl. She loved Shiloh fiercely, and she had since the moment of her birth. Duke thought she'd do just fine raising a whole gaggle of girls, but he kept his mouth shut about such things. Zona wanted boys, and Duke let her say what she wanted about the morning sickness and what that might mean for the gender of their baby.

They hadn't told anyone about the pregnancy in the Glover family yet. Zona wanted to step them into it or tell someone else and have the word spread quietly. For someone as fiery as she was, she didn't really like being in the limelight that much.

They had a dinner date with Preacher and Charlie that night, and Duke knew Zona would tell them then. She already had the new T-shirt she'd bought for Shiloh to wear that night laid out on the bathroom counter when he'd left for this meeting.

New big sister.

Joy ran through Duke at the idea of becoming a father

again. He sure did love his little girl and the tiny family he and Zona were building.

"Come on, boys," Daddy said. "Daylight's burning."

* * *

An hour later, Duke jammed on the brakes as he approached the house. Zona came running down the steps, Shiloh in her arms, and Duke jumped from the truck, laughing.

"I can't believe it," his wife said, meeting him halfway down the sidewalk and holding him tight. "What happened? What changed his mind?" She pulled back, pure wonder and plenty of anxiety in her expression. Duke caught hints of gratitude and relief too, and while they didn't need the money or this ranch at all, they'd both wanted it.

"I think it was just having these conversations," he said. "I don't think Daddy knew how badly I wanted Rhinehart. I think he thought I *didn't* want it." He took Shiloh from Zona and gave her a kiss on the cheek. "Mornin', baby." She looked like Zona had just woken her, with a crease on her cheek from her sheet or blanket still impressed on her face.

"Dad," Shiloh said, smiling as if she'd just recognized him. "Egg."

"Yes, Mama said she'd make eggs."

"Come on," Zona said. "Tell me everything." She started up the walk toward the house.

"We met." Duke followed her, his heartbeat still vibrating in his chest in weird ways. "Daddy's not feeling really well. I'm going to call the doctor today and get an appointment. He wants me to go with him."

Zona paused, her foot on the bottom step of the case that went up to the porch. "You're kidding."

"I think he's...changing," Duke said. "I think he's finally realizing that he's sixty-four years old, and he's not going to be around forever." He went up the steps, saying, "Especially if he doesn't take care of himself."

He'd seen his dad smash his thumb with a hammer and stay out on the ranch. He'd once sliced a good five-inch-long gash on his arm and didn't even go to the hospital. His father was as tough as nails and as stubborn as a mule, and that combination didn't bode well for him as he aged. "Abby said he needed to go to the doctor, and I think he listens to her the best."

He certainly hadn't been listening to Duke until their big blow-out last fall. He'd come along in steps since then, and Duke had to give his dad credit for that. It was incredibly hard to change, as Duke well knew, and his dad had needed some time.

"Anyway, he started the meeting by saying he was going to step back slowly over the next nine months. He'd like to be almost non-existent on the ranch by the end of the year. To do that, he needs a foreman." Duke opened the door and went inside, holding it for Zona to walk through. The house smelled like coffee and sugar, and he took a deep breath of it.

He took a moment to lean down and kiss his wife. "Then he just sat there. My heart was going so fast." He gave her smile. "And then, it was just like heaven opened, and all this light poured into my mind. And I thought—*tell him—tell him right now that you want the job.* So I did. I don't even remember thinking of the words. I just opened my mouth, and I said, 'I'll do it, Daddy. I want to be foreman of Rhinehart Ranch.'"

"What did Dawson say?" Zona asked, her voice awed and hushed. She closed the door behind her and met his eyes again. "Anything?"

"I don't think Dawson wants the ranch or the responsibility," Duke said. "I really don't." He went into the kitchen and started buckling Shiloh into her highchair. "I looked at him, and I asked him, right up front. *What do you want?* He said he'd rather have me run it."

Zona took a pan from the hanging rack over the island. "Wow. What has been the point of these meetings then?"

Duke didn't know how to answer that. "I think everyone just needed time. Dawson's been told his whole life what he's going to do and what he has to be. He's just like I was at that age. He's trying to figure out what *he* wants and who *he* is."

"Mm." Zona started cracking eggs into a bowl. "And Abby?"

"Daddy says Abby doesn't care what happens on the ranch. They'll have a house to live in no matter what. I told him everything, Zona. That I wanted the ranch. That we'll buy it from him if we have to."

Zona looked up, her eyes wide again. "Is he going to make you do that?"

Duke grinned, his face almost cracking he'd been smiling

so widely for the past several minutes. "Nope. He said he's going to email his lawyer and get the will changed. He wants us to make sure Dawson and Brandon have a place here if they want it—like your family does. They can build houses here. They can work here. They can be on the administration team. But that I'll be the owner of the ranch after Daddy dies, and by the end of the year, I'll be the foreman."

Zona abandoned her whisking and threw herself into his arms. "I'm so proud of you, baby." She held him tight, and Duke hugged her back, once again letting his feelings of inadequacy go and embracing the ones that made him feel strong and capable, worthy of her love, and like the man she needed in her life.

"How was this morning?" he asked, stepping away slightly and putting his hands on her belly. She was only eight or nine weeks along, and because of her height and how much she worked around the house and Shiloh Ridge, there was no baby bump to be felt.

"Still sick," she said. "In fact, you're going to have to scramble those eggs. I can't even look at them." She turned away from the bowl and reached for a bib to put on Shiloh.

Duke took over, zings of disbelief still moving through him. *Thank you*, he thought. *Thank you for the gift of forgiveness. Thank you for the blessing of families. Thank you for Thy mercy and grace.*

"Charlie says dinner at seven is fine," Zona said. "Preach doesn't come in too much sooner than that."

"Okay," Duke said. "I'll do my best."

"You can meet us down there if you need to."

"Might," he said. "With the meeting and now all this egg-scrambling, I haven't even started work yet." He gave her a smile as he poured the eggs into the pan. They hissed slightly for a second, and Duke turned away from the stove to get a rubber spatula. Zona met him in front of the drawer, and she reached up and cradled his face in both of her hands.

"I love you," she whispered.

Duke leaned down and kissed her, feeling so complete in a life he'd never been satisfied with. He let that feeling encompass him while Shiloh banged something on her tray, and the eggs cooked too fast. None of it mattered, because he had Arizona in his life, and he loved her with his whole soul.

In fact, in many ways, Zona had reminded him that he *had* a soul, and while he'd already started healing and changing and fixing the broken things in his life before he'd returned to Three Rivers, she'd been a major reason why he'd continued doing so.

"Dad, egg, dad, egg," Shiloh babbled, and Duke broke the kiss with a chuckle.

"Yeah, baby," he said. "I better not let momma distract me from these eggs." He gave her a look that he hoped told her he'd like to pick up that kissing later, got his rubber spatula, and returned to the task of trying not to burn breakfast.

Chapter Twenty-Two

Bear Glover reached down and lifted his son into his arms. "This is where granddaddy is buried," he said to Russell, the two-year-old he'd needed to get out of the house that evening. Apparently, he'd been fussing and crying all afternoon, and Sammy had nearly been in tears too. And she wanted *more* children.

It didn't make sense to Bear. She wasn't overwhelmed with the four they had, but some days were busy and chaotic, and adding another baby to that when Heather wasn't even one yet didn't make a whole lot of sense to Bear.

"He's right here," Bear said, still walking toward the headstones. "Remember his name?"

"Stone," Russ said, and Bear grinned at him. He had been whiny when Bear had taken him from the house, but he'd calmed down in the stables and he'd let Bear hold him while he fed the horses a couple of Bishop's favorite strawberry candies.

They'd just been walking since, and Bear's right hip actually ached from how slow he had to go so the two-year-old could keep up. He made it to the graves and set Russ back on his feet. "Yep. Stone." He reached out and traced the S in his father's name. "See the S? T-O-N-E." He put one hand on top of the stone and held it there, feeling the breath and life of his father.

Bear had spent a couple of years thinking he couldn't miss his father. He couldn't acknowledge that he was gone or admit that Bear felt lost without him. Then he'd realized how ridiculous that was, and he'd started coming to the family cemetery to just sit with his dad. It had taken him a while to work up talking to him, but Bishop had needed that, and they'd started coming together.

It had been at the cemetery when Bear had felt the need to get out to the Edge and check on Cactus. At the cemetery when he'd finally decided he better ask Samantha Benton on a date. At the cemetery when he'd found a way to forgive Duke Rhinehart.

"Your granddaddy worked so hard around here," he said. "He loved this land, and he believed it was a gift from God. He wanted to do everything in his power to show the Lord how he could be trusted with the things he'd been given." Bear wanted that same thing, not only for the Lord, but for his father and his uncle. They'd left him and Ranger this ranch, and when he saw them again after this life, he really wanted to be able to look them in the eye and say, "I did the best I could."

His chest squeezed, because he often felt like there was

so much more he could be doing. He grappled with the idea, because he didn't know what those things were. Sometimes they would enter his mind, and he did his best to grab them and do them when that happened, the way Sammy baked gluten-free brownies for Ace, and double-chocolate for Duke, and blondies with walnuts for Preacher.

His wife was so amazing, and in that moment, Bear had the answer to one of his big questions. He sighed and bowed his head. "Give me strength and longevity to raise another baby to adulthood," he whispered. Russ toddled forward and put his hand over Bear's, and he lifted his head and smiled at his second son.

"Daddy," Russ said, his smile bright and big and boyish.

"Yeah, Rock," he said, startling even himself. He drew in a long breath and looked at the name on the headstone where his hand still rested, pinned there by his little boy's. Stone.

Rock.

"Oh, your momma isn't going to be super happy about this." But a feeling like an electric current ran through Bear. The Glover family had a lot of nicknames, and they'd already given Smiles to his son Stetson. Bear called him either name —everyone did. The boy answered to both. Bear's mother had given Stetson the nickname at an early age, though most of the Glovers didn't earn their name until later in life.

His grandmother had been the one to dole them out, but as Bear looked at his son's perfect five fingers splayed over the back of his palm, he simply knew the boy should go by Rock.

"It'll remind you of your granddaddy," he said to the boy, though Russ just looked at him with wide, innocent eyes. "He was tough as stone. He knew how to let others chip pieces of him off though, and while he started out rough, by the end, he was polished."

Bear had felt himself going through that refiner's fire for the past few years, and he hoped this nickname would remind his son of how important it was to be moldable. To change and adapt, while still trying to keep important family traditions on the ranch. The buzz of an ATV met his ears, and while it normally annoyed Bear to no end, today, he just lifted his head and watched Preacher arrive at the top of the hill.

He looked left and right, his eyes coming back to Bear. Bishop rode on the back of the machine, and the two of them came down the lane and parked just outside the gate of the cemetery.

"Can we join you?" Bishop asked after the ATV's engine had been killed. He swung off the back first and turned to help Preacher.

"Of course." Bear straightened and watched his two brothers. Preacher had graduated out of his crutches and his cane, but he still took precious seconds to put his hand in Bishop's, steady himself, and then get down. Bishop didn't let go of him then either, only pulling his hand away after Preacher had made it down the grassy incline from the road to the sidewalk that led through the gate to the cemetery.

"Talkin' to Dad?" Bishop asked. "What are you saying?"

"Nothing," Bear said. "Just listening today." He hugged

his youngest brother, and then the middle child in the family, all three of them smiling. "Heard Zona's expecting again."

"She is?" Bishop asked, looking from Bear to Preacher.

"Yeah," Preacher said. "She told me and Charlie a week or two ago. She doesn't want to make a big announcement. It's just been going around by word of mouth."

Bishop shifted his feet, and Bear's attention came back to him. "Ah, I see."

"Haven't seen you around lately," Bear said, seizing onto the opportunity to perhaps find out why.

"Yeah, Montana's been...we're busy with Mister's house."

Bear gave him a smile and cocked his head. "I find it amusing you think you can lie to me."

"Ditto," Preacher said dryly. He didn't look straight at Bishop, and that was probably why people told Preacher things. He gave them room to breathe. He gave them space to be themselves. He gave them time to think.

Right now, he moved past Bear and bent to pick up Russ when the boy lifted his arms up, his way of saying, *Pick me up Uncle Preacher.* He said something to the boy Bear couldn't hear, and he looked past Bishop to True Blue further down the road.

Bear kept the nickname to himself for now. He needed to talk to Sammy and Mother first. He needed to make sure the feelings he had were true, and he liked to give himself time to do that.

"Anything you want to tell me?" Bear asked quietly. "I

could just pray for you if you're having a hard time. I don't need details." He and Sammy had talked about how Montana had been quietly disappearing from the family over the past couple of months, but Bear hadn't thought much more about it.

Sammy had taken her dinner, but she hadn't stayed for long. She hadn't reported anything out of the ordinary at all, other than Montana's gratitude. They'd then eaten the same thing for dinner at their own table, and Bear was sure someone had ended up crying or covered in some sort of sauce. That was about how dinnertime went at his house.

"Prayers would be great," Bishop said, his voice tight. "We've—" He cleared his throat and turned away from Bear. He walked over to the edge of the cement and looked out over the rolling fields below. Bear gave him the space and the silence, his prayer already started to help Bishop with whatever he needed.

Preacher returned to his side, and Bear took Russ. "Come on, baby," he said. "Let's go see if Auntie Etta has anything to eat at the homestead."

"Keeping him out of Sammy's hair?" Preacher asked.

"Yeah, he's had a rough day." Bear wouldn't have been able to tell from looking at Russ now, but he'd seen both his son and his wife when he'd walked through the back door. It had not been pretty, and he considered asking Etta if the child could sleep over with her. If she didn't already have a niece or a nephew, she'd keep Russ.

"I think Etta's out with August tonight," Preacher said. "I saw his truck leaving the ranch when Bish and I came out of the farmhouse. I couldn't tell if she was in the truck with him or not, but we have Hailey, so my guess is she was."

"Guess we'll find out," Bear said, giving Preacher a smile. "What about you? Anything you need?"

"I wouldn't say no to your wife's Boston cream cake," he said with a sly smile, his eyes fixed on Bishop's back. "Why don't you guys come to dinner?"

"Because Charlie hates it when you invite people to dinner without asking her first," Bear said with a grin.

"So I'll ask her, and then I'll text you."

Bear nodded. "I'm sure Sammy would love it." His wife spent way too much time trying to make sure everyone on the ranch stayed happy and felt like someone loved them. He really admired her for her wide open heart and her ability to welcome everyone to Shiloh Ridge, but he also knew it took a toll on her. One she might not be able to keep paying.

"All right, baby," he said. "Let's go see what's cookin' at the homestead." He gave Preacher a side hug and said, "Love you, brother."

"Love you too, Bear."

"Bish," he said. "I have to go."

Bishop turned around, so much unrest in his gaze. "Okay." He came toward him and hugged Bear again, sandwiching Russell between them. "Love you."

"Love you too. I'll pray for y'all." Bear liked having someone besides himself to talk about with the Lord. Not only that, but he'd gotten a pretty major answer for himself while kneeling in front of his father's grave.

His footsteps crunched over the gravel, and he set Russ

on his feet so their journey to the homestead would take a few minutes. Then he dialed his wife.

"Hey," she said. "Heather's in the tub, and Smiles already has his pj's on. You guys are fine to come back."

"I'm taking Russ to the homestead," he said. "If Etta's there, she'll keep him."

"I'm really okay."

"I know you are." Bear took a big, deep breath. "This might not be the best time to bring it up, but I just visited Daddy, and I think...I'll have another baby."

Silence came through the line for several seconds—long enough to take three Russ-speed-steps. Then Sammy started to laugh. "Yeah," she said through giggles. "Definitely not the night to bring it up."

Bear chuckled with her, the moment lightening and turning fun. "Let's get away from Shiloh Ridge for a bit," he said.

"What?"

"We celebrated our six-year anniversary with a pot of mac and cheese laced with hot dogs."

"The kids like hot dog mac and cheese—and you can blame Mister for that."

Bear smiled into the sunset. "Yes, baby, I know what the kids like." This wasn't about the children. "This is about us. Let's just go away for the weekend. We can even just drive to Amarillo and stay in a hotel there."

Sammy hesitated, and Bear wondered why. "Why can't we?" he asked. "And do not say because of the kids. There are a plethora of people who would take them in a heartbeat.

It's not because of the shop. You don't own it anymore. The ranch doesn't need me at all."

"It's planting season," she said. "You work overnight sometimes. Are you saying that's not necessary?"

"Yes," he said instantly. "I'm saying someone else can do it for a weekend. I do it so my guys don't have to."

"Hm."

"Hm, what?" he asked.

"I just think it's interesting you admitted it's not necessary for *you* to be out all night on the tractor."

Bear looked left, toward the barn and the equipment shed. "Honestly, Sammy, I'm not necessary here at all. I just like to pretend I am."

"That's not true," she said quietly.

"You just said it was."

"I didn't," she said. "But I think you're right—you don't need to be out all night anymore. There are men far younger than you, with no small children at home, who can do it."

"You're worried I'll get hurt out there."

"Yes," she said, and he wondered how this conversation had gone from him telling her he'd have another baby to her admitting she didn't want him planting or mowing all night long anymore. "And I need you, Bear. Especially if we're going to have another baby. I *need* you."

It was nice to be needed, and Bear felt the strength of her words way down deep in his soul. "All right," he said quietly. "I'll put someone else on the overnight work from now on."

"You really can come home," she said. "I just needed an hour, and you gave me that."

"I will give you whatever you want," he said, his voice sinking the way the sun did in the west.

"I know, Bear. Come home."

He looked at the homestead as he neared and then kept going. "Okay," he said. "We're on the way, but do you know how slow Rock walks? We're gonna be a minute still." A long minute. Maybe thirty minutes.

"Rock?" Sammy asked, and Bear grinned this time.

"Okay, hear me out...."

"Not if you think we're going to call Russell, our son, a human being, Rock. Mm, nope. *No.*"

Bear just kept walking at a snail's pace, Russ at his side.

"Bear," Sammy said with plenty of warning in her voice. "Bartholomew."

"Baby, it'd be after my daddy," he said. "Get it? Stone? Rock? We were just in the cemetery, and it'll remind him of who he is. What name he carries."

"The surname Glover tells him that," Sammy said.

Bear watched the ground go by, step by step, silent. Finally, Sammy sighed and said, "Grizzlies and *pandas.* I curse the day your grandmother nicknamed you Bear."

He burst out laughing, feeling his spirits lift as he did. His daddy had inspired him to get himself in gear and figure out how to get Sammy to go out with him. Their relationship hadn't been great in the beginning. Their first date shouldn't have ever led to a second.

Somehow, he and Sammy had made things work, with a lot of prayer, a lot of forgiveness, and a lot of love.

"If you hate it," he said after he sobered. "It's fine. It was just an idea."

"Maybe I just need time to think on it," she said. "The way you did with another baby."

"Okay," he said. "He's two years old. I think we have time."

Someone on her end of the line squawked, and she said, "Hurry home, Bear. I miss you, and we can start planning our weekend getaway once the kids go to bed."

He grinned up into the sky, the clouds creating a gorgeous painting with the golds, reds, and oranges in the sunset. "Baby, I can't stay up until midnight the way Link does."

"It's a school night," Sammy said. "He'll be in bed by ten, I promise."

"We're on the way," Bear said, and he scooped his son into his arms and up onto his shoulders, so they could get home faster.

Chapter Twenty-Three

Oakley Glover stayed in the brand-new, two-seater car she'd just bought for herself and watched as Etta and Holly Ann went inside the restaurant. The moment she got out, she'd be expected to have a smile on her face, and she told herself she could do it.

She *could*.

Ranger had been down at the fast-food joint with their kids for about twenty minutes now—and she'd been in the parking lot for half that. She just needed another moment to figure out how to appear happy and like she was having a grand time when she really just wanted to go home.

But go home, she couldn't. This was the family birthday party for Wilder, Smiles, Gunnison, Robbie, and Shiloh. They all had February, March, or April birthdays, as did Ace, June, Cactus, and Oakley herself.

Sammy had worked with Dot and Willa to put the whole thing together, and Oakley had been told to show up and be ready to have a good time. The Glovers continued to pour into the restaurant, and Oakley would've worried about what they'd do to other guests, but she'd seen the huge, bright orange signs that said this place would be closed for a private party until seven-thirty.

The drive-through remained open, and Oakley wondered who'd notice first if she simply drove on through and kept going. Kept going south, past the turn-off to Shiloh Ridge. Past the next town. Past the point of empty in her gas tank.

Her husband would notice, and Oakley wouldn't do that to Ranger. Her phone rang, and she looked at it with a measure of calmness moving through her. His name sat on the screen, and she lifted the phone to answer it and hold it at her ear. "Heya, sweetheart," he said, and he came through the door and into the parking lot, clearly looking for her. "Where are you? Everything okay?"

Etta joined him, a cupcake in her hand. Ranger smiled as he took it from his sister, and it was surreal to watch her mouth move from so far away and still be able to hear her voice. "Is she almost here? I can hold the kids. It's not a problem."

"I'm coming," Oakley said as Ranger said, "She'll be here. Five minutes, Etta."

His sister nodded, and Ranger now held a cupcake while he stood there, looking for her.

"I'm out in the shade," she said. "I can't come in."

"I'm on my way." Her husband lowered the phone, obviously still searching for the metallic blue sports car Oakley had brought home from Mack's Motor Sports one day only a couple of weeks ago. Men usually had some sort of midlife crisis with cars like these, but Oakley loved cars with her whole heart and soul, and the moment she'd seen the Italian-made car, she'd bought it.

Recognition lit Ranger's face when he spied the car, and he jogged toward her. He opened the passenger door and slid inside, breathing hard and bringing the April wind with him. He sighed as he sank nearly to the ground, and he extended the cupcake toward her.

Oakley shook her head, and Ranger reached up and put the treat on the dashboard. "It didn't go well?"

She shook her head and couldn't look at him. "My dad...." She blew out her breath, the faint reflection of herself in the glass showing her how sad she was. "He said he's not interested. Just like that. He doesn't want to even try."

Ranger reached over and took her hand in his, his fingers long and strong. "I'm so sorry, sweetheart." His voice flowed like calm water over a short drop. It was sweet and soft, and Oakley closed her eyes, wishing she could find somewhere outside to just breathe for a minute.

"I'm holding up the party," she said, sniffling. "I'll be fine. I just need a moment." She drew in a deep breath. "He answered the phone this time. That's something." Oakley wished she'd recorded her father's voice, because she hadn't heard it for so long. He hadn't been cruel during the conversation, which had been a lot of pausing, his accented words, and awkwardness.

He'd simply been indifferent. He had no desire to see her, meet Ranger, or his two grandchildren. That kind of attitude lay so far outside of Oakley's normal that she couldn't process it.

"In other news," she said. "Heath has secured the funding to buy Mack's. His agent is sending Nile the paperwork this week. Once everything is signed, that's done." Honestly, Oakley couldn't wait to be out from underneath the huge dealership. At any given time, she had three hundred cars and trucks on the lot, some new and some used. Over a hundred ATVs or OTVs. Campers, RVs, fifth wheels, rentals, parts to order, and more.

She closed her eyes again and exhaled it all away.

"That's great," Ranger said, his voice taking on a touch of brightness. "You can stay out here as long as you like. I'll bring out your food."

"It's a birthday party for our son," she said, finally facing him. "I'm not going to miss it."

He wore compassion and understanding, love and anguish, on his face. He reached over with his free hand and cupped her face in his palm. "I love you so much," he whispered. "I'm so sorry about your father."

But I love you, and you'll always have me.

Ranger didn't say that last part, but Oakley heard it. He gave her a timid smile that seemed brave along the edges. "Your mother will be here in a month or so, and you'll probably want her to leave soon enough."

Tears filled Oakley's eyes. "I love you too," she said, her voice cracking.

Ranger pulled her toward him and held her in his arms while she cried. Thankfully, Oakley wasn't an overly emotional woman, and she emptied the tear ducts quickly. She straightened and ran both hands down her face. "I hate crying." She scrubbed her eyes clean and pushed her fingers into her hair.

When she looked at Ranger again, he simply smiled at her. "I know we're not much, and I know you'd have more kids if you could, but you'll always have me, Wilder, and Fawn. You'll show them what a good mother looks like, and I'll do my best to be the father you wish you had for our kids." He leaned his forehead against hers.

"Could we have another baby?"

"Oakley," he said, and that was all.

She let the silence pass between them, and then she said, "You, Wilder, and Fawn are everything to me." They'd just scheduled to have their family pictures done with Whitney Walker. "I don't need more kids. I don't need anyone else."

"Everyone inside that restaurant loves you," he said. "I know they're not your blood relation, but Oakley, the feelings are the same."

"Your sisters are my very best friends," she said, opening her eyes and sitting up straight again. "Okay, let's go. I don't want to ruin anything Etta's done." Or Willa or Sammy for that matter. She and Sammy had married their husbands on the exact same day, and Oakley would not do anything to make Sammy's life harder.

She opened the door and got out, taking a moment to stretch her legs. Ranger met her at the front of the car and took her hand in his. "Just stay beside me, my love. We'll get through tonight, and then you'll get some relief. A reprieve."

She nodded and stepped toward the entrance of the restaurant. The scent of cooking meat and frying potatoes met her nose, and she wiped her face one last time before Ranger opened the door.

Someone had stuffed the entire place with balloons, and Oakley's happiness lifted as if that same person had just pumped her full of helium. Etta saw her and hurried over. She had a special way of seeing things no one else could, and she drew Oakley right into a hug and said, "I love you, Oak."

Nothing else, and somehow with those words from such a sweet woman—a woman who'd been through a lot in her life too—it didn't matter that Oakley's dad didn't want to be involved in her life.

Oakley also didn't care who saw her crying, and she hugged Etta with all the muscles she possessed. As she stepped back, Ida was right there to take her place, and she said the exact same thing.

I love you, Oak.

Nothing more.

Oakley didn't have to say anything, and as she accepted hug after hug, and heard the same words spoken time and again, she realized how many wonderful blessings the Lord had given her. She didn't know who had told the family what, but someone had said something. She hadn't noticed Ranger sending any texts, but anything was possible with that man.

Sammy took her into her arms last, after every other

brother-and-sister-in-law. "I told them you must've had a hard day at Mack's," she whispered. "I'm so sorry, whatever it is. You don't have to tell me." She stepped back and held onto Oakley's shoulders. "We love you so much. I would do anything for you."

Oakley nodded, her chin shaking and Sammy blurring through her tears. The blonde woman wore such a kind smile. "Could Heath not get the funding? Because Bear and I, we'll fund it."

Oakley half-laughed and shook her head. "Heath is going to come through," she said as Cactus walked by with a huge tray of hamburgers.

"Here's one for all the kids," he yelled, and the children in the Glover family swarmed him. Oakley grinned at them, especially her sweet boy who'd just turned four a couple of weeks ago.

"It's my dad," she said to Sammy, getting rescued from having to explain more by Ranger, who slipped his hand into hers. Sammy fell back a step, her eyes still searching Oakley's face.

"Sweetheart," he said. "I've got our food over here." He glanced at Sammy. "Is Fawn okay with you?"

"Absolutely," Sammy said, though Oakley hadn't even seen her daughter yet. "I'll be over in a few minutes."

"Bear got your chicken," Ranger said, and then he tugged Oakley away from her best female friend in the world. Oakley had understood why Sammy and Bear needed a place of their own, but she still missed living in the homestead with them.

At a table in the corner, the furthest from the fray of children's cheeseburgers and French fries, Ranger let her step into a booth first. Etta sat directly across from her, with August at her side. They had their heads bent together, but they wrapped up their private conversation a moment after Ranger had sat down.

Oakley suddenly had plenty of questions for the other couple, but it wasn't her style to pry. She smiled at Etta and looked at August. "You're brave, coming out in public with all of us. We usually like to contain our crazy to the ranch."

"Yes, right there," Ida said, causing them all to turn and look. "Just slide the table up to theirs, baby."

Her husband, Brady, did just that, and Ida dragged over two chairs. "Grab a couple more, babe, and we'll be fine." She sat down while he did that, and then he sat beside her.

"Can we sit here?" Judge asked, holding a tray with more hamburgers than any two people could eat. "June wants a hard chair."

"Of course," Ida said, and they took the two seats on the same side of the table as Oakley and Ranger. Just like that, she had her people with her, and all seven of them protected her from questions and glances—not that anyone in the Glover family would press her.

Any of them—Bishop and Montana, Holly Ann and Ace, Willa and Cactus, Dot and Ward, Zona and Duke, Bear and Sammy, Preacher and Charlie, or Mister and Libby— could've sat down and done the exact same thing.

In fact, Preacher put a tray down on the booth in front of theirs and looked at their group of eight. "You guys have the right idea." He'd held Oakley and whispered *I love you, Oak*, just like everyone else, and she reached for one of the foil-wrapped hamburgers so she wouldn't have to think too hard about these men and women who'd rallied around her.

Preacher motioned for others to come join him, and more tables got added to the booths, and before she knew it, all of the adults had congregated in this quieter part of the restaurant. Sammy, Bear, Cactus, and Willa all stayed in the Play Zone with the children, and Oakley ate while the conversations happened around her.

Every single person here had suffered through some sort of heartache. Preacher had been through terrible pain physically. Zona and Duke hadn't had an easy time with his family at Rhinehart Ranch.

Holly Ann and Ace dealt with his health every single day. She didn't even know what Ace could possibly eat at a place like this, and yet, he'd come. Smiling, he'd come.

Cactus had buried his four-day-old son once.

Judge had fallen off a roof.

Dot had diabetes she had to manage each and every day.

June had gotten pregnant before she'd been married when she was eighteen years old. Willa had been injured in a car accident that was her fault, because she was texting.

Sammy had lost her sister and her brother-in-law in one fatal accident, then become a mother to her seven-year-old nephew.

Even August, who wasn't officially a Glover—*yet*, Oakley thought—had lost his wife to a terrible accident on their ranch.

Every single person here had something they were dealing with. Something physical that prevented them from doing what they really wanted to do. Something emotional that they'd had to work through.

She wondered how they'd done it, and the answer came instantly.

With God, all things are possible.

She could get through this, because she had twenty-five examples of pure strength and pure faith in God, right here, right in front of her. She put her hand on Ranger's leg, and he curled his fingers around hers. She leaned against his bicep, and he turned toward her. "Okay?"

She met Etta's eye, and she was okay. She looked at Ida, who had to deal with their mother's health problems on a more frequent basis than anyone else, and she was okay.

She watched Dot laugh with her baby girl on her lap, and she thought of the woman driving her big dump truck down to work every morning, and she was okay.

Thank you for this family, she thought.

To her husband, she said, "Yes. I'm okay."

"Momma, Momma," Wilder said, racing toward them. "Come see Fawny go down the slide." His joy couldn't be contained in such a small body, and Oakley grinned at him.

"All right," she said. "I'm coming." She caused several people to have to get up, and Ranger didn't leave her side as they went into the area where the slides and toys were. Fawn didn't much like slides, and Oakley didn't make her play on them if she didn't want to. She'd rather swing or chase after

The General in the front yard, though she never could catch the crotchety cat.

Benny, Sammy's dog, somehow knew when Oakley took Fawn outside to play, and he'd come play with her.

The little girl didn't say any real English words yet. She was only sixteen months old, and she'd been a bright, bubbly baby so far. She simply didn't like slides.

But Oakley heard her giggling girl coming down the tube slide, and she came out the end of it with an expression of pure happiness on her face, her cousin Link right behind her.

"Geen," she said as she scooted to the end of the slide. Link smiled down at her and took her hand as she nearly fell forward.

"Again?"

"Geen," Fawn said, already toddling toward the steps to get back up to the top of the slide, and Oakley knew in that moment that her life was complete. Her family was complete. She didn't need another baby to fill the hole in her life. God had already given her everything and everyone she needed.

She didn't need her father to accept her life in the Texas Panhandle. She was living it, and she was proud of who she was, and what she'd done with her life.

"Can I go down with you too, Link?" Wilder asked, and he looked to Oakley for a translation. Wilder could talk fast when he was excited.

"He wants to go too," Ranger said. "Make a train of three."

"Sure, bud," Link said, and Oakley knew the teenager was a gift straight from heaven. "You can come too."

Oakley stood in the Play Zone and watched her kids come down the slide with Link, clapping with Fawn and giving her son a high-five, until Etta yelled, "Time for cake! Everyone, come on down. It's time for cake!"

Oakley turned to find the petite woman on top of a table, the one next to her covered with birthday cakes—one for each person. She spotted a bright yellow dump truck—that would be for Robbie. He loved trucks of all types, and Dot sometimes took him for rides in Brutus, her truck, just to make him smile.

"Mama," Smiles said. "Look at that dinosaur one." His voice held wonder and awe, and Oakley grinned at him as his mother told him that cake was for him. Willa put five candles in it and moved on to a three-layer cake that had been decorated to look like the hide of a paint horse.

"This one is for Uncle Cactus," she said to Smiles. "Do you want to come put in the candles?"

Smiles nodded and went to help while Willa explained they couldn't put on all of the candles for his age, because the restaurant had limits on the amount of fire they could have in the building. Cactus rolled his eyes, his wife clearly teasing him for how old he was, and Oakley basked in the goodness of their relationship.

She looked around for Wilder as he came out of the slide with Gun, and the two of them beelined for the tables. Ranger intercepted their son and lifted him into his arms. "Which one do you think is yours?" he asked.

"The lion," he said right before making a huge roar that caused a few people nearby to laugh.

"I bet you're right, bud," Ranger said, chuckling. "What about for Momma?"

"The racecar," Wilder said.

Someone had made a very life-like rendition of a racecar, and they'd frosted it bright red. Etta pointed to it, and August put in the two numbers for Oakley's age. Thirty-eight.

Shiloh had a bright pink unicorn cake, and Gun had a cake shaped like a cartoon cow. Ace's was a big, yellow emoji face with the widest smile on the planet, and June had been given a computer cake.

Oakley wanted to belt out a song from her heart, but as the very large, very loud, and very lovable Glover family sang *Happy Birthday*, she simply stood there and took it all in.

She hoped she'd be able to make someone else's birthday as good as Sammy, Willa, and Etta had made this one for her. Or just their day, by the way she interacted with the men and women around the ranch or around town.

All of the birthday boys and girls, men and women, got to step forward and blow out their candles, and then a massive cheer went up. Cowboys could whistle so loudly, and someone started stomping their boots on the hard, brick floor, creating a new kind of ruckus Oakley wouldn't soon forget.

She laughed, so glad she'd come inside. Beyond grateful for a husband who'd come to get her, and a sister-in-law who'd told the family exactly how to love her. She helped pass out cake until the crowd dwindled, handing a piece of his own cake to Cactus.

"Thank you, ma'am," he said with a huge smile. It faltered a little, and he added, "I'm sure glad you're one of us."

"Me too," Etta said, stepping over from August's side to hug Oakley again.

"What about him?" Oakley asked. "Is he going to become one of us?"

"I'm working on it," Etta whispered, and she wore a look of excitement and hope when she stepped back to her boyfriend's side.

Chapter Twenty-Four

Judge woke when his wife gripped his bicep, a groan coming from her side of the bed. His first reaction was to throw her arm off and roll over so she couldn't touch him. He was just so tired.

His exhausted, still-sleepy brain fired at him that June was his wife, and she might need him. She was getting bigger and bigger with their baby by the day, sometimes by the hour, and she often used him as support to get up, sit down, and roll over.

"Judge," she said, his name coming out in a pant. "I'm having a contraction."

That woke him all the way up, and he noticed the urgency in her grip now. "That can't be right," he said, his brain misfiring. He had no idea what day it was or what time, but June wasn't due for three more weeks. He knew that much.

"It's right," she growled at him, and Judge reached to

snap on the lamp on his side of the bed. June already sat up in bed, her knees bent in front of her. Her face bore a resemblance to bland oatmeal, the kind without any cream or brown sugar, and she breathed in a quick fashion.

Panic streamed through Judge. He'd never had a baby before, and he sure as heck wasn't going to let his wife go through labor right there in the Ranch House. He jumped up and hurried around to her side of the bed. "Okay," he said, putting his hand in hers. "How long has this been happening?"

"I think this is the second or third one," she said, and as quickly as he'd woken, the pain left her face. She relaxed completely, her shoulders going down and the clenching of her fingers around his loosening. "Okay, it's done."

"We're not anywhere near done, June-Bug," he said. "Let's get to the hospital."

"They have to be close enough together," she said.

"We're thirty minutes away." He stepped over to the dresser, where he draped his clothes most days. He pulled on a pair of pants and rushed into the closet to find a shirt. "Stay there," he called over his shoulder. "Time how long between each one." He should've done that, but Judge's mind ran in fifteen different directions, and he didn't know which avenue to pay attention to.

He needed to be dressed and shod to enter the hospital. June too. He'd work on that first. He pulled down the first shirt he saw and yanked it over his head. "What do you want to wear?"

"My stuff is on the settee," she said, and when Judge

returned to the bedroom, he found June sitting on the edge of the bed, preparing to stand.

"Wait for me," he said, swiping up her clothes and jogging over to her. "Here, let's get the nightgown off." He lifted it over her head and handed her the maternity shirt she loved. It was pale pink, with a giant heart over the chest and belly. "Okay, nice and slow, love. Did your water break?"

"I don't think so."

Judge didn't either, and he let her steady herself with her hands on his shoulders while he helped her into the pants. "How long?"

"Three minutes," she said. "It's too soon to go."

"I'll get your shoes," he said. "In the kitchen?"

"I'll follow you out there."

He nodded and started for the door. His boots sat by the back door too, and he pulled them on before grabbing June's sneakers. She still hadn't come out of the hallway yet, and Judge went back toward it, calling, "June?"

She leaned against the wall, one hand on her belly and the other supporting her against the plaster. "This one just started," she said, her voice pinched. "I think they're four or five minutes apart."

As Judge stood there, wondering how he could help his wife, he had the very distinct thought that he couldn't. This was not his burden to bear. He could not have this child for her.

Get her to the hospital, streamed through his mind, and he took a step toward her. The discoloration in her jeans stopped him, and he said, "Uh, Juney, we need to go now."

"I don't think I can move," she whimpered, and Judge wasn't sure he could lift her. Before she was nine months pregnant, sure. Her eyes met his, and he was surprised by the level of fear there. She'd had a baby before, at a much younger age. "I don't have a baby bag ready or anything."

"We don't need a baby bag," Judge said, making an executive decision. "We're going to the hospital right now. I'll bring your shoes, but I don't care if you wear them." He took another step toward her and met her in the hallway as she groaned and closed her eyes. He cupped her face in his hands and said, "I'm going to get my wallet, and we're going to go. Stay right here. Do not move."

She panted in and out and nodded.

Judge hurried back into the bedroom, grabbed his wallet and then his phone, and rejoined his wife in the hall. "As soon as it's over, tell me," he whispered, keeping one solid hand on her back.

She nodded almost frantically now, and Judge stepped even closer to her so she could lean into his body for support too. She did, and he wrapped his arms around her and put both hands on their baby. "I love you," he whispered. "This is going to be fine."

"We still don't have a name for him," she whispered, her voice full of agony. "Please, tell me what you want to name him."

Judge had said June could name their baby boy whatever she wanted, but she didn't like that. She wanted him to have an opinion. He'd held out, because she and Lucy Mae had wild ideas for male tree names, and he hadn't wanted to admit he actually liked a couple of them.

Now, in the quiet, country stillness of their hallway, in the darkness of early-early morning three weeks too early, he leaned closer to her ear and said, "I sure do like Birch, June-Bug."

"Oh, I love Birch," June said with a sigh, all of the tension leaving her body.

"Time to move," he said, nudging her forward.

"What can we pair with Birch?" she asked, and Judge wished she'd focus on putting one foot in front of the other.

"The truck's out front," he said. "Can we talk about it once we're on the way?"

"Okay." June walked then, and Judge managed to help her into the truck and get behind the wheel without another contraction coming.

He started the vehicle, turned off the radio, and adjusted the air. "Hot? Cold?"

"Cold," June said. "I'm dying already."

Judge let her fiddle with the dials and the temperature, and he got them moving down the road that went around the ranch. June didn't have another contraction until they hit the road leading down, and with the pilgrimage out of the house, into the truck, and along the ranch road, he figured that was about four or five minutes.

"Oh, boy," June said, reaching up to hold onto the handle above the window.

"It's a dirt road," Judge said, easing up on the accelerator. "I'm sorry. Should I stop?"

"Don't stop," June said through clenched teeth. "They're coming faster and harder. I am not having this baby in the truck." She glared at him like it would be all his fault if that happened, and Judge got the vehicle moving again.

Once on the smoother highway, he could pick up speed, and just as they passed Seven Sons Ranch, the contraction abated.

"I think his middle name should start with a B too," June said.

"You know if he gets a nickname, it'll be a B too," Judge said, looking at her. The sheen on her face made him love her even more. He reached over and took her hand in his. "I love you so much. You are my queen."

June lifted his hand to her lips and kissed the back of it. "I love you too. I love babies, and I'm excited to have a boy."

Judge focused on the road, a smile touching his lips. "B-names for a boy," he mused. "Brian?"

"No," June said. "Bradley?"

"No," Judge said. "I knew a Bradley once who was the high school quarterback, and he was so ridiculously arrogant."

"Brrr—" June said. "I have no idea."

"Bob?" Judge guessed, immediately saying, "I lost my mind for a second. Sorry."

June burst out laughing, and Judge was glad she could still do that at two-twenty-four in the morning, his headlights the only source of light in the world right now. He pushed the truck to sixty and then seventy, not caring that the speed limit out here on the south highway was fifty-five.

He glanced at the clock. It had been four minutes since the last contraction had ended, and sure enough, on his next breath, June sucked in a tight breath, reached up for the handle, and said, "Here we go again."

"Let's see," Judge said, hoping to distract her through this contraction. The speedometer climbed to eighty, and he flipped on his brights so he could see further down the road. "Bryant. Bill. Brick."

"No," June said. "And Brick sounds like one of your family nicknames, and I'm vetoing that right now too." A horrible, guttural groan came from her mouth, and she added, "We should've brought a towel. I think I'm bleeding."

"It's fine," he said. "Just a truck." He glanced over at her but couldn't look long because of the speed at which he drove. "Bear? Bartholomew. Blake. Brooks. Brandon." His mind seemed to be working now.

"Bennett. Bruce. Benson."

"That's a last name," June said, her voice grinding in her throat.

"And Bishop's real name," Judge said. "Can't do that." He wished the Lord would fill his mind with light. "Boone. Brett. Uh, Bridger."

The lights in Three Rivers came into view, but Judge didn't ease up on the gas pedal. He kept barreling toward the town, knowing all the turns to take to get them to the hospital. Lord knew he'd been there plenty of other times for his siblings and cousins.

"Boyd," June said.

"I think that's worse than Brick," Judge teased, and June giggled as the contraction eased.

"Branson," June said, relaxing into the seat. "Bodey. Brody."

Judge just looked at her. None of the B-names she suggested were the right ones. She looked exhausted already, and he wished with his whole heart that he could ease her discomfort. If he'd timed things right, she should only have to endure one more contraction before they got to the hospital.

She can do it, he thought. *Keep talking to her.*

So he kept naming off as many names as he could think of that started with the letter B, even delving so far into things like Boaz and Bjorn.

June did make it through one more contraction before Judge pulled up to the hospital, and he got her in a wheelchair and up to maternity as quickly as he could. "She's in labor," he told the nurses there. "Contractions that last almost a minute, coming every three to four minutes."

Three nurses came around the desk, one of them firing questions at him while the other two whisked June off.

"I can go in with her, right?" he asked. All of his brothers had gone into the delivery room with their wives.

"Yes," the remaining nurse said. "We just want to get her information so we can band her. It takes two minutes. She won't have the baby in the next two minutes."

Judge wasn't so sure, as June was due for another contraction any second now. As she got wheeled out of his sight, he blinked and focused on telling the nurse her name, birthdate, address, and the name of their doctor.

"Let's go," she said once all of the information was in the system, and he followed her down the hall. She made him scrub his hands and arms up to the elbow and put on a gown over his shirt. It hung down over his jeans too, but he didn't care. She then led him into a room where June was just getting into a bed. She'd changed into a gown completely, and she looked to him.

"Are they calling Doctor Stephenson?"

"The system alerts him when we put it in," the nurse who'd stayed with Judge said. "He knows. Look, he's even responded." She turned the tablet toward June. "It says, on my way. Ten minutes."

"I have ten minutes, right?" June asked. "I want an epidural."

"Feet up," another nurse said, actually taking one of June's feet and placing it in the stirrup. "Let me check you, and we'll see how things are going." She gave June a fiercely kind smile, and the nurse with Judge guided him to a spot directly beside June's right shoulder.

"That's where you go, Dad." She leaned in closer. "She definitely has ten minutes. No worries."

He nodded and looked at June. She seemed calmer now, but there was a sense of urgency as the nurses hooked her up to an IV, to a machine that monitored her pulse and oxygen rate, and started asking her if this was her first baby.

"No," she said. "I have an eighteen-year-old."

"No other children?"

"No." June looked up at Judge, and he smiled down at her.

"It's okay," he whispered. "We've got this."

"You're at about a five," the nurse said. "Your water broke. I'll call the anesthesiologist. As soon as she gets here, you can get that epidural."

"Great," June said, relaxing back into the bed. "Thank you."

"Yes," Judge said as two of the nurses started to clear out of the room. "Thank you."

*　*　*

Later that morning—about ten hours later—Judge accepted the bundle of baby boy from the nurse and gazed down at the perfect human being who'd come partly from him. He could barely believe this was his son, and that his life included a wife and baby. It felt so surreal, after so long of waiting for June, just praying and knowing that she was the woman for him.

"Let's go meet your aunts and uncles," he whispered to the baby. "I'm sure they're about as restless as caged tigers who haven't been fed yet." He grinned at the boy and looked up. June was asleep, and he wanted her to rest for as long as possible.

She'd just fed their son, and he should be good for a visit for a little while.

"They're down in the main waiting area," a nurse said. "Did you know I've helped to deliver seven of the Glover babies?" She smiled fondly and reached out to stroke the boy's hair on top of his head. "This one's the cutest."

Judge grinned at her, his heart so warm and so full. "Thank you." He went down the hall and past the check-in desk. Out of maternity and toward the waiting area. Smiles appeared, and he yelled, "Here he comes, Gramma! He's comin'!"

Judge chuckled and whispered, "That's Smiles. He's the oldest of the cousins that we started having once people got married. There are a couple of older cousins that we love too, even if they don't have all of our Glover blood."

His mother came around the corner, and Judge dang near burst into tears. She held Smiles' hand in hers, a look of absolute love and wonder on her face. Sammy, Oakley, Holly Ann, Willa, and Zona crowded in around her. The taller men—Bear, Ace, Bishop, Ranger, Cactus, Ward, Mister— stood behind them.

"They love you already," Judge whispered. "They love June and me so much."

He approached Mother, who would get the baby first. He cleared his throat, wishing his emotions would go as easily. They never had, and he'd been trying to embrace them more and more in recent years.

"Here he is," he said in the loudest voice he dared to use in a hospital, while holding his newborn son. He turned the baby so he faced all of them. "He has a lot of hair," he said while several of the women sighed and commented on the wild, sticking-straight-up hair the color of dark, freshly turned earth.

"We named him Birch Bennett Glover," he said, leaning down to press a kiss to his son's head. Then he passed him to Mother, who smiled and smiled and smiled as she swayed with him, hummed to him, and kissed him too.

Judge moved into the crowd and started hugging his brothers and cousins. He noticed Dot, Charlie and Preacher, Montana, Ace, and Libby over on the couches with the other children, and after he'd hugged everyone who'd gotten up to greet him at the end of the hallway, he went that way.

Preacher stood and gathered him into a hug. "Congratulations," he said in the quiet way Preacher did. "You're going to love being a dad."

"I think so too," Judge said, clapping his brother on the back. And thankfully, he had plenty of good examples right there around him to go to should he need help.

Mister sat beside Libby and put his arm around her. "He's the cutest baby in the world," he said, and he grinned at Judge. "I knew Judge and June would have the cutest kids."

Judge chuckled and shook his head. "Whatever. All the Glover babies are cute." He glanced over to his son as the crowd started breaking up. None of them would leave until they'd had their turn with baby Birch, and he decided he better rest while he could.

So he sat beside Mister and asked, "So when are you going to have a baby?"

"Hey, me and Libby are far younger than you," he said, clearly teasing. "We're not in any hurry."

Judge nodded and closed his eyes. "Mm, good for you. Enjoy each other first." He sure did love June, and he wasn't afraid that this baby would change their lives. Of course he would, but Judge knew it would be in the best ways possible.

"Yes, here they are," a man said, and Judge opened his eyes. August Winters had arrived, and he had Lucy Mae with him. Judge jumped to his feet, another round of adrenaline hitting him at the arrival of the girl.

"Lucy Mae," he said, and she stepped into his arms. "Hey, how was the flight, baby? You got in okay?"

"Yeah, totally fine." Lucy Mae stepped back, her eyes still searching for something.

"Your mother is sleeping," Judge said. "But I can take you back. Or I can grab Birch for you, if you'd like to see him." He paused to shake August's hand. "Thank you for getting her, August."

"Of course," the cowboy said as Etta moved to his side and they put their arms around each other.

Judge saw a path to Mother, and he moved that way, Lucy Mae going with him.

"I don't want to take him from your mother," Lucy Mae said behind him.

"Mother," Judge said anyway. "Can Lucy Mae see him for a moment?"

"Of course, dear." Mother passed the sleeping boy to Lucy Mae, who gazed at him with so much adoration in her face.

"Judge," she whispered. "He's so wonderful." She leaned down and kissed the baby, and when she looked up, tears rode in her eyes.

Judge's eyes turned hot too, and he put his arm around Lucy Mae and squeezed her tightly. "Love you, Lucy Mae."

She laid her head against his chest, still gazing at her new half-brother. "I love you too, Judge."

Chapter Twenty-Five

Willa turned from the oven and put the cookie sheet full of treats on the counter. "Lynnie, close that up for Mama, please."

The little girl closed the fridge and turned toward Willa. "I want juice."

"I already have your juice in your bag," Willa said, removing her hands from the oven mitts. She leaned against the counter, her stomach aching behind everything she did. She felt too hot for the temperature in the house, and she told herself it was because she'd been boiling water for pasta and then baking cookies in a hot oven.

"Go get your jellies," Willa said to the little girl. "Daddy's going to be here in a few minutes." Just as she finished speaking, her phone rang. Cactus's name sat there, and Willa picked up the phone with relief. "Hey," she said.

"Heya, Willie," he said, his usual cheerfulness evident. Then he sighed. "I can't get away from the branding to come get y'all. Can you come over to the picnic with Lynn and Chaz?"

He'd taken their older boys over to the big weekend branding extravaganza the ranch was sponsoring today and tomorrow. They'd left before dawn to get cattle moved into the right pens and equipment out and cleaned.

Willa had signed up on the family sheet to bring some of the food, as the ranch wives would feed everyone who'd come to help with the spring branding. The Rhineharts came up from their ranch; Libby's father and brothers would come; all of the Walkers had signed up to come help; even Squire Ackerman and Pete Marshall would make the long drive from Three Rivers Ranch.

Sammy had coordinated all of the food between all of the men and women from the five ranches, and Willa didn't even think her potato salad or oatmeal raisin cookies would be needed.

"Willa?" Cactus asked.

She jerked back to attention, wondering where her brain had gotten to. "Yes," she said. "I'll find a ride."

"The car should be done soon," he said. "Then you won't be stranded out there."

"I'm sure Sammy or June can come get me," she said, though she wasn't going to ask either one of them. Sammy had probably been over at the branding pens for hours already, setting up tables and making sure the cowboys and cowgirls involved had plenty of water and punch to keep them hydrated.

June had just had a baby only ten days ago, and Willa

hadn't been a functioning adult ten days after having her baby. She still barely felt like a functioning adult, in all honesty. She loved June, especially after they'd gone over to Montana's together. The three of them had been spending more time together with planned walks in the mornings—at least until June had gone into labor three weeks early. They hadn't gotten back to those walking dates yet, but Willa was sure they would.

The next closest person to the Edge Cabin was Dot or Ward, and Willa thought they'd both be out branding. Ward would be, as he was one of the foremen of the ranch. Dot liked to strap their baby girl to her body and do everything with her husband. Willa had marveled at her drive and energy since having Glory only four and a half months ago. She still went down to the landscaping company she owned every day too, and either she or Ward kept their little girl with them.

At the homestead, she could ask Oakley or Etta, and Willa said goodbye to her husband and immediately called Etta.

"You're on speaker," the woman said. "Mister and Libby are in the kitchen with me, just so you know."

As if Willa was going to say anything inflammatory. She still appreciated knowing, and she said, "Cactus took the truck over to the branding," she said. "My van is in the shop. Is there any way someone could come get me and the two littles I've got with me? I have a bunch of cookies and a huge vat of potato salad that need a ride too."

"I'm sure there's someone," Etta said.

"I can go," Libby said.

"I'm finishing up with these pizza pockets," Etta said. "Libby and I will come. Mister needs to get back outside anyway."

"It's hot, Willa," Mister said, plenty of joviality in his voice. "Just so you know."

Willa smiled, and said, "Noted, Mister. Thanks for cluing us all in." They all laughed, and a sharp tug inside Willa's stomach told her she was hungry. If it was hot outside, she should eat before the luncheon.

That made no sense. Besides, Willa had only eaten breakfast an hour ago. She couldn't be hungry again.

"Give us about thirty or forty minutes," Etta said. "I need to finish up here, and we'll drive out."

"Thanks," Willa said, and she hung up. She wouldn't be late with the food when she arrived in an hour. She simply wouldn't be early the way she'd planned to be. She wanted Chaz and Lynn to be able to see their father at work, see what cowboys did, and experience life on a working cattle ranch.

She'd enjoyed the past years' of branding, and she thought her children would too.

A wave of exhaustion hit her, and Willa moved toward the hall saying, "I'm going to go to the bathroom and lie down for a few minutes. You two come with me."

Her two-year-old and her four-year-old did what she said, and she lifted them both into the bed on Cactus's side. She handed them her phone and told Lynn to put on the cartoon they liked. In the master bath, she closed the door and sighed as she leaned into the counter. The bathroom had an air conditioning vent that pumped constantly, and she reached up and wiped the sweat from her forehead, feeling clammy and just...not right.

She just needed to use the bathroom. She did, but she didn't feel any different. She went to get a banana and ate that, but she still felt unsettled and just jittery. Her stomach didn't seem to like bananas, and she hurried into the bathroom only moments before it came back up.

"No," she moaned as she sat on the bathroom floor. She did not want to be sick on branding weekend. She didn't want to be sick moving into summertime. Her children were almost finished with the school year, and she wanted this first summer with Cameron, Kyle, and Lynn to be full of Texas day-trips, laughter, and fun. She loved the three kids she and Cactus had the great privilege to foster, and with their dad's trial underway, they'd know by fall if they could adopt them or not.

"Hopefully," she reminded herself. The legal system sure did move slowly sometimes, not at all like the movies and TV shows she'd seen.

"Mama?" Lynn asked, coming into the bathroom. "You okay?"

"No," Willa said, gesturing the little girl closer. "Mama is sick. I might send you over to your daddy with Libby and Etta, okay?"

Lynn sat in her lap and faced her. "I stay with you. Bring you a cookie until you feel better." She smiled at Willa, whose heart melted at the kindness in this child.

"We'll see," she said. Chaz and Lynn could easily stay here with her. She had a hook on the front and the back door she could latch that was too high for either of them to reach. Chaz had tried on more than one occasion by pushing a chair over to the door and stretching up as high as he could. That boy was going to be real trouble one day, that was for sure.

But she could at least keep them in the house while she napped. At the same time, she knew she didn't need to do that. There were plenty of people who could help, and her stomach took a dive again.

She didn't want to miss out on the festivities. She didn't get to see the cowboys and their wives and families from the other ranches all that often. She *wanted* to be at the branding this afternoon.

A touch of desperation filled her heart and caused tears to prick her eyes. "We'll see, my darling," she whispered to Lynn and touched her lips to her forehead. "Go keep an eye on Chazzy, okay?"

The dark-haired girl skipped through the bathroom and Willa could see through the two doors as she climbed back into the bed. She leaned her head back against the wall, her thoughts churning.

All at once, she froze.

A wail started somewhere in the back of her mind, and she tried to push out the horrifying thought. It wouldn't go.

You could be pregnant.

It morphed into a question.

When's the last time you had your period?

She didn't know. Couldn't think.

You're pregnant.

It wasn't that Willa didn't want more children. She did. Cactus desperately did. They'd decided to foster, however, because of her physical limitations. Chaz had been a very difficult pregnancy for her, and the very thought of having to endure nine months of pain, nausea, no sleep, and sickness made Willa's tears overflow on the spot.

Just the very *idea* of it.

Using the wall for support, she got to her feet. She had a pregnancy test here somewhere, as she'd bought them a lot before getting pregnant with Chaz. Sure enough, she found a box of two in the bottom drawer of the bathroom vanity, and she took one into the toilet room, closed the door, and locked it.

She didn't want to see the results of this test. But she had to know.

Only minutes later, Willa sat on the closed toilet and sobbed. She sobbed and sobbed and sobbed, wondering why the Lord had given her a baby when He wouldn't give one to Montana and Bishop.

"How can I ever tell her?" she said aloud, her voice so strangled it didn't even belong to her.

Now that she had the two pink lines staring her in the face, Willa's back hurt. Her hip twinged with pain. She couldn't sit up straight, and she absolutely couldn't let anyone else know about this for a good, long time.

She hated these feelings, because they mirrored so closely how she'd felt when she'd found out she was pregnant with

Mitch. She hadn't been the best of people then, and everything about his pregnancy had been shrouded in shame and embarrassment.

Willa straightened her shoulders and wiped her face. She was not going to put any of that on this baby. This baby was a huge blessing, and she tilted her head back and looked up at the stark, white ceiling.

"You gave me this blessing," she murmured. "I must be strong enough to bear it." She didn't *feel* strong enough, and she instantly prayed for that strength. Mentally and physically. An overpowering feeling of love drove through her, and she reminded herself that she didn't have to go through this pregnancy alone. She had an amazing husband. All of her ranch wives. Three older children who could and would help her.

"How can I tell Montana?" she asked next, but the Lord stayed silent on that question.

"Willa?" Etta called, and she'd run out of time. She couldn't wipe her tears or wash away the evidence of her sobbing.

In fact, when Willa managed to stand and get the door open to leave the toilet room, Etta stood in the bathroom doorway, Chaz on her hip. His face was covered in cookie residue and chocolate, which meant he'd climbed into the pantry somehow.

"In the tub," Etta said with authority, and she swung the two-year-old into the bathtub. He started to cry, but Etta trained her eyes on Willa and marched toward her. "What's wrong? Are you okay?" She scanned Willa from head to toe, trying to find the source of bleeding or unrest.

But it couldn't be seen, at least not yet.

Willa held up the pregnancy test, a fresh set of tears coating her cheeks. "I wonder if you might be so kind as to fetch Cactus for me."

Etta took the pregnancy test, her eyes rounding. She only looked at it for a moment and then she engulfed Willa in a tight, enormous hug. "Oh, sissy, you're going to be fine."

"I don't see how," Willa said, leaning on the other woman's strength. "And how can I possibly tell Montana? She and Bishop have been trying for a baby for so long, and it seems wholly unfair."

Etta said nothing, because there was nothing to say. When she stepped back, her expression held tears too. "I'll take the kids and get Cactus."

"I don't feel good," Willa said. "I want to come so badly, but I don't know...." She let her voice trail off, as everything seemed to make more tears arrive.

"Libby and I will handle it all." Etta moved to the doorway and called, "Libs. She's in here. Come on back, would you?"

Willa didn't want to face Libby—the newest Glover in-law—in her bathroom, with fresh tears running down her face, and a positive pregnancy test being waved around by Etta.

Libby came through the door just as Etta started the tub to clean up Chaz, who sniffled and looked at Willa like she'd save him. "Everything okay?"

"I can just call Cactus," Willa said.

"I have your phone." Libby held it out to her, her big, brown eyes filled with concern and compassion. Willa stepped over to her, and Libby backed up out of the doorway. "Are you okay?"

"Sort of," Willa said, trying to smile. She should be strong for the younger women in the family. As a pastor, shouldn't her faith be perfect? What would they all think of her if she showed any weakness at all?

"Lynnie," Libby said, falling back to the bed. "Come with me, okay? We're going to go see Uncle Mister, and I'll bet he has some candy in his pocket for you." She smiled broadly at the girl and picked her up. She looked like a natural nurturer with Lynn in her arms, but when her eyes came back to Willa's, she sobered.

"I love you, Pastor Glover," she said. "If I can help, I will."

"You're helping," Willa said, giving her the best smile she could conjure up. "Thank you for coming all the way out here."

The tub turned off, but Etta continued with her stream of talking, telling Chazzy he better not cause any problems for her during the picnic or she wouldn't let him stay the night with her. He sniffled and kept saying, "Okay, Auntie," or "I will, Auntie."

She came out into the bedroom with the boy wrapped in a fluffy, blue towel, and Willa just looked at her and Libby. "I'm sorry," she said, her voice breaking. "I'm going to call Cactus, and maybe I'll come over."

"You have nothing to be sorry about," Etta said. "I'm a little nervous leaving you here alone." She looked at Libby, who nodded.

"I can load up the food and the kids and take them to the branding," Libby said. "Maybe Cactus and August could come back here?"

"No," Willa said firmly. "I can't take two cowboys from the branding. Let me just call Cactus really quick. I'm feeling better." She drew in a deep breath and pushed it all the way out. Her stomach still didn't feel totally settled, but the tears seemed to have gotten the hint that they couldn't just show up whenever they wanted.

"We'll load up the food and kids," Etta said. "Come on, Chaz. You show Auntie Etta where your big boy pants are." She and Libby left, and Willa dialed her husband, praying with everything inside her that he could answer.

"Hey," he said just as someone else on his end of the line yelled.

"Hey." Her voice trembled. "Charles," she started, but the rest of the announcement wouldn't come.

A few seconds of silence came through the line, wherein Cactus finally realized Willa was in trouble. "What's goin' on?" he said. "Are you hurt? One of the littles?"

"Neither," she said, clearing the lump from her throat. She wanted this baby. She would do whatever she had to do in order to bring he or she into the world surrounded by love, adoration, and family. "Charles, I'm pregnant." She sniffled, because she'd never thought she'd be blessed enough to say those words again.

Cactus let more silence fill the line, and then he drew in a breath. Willa pulled the phone away from her ear, because she knew what came next. The cowboy—*her* cowboy—whooped and laughed, and said, "I know you're scared, my love, but you can do this. You *can*."

She nodded though he wasn't there to see it, and she let more tears wet her face. "I love you."

"And I love you. I'm on my way right now."

"No," Willa said. "Libby and Etta are here. They're loading everything up, and I think as long as I don't get too hot or eat too much, I won't throw up again."

"Oh, my love," he said, and that was Cactus-code for *I'm so sorry you're throwing up. I wish I could be there. I love you as far as I can see and as deep as the ocean.*

"I'll see you in a few minutes," she said. "Now, Charles, I do not want this to be made into a big deal. It's too soon to tell others, and I don't want to hurt Montana or Bishop. I will not cry. You will not sweep me off my feet and kiss me."

"Come on," he said, a light lilt in his voice. "I can't kiss you?"

"No, sir," she said. "You'll get in line with the other cowboys and get your lunch, and when we can, we'll sneak off to the side of a barn or something, and you can kiss me then."

He laughed, but Willa was serious. "I mean it," she said. "I will not hurt Montana with this news."

"I know, Willa," Cactus said. "We'll be discreet."

"Thank you," she said just as Chaz went running past the master bedroom door. "Your son needs a leash for the branding, and we need to put the chocolate higher in the pantry."

Cactus burst out laughing again, and even Willa managed to smile. Libby paused in the doorway, and she added, "I need to go. I'll see you soon."

"I love you, Willa."

"Love you too." She hung up and stepped over to Libby, gathering her into a hug. "Thank you for coming. I'm sorry if I scared you."

"Everything is okay?"

"Everything is great," Willa said, moving back and smiling. She wasn't entirely sure that was true, but she could still walk and she was still breathing. So yes. For right now, everything was great.

As she followed Etta and Libby out to the car and let Etta deal with Chaz, all she could do was pray that the Lord would be as merciful and kind to Montana and Bishop as He'd been to her and Cactus.

Chapter Twenty-Six

Etta rolled over in bed, the light coming in her window greeting her on the first day of her thirty-seventh year on the earth. She smiled into the white light, hoping today was one of the most amazing days of her life.

She hadn't particularly enjoyed her birthday over the past couple of years, because all it did was mark another year alone. Another year older, and closer to being barren. Another year without all of the things she wanted.

After picking up her phone, she found she had dozens of texts. She hadn't been expecting anything less, actually. She tapped on Ida's first, because her twin should be the first person she texted on their shared birthday too.

Etta was older than Ida by six minutes, and she smiled at her sister's messages of cake, lunch at their favorite restaurant, and "the best year yet!"

I want dessert first today, Etta sent. *And yes, this is going to be our year!*

She navigated back to her main screen and sent smiles and hearts to Ward, Ranger, and Ace, all of whom had texted her before six a.m. Now that May had arrived, so had the summer temperatures, and everyone who worked outside got up with first light and worked in the coolest part of the day. Anyone with any sense at all, that was.

Several of her cousins had texted, and Etta sent them the same emojis. At the bottom, the very last unread text had come in very first overnight. It was from Mother, and Etta's eyes filled with tears as she read the timestamp on the message. Three-fourteen in the morning.

Mother had been texting her and Ida at that time on their birthdays every day since she'd learned how to use a cellphone. Well, Etta got a text at three-fourteen. Ida got one at three-twenty a.m.

Mom, Etta typed out. *I can't believe you were up in the middle of the night to send this. I love you so much, and I hope to be as good of a mother as you've been one day.*

She couldn't believe how emotional such a statement made her, but she found herself silently weeping as she sent the text.

Happy birthday, darling, Mother said. *Enjoy your lunch with Ida. Perhaps we could go tomorrow.*

Etta tapped on her home button and went to her calendar to see what tomorrow held for her. She always took her birthday off, and because she and Ida arranged their own schedule with the schools and community programs, they could do that.

I can do lunch tomorrow, she sent to her mother.

Maybe you'll have a new ring to show me.

Etta's pulse positively stopped. Just came to a screeching halt. "What?" she said out loud, her fingers frozen above her screen. She hadn't even *thought* about August proposing to her on her birthday.

In fact, she immediately recoiled against the idea, and she tapped to call Mother. "Hello, dear." Her mom's voice shook, and that was a side-effect of one of her heart medications. Unfortunately, there was nothing she could take to stop or slow the dementia, but she had been working with an art therapist who'd had great results in retaining or refreshing memory.

She came to Nestled Hollow, the assisted living facility where Mother lived, and Ida had made sure Mother had been attending the classes. Not only that, but they had an animal therapist come every week too, and as Mother had always loved dogs, she'd been benefitting from simply holding a little, white dog on her lap and telling it all about her life.

"Mother," she said. "Did you encourage August to propose today?"

"Of course not." She sounded lucid and firm, and Etta sat up in bed to hear her better.

"But he came with Ranger and Ward last week," Etta pressed. "Are you sure you didn't say anything to him?"

"I wondered when the wedding might be, that's all."

Etta let out a sigh. "Mom." She didn't know how to explain that she didn't want anything else to celebrate on her birthday. Yes, she and August had been dating for a while now. Going on seven months. Yes, she was a touch frustrated with how their relationship had slowed over the past two of those. No, she had not said anything to August about it... yet. She didn't see the point.

He wanted to make sure everything between them was perfect, including Hailey's comfort level with him getting married again, and with the person he married. Etta had no idea what such a thing looked like or felt like, though she had spoken to Sammy and Willa about it.

They'd both said it might be different for a man, but that yes, they'd spent plenty of time on their knees, praying to know if they should let another father-figure into their child's life. Willa had said because of Cactus's amazing ability to love children, that she'd known early on that Mitch would be fine with him. Sammy had admitted that she'd worried about Lincoln and Bear often in the beginning.

August was not abnormal. His feelings were valid and completely regular, and Etta wasn't going to press him to make decisions he wasn't ready to make.

"You don't want him to propose today," Mother said.

"No," Etta said. "I do not." Every time she thought about her and August standing in the Top Cottage, holding one another, she could see the future. She remembered the feelings of pure love and delight, of relief and joy at the thought of finally—*finally*—having a husband and a family.

"I'm sure he won't then," Mother said. "He knows you, Etta."

"Yeah." She gave another sigh. "I have to get ready for the day, Mother. Thank you for the birthday text."

"I love you, darling. I'm sorry if I said something wrong to August."

"I love you too," she said, and the call ended. She hadn't received any texts from him yet, and a pinch right behind her heart accompanied her into the shower. When she got out, she smelled the scent of rich, dark coffee, and that could only be attributed to Mister. He'd gotten some fancy Columbian coffee from one of his rodeo pals, and he only made it on special occasions.

Etta smiled to herself as she dressed and dried her hair. She didn't bother with makeup yet, because she had hours until she needed to leave for lunch, and someone had put bacon in a pan, the smell of that teasing her and drawing her out of her suite with the intent to eat breakfast before she did anything else.

She'd only taken two steps as she looked over the couches and into the kitchen before she came to a full stop.

"Happy birthday!" August and Hailey shouted, and Etta's smile went from zero to sixty in less time than it took to breathe.

She pressed both hands to her chest and asked, "What are you two doing here?"

"We brought you breakfast," Hailey said, skipping around the counter. "It's a waffle bar, Etta. Come see!" She grabbed Etta's hand and started dragging her through the living room. Mister and Libby sat at the huge dining room table, both of them grinning, and as Etta's bare foot touched the first tile, Oakley came rushing into the kitchen.

"I'm too late."

"Not at all," August said, grinning at her. "You were right, though. The bacon totally got her out here."

Etta met Oakley's eyes, cocking her eyebrows.

"I had to go change Fawn," Oakley said, grinning at her. "Happy birthday, Etta."

"Is everyone coming to breakfast?" she asked, taking in the purple and white balloons tied to the backs of the chairs that sat in front of the windows. Someone had hung a huge "Happy birthday!" banner above the windows in the kitchen, and all of the paper plates and cups came in various shades of purple too.

"No," August said. "I just invited the people you live with. And Ida and Brady. I think she said they were just turning off the highway. And your brothers."

"So yes, everyone," Etta said, grinning at him. She finally reached him and took his face into both of her hands. "Thank you, August." She stretched up and he bent down, and she kissed him right there in front of his daughter, Mister, Libby, and Oakley.

The back door opened, and Ranger walked in, his voice alerting Etta to his arrival. Ward spoke too, and whatever they were saying didn't sound like a happy conversation. She minded her manners and pulled away from her sweet, cowboy boyfriend and tucked herself into his side.

"Okay," Hailey said. "Should I go over the bar, Daddy?"

"Let's wait until everyone's here, sweets," he said as the sound of the front door opening and twin two-year-olds entering met their ears. "Sounds like Ida and Brady are here."

"You got Brady to come?" Etta asked. "That is a feat." She suddenly wished she'd put on makeup, though a voice in the back of her mind asked, *Why?* August clearly didn't care.

"It's my birthday," Ida said, clearly overhearing Etta. "He took the day off."

"The whole weekend," Brady said from her side. He grinned at Etta and came toward her. "Happy birthday, Etta." He hugged her, lifting her right up off her feet.

She laughed and said, "Thank you, Brady." As she settled back on her feet, she looked at Ida, who had Mother on her arm. She left August's side to go to them, and the three of them hugged silently for several long moments.

"Mother, you sneak," Etta finally whispered, all she could get her voice to do. "You must've been in the car when I called."

"She was," Ida said. "I'd just gotten her settled. It's a miracle you didn't hear Judy having her meltdown."

Etta leaned forward and kissed Ida's cheek. "I love you, sissy. Happy birthday."

"Love you too. We have the best birthday in the world, because we get to share it." She glanced over to August and Hailey, and when she looked back at Etta, so much was said.

This is pretty spectacular, right?

He did this for you, Etta. That means something.

I think he's in love with you.

I'm so happy for you.

Etta gave a quick shake of her head, the conversation she'd have later with Ida, during their twin-only lunch, already overwhelming her. She went back over to Hailey and August. "I think you can go ahead."

"No," Ward said. "Dot's coming over. And Ace is on his way in with Preacher."

"I maybe invited Preacher too," August said, grinning at her. "He's my boss, and he and Charlie may have helped with the whole concept."

"The waffle bar concept?" she asked.

"I came up with the waffles," Hailey said. "Charlie said, 'you know what Etta would do? She'd have a whole waffle bar!'" She grinned at Etta, who was utterly charmed by the girl. "And she got Holly Ann to make the caramel sauce and the maple syrup."

"Morning," Holly Ann herself chirped, and she arrived in the arched doorway a few moments later, both of her children with her. Etta wanted to reach for Pearl Jo, the precious baby that had joined the family a couple of months ago. Instead, she stayed right under August's arm, enjoying the weight of it across her back, the way he curled his fingers along her hip.

"Look," Hailey said, running toward her. "Look how we laid it all out."

Holly Ann beamed down at her and then came over to the island, where the waffle bar had indeed been carefully laid out. "It looks amazing," Holly Ann said. "Like a real caterer would do." She reached out with her free hand and stroked Hailey's hair back. "You're a pro."

"I followed your map." Hailey's face held only

sunbeams, and Etta admired the lengths she and August had gone to for her birthday.

"Okay, we're here," Ace said as he opened the side door. Dot preceded him, handing a very sleepy-looking Glory to Ward, who kissed the baby and tucked her into his chest. Etta would be surprised if the girl didn't fall right back asleep, a fact that made her smile.

Behind him, Preacher entered the homestead, Charlie and Betty hot on his heels. "I may have said something about waffles to Judge," he said, his eyes searching out August's. "Sorry."

"It's fine," August said. "There's plenty."

"Plenty," Holly Ann echoed, and she moved toward Ace, not even offering Pearl Jo to Etta. She let her go, because this was her birthday, and it was obvious that no one was going to let her hold a baby while they ate and she stood out of the way.

"Go over the bar, sweets," August said, nudging Hailey. "If others come, they'll know what to do, I'm sure."

"Okay." Hailey cleared her throat as she stepped up onto the stool Etta herself had perched on many times. She couldn't help giggling at the girl, her heart swelling and swelling with love.

"It's a waffle bar," she said. "We've got a bunch of waffles warming in the oven, and we can make more if we run out. There are four choices for toppings. There's fruit and cream. Butter and syrup. Caramel sauce, or a salted chocolate sauce."

Etta's mouth began to water. She wanted one of each.

Perhaps she could put a different topping in each quadrant of the waffle.

"Then there's sausage and bacon, a big bowl of fruit, and a ton of scrambled eggs. They have cheese in them for anyone who might be lactose-intolerant." She looked at August, who simply kept smiling at her like she was the world's next Nobel Peace Prize winner.

He turned and looked at Etta, and if she hadn't been fully in love with him before this morning, she was now. He pressed his lips to her temple while she wondered what he saw when he looked into her eyes.

"There's hot chocolate," Hailey said. "Orange juice. Milk—white and chocolate—and this special coffee from Mister." She glanced over to him, and he gave her a single nod. "Oh, and Ace, there are three gluten-free waffles just for you. I'll get them out for you."

"Thank you, Miss Hailey," he said.

"Who made the salted chocolate sauce?" Etta asked.

"That would be me," Charlie said. "I saw it in a live feed, and I thought, I bet I can do that. If it's sick, don't eat it." She suddenly looked worried, but Etta didn't think she had anything to fret over.

"All right," August said, clapping his hands together. "I didn't ask anyone to pray." He glanced around, obviously a little nervous. "Ranger?"

"I'd be happy to." He swept his cowboy hat off his head and gave the other men who'd come in off the ranch the opportunity to do the same. Even then, he paused for a moment, the only sound the humming of the refrigerator, doing its best to try to beat the constant thrum of the air conditioner.

Etta took a deep breath, the vastness of her blessings spreading before her, especially when August slipped his hand into hers.

"Dear Lord," Ranger finally said. "We thank Thee for this beautiful morning in Texas. Bless us all to be safe on the ranch today, and especially bless and sanctify this day for Etta and Ida. They have blessed each of our lives beyond measure, and we love them." He paused, and when he spoke again, his voice carried a hitch.

"Bless the food and those who came up with the concept, contributed to this meal, and sacrificed to be here. We're thankful for Mother's continued health and ask a special blessing on her."

Another pause, this one longer than the last. Etta was just about to look over to Ranger when he said, "Amen," and several others chorused it back to him. Etta took a moment to reach up and wipe her eyes, lest any of the tears that had gathered there should leak out.

Sometimes, it was easy to think of her brothers as tall, tough cowboys, without emotions or feelings. Of course, she knew that wasn't true. They'd all been nervous when their children had been born. They'd all experienced hard things in their lives. Their own health issues, their own trying times in their marriages, their own mistakes and blunders.

Sometimes, Etta simply forgot about all of that. She moved over to Ranger and hugged him, saying, "Thank you, Range." She knew he'd been going down to town a couple of times each week, and his wife went more often than that, just to be with Mother. Since Christmas, when Ida had told them about the dementia, they'd all tried to find ways to help their mother, and help Ida, who lived in town and bore most of the day-to-day burdens of Mother's care.

"Happy birthday, sissy," he said just as the door opened again.

Bear said, "Looks like they're just getting started."

"I ran into Bear," Judge said just as his darling baby gave the cutest, almost-not-a-newborn wail.

"I didn't know it wasn't a whole-family thing," Bear said, glancing at Etta.

"It's fine," she said, though she wondered just how many waffles sat in the oven.

"I put it on the ranch text," Bear said, his eyes full of apology.

"That's okay," Holly Ann said, stepping into the kitchen with August and Hailey as more cowboy voices filled the foyer from the direction of the front door. "Etta, Ida, get up here at the front of the line, and let's get you fed first."

Etta did what Holly Ann said, and she enjoyed her waffle with caramel, chocolate, and fruit, her bacon, the rich, dark coffee, and plenty of eggs while the homestead filled with people. She'd likely have to clean up after them all, but she didn't care.

She loved her family, and the ranch family that extended out into the cowboy cabins here at Shiloh Ridge.

But most of all, she loved it when August put his hand on her leg under the table, nodded toward the back door, and they snuck out while people still moved through the line to get food from the waffle bar.

Outside, he led her around the deck to the front of the house where they'd first sat to eat the miniature meatloaves she'd once fed everyone. "Happy birthday," he said honestly, his voice set on low and husky. "That kind of got away from me."

"My family is to blame for that."

"Mm." He smiled down at her and took her into his arms. "I hope this day is everything you want it to be."

"It already is." She loved holding him in her arms too, and she inhaled the clean, crisp quality of his shirt. He hadn't been out on the ranch yet that morning, obviously.

"We're still on for dinner tonight?"

"Absolutely," she whispered.

"Good." August lowered his head and kissed her, a proper birthday kiss that said so much more of how he felt than his voice ever had.

Etta kissed him back, hoping he'd know that she'd say yes if he asked her to marry him. And this time, she'd make it down the aisle to his side, and she'd say the I-do.

She wasn't going to bring it up right now, or even that night, or even in a week or two. *Whatever time August needs to be ready*, she told herself. At the same time, she couldn't help pleading with the Lord to, *Help him hurry up and get ready*, so she could kiss him like this every morning, noon, and night. So she didn't have to sleep alone anymore. So the future she'd been waiting for and planning for would finally arrive.

Chapter Twenty-Seven

August pulled hard on his end of the rope, his muscles screaming at him to stop. He didn't stop, but put a little more lean into the motion, his teeth grinding together. Around the other side of the barn, Jess yelled, and in the next moment, the rope released.

August stumbled backward, the whistling sound of metal slicing through air meeting his ears. He let himself fall to the ground, and he rolled to protect his face and head. Everything *moved* around him, something hit the ground nearby, and then...stillness.

Boots came running toward him. "August!"

The scent of dirt, heat, and his leather gloves filled his nose as August tried to decide if he'd been hurt or not.

"You okay?" Jess put his hand on August's shoulder, and he lowered his hands.

"Yeah, I think so."

"Careful," Jess said, stepping over him, and August held

very still as he picked up a piece of barbed wire that lay only about a foot from his eyes. "Let me move this first."

August waited for him to do that, and then he got to his feet and dusted himself off. "I guess the post came up."

"You almost got stuck a bunch of times." Jess cast him a look that said so much, and August automatically looked toward the farmhouse, as if Preacher would be standing there, watching the whole thing.

August swallowed, wishing he had a big bottle of ice cold water. "Yeah, well, I didn't."

"Let's not tell the boss about this all the same," Jess said, rolling up the spent barbed wire. They had to get the new fences in and restrung, and fence-building was one of August's most-hated chores. He'd do anything to keep this job, however, and if Preacher needed him to dig holes in the dry Texas earth, set posts, and string wire, he'd do it. Ward wanted another huge pasture down here, and it had to be completely fenced, as Shiloh Ridge did rotational ranching. They put sheep, goats, pigs, turkeys, chickens, and cattle in the pasture to help it turn over faster, and the last thing they wanted was a coyote or a fox stealing away their fowl.

Thus, August had new posts and tons of wiring in his future.

Also in his future was a horseback riding date with Etta. Since his successful birthday breakfast surprise, he'd seen her less than usual. Her niece had returned from college in Georgia, and the two of them were running a massive horseback riding program this summer. Apparently, Aurora had taught lessons previous to her going to college, and Etta had helped out.

They'd been making calls, refreshing the website, and readying the horses for a week or two now, and the lessons started the Monday following the last day of school.

Etta had secured a spot for Hailey, and while August hadn't asked her if his daughter could tag along with her most days this summer, he suspected she would. *You should also talk to her about it*, he told himself.

He would.

Tonight. She'd promised him a picnic dinner, complete with a red-checkered blanket and delicious food, and he'd promised to show her part of her own ranch she hadn't seen in a while.

He also wanted to ask Etta about having Hailey work around the ranch. She'd turned ten already, and Cactus's boys around that age carried their weight. Hailey could too. She could feed chickens or herd goats from one field to the next. She could push a lawn mower or rake rocks back where they belonged.

He mentally added that to his to-talk-to-Etta-about list, which already had a great number of things on it. His parents wanted to meet her. Like, in-the-flesh, look-her-in-the-eyes, meet her. He'd told them that no, he and Etta wouldn't be returning to Southern Texas if they got married, and his mother had started asking when they could come to Three Rivers or when August could bring everyone for another visit.

He hadn't brought it up with Etta or Preacher yet,

because he knew it was hard to get time off in the summer. In fact, Preacher had just filled the last two cabins on the lane where August lived, because he needed more hands and more help.

Hailey kept Josie's parents up to date, and August had answered a lot of questions after Etta's birthday party. He'd been honest, and they'd expressed their love for him and Hailey, and yes, Shannon had started asking when he and Etta might get married. She'd hinted that she and Daniel would like to come if they could.

Even Etta's mother had mentioned a wedding, and August blew out his breath as he realized Jess had gone ahead of him, rolling up the wire onto the huge wooden spindle. He caught up to him and helped push it as the last of the wire came into view.

"Are you really okay?" Jess asked, giving him a look. August had gotten to know him quite well over the past several months, and he liked the man a lot. He worked hard. He didn't gossip. He laughed at appropriate times. Walt, his cabinmate, had nothing but good things to say about him, and he'd ridden along to church with August and Hailey a time or two.

"Just thinking about Etta," August said.

"Ah." Jess tied off the end of the wire with a plastic zip tie and looked up toward the homestead. The whole thing oversaw this part of the ranch, and August gazed at it too. "Things okay with her?"

"Yeah," August said honestly. "I...I think she thinks we should be moving faster. Everyone seems to."

"But...?" Jess prompted.

August shrugged, not quite sure what sat on the other end of the sentence. A *but* existed, but he couldn't identify why. Etta wanted children, and she'd just turned thirty-seven. He knew she couldn't have babies forever, and he wasn't opposed to marrying and having more kids.

"Don't do that," Jess said. "I know I'm young, but I get things." He lifted his hat and ran his gloved hand through his messy, unruly hair. August had teased him about it a few times, and he swore Jess had grown it longer on purpose. "Are you not feeling things with her?"

"No," August said. "That's not it. I...feel all kinds of things for her."

"Then what's the problem?"

August tore his gaze from the ridge above them, from the homestead, from the spot where the family cemetery stood. "I think it's a couple of things." He removed his gloves and let his fingers breathe in the breeze. "First, I'm having a little bit of anxiety about my worth compared to hers."

"Which is ridiculous," Jess said.

"Even so." August spoke barely loud enough to hear himself, and he put his gloves back on to push the spindle of wire where it needed to go. "And second...this one might be even more ridiculous." He didn't want to say it out loud.

"Jess," someone called, and both he and August lifted their heads as Arizona came riding toward them. "August." She swooped out of the saddle while the horse was still moving a little and smiled at them. "I need to talk to you about something."

"Okay," they said in tandem, exchanging a glance with one another. August knew Arizona, of course. He'd heard she was pregnant and due in October, and while she still had five months to go until she delivered, she already sported a small bump in her midsection.

"I don't have much time. If Preacher asks, I was not here."

"Okay," they said again, and August heard the wariness in Jess's tone. He felt it moving through his soul too.

"My brother's birthday is coming up," she said. "He does not like a fuss being made, but I need you guys to get him off the ranch for a few hours that day. Morning, afternoon, I don't care when."

August looked past her, but he didn't see Preacher anywhere. No dust trails lifting into the air anywhere.

"Why us?" Jess asked.

"Because he'll say no to family," Arizona said. "I have the perfect set up. Have you guys been out to Three Rivers Ranch and done the equine therapy riding there?"

"No," August said. "Heard about it, though." He looked at Jess and swatted his chest. "Remember we met Pete Marshall at the branding? He owns Courage Reins and the therapy unit."

"Right," Arizona said. "Preacher loves it. I need you to tell him you want him to take you. Ollie's back, and he goes with his dad. So Preach won't think anything of it. All of you can go." She held out a card. "Here are all the details. Let me know what time your appointment is."

August took the card, and Arizona walked away. She swung onto her horse, nickered at it, and trotted away. He flipped the card for Courage Reins over and saw the date. "This is in another month," he said, frowning. "We have to call that far ahead?"

Jess peered at the card, and August tilted it toward him further so he could see the details. "Let's give it a go." He pulled out his phone and August held the card while he dialed. "Yes, hi, this is Jess Cochran, and I'd like to make an appointment for some...riding." He looked at August with wide eyes, gesturing like *what do I say here?* "How many?"

August counted quickly—him, Jess, Preacher, Ollie, and his dad. He held up five fingers.

"Five," Jess said. "Oh...groups of eight. Okay, eight." He shrugged, smiling now. "Let's see, I'd love to come on—" August held up the card. "June twentieth."

A pause, wherein August wondered how much therapeutic riding cost, and if anyone was really allowed to do it. Seemingly able-bodied men.

"Any time," Jess said. "Morning, night, whatever."

"Afternoon," August hissed, and Jess said that too.

"Almost booked?" Jess asked, his eyebrows going up. "Well, it's for my boss's birthday. Preacher Glover? I know he'd love to get in on his birthday."

August smiled and shook his head. Jess was good, he'd give him that.

"Great," Jess said, beaming. "Sure, eight is great. Mm...

yeah. Yes, we'll pay when we get there. Thank you." He hung up, and both of them started laughing. "I'll tell you what," Jess said. "Arizona needs to give us a credit card too. That's going to be hundreds of dollars for eight people."

"Yeah, but you said Preacher Glover, and bam. They had openings." August bent to start rolling the spindle again.

"I mean, the Glovers *are* kind of like royalty around here."

He was right, and that only spoke to August's first point about not feeling worthy of a woman like Etta Glover. He'd only admitted his second reason for his hesitation to tie the knot tomorrow to himself, and only in his very quietest of moments.

Thankfully, Jess didn't bring it up again, and it wasn't very quiet inside August's head right now.

* * *

"You're right," Etta said later that evening, leaning back into August's chest as they faced west to watch the sun set. "I don't think I've been to this part of the ranch, ever."

"Ever?" The gold in the sky reminded him of God's glory, and as the pink and navy tried to steal the majesty of it, August finally allowed complete contentment to move through him.

"Are you sure we're still on Shiloh Ridge property?" Her voice carried a teasing lilt, and August closed his eyes and smiled into the sky.

"If we're not, I tended to a well out here for no

reason." According to the map Preacher had given him, the well sat right in the southwest corner of the ranch, and one could only access it by a footpath that went into a small meadow, with trees bordering it on the south and east.

August had been utterly charmed by the spot, and it was large enough to hold the now-cleared well, as well as probably five or six blankets. So others could come here and spread out and August would be able to talk softly to Etta so only she could hear.

He had no intention of telling anyone else about this spot, and his heart felt fuller than it ever had before. Etta currently sat between his legs, leaning her back into his chest, and he braced both of them with his palms flat against the ground.

"Etta," he murmured, opening his eyes and noting the shiver that ran across her shoulders. It made him smile and added courage to his small store of it. "I wanted to talk to you about Hailey and this summer."

"Okay."

"You don't have to take her every day," he said. "But could she tag around with you a few days a week? I know you have the lessons and all of that, and I'm going to talk to...someone about actually putting her to work."

"I'll put her to work," Etta said. "She can work around the homestead, the yard there, and on the riding program with me and Aurora."

"Are you sure?"

Etta turned her head to look at him, but August kept his

gaze on the horizon as the sun kept sinking toward the curve of the earth. "Of course I'm sure, August."

He nodded. "If you can't one day, just let me know."

"I'll let the ranch wives know," Etta said. "Someone will take her. Heck, Dot will take her and put her to work at the landscaping company. Or Holly Ann will make her carry trays of food to her catering van."

"I'm not opposed to either of those," August said. "I do want her to have time to play too."

"There will be time for all of it," she said. "It's summer-time on a ranch."

"Mm." He'd spent plenty of summers on a ranch, as had Hailey. Not with as many children, and not with as much purpose as it sounded like this summer would hold.

"August?"

"Yeah?"

Etta didn't speak immediately, which clicked his internal alarms up a notch. She hadn't pressured him about a proposal or an engagement or a wedding. He hadn't asked her what her ideal wedding would entail. Knowing Etta, she'd have planned the whole thing already, and it was just a matter of execution.

She'd already put on one wedding where she hadn't made it down the aisle, and he wondered if that had altered any of those plans.

"Remember when we went up to the Top Cottage?" she finally asked.

His tension bled from his body now. "Yeah."

"You do want to marry me, right?"

"Yeah."

"Are you going to say anything but yeah?" She sat up and scooted away from him. Her gaze felt too heavy for him to hold, and he ended up dropping his head to block her view. His heart thundered like galloping horses' hooves, and he didn't know how to tell her what sat in his mind.

He also knew she wasn't going anywhere, and he better start talking, like, now.

Chapter Twenty-Eight

Etta didn't like the way August just sat there. Frustration built beneath her tongue, despite her commitment not to say anything to him about his intentions. Noah had known before her that he wanted to marry her; everyone worked at their own speed, on their own timeline.

"August," she finally said, when it felt like way too much time had passed. "Remember how I said I would tell you if I wasn't feeling good about us? Remember how we were going to be honest with each other?"

"I remember."

Of course he did. She didn't know how to be delicate, and she decided it was past time for such things. "There's something holding you back, and I'd like to know what it is."

He lifted his head, those eyes filled with emotion. Etta fought the urge to reach for his face, smile softly, and tell him it was all okay. He could take as much time as he wanted. He actually couldn't, and Etta felt every second ticking by incredibly slowly.

Tick...ti—ck...ti...ck.

"I don't think I deserve you."

Etta glared at him, feeling all of the softness inside her harden. "That's ridiculous."

A pained smile flashed across his face. "It's true."

"It's more than that." Etta refused to believe that his self-worth was this low. "All of my brothers feel like that about their wives too." She turned her attention to the picnic dinner she'd brought and started cleaning it up. She couldn't look at him right now, and the chore gave her the opportunity to throw some things in an innocent way. "And yet, they managed to date, propose, and get married."

She tossed him a dirty look and went back to the container of watermelon wedges, snapping the lid on with far too much vigor. "It's something else. I can feel it seething between us. If you don't want to say, that's fine. But I don't want to keep doing this." She gestured between the two of them, abandoned the quest to clean up, and stood.

"Wait," he said. "Are you leaving?"

"I'm quite certain I can get back to the homestead on my own," she said, lifting her chin.

"What don't you want to keep doing?"

"This dance," she said with a sigh. "You light up when you see me, and then you pull back. As long as we're not talking about anything too serious, everything is great. But August, I'm not...I'm *serious* about you." She swallowed, her next thought stabbing through her brain. "I thought you were serious about me."

"Etta." He ran his hands up her arms, but she didn't shiver this time from his touch. "I am."

She simply looked at him, silently begging him and the Lord to talk to her.

"Is it a proposal or nothing?" he asked.

"No," Etta said. "Of course not." He knew what she wanted. He *knew*. "Can you—could you at least let me know where your head is? We've been seeing each other for almost nine months. Even Preacher knew by nine months that he was in love with Charlie and wanted to spend his life with her."

Something marched across August's face, but Etta couldn't identify all of the soldiers. "My parents want to meet you."

Etta threw up a wall to that, but she held her tongue while she thought about what to say. Sarcasm wasn't welcome in this conversation, though she did want to hurl something at him that would get him to see how completely ironic that statement was.

"Well, August," she said slowly. "I think driving several hours to meet someone's parents should happen only if they're going to be my future in-laws."

"People meet each other's parents before an engagement all the time."

"If they live nearby," she said. "You're talking several days off, a massive road trip, and tons of introductions."

Displeasure entered his expression, and she'd definitely

seen that before. "I've met your whole family. More than your family."

"They live right on top of me," she said. "There's no room to breathe here." She moved away from his touch, and his arms fell back to his sides. "You want to go see your parents? Fine, I'll go. Figure it out with Preacher, and I'll figure it out with Aurora, and we'll go."

She met his eyes again, and his eyes dropped to the ground. He wasn't going to figure anything out with Preacher.

"Okay," he said anyway, and Etta thought she might be surprised. August had certainly shown her how he felt about her. She could feel his desire, passion, and love in his touch, his kiss.

There was still something not quite right between them, and it flowed from him.

"I don't want to be pushy," she said, bending to pick up the blanket they'd been sitting on. "You'll tell me when you're ready." All she could do at this point was hope she wasn't old and gray when August decided he could marry her.

Help me to be patient, she prayed. *Or clear my mind and give me courage if he's not the one for me.*

Etta had felt very strongly that August Winters was absolutely the man for her. She loved him, and while she hadn't told him that in those exact words, they'd talked about children, where they'd live, if they could get married—all of the things that Etta thought testified of how she felt about him.

Something nagged at her, and she folded the blanket

with a trumpeting heartbeat. She sniffled and placed it on top of the basket before linking her arm through the handle. She'd only told one other man—exactly one other man—that she loved him. It had been a wonderful, glorious moment between her and Noah, and standing in this beautiful meadow with August felt like the opposite of that.

If she told him now, what did she hope to accomplish? Would it be pushy? Bullying him to say it back to her? A desperate move by a desperate woman?

She wanted to tell him, but now didn't feel like the right moment. She stepped over to him and cradled his face in her free hand. "Okay? You'll tell me when you're ready?"

He nodded, and Etta had to accept that, even if she didn't like it. "I'm sorry, Etta."

"Don't be sorry," she said. "I'm sorry I ruined tonight." She dropped her hand and turned toward the path that led to the ATV they'd ridden out here. "It's getting dark, though. We better head back."

They did, and Etta leaned into the strength of August's back on the ATV as he navigated them to the homestead. She didn't want to even think this might be the last time she'd be this physically close to him, so she put it out of her mind.

He walked her up the sidewalk to the wrap-around porch, where he stalled. "Etta," he said. "You are an extraordinary woman."

"August, please don't say anything you don't mean."

"I won't," he said.

Tears pricked her eyes. "I don't want to talk anymore

tonight." She turned to face him, pure exhaustion running through her blood. "You had the chance to tell me, and you didn't want to. It's fine. I'm reassured that you're working through something, and that if something between us is all wrong, you'll tell me."

Right? she added silently.

"I want you to know this is nothing about you," he said. "It's entirely within me, and it *is* something I'm going to figure out."

She gave him the best smile she could, but it wobbled in all the wrong places. "I know you will." She tipped up and kissed him squarely on the mouth, hoping he would know he really could take his time.

She had been on so many bad dates. She had been out with over a dozen guys she'd never seen more than once. She could give August more time.

He held her close and kissed her back, and Etta knew he loved her. She just *knew* it, despite the lack of words that came from his mouth.

Be patient, she heard in her head, and she broke the kiss.

"Don't cry," he whispered, wiping his thumb across her wet cheek.

Etta ducked her head and sniffled. "Don't kiss me like that then." She reached for the doorknob and opened the front door. "Good-night, August."

"Good-night, sweets," he said, and Etta forced herself to go inside the house and close the door behind her. She pressed her back to the wood and breathed out slowly, his voice repeating in her head. *Sweets.*

Sweets, sweets, sweets.

That was what he called his daughter, the person in his life he loved unconditionally. Why had he called her that?

A couple of weeks later, Etta swung out of the saddle and bent to hug the girls who'd been with her on their riding lesson that day. "You three did *amazing*." She grinned at them like they'd be the rodeo's next barrel racing champions, and all of them hugged her. "Now, let's go over the after-care for the horses."

She led them through removing the tack, cleaning it, and hanging it properly in the stables. She taught them how to brush down their horse and lead it with a line when they didn't have reins. She put her horse away first and smiled proudly at the trio of twelve-year-olds as they did the same.

"Okay," she said. "Done for today. See you next week."

"'Bye, Etta," they chorused at the same time, and all three of them giggled as they hurried toward the big SUV waiting to pick them up. Etta waved and smiled until she didn't have to anymore, and then she turned back to the stable with a sigh.

Aurora Osburn looked up from her clipboard, looking completely cowgirl-country in her cowgirl hat and boots. Even her shirt boasted blue-and-white plaid today. "What's wrong, Etta?"

"Nothing," she said as cheerfully as she could, which was about as happy as a prince who'd been turned into a frog.

Aurora hung the clipboard on the side of the stable and came a little closer. "Oh, you would've called me out on that ten times out of ten." She put her hands on her hips, a very serious expression on her face. "Or have you forgotten how many times you caught me and Ollie in the barn, separated us, and then asked me why I was so unhappy?"

Etta didn't want to talk about her adult relationship problems with Aurora. The girl was barely older than half her age, and she'd been married for over a year already. Looking at her, Etta felt the full weight of unfairness descend upon her, and she clenched her jaw against it.

She would not be jealous of Aurora. Everyone had their own path to trod, and Etta had made different choices in her life. Still, she could not hold up the world, the unfairness of life, and all of her envy at the same time, and she started to crumble.

Aurora saw it, and she stepped into her and hugged her tightly. "Tell me why you're so unhappy."

"I'm worried August is going to break up with me," she whispered, gripping the girl with everything she had.

"He's not," Aurora said, stroking Etta's hair the way she'd done so often for the girl. "What did you used to tell me, Etta? I've seen the way he looks at you. He's not going to break up with you."

"His life...." She shook her head and stepped back. "Things are more complicated for us than they were for you and Ollie."

Aurora nodded and didn't try to say they weren't. She

glanced to her left as footsteps approached, and Etta spun away as Hailey came around the corner.

"Not a word," she hissed at Aurora, who immediately stepped away and said, "Hailey, are you done with the all-stars already?"

"Yes, ma'am," August's daughter said. "My daddy asked me to find Etta. He said he has something for her at True Blue, and I said I knew right where she was."

Etta could feel the girls' eyes on her back, and she took another moment to make sure her face was completely dry before she turned. "He has something? What?"

Hailey grinned like the cat who'd just caught the canary. "It's a surprise."

Aurora's eyebrows flew toward the sky, and Etta's pulse fired through her like a twenty-one gun salute. She would not hope for a proposal. She would *not*.

He hadn't even told her what the issue was, and things between them over the past couple of weeks had been... strained at best.

They'd been distant. Quiet. Etta hated distant and quiet when it came to the man she loved, and she reached up to brush her hair out of her face. "All right," she said. "That was our last lesson for today, so I suppose I have a few minutes to go over to the barn."

"I suppose you do," Aurora said. "I'll come by the homestead tonight to go over tomorrow's lessons."

"Yes, ma'am," she said, just like Hailey had, and then she turned south. She could just barely see the roof of True Blue from the stables, and she took the first step in that direction. The scent of wood smoke met her nose, and as she came around the hay loft, she found Ward, Dot, and Glory getting ready to build a fire.

"Hot dogs tonight," Ward said, tending to the fire lovingly. He loved this firepit spot with his whole heart, and he and Dot came out here quite often. "If you want to come."

"Thanks," Etta said. "I'm starving, and I'll be back."

"Ace and his family all coming," Ward said. "And Judge and June. That's all I've heard back from."

"It's last-minute," Dot added, smiling at Etta. She saw something on Etta's face, if the way her eyes widened was any indication. Etta nearly stumbled in the gravel, her panic influencing her step.

"You okay?" Dot came toward her, glancing at Ward and positioning herself between him and Etta.

"Do I look all right?" Etta whispered. "You looked like maybe I have an extra eye growing out of my forehead or something."

"You look...upset." Dot reached out and put her hand on Etta's bicep. "Why are you upset?"

"You're upset?" Ward asked, twisting from the fire. How he'd heard from all the way over by the crackling, dancing fire, Etta would never know. His boots crunched over the gravel as he strode closer. "What's happened?"

"Calm down," Etta said.

"Who do I need to talk to?" he asked.

Glory started to fuss, and Etta reached for the baby. Dot

gave her to Etta, but the concern didn't leave her eyes. Ward's either.

"I'm fine," Etta said, her focus on the dark-haired girl.

"Oh, she said fine."

"We're here," Ace said, approaching from around the barn too. Etta glanced over to them and passed Glory back to her mother.

"Please, don't make a big deal of this."

"No one has the right to upset you," Ward hissed. "You do more for everyone around here than anyone else. Was it Ace? Did he say something rude about the gluten-free stuff you slave over?" His eyes fired dangerously, and Etta quickly shook her head.

"Of course not," she said. "Ward...." She sighed and shook her head. "It's August, and you will *not* say a word to him about anything." She held up one finger the way she had as a child when she'd lectured her brothers about staying out of the kitchen while she and Ida cooked with Mother.

"I will say whatever I want to him," Ward said, though his voice had calmed considerably. "What's he done?"

Dot put her hand on her husband's chest and pushed him back a step. "Baby, it's about what he *hasn't* done."

Ward looked confused for only a moment, and then his eyes widened. "But you've been seeing him forever. He doesn't want to get married?"

"Howdy," Judge called, and more feet on the gravel filled the sky with noise. With people that were getting too close. With way too many ears to be having this conversation.

"Let me handle it," Etta said.

"Handle what?" Ace asked.

She put a ginormous smile on her face. "Nothing. I just have to run and change, because I smell *so* horsey. Then I'll be back with a whole bowl of cantaloupe. Save me one of the cheddar dogs." She beamed at both of her brothers, silently begged Dot to contain this disaster-waiting-to-happen, and turned to leave.

Every step toward True Blue felt hesitant, like she wasn't sure if she wanted to take it or not. A surprise.

Surprises were good, right?

He wasn't going to break up with her and call that a surprise.

Right?

Chapter Twenty-Nine

August paced in front of the back door of True Blue, wondering where Etta was. Hailey had texted fifteen minutes ago that she'd found her at the stables, and she was on her way. It was maybe a five-minute walk, not fifteen.

He checked on the setup in the main hall, and the single table he'd gotten out still sat there. He'd put a white tablecloth on it and set two places for dinner. The food waited in the kitchen, and his stomach roared at him about more than eating.

"It's fine," he muttered to himself. "You're going to be fine. Everything is fine."

Really, he felt like he'd been run over by one of those machines that aerates lawns, and he had inch-wide holes all over his body. He paced back to the windows and looked out. No Etta.

"August?" she called from behind him, and he spun before breaking into a jog.

He burst through the doorway at the back of the hall to find her only a few steps inside, having used the front door and come in through the lobby area. "Hey," he said, more breath than voice in the word. "You made it."

"I do know where True Blue is."

"Hailey said you left a while ago."

"Oh, I got stuck talking to my brothers," she said, hooking her thumb behind her. She was gorgeous in her riding pants and boots that went all the way to her knee. "They're doing hot dogs at the firepit." She looked past him to the set table. "I suppose we won't be joining them?" When she looked at him again, August found the familiar glint in her eye. Etta Glover liked surprises. She liked parties. She liked being taken care of.

"We can if you'd like," he said. "But I drove to Giuseppe's and got paninis and gelato."

"I don't even like hot dogs." She grinned at him, and August laughed. In moments like these, it felt like he and Etta didn't have a wedge between them.

"You adore hot dogs," he said, taking her into his arms. She came willingly too, and as she smiled up at him, he leaned down to kiss her. This moment felt so real and so true and so familiar too. He hadn't kissed her like this for a while, and he really wanted to get back to it.

"Let me show you something," he said, pulling away and lacing his fingers through hers. She came with him a bit grudgingly, and August added, "It's not a diamond ring, so don't worry."

"Okay, good," she said.

His eyebrows went up, but he kept on toward the table. "Good? I thought you wanted me to propose."

"Not if you don't want to."

"Trust me, Etta," he said. "When I propose, I'll want to." If she noticed he'd used *when* and not *if*, she didn't comment on it.

He reached the table and pulled out her chair for her. "Let me grab the food." His stomach quaked as he all but ran into the kitchen. He'd already plated their meals, and he picked up the envelope with her name on it and placed it on top of the cloche hiding the turkey-bacon-spinach panini she loved.

After setting it in front of her, he took his seat. She eyed the envelope warily and made a big show out of unfolding her napkin and putting it on her lap.

He grinned at her. "Go on," he said. "Open it."

She reached for the envelope and slid her finger under the flap on the back. He couldn't help staring at her as she pulled out the two airplane tickets, the printed itinerary, and the receipt for her own hotel room. She looked at all of it, the vein in her neck picking up a throb that made him smile.

"I talked to Aurora and Ida," he said. "Dot and June. Montana and then Willa. Oakley and Sammy. Holly Ann and Zona and Libby and finally Charlie and Preacher. Those dates work for both of us."

She finally lifted her eyes to his. "You're taking me to San Antonio?"

"And Dripping Springs," he said, his smile stuck on his

face. "It's only four days, but trust me, Etta. That's long enough."

She blinked at him, looked back at the papers and tickets, and when their eyes met again, that magnetic charge that had always arced from her to him pulled him out of his chair. He didn't care that his napkin fell to the floor as he dropped to his knees. He didn't mind that the floor was so dang hard against his bones. He didn't want to be anywhere but where Etta Glover was.

He cradled her face and said, "I want you to meet all of them. I know you said it was something a fiancée would do, but I'm really hoping you'll come with me anyway." He swallowed, because he hadn't asked her to marry him, and he wasn't going to before their trip south.

She nodded, leaning her forehead against his. "Of course I will," she whispered, and August fell all the way in love with her. Now he just had to figure out how to tell her what he was truly afraid of—and pray that it wouldn't break them when he did.

* * *

"All right," August said, easing the rental car to a stop in front of his parents' house. The driveway held three trucks, which meant he'd parked on the street. He didn't think for a second that his mother didn't already know he'd arrived, but to her credit, she hadn't come out onto the porch yet. "Here we are."

Etta smiled at him, tucked her hair, and reached down

for her purse. "Let's go." She got out of the car first, and August admired her on so many levels. She claimed she hadn't done much traveling, but she knew what to pack for the airplane, which had been cold, and she looked like she'd just woken from an amazing nap and could go for hours.

On the opposite end of the spectrum, August felt like he'd flown here with only the strength of his arms, and as he straightened from the sedan, he caught sight of his brother coming down the driveway. Christian wore an apron over his shorts and tee, and he carried the longest pair of tongs known to man.

"Hey," he said, chuckling. "Come on back. We're in the yard; the grill is nice and hot."

Etta stepped to August's side as he came around the front of the car, and he took her hand in his. Her grip told him of her nerves, but she wore a professional smile on her face. He'd seen it before, and he hoped she'd be able to relax.

Christian's eyes moved from August to Etta and back. "How was the flight?"

"Great," August said, dropping Etta's hand to hug his brother. He clapped him on the back, starting to release the tension in his own muscles. He'd told his family that things were incredibly serious with Etta, and he wanted them to meet her.

He stepped back smiling and reached for her again. She came right to his side, her fingers sliding into the empty spaces between his. "Christian, this is Etta Glover. Etta, Chris is the middle brother. Four years older than me."

"Nice to meet you," she said, extending her hand for him

to shake. But Christian was Texan, and he grabbed onto her and hugged her. Etta laughed, as did Christian, and when they separated, August could taste the joy in the air.

"Aren't you just perfect?" he asked as Etta reseated her hand in August's. "Momma is going to lose her mind. Come on."

Etta raised her eyebrows as Christian turned and walked up the driveway again. "Wow," she said. "Lose her mind."

August could only grin and press his lips to her forehead. He'd know after tonight if his fears had been founded or not. *Please, please,* he pleaded. *I don't want to have to explain things if it's nothing.*

He followed Christian around the corner of the house and the backyard opened up before him. He whistled through his teeth. "Mom's been busy back here," he said.

"August," she exclaimed. She rushed at him and hugged him, and August had always enjoyed hugging his mother. She stood a few inches shorter than him, and she'd kept the grass, the bushes, and her hair trimmed neatly.

When she stepped back, her dark eyes glittered, and she reached up and swept her chin-length hair from one side of her head to the other. She faced Etta, her smile on high. "Hello, dear. You must be Etta."

"That I am." Etta shook her hand with both of hers, her smile shaking for how hard Mom rattled her.

"Okay, Mom," August said, chuckling. "Let her go."

His mom could chat up a deaf man, and she said, "It's so nice to meet you. I was telling Cliff just the other day that I thought August would cancel."

"Mom," he said, plenty of warning in his voice.

"He doesn't like to fly much," she continued anyway. "I was actually surprised he booked tickets." She looked at him, her eyes wide. "He usually drives to save money."

Etta looked at him too, plenty of understanding streaming between them.

"My mother," he said dryly. "Mae. May we all hope she learns how to stop talking one day."

"Oh, you." She swatted at his chest and turned toward the grill. "Cliff, come meet August's girlfriend." She swung back to the pair of them with lightning speed. "It is still girlfriend, right, Etta? August?" She looked between the two of them, hope high in her expression. "He didn't propose on the plane, did he?" She trilled out a laugh as Daddy came over.

"Oh," Etta said, plenty of surprise in her voice. She linked her arm through August's and blinked in rapid-fire fashion.

"Daddy," August said with all the patience of a diplomat. "This is Etta Glover. Etta, my father, Cliff Winters."

"Howdy, ma'am," he said, right proper-like despite the enormous hat on his head. It honestly looked like a costume or a prop, but he lifted his hand to tip the hat at Etta.

"Lovely to meet you, sir," she said. "I see where August gets his height and his hair color." She looked at August and reached up to touch the back of his neck, where barely any hair showed beneath his own hat.

"They're not engaged," Mom said, still smiling like this was the greatest news ever. She started to turn toward the oasis behind her. "Come meet Lawson. He's stewing over something the Astros did this afternoon. Meeting Etta will cheer him up."

August wanted to ask her how meeting Etta would possibly influence his oldest, married brother, but he kept his mouth shut.

"I wouldn't think so," Daddy said, turning with her. "Didn't he bring her so we could tell him what we thought?"

"Wow," Etta said, plenty of surprise in her tone. Or maybe that was shock. August wanted the ground to open up and swallow him whole.

Especially when Daddy followed his already embarrassing comment with, "She sure does remind me of Josie, don't you think?"

August pressed his eyes closed, his heart falling all the way to his boots. Then further.

Etta delicately removed her arm from his, her voice low and only meant for his ears when she said, "I see why you brought me now."

"Etta," he started, but one look at her silenced him. Fire and lightning moved through her gaze, and she might as well have been shooting ninja stars from her eyes. His chest shredded with every labored breath, and he wanted to march out of the backyard and return to the airport immediately.

And this was the first day of their trip. She hadn't even met Josie's parents yet.

She didn't need to now.

August had the answer to his plaguing question, and it felt like his father had sliced him in half, the serrated knife going in through his bicep, separating the front half of his body from the back.

"Etta," he said again, but she stepped away from him and over to his sister-in-law, who'd just come out of the back door with a huge bowl of cubed watermelon.

"What can I do to help you?" she asked, slipping into party planner mode. August stood helplessly on the side, wondering how he was ever going to explain now.

* * *

By the time they left the backyard barbecue, August felt like crying. He pressed his teeth together and gave one more wave. He'd get a slew of texts, and as he walked through the semi-darkness toward the rental, he vowed to delete them all without reading them.

In fact.... He pulled out his phone while Etta opened her own door to get in the car and sent a text to the same family string he'd used to let them all know he and Etta had landed and were on their way.

I don't want a single text about her, he typed out furiously. *I don't care what any of you think. Please, don't say a word.*

He sent the message without re-reading or second-guessing.

When he got behind the wheel and started the car, August couldn't hold back any longer. "I'm so sorry."

Etta folded her arms and looked out her window.

"They're really great people."

"Yes," she clipped out. "I can see, in a different circumstance, where they haven't been asked to make a judgment on a person within twenty seconds of meeting them, that they'd be great people."

The headache he'd kept at bay with diet cola and potato chips roared forward. He flipped the car into gear, because they couldn't sit in front of his parents' house and argue.

"It's my fault," he said. "I'm the idiot."

"What did you say to them?"

He might as well just lay it all out. "I have this mental block with you," he said. "I've been hoping and praying, *praying*—my Lord, I've prayed more about this than anything in my whole life—that I was just being stupid."

Etta said nothing, and she wouldn't look at him either. August gripped the wheel and focused on the road. If he got everything out now, maybe he'd be able to sleep tonight. Maybe the whole trip wouldn't be a complete loss. *Maybe Shannon and Daniel will have a different opinion.*

He seized onto the thought, because he really needed it to be true.

"See, when I first met you, I didn't think you were like Josie at all. Sure, you worked on a family ranch, and so did she. But she was this tall, tough, cowgirl, you know? She worked right alongside the men, and she loved it. But once summer came, and you started organizing all of these horseback riding lessons...." August shook his head. "You reminded me more and more of her. And I started to panic that I was going to find myself in the same situation I'd been in before."

"I thought you loved your wife," Etta said quietly.

"I did," he said. "We lived on *her* family ranch, with *her* family. Sound familiar?" He didn't mean to sound so bitter. "There suddenly came a time when I wasn't sure if I was falling for you or trying to recapture what I'd lost."

Etta turned toward him, plenty of challenge in her face. "And?"

"And I don't know," he said, the words exploding out of his mouth. "And you wanted to meet my family, and they wanted to meet you, and I asked them for two things: to be on their best behavior and to tell me what they thought of you." He shook his head, his anger growing with every passing second. "I didn't think my father would just blurt it out."

He came to a halt at a four-way stop where no one else waited. He looked at her, plenty of desperation streaming through him. "You don't look like Josie."

"Don't I?" Etta asked. "Why else would your dad think that? I'm not wearing anything remotely cowgirl-ish." She even looked down at her dark blue cotton shorts and bedazzled sandals.

"I'm not trying to replace her."

"Aren't you?" she challenged again. "You want a mother for Hailey. You want a companion in life."

"Etta," he said, not sure how to explain.

"Just tell me the truth," she said. "Am I just going to be a replacement for Josie?"

August said the first thing that came to mind. "I don't know."

The moment he said it, he knew it was the wrong thing to say, and he opened his mouth to call the words back, but Etta said, "I'd like you pull over right here, please," in the calmest, most deadly voice he'd ever heard a human being use.

So he did what she asked.

As she gathered her purse and got out of the rental car, pure defeat weighed August down and pinned him to his seat. "Etta."

He couldn't just leave her on the streets in a suburb of San Antonio. She paced away from him, her phone in front of her. He stayed right where he was, parked against the curb, as she made a phone call.

Fifteen minutes later, she climbed into the back of a cab without another glance in his direction. She'd kept her back to him for the majority of the time, but he hadn't seen a single tear slide down her face.

No matter. He stayed on the side of the road and cried plenty for both of them.

Chapter Thirty

Preacher Glover let his mind wander as Jess drove, the miles between Shiloh Ridge and Three Rivers Ranch melting away without the stress of work. He couldn't do anything about moving the hay from one barn to another during the drive. He wouldn't know what his cowboys were or weren't doing. He'd silenced his phone, which he'd probably pay for later.

Charlie knew that if she needed him, she only had to call three times within five minutes, and his phone would wail an alarm at him. He'd also activated her pin and his on their map program, so he could see where she was, and she could find him anytime, anywhere.

He loved going to Courage Reins to ride, though he'd put up a bit of a fight in the beginning. Pete Marshall and Reese Sanders and the doctor at the equine therapy unit had sat down with him and his medical reports, his chiropractic recommendations, and his physical therapist notes, and they'd made a plan.

Several months ago, Preacher had driven out to Courage Reins twice a week. Well, he couldn't drive himself, so his wife or Ward had brought him. Sometimes Judge or Bear. They'd worked together to get Preacher to the point where he could drive himself. He could walk without a crutch or a cane. He felt better than ever now, though he still exercised caution around the ranch and the farmhouse.

He absolutely did not want to get injured again. Each time seemed to take longer to recover from, and he didn't want to swallow a ton of pills just to get out of bed in the morning. He'd thrown away his walker, cane, and crutches, telling Charlie he wasn't going to need them again, and he wanted to keep that vow for as long as possible.

Beside him, sitting between him and Jess, August rode with his arms folded and his eyes closed. Preacher glanced at him and away, his heart tearing a little at the unhappiness pouring off of him.

He'd asked for time off last week so he could take Etta south to meet his folks. They were supposed to be gone for five days, but August had returned the next day. He'd asked Preacher and Charlie to take Hailey, and when he'd come to collect her, he had no explanation for his early return.

Etta had not yet returned to Shiloh Ridge, at least to Preacher's knowledge. He had a spy on the inside in his wife, who was connected to all of the ranch wives via text, and the word inside that string was that Etta was staying in town with Ida.

Preacher drew a breath, praying the Lord would give him something to say. Anything. Maybe if he knew more, he could help August past whatever had happened between him and Etta.

No words came, and Preacher closed his mouth again. When he and Charlie had broken up after his car accident, he hadn't wanted to answer any questions or listen to unsolicited advice. August Winters reminded him a lot of himself, and he just wanted him to know how valuable he was. How loved.

"Have you ever done an equine therapy ride?" he asked, and August's eyes came open.

Jess looked over to him, the highway in front of them clear and going on for miles and miles. "I haven't."

"I haven't either," August said. "I've heard you like them."

"They're fantastic," Preacher said. "Of course, I have physical things as well as mental and emotional things to work out. But I always feel better in all ways after the ride."

"What's it like?" August asked.

"Oh, and Wyatt, Tripp, Liam, and Ollie Walker will be there, besides us." Jess reached over and turned down the radio a click. Previous to Preacher's question, it had filled the silence between the three of them.

"The Walkers are good men," Preacher said, looking out his window. "Wyatt's had a lot of back problems from the rodeo. Mister too." His brother rode in the truck behind them, and Preacher saw the hulking black thing in the rearview mirror. He'd wanted to drive separately, because Libby had an appointment in town before noon, and he wanted to meet her there after their ride.

No one said anything, and Preacher opened his mouth again. "The ride is...hard to describe. There's just you and the horse. You guys ride horses, but it's different. They have different spirits than the ones we use around the ranch for work. It's like they know you have something on your chest you need to give them, and they're happy to take it."

"Do you ride the same one every time?" Jess asked.

"I do, personally," Preacher said. "You guys must've called pretty far out to book this for me, which I appreciate, by the way."

"When we found out it was your birthday, we wanted to do something," Jess said, and Preacher noticed that August was perfectly content to let him be the voice for the two of them.

"I don't get birthdays sometimes," Preacher said. "I'm old. I don't need it to be a big deal."

"My wife used to say every birthday was a big deal," August said, his quiet voice reaching its fingers right into Preacher's soul. "Because you lived another year on the earth. Another year of ups, downs, and in-betweens. Another year of laughter and love and sadness and tears and experiences. She said every year should be celebrated."

"That's beautiful," Preacher said.

"It meant more when she didn't get to her next birthday, I'll admit," August said, his eyes closing again.

"I'm sorry." Preacher reached over and patted his leg. "I can't even imagine."

"My sister died when I was growing up," Jess said. "She was born with a birth defect, so she was only three. But I really like the idea of celebrating every year, whether good or bad."

"We sometimes only celebrate the good things," Preacher said, and August opened his eyes. "I've never thought about thanking the Lord for the experience of the bad things." He smiled at August. "Thank you for that."

August gave him a brief smile, there one moment and gone the next. A smile that told Preacher how very unhappy he was.

He had not asked August why he'd come back early, but the question pressed against the front of his skull. He told himself he was not going to ask it. The man deserved some privacy. He also knew August and Jess were close, but August had asked Preacher and Charlie to take care of his daughter while he was gone.

If anyone could ask, Preacher could.

The sign for Three Rivers came up on his right, and he cleared his throat. "August," he said. "You don't have to say, but I'm wondering if there's anything I can do to help you with Etta."

Jess drew in a breath and looked first at August, clear anxiety in his eyes. He looked at Preacher, who gave him a single, barely-there nod. "I would help too," he said. "You two seemed so very happy, and since you came back from San Antonio...you're miserable."

"I'm fine," August said quietly, but Preacher saw the tremble in the man's chin. "We broke up."

"I'm sorry," Preacher said again. "I know my cousin sure

did like you. I've only seen her look at one other man the way she looked at you, and she nearly married him."

August shook his head, tight little movements that had to send pain down into his back. Then Preacher remembered that it was *his* spine and neck that were all messed up, not August's.

"It doesn't matter."

"That's just not true," Jess said, easing off the accelerator as the turn came into sight. "Preacher's right. You don't have to tell us everything, but if we knew what happened, maybe we could help you."

"What happened is I said some really stupid, hurtful things," he said, his voice powerful and yet quiet too. "I can't take them back. I can't fix them."

"You couldn't have met everyone in the Hill Country," Preacher mused.

Jess made the turn, and August leaned into him. "Just my parents," he said. "And I'd been worried about something specific, and I'd asked my family to let me know if my fears were founded or not. My dad said them right out loud in front of Etta, and it was downhill from there."

"What have you been worried about?" Jess asked. "Not the inadequacy thing."

"You are one of the best cowboys we've ever had at Shiloh Ridge," Preacher said, pure sincerity in every syllable. "You are completely worthy of Etta."

"It wasn't that," August said quietly. He looked so lost for a moment, and Preacher searched for something to say. Nothing came. He hated feeling so out of control and so helpless, but he'd had plenty of experience with that over the past few years.

"After my accident," he started. "I couldn't do anything myself. My brother had to come help me out of bed. My cousin came every day and walked with me to the barn and back. He put my whittling tools out in a bench there, because I couldn't make it there and back without resting in between."

The landscape out here in the middle of June was quite different than Shiloh Ridge. Three Rivers Ranch sat out in the wilds north of town, and everything was a shade of beige, tan, or brown except for exactly where Squire Ackerman, the owner of the ranch, had his people water. It was one of the larger ranches surrounding Three Rivers, and had thus taken on the same name as the town.

Preacher watched the drab landscape, thinking he'd once felt just like it. Dry. Barren. Useless. "For some reason, Charlie forgave me for all the stupid things I'd done, and we got married. I was still really...inadequate. There were so many things I couldn't do. There are things to this day that I can't do that she helps me with. I hate it, but at the same time, it's been very, very good for me."

"How?" August asked.

"It's helped me to allow others to serve me," Preacher said, a small smile touching his face. "My relationships with my family members who've done that have bloomed and improved to the point where I'm pretty sure my sister—who I barely spoke to a few years ago—is planning something I'm going to pretend to be upset about for my birthday."

He looked at the other two men in the truck, and their wide-eyed glance at one another confirmed it. He laughed and said, "It's fine. I'm not going to ask you what it is."

"Good," August said. "I'm a little scared of Arizona."

Preacher belted out a laugh then, though he could completely see Zona from August's point of view. She was intense about some things, that was all. He'd enjoyed getting to know her and spending time with her, her husband, and her daughter over the past few years.

"My injuries and the way I have to rely on others has made me stronger," Preacher said honestly. "Not physically, obviously. But spiritually. They have opened my eyes to others who are in pain who I can help. They have made me mentally stronger. They have humbled me and allowed me to show my gratitude in a variety of ways. There is more to being strong than lifting a lot of weight or knowing all the answers or, in Etta's case, planning the perfect party and having every child within a fifty-mile radius of the ranch love you."

He smiled, glad when August did too. "She has a very big heart," he admitted.

"She'll forgive you for whatever you said," Preacher said, a scripture coming to mind. "She knows keenly both sides of forgiveness, August."

"I know," he whispered.

"If you forgive others for their transgressions, your Heavenly Father will also forgive you." Preacher drew in the power of the words and held them in his chest. "She'll forgive you."

Jess eased to a stop in front of a big building with windows from ground to roof along the front of it. "This is it."

"I was worried Etta was too much like Josie," August said. "At first, she wasn't. She's completely different. But as time went on, I started to see all these similarities, and I started to worry I'd fallen in love with her, because she was just a replacement for my late wife." He reached up and removed his cowboy hat, clear anguish pouring from him.

Preacher held up his hand as Jess opened his mouth, and he closed it again.

"There was a lot said," August said into the silence. "At the very end, she asked if that's what she was. A replacement. Not a person of her own. Not someone who I loved for her, and not the woman I wanted to share my life with. To raise my daughter. But just a Josie-replacement."

Preacher's heart hammered in his chest despite Mister getting out beside him and clearly waiting for someone in their truck to get out.

"I said I didn't know," August said, studying his lap. "My dad had just said she even looked like Josie, and I didn't know."

"It's been a week or so," Preacher said. "How do you feel now?"

Mister moved to the front of the truck, and Preacher signaled to him to give them a minute. He scanned everyone in the truck and seemed to get the message. He walked over to the door and opened it, hopefully to get them all checked in.

"I love her," August said. "Jess is right. I'm completely miserable without her. There are similarities between her and Josie. There are similarities between the situations—I lived with my wife on her family ranch, which we both worked. But...but she is not Josie, and she's *not* just a replacement for the woman I can't have." He looked at Preacher, hope and desperation such a dangerous cocktail on a man's face. "How do I tell her that?"

"I have no idea," Jess said. "Maybe just telling her you love her is enough?" He looked at Preacher for confirmation, but Preacher didn't know either.

"Our family motto around the ranch is reuse, repair, and recycle," he said. "We don't replace until it's absolutely necessary to keep things running. You can't reuse, repair, or recycle your wife. You can't even replace her. There is no one like her—and no one like Etta. What you want, I suspect, is a life where you feel safe, loved, and accepted, and you feel like your daughter will be safe, loved, and accepted."

"I do want that," August said.

"Women are exceptional at making others feel safe, loved, and accepted," Preacher said. "I've seen that from all of the ranch wives in my life. Sammy still brings me a box of cereal at least once a month." A scoff came out of his mouth though he smiled with fondness for his brother's wife. "It's little, and I know she does it for everyone. But for that moment—that one moment in time when she bought that silly box of puffs, I was important to her. I was loved and accepted, and that's what the cereal represents. It's not just cereal."

"So...should I take Etta some cereal?" August asked.

Preacher chuckled again and reached to unbuckle his seatbelt. "No, but I do think you should go talk to Etta. Tell her that she is *not* a replacement, but that she is your whole future. That somehow, she's been saved all this time just for you, just so *you* could meet her, and just so the two of you could have a life together." He opened his door and looked back at August. "At least, if that's how you feel."

He thought that was exactly how August felt, and as the man thought about what Preacher had said, he started to nod slowly. "There have been extraordinary circumstances that brought us together."

"She could've been married to Noah Johnson," Preacher said.

"Your wife could still be alive," Jess added.

"And if you need help finding out some of her favorites, I know plenty of people who know Etta real well." Preacher provided him with a smile and got out of the truck. "Now, come on. We don't want to miss a minute of our riding time."

"Howdy, stranger," a man said, and Preacher stepped up onto the sidewalk and right into Tripp Walker's arms. They laughed and clapped each other on the back, and Preacher pulled back to introduce his cowboys.

"Two of my best," he said, indicating August as he closed the door. "August Winters and Jess Cochran. Boys, this is Ollie's dad, Tripp Walker."

Ollie stepped around his father and shook Jess's hand,

then hugged Preacher too. "And my uncles. Wyatt, the Rodeo King. And Liam, who is clearly my dad's twin."

Hands got shaken all around, and they all moved into the building. Preacher couldn't wait to get outside to stroke Mint Brownie's cheeks and tell the horse how good he felt on this day he was turning forty years old.

* * *

Preacher rode in the middle on the way back to Shiloh Ridge, and he'd just finished the last bite of his peanut butter cup shake when Jess made the turn.

"Oh, boy," August said, which caused Preacher to look up.

Someone had threaded streamers across the roadway that led up to Shiloh Ridge, linking the bright blue, red, yellow, and green banners from the roof of the equipment shed on the side of the road where Preacher's house stood to the roof of another shed across the lane.

In all, the colors streamed through the sky for probably a hundred yards, and they made his whole soul light up. "It's my birthday."

"Forty," Jess said. "You guys make a big deal out of big milestones. I heard about Bear's birthday last year."

"Forty is old," Preacher said as Jess turned to go down the road that led to the farmhouse and the cowboy cabins. "Oh, holy brands and saddles, stop the truck." He hated that he was in the middle, because he needed to get out of the vehicle right now, moving or not.

"What?"

"Stop the truck," Preacher said. "August, you better be unbuckling. That's a 1966 Ford GT Coupe." A red one. With the silver glinting in all this summer sunshine too. "She can't have bought that for me."

Jess brought the truck to a shaky stop, and August jumped down. Preacher slid over and out, moving toward the car sitting in front of his house as fast as he could move. "Zona!" he called. "Get out here!"

She came through his front door, his daughter on her hip. "You're back." She walked down the steps, her smile huge.

"Da dad," Betty said, and Preacher took the little girl from his sister, their eyes meeting.

"Tell me you didn't buy this for me." It was too much. Way too much.

"It doesn't run yet," she said. "Don't get all excited." She bumped him softly with her hip. "I thought you and I could work on it together, the way we used to work on old stuff with Dad."

He looked back at the car of all cars. It might not run yet, but they'd get it fixed up and when she could go, she'd purr like a kitten. "I'll pay for all the parts." He started around the car to examine what he'd be dealing with.

"I was counting on that," Zona said after him. "Charlie has approved a space in your massive garage for us, but I wanted you to see it when you got back from your ride."

"Thank you." He looked over the top of the car and met his sister's eyes. "This is incredible. Thank you."

"Did he like it?" Charlie called down from the porch. She skipped down to him, and he went around the trunk of the car to give her a squeeze and kiss.

"He liked it," Preacher said.

"Happy birthday, cowboy," Charlie said, and Preacher kept her tucked into his side as he focused on the car again.

"It's incredible," he said. "I wish we weren't in full summer swing so we could get started."

Zona joined them and said, "We'll find time. Even twenty minutes is twenty minutes, and it's not work if it's fun."

"Tonight?" he asked, glancing from his wife to his sister. "I don't think there's any plans."

"That's where you'd be wrong," Charlie said. "Your day is packed full, cowboy, and I can smell the peanut butter and chocolate on your breath, but you better not have eaten any lunch."

"No?" He kissed his baby's cheek. "Why's that?"

"Because we're having your favorite for lunch. Well, yours and Betty's. It's her birthday month too, you know."

"So now I have to share my birthday with a baby?" he asked, clearly teasing his wife.

Charlie just beamed up at him and said, "Come get your chocolate-covered strawberries, and celebrate your daughter's first birthday. I made everything myself."

"I can't wait," he said, going with her. "Thank you, Charlie." For everything. For how she'd taken care of him. For how she'd let him heal. For loving him even when he was very hard to love.

Chapter Thirty-One

Bishop Glover pulled up to his house, relief filling him. He loved coming home to his wife and son, both of whom had arrived ahead of him this evening. He'd stayed down on the construction site with Libby and Mister as he walked them through the timeline and schedule, which seemed to constantly change.

Montana, his wife, had left at least an hour ago, and she'd stopped by Holly Ann's to get their son Robbie. Her truck, dusty as it was, sat out front, and Bishop ran his fingers along the side of it, getting plenty of dirt and grime.

Their sprinklers came on in the middle of the night to keep their patch of grass green, and that made for a muddy morning almost every day. He glanced past her truck to see if Ollie and Aurora were there, but the spot where they parked sat empty.

Rory was probably still doing her riding lessons, which went late on Thursday nights. Ollie, after he'd spent the day working down at Seven Sons, his family ranch, went to help her clean up faster.

So Bishop was anticipating finding his wife and son in the kitchen, where hopefully Montana hadn't spent the last hour. Bishop had put a few chicken breasts in the slow cooker that morning, and all he had to do was boil some noodles and mix in some cream cheese to make the Alfredo sauce with shredded chicken.

He climbed the steps and opened the door, a long exhale coming from his lungs at the tightness in the back of his legs. "Hey," he called. "I'm home."

His wife wasn't in the kitchen, though Robbie was. He came out from behind the counter, a wooden spoon in one hand that looked dangerously like it had chocolate on it. His son bore the sticky sweet on his face, his shirt, his hands. He wasn't even wearing pants, as Montana had been trying to potty train him for about a month now.

"Buddy." Bishop dropped his tool bag and hurried toward his son. "What are you into?"

"It's okay," Montana said, coming down the hall. "I gave him the frosting."

"It's everywhere," Bishop said, not even glancing at Montana. He swept the boy into his arms and smiled at him. "Don't you know food goes in your mouth, bud?" The floor had a few streaks of frosting on it, but mostly the container of it looked like a badger had tried to eat it with his paws. "Ooh, German chocolate. That's Momma's favorite, so something must've...." He trailed off, his mind firing at him.

Montana had kept the house stocked with German

chocolate frosting a lot over the past few months. Several months. Fifteen months now, if Bishop wanted to be accurate. Fifteen months since they'd been trying to get pregnant and couldn't.

He'd come home to his wife crying more than once, and he turned toward her now to find her in tears again. "Baby," he said, sadness pulling through him too. Maybe they'd never get another baby. Maybe Robbie was all they would ever get. He wanted that to be enough, but in a family like his, it only felt like failure.

"I gave him the frosting," Montana said, tears trickling down her face. "Because I don't need it anymore. I mean, I have to eat for two now, and that much sugar always made him so wiggly inside."

Bishop blinked, sure he'd heard her wrong.

Eat for two now.

Wiggly inside.

I don't need it anymore.

He put Robbie on the counter next to the sink and bent to pick up the container. "You stay right here, bud. Eat whatever you want."

Montana grinned at him as he approached, and Bishop's swooped her into his arms. "You're pregnant?"

She laughed as he twirled her around and said, "Yes. I just did the test. I'm *two* weeks late, Bishop."

He set her down, instant concern spiking inside him. "What if it's false? We have to go to the doctor. Get them to confirm it." He looked around as if he'd pick up the phone and make an appointment right now. They'd waited so long, and he had to know for sure. He had to also ensure that she was healthy and well enough to carry the baby to term.

"I can finish Mister's house by myself. I'll call the twins. I'll call anyone." He took her face in his hands. "I don't want you to be stressed at all."

"I haven't miscarried," she said. "I should be fine to work."

"Can you please go to the doctor anyway?"

She smiled at him and touched her lips to his. "For you, I will." She put her arms around him and held him, and Bishop felt like everything had suddenly been coated in candy. Pink candy, and the whole world was different now than it had been five minutes ago when he'd stood outside, wiping his hands through the dirt on her truck.

"I can't believe it," he said. "I think I've forgotten what true joy feels like."

"I know," Montana said in his arms. "I'm not sure if I'm happy about the pregnancy or sad that I know how stark of a difference there is between happy and sad now."

He pulled back and leaned his forehead against hers. "You've always known that. You've worked so hard to be where you are now." He kissed her again, a slow, sweet, I-love-you-with-everything-I-have kiss.

"Boy or girl?" he asked.

"We have one of each," she said. "I don't know. You?"

"I want a girl," he said. "Because now that Ward and Preach have girls, I see how absolutely adorable they are."

Her smile filled her whole face. "You'll spoil her rotten."

"I hope so."

"You won't bark at her about bein' good while you work. You'll just give her suckers."

He couldn't deny anything right now. "Probably."

"Yeah, I've seen you with Aurora, and she's a big girl."

The front door opened in that precise moment, and Robbie said, "Rowa," at the same time Bishop and Montana turned toward the front of the house. Rory entered first, saying something to Ollie, who came behind her.

"That's all," Rory said and the door closed. She looked up and froze. "What's going on?" She looked a little sunburnt, though Bishop knew she wore her hat every afternoon and evening while doing the riding lessons. "Mom? Are you crying?"

Aurora started through the living room toward her mother, while Ollie approached at a slower clip.

"I'm going to have another baby," Montana said, stepping away from Bishop to receive her daughter. "So yes, I'm crying."

Aurora hugged her tightly, her eyes closed and her smile as big as the moon too. "Congrats, Mom." She stepped over to Bishop and drew him into a hug too. "I'm so happy for you, Dad."

Bishop's whole heart swelled as she called him her father, and he lifted her up off her feet. "Thank you. How were the lessons?"

"Long tonight," she said as she stepped back. "But I love it. I'm not complaining." She melted into Ollie's side as he slid his hand along her waist. She beamed up at him. "They're having another baby, in case you missed it."

"I heard." He nodded over to Montana. "She told me while you hugged your dad."

"How's Seven Sons, Olls?" Bishop asked, moving to the sink to get Robbie cleaned up. "I just need like twenty minutes to make pasta, and we can eat."

"The ranch is great," he said. "Uncle Jeremiah actually went in early this afternoon and let me finish things alone."

Bishop twisted and grinned at the young man. "Wow, he's trusting you with more and more."

"I think he's just really tired," Ollie said with a laugh. "They just brought home their fifth baby, and he's nowhere near as young as you guys."

"That's why you have babies early," Montana said.

"Mom," Aurora said. "We're not having a baby anytime soon."

"I didn't even ask."

"You *suggested*," Aurora said, and Bishop put his head down and kept wiping at the chocolate on Robbie's face.

"I'd have a baby," Ollie said. "I love babies."

"Oliver Walker," Aurora said. "Stop it right now."

Bishop turned then, something catching in his ears. "Oliver Walker?" Ollie's last name was not Walker, though he'd been raised for over a decade with Tripp Walker as his step-father. He'd tried to adopt the boy, but his biological father wouldn't give permission.

Of course, Ollie wasn't a child anymore, and he could make his own decisions now. Aurora moved back to his side and looked up at him. "Tell them."

"Now that I don't need my dad's permission, I asked

Tripp if he'd adopt me. Legally and all that. For some reason...it matters to me." He gave a shrug, but Bishop knew he wasn't anywhere near casual about this. That last name—that family—meant a lot to Oliver, and they always had.

"We got the change done this past week. I got the email this morning, and an official certificate and everything is on the way." He beamed at Bishop, Montana, and then his wife, leaning down to kiss her forehead. "Rory is going to change her name too. We've even been talking about doing a little vow renewal with the right name."

"Do you think we need to?" Aurora asked, looking to her mother first. "I mean, we're married. That's not new or anything. But I married Oliver Osburn."

Montana looked at Bishop with wide, blue eyes, and he hoped their daughter would come with the same set. "What do you think?"

Bishop had no idea what to think. "I think," he said. "That this deserves so much more than cheap, knock-off chicken Alfredo. Let's go get something good to eat in town."

"Buck's," Robbie said, his only contribution to the conversation so far.

"No, bud," Bishop said, laughing. "I said something good."

"Buck's is good," Aurora said. "They have good pizza at least."

"If you want good pizza," Ollie said. "You go to Margherita. Not Buck's. *Please*."

"Do not insult Buck's." Aurora spun on him, her finger up in his face.

"Are you kidding right now?" Oliver asked, laughing. "Last time we ate there, you actually got sick."

She backed down. "Oh. Was that Buck's?"

"Yes." He laughed and laughed, and Bishop sure did love the two of them.

"I don't want fast casual," he said. "My wife is pregnant, and my son-in-law got the family he wanted. My son has only had chocolate frosting for who knows how long, and we have the best fashion designer in the country in our midst." He beamed around at these people he could call his, and his love for them grew, expanded, and warmed him from the inside out.

"I say we try somewhere nice," he said. "Somewhere like The Chef's Table."

"Oh, nice-nice," Aurora said.

Montana sucked in a breath, and her eyes flickered from Bishop to Robbie. "Can you imagine him there? They won't even know what hit them."

Bishop looked at his son too, his emotions overflowing and creating a waterfall through him. "Well, he *is* going to need some pants."

"Buck's," Robbie said again, frowning as he folded his arms.

"No," Bishop said. "I said *pants*. Let's go get you some pants, buddy." He swooped his son off the counter and into his arms, both of them laughing.

He paused in front of Montana, the woman who'd

changed everything in his life for the better. "I love you, baby," he whispered, and he kissed her again before going to get his son properly dressed for the five-star restaurant where they'd be dining tonight.

He did some simple math as he went down the hall, and seeing as how it was the beginning of July and Montana was two weeks late, he figured she'd be having their second child in late February or early March.

He absolutely could not wait, and as he opened his son's dresser drawer to look for a pair of clean pants—and get another shirt—he thanked the Lord for His bounteous blessings.

Help me to continue to be patient, he prayed silently, something he'd been asking for over the past several months. "Help me with Montana," he whispered. He'd do anything for that woman, and Robbie looked up at him.

"Momma?"

"Yeah, buddy," Bishop said. "We have to be a big help to Momma from now on. Okay?"

"No Buck's," Robbie said, lifting his arms so Bishop could pull off his frosting-stained shirt.

"No Buck's," Bishop confirmed. "You've gotta be on your best behavior tonight, all right? For Momma."

Chapter Thirty-Two

Dorothy Glover ripped at the weeds in front of Bull House, wishing they were a metaphor for the things that had crowded into her life that she could so easily get rid of. Not that these particular weeds were giving up easily.

They had long, deep roots that Dot had soaked the ground to try to convince them to let go of. She managed to get one where the root didn't break off so the errant plant couldn't grow back, and she tossed it into the big wheelbarrow nearby.

Her daughter, Glory, sat on a blanket several feet away. Ward, her husband, had staked a huge umbrella in the ground to keep the tiny girl out of the sun, and Dot had slathered her fair skin with plenty of sunscreen. She wore a big beach hat for babies in red, white, and blue too, and she currently clapped together two of her teething rings.

Dot grinned at the tiny human she'd had a part in creating. She'd never considered herself very maternal, though she'd wanted to be a mother. The very moment Ward had passed their daughter to her, everything in her life had changed.

She now had weeds clogging up her schedule that she needed to get rid of. She had things she didn't want taking her time that currently took too much of it. She needed to soak the ground, put on her gloves, and get to work.

She sat back on her haunches and wiped the back of her dirty glove across her forehead. Dot was very used to being knee-deep in mud, and the scent of it actually calmed her. She looked up into the sky and then at the homestead, where two of her sisters-in-law lived, one with a husband and one without.

Oakley had sold Mack's a couple of months back, and Dot had seen the change in her. She no longer had so much hanging around her neck—invisible things that Oak hadn't even known weighed her down.

That was how Dot felt about From the Ground Up, her landscaping company. At the same time, she'd poured so much time, sweat, tears, and money into the landscaping company. Before, it had brought her much joy and a sense of satisfaction. She still felt at home every time she drove onto the property and saw the big piles of barks, rocks, stones, and mulch.

She loved Brutus with her whole soul, and so did a lot of the children here at Shiloh Ridge. The fleeting thought that she could sell the landscaping company without her dump truck as part of the assets ran through her mind, not for the first time.

"Talk to Ward," she muttered to herself, also something she'd been doing more and more of lately. She still hadn't mentioned how she felt to her husband. He was one of the foremen here at the ranch, and they didn't need the money generated by From the Ground Up. In fact, Dot had been donating her monthly salary to the women's shelter in Three Rivers for the duration of this year.

She stood and rinsed her hands in the hose, then took a long drink of the cold water while Glory babbled, "Ma ma ma ma ma," at her. Dot dropped the hose on the next section of land that she'd try ridding of weeds and went to sit in the shade with her baby.

"Heya, my darling baby," she said, picking up the girl and pulling her onto her lap. Glory put a ring in her mouth, which silenced her. "Should we talk to Daddy today? Find out what he thinks about having us here at home all the time?"

Right now, she either took Glory to work with her, as the infant could ride around on deliveries or play in a play pen in her office, or Ward put the girl in a sling and took her with him. There were only rare times he couldn't have her, and they'd only asked Oakley or Etta to tend to her a few times.

For some reason, Dot wanted her and Ward to manage their child. They'd chosen to have her, and while everyone needed help from time to time, she didn't want Glory in daycare full time or with one of the ranch wives every single day.

She was a little over seven months old now, and she

changed so much in a single day. Dot didn't want to miss any of her milestones, even the ones as slobbery as getting a new tooth.

"Howdy, Dot," Holly Ann said from the road, and Dot looked up from her baby's chubby legs.

"Howdy, Holly Ann." She'd married another of Ward's brothers, and Dot sure did like all of the women in the Glover family. She and Ward hosted meals and activities at Bull House for his core siblings, of which he had four, and Dot knew them the best. She was also particularly close to June, who just lived down the road and around the corner at the Ranch House, and Charlie, as they seemed to be the three quieter women in the overall Glover family at Shiloh Ridge Ranch.

Sometimes the three of them got together on their own, each with a single baby now, and they enjoyed brunch without a lot of good-natured bickering or any yelling at all. It was downright peaceful. In fact, June had invited her and Charlie for "afternoon tea" tomorrow, in the hopes that the babies would nap while they had cookies and lemonade in the shade.

Dot couldn't wait to go, but a flicker of guilt stole through her that Holly Ann hadn't been invited. She indicated the huge blanket in the shade. "Do you want to sit for a minute?"

"Sure." Holly Ann pointed for Gun, who came running toward Dot.

"Auntie Dot," he said. "My cousin be coming."

She grinned at the little boy. "Which one?"

"Cousin Garrett."

"My sister is almost here," Holly Ann said. "Someone was so excited, we couldn't wait in the house." She smiled at Gun as she pushed the stroller with her little girl into the shade and knelt beside it. "Weeding?"

"Trying," Dot said.

"I hire someone to do that for me," she said as she got to work on unbuckling Pearl Jo.

"Yeah, I know," Dot said, grinning at her. "Almanzo says he loves coming to work on your lawn." They laughed together, and Dot knew she didn't have to take care of the yard at Bull House. She *wanted* to, and that was why she did it.

"I can't believe it's July," Holly Ann said. "It feels like this year has gone by so fast, doesn't it?"

"It sure does," Dot said. Maybe she could ask Holly Ann how she managed to have two kids and keep running Three Cakes. "Hey, can I ask you something?"

"Yeah, sure." She reached for one of the teething rings Glory had discarded and tried to entertain Pearl Jo with it. The girl didn't seem terribly interested, and Glory grunted and tried to swipe it.

Holly Ann smiled and gave it to her while Dot tried to organize her thoughts. "Do you ever think about quitting the catering?"

Holly Ann's dark, deep eyes locked onto Dot's. "From time to time," she said, her voice somewhat cool now. "But I really love it, and I can do a lot of it from home." She dug in the bottom of her stroller and came up with a bag of crackers. "Gun, sit down for a minute. Garrett will get here when he gets here." She handed him the snack, and Gun did what she said.

"Are you thinking of selling From the Ground Up?"

"From time to time," Dot said, which was a complete lie. The words even tripped coming out of her mouth. Holly Ann cocked one eyebrow at her, and Dot sighed. "It's all I think about. It's just...I worked so hard on that place, and what am I going to do instead? This?" She gestured to the blanket on the front lawn, the umbrella, the hose quietly soaking the ground so she could weed along the front of the house.

"Yes," Holly Ann said. "This. And all those hot dog roasts you and Ward do. Dutch oven night was spectacular. I think we should do a dessert-only night. Campfire desserts. Eat dinner first; join us at the ranch firepit for a dessert bar not to be missed." She grinned with the strength of gravity, and Dot gave the same smile back to her.

"I love that idea," she said.

"You and Ward are cornerstones of the ranch," Holly Ann said. "He's the foreman, and you're the foreman's wife. Those events at the firepit? They're important for ranch unity."

Dot shook her head about the time Holly Ann said *cornerstone*. "Anyone could do them."

"Anyone *could*," Holly Ann said. "But they don't. You and Ward do them, because somehow, you know we need it as a family, and you know the cowboys and cowgirls who live in the cabins here need a community to belong to. Who do you think provides that?"

"Sammy," Dot said instantly. "I see her out every week, pushing that stroller around with treats in the bottom of it."

"Well, no one's Sammy," Holly Ann said, looking out toward the road that ran in front of the house. The breeze stopped, and it was so quiet. The stillness up here at Shiloh Ridge had been something Dot had definitely had to get used to. Sometimes she fired up Brutus just to infuse some rumble into the world.

"But what she does is behind-the-scenes. It's personal, and important," Holly Ann added at the end. "The big events are twice as important, in my opinion. They bring people together."

"So you're saying I shouldn't be dreading tonight's s'mores extravaganza."

Holly Ann giggled and shook her head. "Oh, no," she said. "You should be dreading it. I'm dreading it, but for an entirely different reason."

"Marshmallows and little boys," Dot said, because she knew Gun, and sure enough, he perked up at the M-word.

"Marshmallows?" he repeated. He got to his feet and went over to his mom. With her kneeling, they were about the same height. "Momma? I have marshmallows?"

"No, baby," she said. "Not right now. That's tonight. That's why Auntie Bethany Rose is bringing Garrett."

"How long tonight?" Gun asked, his face scrunching up as if he could truly understand how time passed.

"Let's see." Holly Ann plucked her phone from her back

pocket. "It's eleven hours till tonight, Gun." She smiled at him and looked at Dot, clearly saying that her son had no idea what that meant. She'd humored him though, and he looked at his hands.

"I have ten fingers."

"Right," Holly Ann said. "It's one more than that." She looked down the road as the tell-tale sound of tires over the gravel roads met their ears. "I bet that's my sister. It was good to chat for a minute, Dot."

"Yes," she said as Holly Ann took the crackers from Gun and put Pearl Jo back in the stroller. They left, with Dot waving to them, and she was once again left alone with Glory. She hadn't thought of herself as "the foreman's wife," and she wondered if Charlie did.

She and Preacher lived down at the bottom of the hill, somewhat removed from this part of the ranch. They did come up to everything at the firepit and True Blue, and as Dot truly thought about it, she and Ward had gone down to the things Preach and Charlie planned for their cabin community around the farmhouse.

Sudden joy burst into her life, and she set Glory back on the blanket. She'd finish the weeding, and when Ward came home for lunch, she'd talk to him about doing some personal weeding in her life too.

* * *

"Just toss them in there," she said to Hailey Winters a few days later. The ten-year-old had been helping Dot with the yardwork around Bull House and the homestead for the past several weeks, since school had gotten out.

Today, they were finishing up with the roses at the homestead, and then Dot would fertilize the lawn and they'd be done.

Hailey put the dead heads—the roses they'd clipped from the bushes along the south side of the house—into the wheelbarrow and watched as a truck came up the rise to the top of the hill. "Dot," she said, but Dot had already seen Etta's truck.

She abandoned the clippers in the green waste that would go into their compost pile and headed for the front of the house. Hailey ran along behind her, catching her pretty easily as Dot didn't move all that fast, even when she was in a hurry.

Today, Ward sat on the front steps with Glory in his arms, and he rose as Etta parked in front of the homestead.

"Did you know she was coming today?" Dot called to him, but she could tell from the shock on his face that no, he did not.

Dot grabbed Hailey's hand and kept her at her side. "Hailey," she whispered. "Let's give her some space."

"I haven't seen her in so long," Hailey said, only a touch of whining in her voice. Dot hadn't either, though she'd gotten lots of texts from Etta. She'd been staying down in town with Ida and tending to their mother for weeks now.

Since she left to go to San Antonio with August. She'd never come back from that trip—well, she had, but not to the ranch. In truth, she'd only been gone for a single day's time, and then she'd come to the homestead while others slept, packed a few things, and retreated to her twin's side.

Dot knew she and August had broken up, but she didn't know why. She had no idea what version of Etta would emerge from the truck, and she turned toward Ward as he came down the sidewalk.

"Hailey," he said gently. "I want you to stay right here with Dot, okay?" He gave her a warm smile and passed Glory to Dot. "Let me talk to her for a minute." He turned serious again with his arms free, and he headed for the gravel parking area in front of the house.

"Come on," Dot said. "Let's go get something to drink. We don't need to stand here and stare." She guided Hailey toward the house, throwing one last look over her shoulder before she ascended the steps. Etta sat in the truck, but she'd rolled her window down and was talking to Ward.

"I miss her," Hailey said. "Daddy won't tell me what happened, but he's sad too. He misses her too."

"I'm sure he does," Dot said gently. She didn't want to speak for Etta or August or anyone. She'd enjoyed the man, because he seemed like a good match for Etta. Though she loved a good party, she was one of the quieter Glovers too, and Dot knew her heart. She was a kind woman, with a pure soul, and she'd been devastated to learn that Etta and August had broken up, if only because she knew how upset Etta would be.

But Etta had respectfully asked the ranch wives to leave her be, and as far as Dot knew, they'd done it. Dot herself certainly wasn't brave enough to drive down to Ida's and press her presence on Etta if she didn't want it.

"I miss her too," she said. "She hasn't been around the ranch for weeks, and she left a big hole here."

"Yeah." Hailey accepted the bottled lemonade Dot gave her, and they'd both barely taken a drink when Ward's voice entered the house.

"...in here." He came through the arched doorway, plenty of anxiety in his eyes. Etta followed only a couple of steps behind him, and she set down her purse and her overnight bag and looked at Dot, Glory, and Hailey.

"My Hailey," she said, plenty of love and happiness of her face. Hailey burst into tears and ran to Etta, who gathered her up into a hug. She held her close, stroked her hair, and whispered in her ear.

Ward came toward Dot and took the bottle of lemonade she offered him. "She says she's back, and she expects a big party tonight in her honor." He frowned as if that news made him quite unhappy indeed.

"Let's do a campfire dessert bar at the firepit," Dot said. "I can run to town and get everything easy."

Ward looked at her, admiration growing in his eyes. "That's a great idea, sweetheart. I'll go with you." He touched his lips to her forehead. "She's putting on a brave front."

"People will have questions."

"She said she can handle them."

Etta released Hailey, her eyes wet, and she came toward Dot. "Oh, I missed you so much," she said, taking Dot and

Glory into her arms simultaneously. "How are two of my favorite people?"

"Amazing," Dot said, holding Etta with her one arm as tightly as she could.

"I heard you're going to pull back from From the Ground Up." Etta pulled away from Dot and took Glory right from her. She kissed the baby, who grinned and flailed her arms, because she knew exactly who Auntie Etta was.

"I am," Dot said, glancing at Ward. He'd been the one to suggest perhaps just scaling back her role. Moving some of her employees into management positions, hiring more people, and then simply doing the paperwork, the behind-the-scenes owner work. Dot had liked that idea, as it eased her away from the company while still allowing her to have a part in it. "Oakley did that with Mack's for a while, and I talked to her too. She said it was a good first move."

"I'm happy for you." Etta kissed Dot's cheek. "The yard here looks wonderful." She smiled as Hailey came to her side. "I'm to understand that the two of you have taken over for me? I really appreciate it."

"Dot is really good with things," Hailey said. "Oh, my goodness, Etta. You haven't seen the fairy garden. Come on." Her whole face brightened, and she tugged on Etta's hand as she went toward the back door. "Come *on*! You're going to *love* it."

"Fairy garden?" Etta looked at Dot with surprise, but she turned and followed Hailey before Dot could say anything. They left, and Dot knew what Ward meant.

"That's a really big façade," she said. "She's hurting so much, and that fairy garden...isn't going to help."

"I thought you and Hailey built it for her."

"We did," Dot said miserably. "And how do you think she's going to feel about that?" She looked at her husband. "Every time she sees it, she's going to think of that girl. She's going to feel lonely and guilty and heartbroken over and over again." She shook her head. "I didn't know." She pressed her eyes closed and prayed for forgiveness right out loud.

"Forgive me, Lord, I didn't know things weren't going to work out with her and August." She opened her eyes and looked at Ward. "What should I do? Take it out?"

Ward looked troubled too, and he'd likely forgotten about the fairy garden. Dot and Hailey had built it in a few hours, the morning Etta and August had flown to San Antonio.

"Let's give it some time," he murmured. "Things might work out between them yet."

"How?" Dot wanted to know. She searched her husband's face, and she wasn't sure what she saw, but it was something. "Ward, you better start talking right now."

Instead, he pulled his phone from his pocket. "Read those texts I got only a few seconds before Etta showed up."

Dot took his phone, stupefied as he casually drained the bottle of lemonade while she unlocked his phone. The top texts were from August Winters, and Dot drew in a sharp breath.

Then she started reading.

Chapter Thirty-Three

Etta was aware of the increased noise beyond the door separating her inside her suite and the rest of the house. She pressed her eyes closed, realizing what a mistake she'd made. She never should've told Ward she expected a big party for her return.

At the moment, she wasn't even sure what she wanted. Her twin had been extremely kind to her to let her stay in her home in a quiet suburb of Three Rivers for the past few weeks. Etta had known it was time to return to Shiloh Ridge about four days ago, and she hadn't been able to bring herself to make the drive until today.

She had to go right by Preacher's farmhouse and the cabin community where August lived unless she wanted to drive all the way to Amarillo and then come onto the ranch via a dirt road. Since it would take three hours instead of thirty minutes, she'd decided against that plan.

Still, driving past August's cabin, which she couldn't

even see from the dirt road, had been incredibly hard. She also had no idea how they could possibly have a party here at the ranch without inviting him and Hailey.

She looked out the window, which faced east and overlooked the land on the ranch that went toward the highway. Thankfully, she couldn't see August's cabin from here. She certainly could feel his presence in her heart, however. Just the fact that Hailey had been working in the yard with Dot testified of that.

"And the fairy garden...." Etta pressed her hand to her heart as her tears reared up again. Hailey had worked incredibly hard on it, obviously, with each patch of rocks and succulents chosen carefully and placed with love. Etta had felt it pulsing from the small space right on the corner of the house.

Dot had apologized profusely in a long text, saying she and Hailey had made the fairy garden the day Etta and August had flown to San Antonio. Dot had wanted to distract Hailey from missing her father, and she'd loved going down to the nursery and picking out all of the things for Etta's fairies.

The text had only hollowed her out further, and Etta didn't think that was possible.

She'd never felt this alone in her life, even after she'd faced Noah Johnson and told him she couldn't marry him unless he could stand to have at least one child with her. Closing her eyes, she got transported right back in time, straight into the brides' room in True Blue.

She stood in front of him, twenty minutes late for her

own wedding, wearing the dress, the crown, the perfect shoes. Ward had come to find out why she hadn't come down the aisle, and he, Ranger, and Ace had collected Noah from the altar and brought him to see her.

She'd told him how much she loved him.

He'd held her tight and said he loved her too.

She'd finally confessed that she wasn't okay with not being a mother, and she'd asked him: "Can you stand just having one more child, Noah? I only need one."

Time slowed then, the clock above the door ticking with each painful second. In the end, Etta had gotten her answer when Noah's eyes had fallen to the floor. His voice only added pins and needles to her organs.

"I can't, Etta. I'm done with children." He looked up at her, those dark eyes broadcasting several emotions at once: desperation, love, loathing, anger. "This is a deal-breaker for you?"

She nodded, pressing her hands together. "I'm sorry, Noah," she said. She'd apologized so many times. *I'm sorry, I'm sorry, I'm so sorry.*

He'd left through the back door, and Etta had changed out of her wedding dress alone. Only then had she allowed her beloved sister, mother, sisters-in-law, cousins, and cousins-in-law into the room.

They'd rallied around her for many long months after that. She knew each of them, at some point in the past few years, had spent time on their knees in her behalf.

"And for what?" she asked bitterly. "For me to be a

replacement mother and wife for someone far greater than me?"

"Etta?" Ranger said, drawing her attention away from the past, from August, and from the window. "Hey, sorry." He came toward her as tentatively today as he had the day she should've married Noah. "I think we're ready to go over."

"Over where?" Etta asked, turning away from the window completely. She let her eldest brother bend and hold her in a hug. She sighed, but she managed to hold onto the tears. She didn't want to spend forever crying.

And she would not cry tonight. Whatever they'd planned was a celebration—her celebration.

"Ward set up a campfire," Ranger said. "We figured that would be easiest on short notice. No cleaning up here afterward. Lots of space for as many people to come as possible." He pulled away and offered her a kind smile. "Come on. We'll stay by you."

"Who all is out there?" she asked, tugging on the end of her blouse. She'd showered and changed since returning to the homestead just before lunchtime. She'd eaten something out of the fridge and disappeared into her suite for the past several hours, and her stomach growled at her for more to digest.

"Just us," Ranger said. "Our core family, Etta." As he watched her, his dark eyes glittered. He was always so calm and so steady. Etta loved him and appreciated him so much, and she wanted all the best things for him and Oakley and their children. "Bear's family will all be at the firepit. We called Simone Walker, and she spread the word through their family."

"Ranger," Etta said. "That's too much."

"Oh, it doesn't stop there," he said. "Duke invited his family. Libby called her mama." He grinned at her. "I think you forgot who Bear was. He put it on the ranch owner's text, and well, the boys from Three Rivers are on their way. Gavin Redd and his family are coming, along with some of their cowboys. Montana's aunt and uncle have been there for an hour, tending to the campfire for Ward."

He nodded toward the exit. "Come on. You never get the credit you deserve, and you said you wanted this."

Etta studied the carpet at her feet and shook her head. "What's wrong with me, Range?" She lifted her eyes to her brother's with as much bravery as she could. "Honestly, now."

"Etta," he said quietly, but with plenty of chastisement. "There's nothing wrong with you."

"There must be," she insisted. "If I knew what it was, I would fix it." She looked away and brushed at her eyes. "I would try, at least. Maybe it's an unfixable problem."

"There is no unfixable problem with you," he said, sliding his hand through her elbow. "Come on now. We're not going to leave you alone for a single moment tonight. You don't need to worry."

Etta went with him, but her heart beat strangely. "You're not going to leave me alone for a moment tonight, because August is going to be there, isn't he?"

"I mean, Ward sent it out on the ranch group," Ranger

said. "So August'll have gotten the memo. He won't come." Ranger led her through the doorway and into the living room. To her left, Ward, Ace, and Ida waited right along the back of the couch. Brady even wore his police uniform, and he gave her a kind smile.

"If there's a problem tonight," he said. "I'll take care of it for you, Etta."

She smiled at him and went around the back of the couch to give him a hug. "Thank you, Officer." She hoped he knew it was for everything he'd put up with over the past few weeks she'd stayed in his guest bedroom. Of course, he and Ida had gone out on several fun dates while she babysat their twins, so he probably couldn't complain too much.

"There's not going to be any problem tonight," Ward said, taking his daughter from Dot. "Everything is over there, and a bunch of people have arrived already. It's just a walk over." He took Etta's hand and squeezed it. "Okay?"

"Is there food?" she asked. "I haven't eaten much today."

"There's food," Oakley said with a smile. "I think you might've forgotten who you're dealing with."

"Been down in town too long," Ace said, grinning too.

"I tried to do just a campfire dessert bar," Dot said. "But Holly Ann insisted on food."

"A party needs food," Holly Ann said. "I'm not going to apologize for that. Plus." She hit the last word hard. "Bob and Jackie brought a ton of barbecue, and the Bellamores brought an enormous suckling pig. You can't blame *me* for having food."

Dot laughed, and Etta knew no one was unhappy about

the party. "I was teasing," she said. "Though I do think we tend to complicate the menu in this family."

"Oh, no one's denying that," Ida said. "Who's going to get up on a chair and explain it all tonight?" She grinned around at everyone, and Etta's heart filled with love once, twice, three times.

"I love you guys," she said, her voice breaking. She opened her arms, and her siblings and their spouses all stepped into her, engulfing her right in the center of all of them. She told herself this was enough. They loved her, and they would never give up on her. She wasn't a replacement for them, and she never would be.

"We love you, Etta," a few of them chorused, with more saying, "I love you," and "You're my favorite."

She held onto Ace's shoulders tightly on her left, and Ida on her right. She wished she was strong enough to weather this break-up on her own, but the fact was, she wasn't. She needed someone to come to her house and take her for a walk, the way she'd done for Preacher last year. She needed someone to remind her to test her blood sugar, the way Ward did for Dot. She needed someone to reassure her that there really wasn't something unfixable inside her, the way Ranger had just done.

"Okay," she said, inhaling all of their strength, courage, and bravery into her own lungs. "I can go now."

"Let's go," Ace said, and the group broke up. She ended up about in the middle of the group as they gathered their children and headed out the back door. At the bottom of the steps, Gun slipped his hand into hers and started talking about the frogs he and his cousin, Garrett, had caught a couple of days ago.

The little boy had a lot of energy, and Etta only had to say a few things on the walk over. She could hear the chatting and music before the outdoor pavilion, tables, chairs, and firepit came into view. Ward and Dot had been working on this spot on the ranch for a while now, and she wasn't surprised to see shades set up, plenty of seating for everyone, and three long tables filled with food.

"My goodness," Etta said, pausing at the corner of the barn.

"I told you there was a lot of food," Holly Ann said. "Bob had a huge gift card at Down Under, and he went the moment he heard of tonight's shindig." She linked her arm through Etta's. "Come on. I'm with you and starving for some real food." She leaned closer. "I missed you like you wouldn't believe. I'm so sorry about August, and you can come sit with me any day you need to."

"Thank you, Holly Ann," she murmured.

"We have a large back deck that sort of shows the whole world. Aurora sits there sometimes when she needs to think. The two of you could come together." She gave Etta a wide smile. "I know how much you love that girl."

"I do love her," Etta said, glancing around to find her. She stood with her husband and three of Ollie's uncles. It seemed like every Walker had cleared their schedule to come up into the hills and eat barbecue chicken and s'mores.

"Now, I would recommend the turkey-bacon-cream-cheese pockets, but I'm a little partial to them." Holly Ann and Etta arrived in front of the spread of food, and Etta hardly knew where to look.

"All right, everyone," someone said, and Etta flinched away from the extremely loud voice. Bishop didn't just stand on a chair—he'd climbed halfway up a ladder. He waved one arm and put the megaphone up to his lips again.

"I think it's time to start. Traditionally, in the Glover family, we can't eat until everyone knows what's available, and that honor falls to me tonight." He grinned like what he was doing was a real honor indeed, and he looked down at the table. "There's barbecue chicken and brisket from Down Under. They sent up mild, medium, hot, and raspberry sauces. Cinnamon butter for their rolls, which I may or may not have sampled to make sure they weren't poisonous."

The crowd twittered, and he grinned out at them. Etta's spirits lifted, and she decided this party was exactly what she needed. She took in the other familiar faces at the party as Bishop talked about the sides that came with the meat, and she caught Bear's eye.

He lifted his fist to his heart, and Etta couldn't help weeping at his love and kindness. Sammy looked like she wanted to come over and talk to her now, but Bear held her hand and bent his head to whisper something to her.

"Auntie Etta," a little girl said, and she bent down to lift Lynn into her arms.

"What, sweetie?"

She held up a rock with a smear of purple paint on it. "I made this for you. I'm glad you're home." She hugged her and Etta tried to hold back her tears, but she could not.

"Thank you," she whispered into the sweet girl's hair, and she met Willa's eyes several people over.

Sorry, Willa mouthed, but Etta shook her head. This was no problem. Cactus stood behind their three boys—none of whom had actually come from him—and he too lifted his fist to his heart.

Etta had seen the men do this for each other at their weddings, and it signified some sort of unspoken brotherhood. She'd adored that about them, but as she received the gesture, it became so much more personal.

It became absolute acceptance of who she was, flaws and all. It represented forgiveness, though she wasn't perfect. It meant pure love, despite arguments or disagreements, past or present.

She wasn't sure if she should make the gesture back, so she just nodded. Lynn squirmed, and she set the girl on her feet and took the rock. "Thank you, baby."

Lynn ran back to her parents, and Etta met Judge's eye. He pressed his fist to his heart, and Etta accepted his love— she accepted him just how he was. Mister grinned at her as he made the gesture, and she touched her fingers to her lips and gave him a soft air kiss.

She could barely look at Preacher, because she'd grown so close to him over the past several months. He wept for her, and that nearly undid her composure completely. Both he and Charlie pressed their fists over their heart, and Etta finally repeated the gesture back to them.

Ranger had his fist over his heart, as did Ward and Ace.

Everywhere Etta looked, in every face, she found love, forgiveness, and acceptance.

"And finally the dessert bar," Bishop said, and Etta looked back to him on the ladder. "Dot's going to go over that." He started to get down from the ladder, and Etta turned sideways toward Holly Ann to let Dot by.

"You owe me so much for this," she muttered to Etta, and sure enough, she got up on the ladder with the megaphone, her face the shade of a ripe tomato.

"We have all the fixin's for s'mores," she said. "But not just the regular kind. There are three types of chocolate. Two flavors of graham crackers. We have regular marshmallows and the ones dipped in toasted coconut. There are peanut butter cups, Rolos, and Whatchamacallits as well. So go wild on the candy bar s'mores."

She grinned, clearly finding her stride. "We have starburst to roast, and about two tons of aluminum foil to make roasted banana boats. There are walnuts, chocolate chips, coconut, strawberries, marshmallows, and about six different toppings—caramel, chocolate, butterscotch. You know what toppings are."

Dot didn't pull the megaphone away from her mouth before she let her sigh out, and Etta grinned at her, a laugh actually starting to form down inside her stomach. She hadn't laughed in so long.

"We have foil packets with personalized apple pies in them, courtesy of Jeremiah Walker. He says they take five minutes in the coals, and I daresay he brought a truckload, so don't hold back with those."

"Yeehaw!" someone yelled, and Etta searched for the Walker who'd done it. It wasn't hard to find Wyatt Walker, especially with Micah giving him a nudge and Skyler shaking his head. Both Skyler and his wife, Mal, held a child in their arms, and that was quite the feat for Mal, who looked like she could deliver her third baby any moment now.

Jeremiah had five little humans either surrounding him or in his arms or his wife's, and Rhett and Evelyn still just had their older boy and the triplets. They'd grown so much, it seemed, since Etta had seen them last, which had honestly only been about a month ago, at church.

She hadn't been able to get herself to go listen to a sermon on the Sabbath Day, and not just because she didn't want to see August there should he happen to go.

"Squire Ackerman put in two Dutch ovens of peach cobbler about a half an hour ago when he got here. He says they'll be done in another thirty minutes, if you want to save room." Dot looked down at her cards, but Etta's attention got stolen by Micah and Simone Walker's little girl.

She had to be close to two now, and she had the biggest, brownest eyes on the planet. Etta's heart yearned for a girl like her, and she suddenly knew that while her siblings loved her, and everyone had gathered here for her, that she still wanted children of her own.

"Tripp and Liam Walker brought three flavors of ice cream to go with your apple pies or cobblers," Dot read from her card, and Etta's gaze drifted to the Walker twins. They stood next to Ollie, who had somehow gotten the

Glover message, and he pressed his hand to his heart and lowered his head in acknowledgment of Etta.

He was such a kind boy, and she loved him so much. Next to him stood Squire, and when her eyes caught his, he reached up and tipped his hat. Beside him stood Pete Marshall, who ran the equine therapy programs out at Three Rivers, and Garth Ahlstrom, the foreman. Their families had grown up so much over the years, and Etta wasn't surprised to find tall, lanky teenagers beside all three men, all of them eyeing the dessert table like they'd attack the moment Dot got down from the ladder.

She saw Gavin Redd and his family. Brit and Gabi Bellamore, who'd brought their family's pig and all the sides. Libby had told Etta about the picnics at Golden Hour Ranch, and they didn't have to uproot their family traditions and bring it here for her.

But they had.

All of these people, they had come here for her.

Gratitude flowed through her, and her tears blurred the faces of Jed, Max, and Royce, all cowboys who lived up here on the ranch. Walt, Bill, and Jess all stood near one another, and they all lived down in the cabins near Preacher.

With August.

As if on cue, Jess shifted to his left, and Etta got a clear view of August behind and to the side of him.

He'd come. Hailey was not with him, and Etta started searching the crowd for her, finding the girl easily with Lincoln and Zona's family. Duke stood next to his father, one hand on his arm, and he and Zona seemed to catch Etta's eye at the same time.

They too both lifted their fists to their hearts, and Etta smiled at them though her heart seemed to beat up and down inside her chest.

"There's lemonade, sweet tea, hot chocolate, and almond punch, the last of which came from Golden Hour Ranch, and I hear people pay a lot of money to get that stuff. There's plenty. I'm going to stop talking now, because I can smell the impatience on y'all." Dot lowered the megaphone and looked down to the step. Her head snapped back up. "Wait. My lovely mother-in-law is going to say a prayer over the food first. She is so fast, you guys."

Etta wanted to giggle the way others did, but her pulse clogged her throat. The men in the group reached up to remove their hats, and still her heartbeat bobbed up and then down, practically landing in her stomach before shooting toward the roof of her mouth again.

She couldn't help glancing over to August, but he'd moved. Panic struck her. Had he left? Where had he gone?

Of course he left, she thought as her mother started praying. *I can't believe he came at all.*

"...thank Thee for this glorious summer evening, on this beautiful ranch in the great state of Texas."

Etta glanced at Mother, Texas-proud as she was. Ranger stood next to her, holding the megaphone in front of her mouth. "Bless the food, and any who brought it. Bless them with health and strength and bless all of us to have the same by partaking of the food. We're grateful for the good people who've gathered her to welcome Etta back to Shiloh Ridge. Lord, we're so grateful for her in our lives. She had touched every heart here, and we ask that Thy influence will be made known in her life. Bless her to know how much she is loved by all present."

Etta squirmed inside her skin, and thankfully Mother moved on to something else. "We're grateful for our Lord and Savior Jesus Christ, and ask Thee to help us to include Him in our lives and live as an example of His name. Amen."

That was all Etta wanted—to include the Lord in her life and show others how He would love them if He were here.

"Etta," someone said, and every cell in her body thrummed. She tilted her head down, knowing who it was and exactly where August had moved. She couldn't breathe; she couldn't speak.

"Can I talk to you for a minute, please?"

Chapter Thirty-Four

"Sir," a cowboy said, and August looked at him. He was clearly a Walker, and his first instinct was to shrink back and fade behind the nearest building. "She's gonna be busy tonight."

"Come on, August," Ward said, putting himself between Etta and August. He looked at the Walker man, the two of them moving to stand shoulder-to-shoulder, and held up his hands in surrender.

He didn't want to cause a problem. He just wanted to talk to Etta. The moment he'd seen her, a whisper had started in his mind. It now screamed at him not to let these men keep him from her. At the same time, she would be mortified if he called attention to her—attention she didn't want.

"Okay," he said, but Etta said, "It's okay, Ward." She put her hand on his arm as she moved to his side. "Really, Wyatt. It's okay."

"Etta." Ward folded his arms and put one leg in front of her again. "I don't think you should go. This is your party."

Etta looked at August, and he stilled. He dropped his hands, and he didn't take another step backward. He wanted to talk to her. He wanted to be with her. Tonight, she wore a pair of soft, blue shorts that fell to her mid-thigh, and a blouse in purple, blue, and white tie-dye. Her hair had been plaited back into pigtail braids, showing her elegant neck and big, dark blue eyes.

He was *so* attracted to her, and he had never wished harder that he could go back in time and fix something. Not even when Josie had died. If he only got one chance to fix one thing in his life, it would be the conversation in the rental car in San Antonio with Etta Glover.

"Are you hungry, August?" Etta asked, his name so even and calm in her voice. Bishop Glover stepped to her other side, and Preacher moved in front of Wyatt.

"Is there a problem here, August?"

"No, sir," he said. "No problem." He started to turn away, and then looked at Etta again. "Maybe another time." He reached up and touched the brim of his hat. "I am quite hungry, ma'am."

"Me too," she said, stepping past the row of cowboys, who seemed to multiply by the moment. August couldn't even take in all the faces, but by the time Etta had taken the three steps between them and reached for his hand, at least a dozen fierce-looking cowboys had joined her bodyguard squad.

Her fingers slipped through his, and August squeezed

for all he was worth. She faced the line of cowboys and asked, "Ward, can August and I eat by you and Dot?" She looked right. "Or maybe Ace? Holly Ann said the turkey-bacon pockets are amazing."

"No," Ranger said, moving in front of all of them. "What Etta wants is dessert first." He kept coming, and he took Etta's hand right out of August's. "You come with me, sissy. August will make you a personalized apple pie and top it with your favorite ice cream." He glanced at August, the kindness and love in his expression changing in a micro-second as he met August's eyes.

Had he not read the texts August had sent that morning? He'd sent them individually to Ace, Ward, and Ranger, and he knew the cowboys had seen them. These men lived on their phones, ran the ranch, and didn't ignore the chirps their devices made.

"Right?" Ranger asked, and August nodded.

"Sure," he said, the tension in the air more than he wanted. He turned slightly toward Etta as her brother drew her away. "Sorry, sweets. I'll be right back."

She nodded in her refined, sophisticated way, and then the line of cowboys swallowed her whole. Ward stepped forward, two tin foil packets in his hands, one of which he offered to August.

"You do know her favorite ice cream, right?" Ward asked.

"We brought fudge ripple, caramel pecan crunch, and strawberry cheesecake," one of the Walkers said, and August assumed it was one of the twins, either Liam or Tripp.

Ace flanked August too, and whispered, "Of those, caramel,"

August's heart took flight, and he said, "I think Etta would like the caramel pecan crunch with apple pie."

"Good man," Ward muttered, and they arrived at one of the three campfires that had been built in the gravel area beside the barn.

Another cowboy stood there, and he turned as Ward, August, and Ace approached. "There's room for a couple more right there by the peach cobbler."

"Have you met August Winters?" Ward asked. "This is Squire Ackerman. Great man. Great cowboy. Owns Three Rivers Ranch."

"Pleasure," August said, reaching to shake the man's hand.

"And his partner in crime," Ace said. "His son, Finn."

Squire grinned at him like it was Christmas morning. "We went to court this week," he said. "Finn really is legally my son." He put his arm around the teen. "And he's going to be a senior this year, and I can't believe it."

Finn grinned too, and August felt like this meeting might have been staged. He decided he didn't care. He knew now that there were plenty of families out there. They came in all shapes and sizes, and some of them were all connected by blood, but there were many, many who were simply bound together by love.

His love for Etta had never been in question. His sanity? Sure. His inability to make decisions? Obviously. His poor communication skills? Of course.

"Two pies?" another cowboy asked, and August handed him the tin foil packets. The man—obviously a Walker—took them and stooped to put them in the fire.

"You okay, Jeremiah?" someone asked, and he took the time to stuff August's packets in the fire before he straightened, a grimace on his face.

"Yeah," he said.

"I'm pretty sure your wife needs you, bro," the man said. He looked at August. "I'm Skyler Walker." He stuck out his hand and shook August's.

"August Winters," he said.

"*The* August Winters?" Skyler asked, looking at Jeremiah, then Ward, then Ace. "The one we're not supposed to like?" He moved his gaze down to August's boots and back to his hat. "I like him." He grinned like he knew exactly what he was doing. "Of course, I've always been the black sheep of the Walker family."

"We like August fine," Preacher said, appearing at his side. "He's an excellent cowboy and a great father." He looked at August, no smile in sight. "He's going to make things right between him and Etta, I'm sure of it."

"I'm trying," August said. "Just waiting for the pies."

"Let's go over it quickly," Ward said, bending down as if he wasn't talking to August. "Do you need any tips? Anything? What's the plan?"

"Plan?" August asked, looking at the few men who'd gathered around. "I was just going to apologize and try to explain."

"Oh, cowboy," Squire said. "You need more than that."

"You need flowers," Skyler said. "I won Mal over with flowers."

"Yeah, I'm sure that's all it took," Jeremiah said dryly. "It's *food* he needs, you guys. Thus, the apple pies and ice cream."

"Food and flowers?" Preacher asked. "She's not a man, you fools. What she wants is to know that she is absolutely the very first thing you think of in the morning, August. She wants to know that you will love her from now until forever. She needs to know that yes, you made a mistake, and it won't be the last one, but that every single time you mess up, you'll fix it."

"Yeah, that's good," Ward said. "I like how that sounds."

"Me too," Squire said. "Say all of that." He looked at Finn. "Take notes, son. You might could use some of this with Edith."

"What are you boys talkin' about over here?" a woman demanded, and everyone jumped.

"Hey, darlin'," Squire said, sweeping his arm around the woman. "Just checking on the cobbler and chatting about that new horse trailer at the IFA."

"Did you see that one?" Jeremiah asked. "The one with the shutters that open at a certain speed?"

"Wasn't it incredible?" Ward said. "I told Bear we needed it, but you know how Bear is."

"How is Bear?" Bear asked, and once again, everyone turned toward him, August included. He did enjoy the camaraderie among all of these cowboys, and under different circumstances, he'd love to stand here and chat with them about ranching, horses, and trailers.

Bear had a way of striking fear into a man's heart, but when August looked at him, he found compassion mixed with determination. "I need to steal August for a minute," he said. "Are his pies done?"

"Forty seconds," Jeremiah said. "That's almost a minute."

"Should do," Bear said. "August?"

August hadn't texted Bear and asked him to just tell him one thing: If Etta could possibly, if the circumstances were right, forgive him. No one had answered him.

"Sure," he said. "Be right back." He stepped away with Bear, and for how little August wanted eyes on him, he certainly felt plenty. They didn't go far, and Bear tilted his head down. "Etta's saving you a seat over there, and she's got it in her head that you two are going to eat and talk. True?"

"I hope so," August said. "I'm in love with her, Bear. I'm not going to make this worse." Well, he might, but he'd been praying for a solid ten hours since getting Ward's text about that night's welcome home party for Etta.

Bear nodded, his eyes skating over to the tables of food and back to the firepit from where he'd pulled August. "All right. I'll do my best to help you with the women." With that, he walked away, putting his arm around Sammy, who clearly wanted to know how the conversation had gone.

"August," Jeremiah called. "Apple pies are up."

He went back over to the fire and took the paper plate with the two tin foil packets on it. "Thanks."

"Ice cream is over here," Liam Walker said. "Did I hear you say you wanted caramel pecan crunch?"

"Yes," August said, following him. He now realized that all of these cowboys weren't against him. They were...on his side. They wanted him to make things right with Etta, and they'd help however they could.

As Ida's eyes tracked him, August knew he needed to win over the women in order to make things right with Etta. He seemed to have gotten the men on his side already, and he nodded his head at Ida. She cocked her hip and folded her arms, her expression saying, *How dare you show up here?*

Her attention got diverted by Smiles, and she bent down to talk to him, releasing her grip on August. He let Liam scoop a healthy amount of caramel pecan crunch onto the steaming apple pies, and he figured he now had food to help win back Etta's affections.

In the end, Preacher would be right. The food, the flowers, anything August could get for Etta—none of it mattered. Everything hinged on what he had to say.

His throat dried right up, especially when Liam nodded to another table and his twin, Tripp, said, "Go on. It's only hard for the first sentence."

Halfway to the table where Etta sat with her back to him, an empty seat on her right, Aurora fell into step beside him. "She adores you, and I can guarantee you don't need to say a whole lot. Lead with *I love you*."

"Thanks," August murmured, because he saw Oakley coming as Aurora peeled off to the side.

She moved in front of him. "Tell her she is nothing like your first wife."

He nodded.

Sammy stepped to her side, both of them facing him now. "Tell her she is the only woman you want for the mother of your children."

"Got it," he said, nodding. He didn't dare move yet, and Sammy and Oakley stepped apart.

"Go on, now," Sammy said. "I can't stand to see Etta hurt for another second."

August's stomach lurched, because he hated that he'd caused any unrest for her at all. She hadn't been back to the ranch in almost a month now, so he knew he had. He loathed himself for the three words that had caused her to get out of the car and fly home alone.

I don't know.

He knew.

He knew for sure.

He arrived at the table and slid the plates in front of Etta and then took the seat next to her. Etta looked at the dessert and then him. He had no idea what to say to her, and he cursed his thick tongue and thicker mind.

He opened his mouth, calling on the Lord for strength and help. *Please, please*, he begged. "I love you, Etta Glover," he said. "I was such an idiot in San Antonio, and I would do anything to go back in time and fix that."

She picked up a plastic fork from the middle of the table and tugged the plate closer to her.

"You are nothing like Josie, and in no way are you simply

a replacement. There is only one woman I want in my life, and that's you. You're the only one for me, and the only one I want to have more children with, and I believe with everything inside me that we've each had a rocky, pothole-filled path to where we sit right this second."

He looked around, noting that there were plenty of people standing there, all of them obviously listening in, including Oakley, Sammy, Ida, Ward, Bear, Tripp, Liam, Aurora, Montana, Dot, June, and Holly Ann.

And even more.

He focused on Etta again as she put a bite of apple pie and ice cream in her mouth.

"But I believe that God has given us those paths so we could understand one another. So you and your big, loud, beautiful—if a little nosy—family could heal me. I know with everything inside me that He led me to this ranch, and that the first person I met here was you."

He took a big breath, his mouth running away from him now. "I love you. I love you so much I can't even quantify it. I'm so sorry for my idiocy and how insecure and unsure I've been. I just...let myself get in the way of being with you, and I'm not going to do that anymore. I'm not. I'm sorry. Please, please...."

He pulled back on the begging. "I'd love it if you could take some time to think about what I've said and perhaps give me a second chance." Done, he reached for a fork too. "Now, how's the apple pie?"

Etta hadn't taken another bite, and she looked up at the

women standing across the table from the two of them. "Ladies?"

August could only blink and stare as everyone lined up on that side of the table held up a paper plate with a number on it. He saw ten, ten, ten, nine, ten, ten, nine-point-five, ten, ten, and he knew what was happening.

Ward held a ten on his plate and wore a huge smile on his face. Ranger too, and he lifted his fist and pumped it as if August had just hit a homerun.

Etta surveyed the crowd, and she looked at August. His first instinct was to apologize again, but instead, he said, "You are the only woman for me. I know this won't be the first time I mess up, but I will work my hardest every time I do to fix it."

"Atta boy," someone whispered, and he recognized Preacher's voice.

"I suppose I could stand to give you a second chance," Etta said. A smile burst onto her face near the end of the sentence, and the huge crowd that had come to Shiloh Ridge that evening for a campfire dessert bar started to whoop, cheer, clap, and whistle.

Etta leaned toward him, and August didn't care how many people were watching, he took her face in his hands and kissed her.

She kissed him back, and everything that had been knotted and gnarled suddenly relaxed. "I love you," she breathed against his lips, and August enjoyed the touch of her fingers in his hair, along the edges of his beard. "I'm sorry I left San Antonio. I've regretted it every day, every hour, and every minute since."

"I have never thought of you as a replacement." He touched his lips to hers again in a sweet, chaste kiss as the cheering continued.

Etta broke the kiss and pressed her forehead to his. He kept his eyes closed and just breathed in this woman he loved so very much. He felt her smile, and a moment later, she lifted her head and then stood up. August went with her, and they faced her friends and family.

They encircled them on all sides, and August smiled and accepted their congratulations, finally feeling like he was worthy of Etta Glover.

Now, he just had to figure out the perfect proposal. As Ace stepped into him and clapped him on the back as they hugged, August said, "I'm gonna need some advice on the proposal."

"No problem," Ace said. "I'll call a meeting of the brothers and we'll work it out."

August faced him, gripping Ace's shoulders. "Thank you, Ace. I mean it."

"You both deserve to be blissfully happy," Ace said.

"And you will be," Ward chimed in, taking August into the next hug. "Good job, brother."

"Yeah," Ranger said. "Welcome to the family, August." He hugged him last, and August finally did feel like he belonged to this family. They were his, and he was theirs. He didn't have to try to navigate life alone anymore, and pure love and relief filled him.

Etta came back to his side with the plate of apple pie and said, "Walk with me for a minute?"

"I'd go anywhere with you," he whispered, and she grinned at him. They walked away from the group, all the lights, all the fires, and all the noise. It wasn't dark enough to fade into nothing, but Etta led him around the corner of the barn and paused in the shade.

She looked into his eyes, dropped the pie, and kissed him again. He grinned against her kiss, because she didn't want to talk or walk. She just wanted to kiss him where no one could see.

He was definitely happy to oblige, and he pressed her into the barn behind her and kissed her the way he'd kiss the woman he loved.

Chapter Thirty-Five

Etta remembered what August had said to her in the Top Cottage months ago. At least it felt like months to her. *I hold everything I want when you're in my arms.*

She'd known that if he came to the party, she'd forgive him. She'd known the moment she saw him, her love for him would erase the past few weeks of isolation and hurt. That was exactly why she hadn't come back to Shiloh Ridge for so long.

Ida had told her it was time, and Etta agreed. Either she was going to move on and find someone else, or she was going to fight for the man she loved.

She broke the kiss with August and took a deep breath of the heated evening air. "I'm sorry I stayed away from the ranch for so long."

"I don't blame you." He ran the tip of his nose down the side of her face. "I don't know why you felt like you needed to, but it's okay."

"I needed to, because I knew once I saw you, everything would be okay again, and I needed to decide if that's what I wanted."

He pulled away, and Etta offered him a smile. "August, I think I knew the moment I saw you bent over, helping Hailey in front of the barn, that you were the man I'd been waiting for." She'd been out with three other men in the months leading up to meeting August last fall, and she'd liked two of them quite a lot. But there hadn't been this urgent, kicking motion of her heart.

"Remember how I asked for your number before I could leave? How Mrs. Lambert was all frowns and folded arms?" He laughed lightly, and Etta's grin widened. "What did she say to you after I ran off to get on the bus?"

Etta loved the feel of his hands in her hair, and she closed her eyes and just breathed in the scent of him. "She asked me if I knew you. I said I didn't, but that you were new to town, so I was being nice." She opened her eyes and looked at him. "I think she knew you'd asked for my number. We've been friends for a while."

"I wasn't trying to hide my attraction to you." He kissed her again, but this one only lasted a moment, as someone came around the corner of the barn with strange shuffling steps, someone else stomping alongside them.

August broke the kiss and stepped away from Etta to let her come away from the barn too.

"Willa?" she asked as the woman leaned against a barrel there. Her hands flew, but she didn't speak her signs to her son the way she normally did. Etta knew sign language, but wow. Willa and Mitch *flew* through the signs, both of them talking at light-speed.

Willa finished and held up both hands, pressing her eyes closed. She drew a deep breath and looked at Etta. Unhappiness and discomfort lived there, and she leaned into the barrel again, panting.

"Are you okay?" She signed slower and looked at Mitch too. His chest heaved, and he was clearly furious. She loved that boy, though he stood taller than her now. He'd turned fifteen this year, and he was all arms and legs, with muscles filling them out as he worked the ranch with Cactus, Bear, and Link.

No, he signed for his mother. *She is not okay. She's pregnant, and she didn't tell me. She's not strong enough for this.*

Etta could barely keep up with him, but she got the signs before switching her gaze to Willa. Thankfully, she spoke this time, and Etta didn't have to read her hands.

"I *am* okay," Willa said. "I just wanted you to help me get home."

She definitely didn't look fine to Etta, and Willa wasn't moving away from the barrel either. "Let me get Cactus," she said, but Mitch's hands flew about how he didn't need Cactus to come in and save the day the way he always did.

"You will not talk about him like that," Willa said angrily. "That man has loved you from the day he met you, and he has done nothing but take care of you and love you and give you everything you want."

Mitch lowered his arms, his dark eyes blazing with energy. Frost, his hearing dog, stood at attention at his side, and Etta had no idea if she could step between Willa and Mitch without getting punched in the face with their angry energy. She wanted to take August's hand and slip away, but she wasn't sure how to do that either.

"Cactus and I are a team," Willa said in a calmer manner. "He is my husband, and your father, and I am okay."

"No," Mitch said out loud, his voice warbled and lower than Etta imagined it would be. She hadn't heard the boy vocalize much, and she looked at him in surprise. "Not okay." He signed something else that looked like *I can't believe this*, and stalked away.

Willa sagged into the barrel, tears flowing down her face.

"August," Etta said quietly, and he didn't need to be asked. He moved over to Willa and put his arm around her.

"I'll get you home, Miss Willa," he said almost under his breath.

"I'll get Cactus," Etta said. Before she could move in the direction of the party, Cactus came around the corner of the barn. He took in the situation and stepped to Willa's side, replacing August.

"Sweetheart," he said. "I thought Mitch was going to help you get home. What happened? Are you okay?"

She clung to him, sobbing, and Etta's heart broke for her. For Mitch too, and she glanced in the direction he'd gone.

"I'm not okay," Willa said. "Cactus, I can't do this. My

back is killing me, and I can't walk, and I'm what? Four months along?" She looked up at him in pure desperation. "Mitch found out, and he is *furious*."

"I'll talk to him."

"Give him some time," Willa said.

Before she finished speaking, a couple of people yelled from the direction of the firepits, but it wasn't a cheerful yell. Etta stepped that way, alarm pulling through her. Bishop appeared and said, "Cactus, Kyle just punched Smiles. We need you."

"Good Lord," Cactus said, and he flew away from Etta and after Bishop, both of them returning to the party at a jog.

The gravel crunched and shifted, and when Etta turned, she found August holding Willa in his arms. Her mind raced. Kyle was such a sweet boy, and she'd literally never seen Smiles without a smile in the past couple of years. What could've possibly happened to cause Kyle to hit him?

There were dozens of adults to handle that, and Etta turned to August and Willa. "Come on," she said, shouldering some of Willa's weight on her left side. "Are you parked far, August?"

"Not at all," he said. "Right over here." They moved that way, and Willa walked in a painstakingly slow way, saying her sciatic nerve had been acting up as the baby grew.

Etta simply let her talk and then said, "I'll bring you some lemongrass and marjoram. It'll help with inflammation."

It took both of them to get Willa in the truck, and both of them to get her into bed. She said she'd be fine there until Cactus returned with the kids, and August and Etta returned to the barn. "Hailey's okay," he said. "We could just walk for a bit."

"I want to find Mitch," she said. "I don't think he should be alone."

"Let's find him then." August put his hand in hers, and they started down the path between the stables leading away from the party. There didn't seem to be any commotion happening anymore, and Etta would certainly hear about it anyway.

"When do you want to get married?" August asked. "Do you want to do it here?"

"No," Etta said quickly. "I don't want to do it here."

"I find that surprising."

"I was supposed to marry Noah in True Blue," she said. "I had that wedding. I don't want it."

"What do you want?"

Etta looked up into the darkening sky and glanced around for Mitch. She didn't see him, and she exhaled out all of the tension and frustration in her bones and body. "I want to be married outside," she said. "With everyone there, of course. I want us to go down the aisle together—I don't need to be escorted or given to you. We'll go together, side-by-side. And Judge will marry us, and I'll have a picture with all the nieces and nephews in my wedding dress." She grinned at him.

"Outside here?" he asked.

"I don't know," Etta said thoughtfully. "What do you want?"

"I want you to have what you want," he said. "There are other farms and ranches around here. Maybe some of them do weddings."

"Mister and Libby got married at Golden Hour," she mused. "I know some of the Walkers got married right on their property."

"It's a good thing you know so many people in town," he said, his voice touched with dryness.

Etta stalled and stared at him. "August Winters," she said. "Did you just use sarcasm?" She laughed, the sound pealing up into the sky and making her heart grow wings.

He laughed with her, and they arrived at the last barn before the fields gave way to the road and then the Ranch House. Etta heard sniffling, and she paused. Another couple of steps, and she found Mitch sitting on the bench Ward had put there for Preacher.

He used to make Preach walk from the Ranch House to the barn, and he needed a midpoint rest to make it back. Mitch sat there, his head down and Frost's head in his lap while he stroked him.

Etta released August's hand and moved that way tentatively. She sat a few feet away from Mitch, both him and the dog looking at her. "Can I sit here with you?" she asked, moving slowly through the signs.

He shrugged, a universal *I don't care. I don't know.*

Etta swallowed, not sure what to say to him. He dropped his eyes back to the dog, and Etta could feel their bond. August sat beside her, and she slipped her hand into his. The three of them simply sat there, and nothing came to Etta's mind to say to the boy. Perhaps just being here with him would remind him that he didn't have to suffer alone.

On the bench beside him, his phone flashed with lights, but he ignored it. Frost put one paw on the phone, but he pushed it back down and shook his head. He obviously didn't care to read his texts, and Etta smiled to herself.

Mitch was growing up, and he had opinions and a personality of his own.

She lifted one hand to try to get his attention, but he didn't look at her. She knocked on the bench, and that got him to turn toward her. "Do you want me to read them?" she asked. "I can tell your mom and dad that you're okay, and you're with me."

He pushed the phone closer to her. Etta didn't reach for it but released August's hand so she could talk with both of hers. "You can come stay with me tonight. We'll sleep in as late as we want, and I'll make the steak and cheese omelet in the morning for breakfast. You don't have to go out to the ranch tomorrow, and I'll deal with Mister Prickly about it."

Mitch started to smile at her, but his face folded on itself as he began to cry. Etta immediately scooted over to gather the boy into her arms, and she held him tightly as he wetted her shoulder with his tears.

"Shh, shh," she soothed him.

Mitch straightened, and he signed to her. *How do I help*

my mom? And I'm a monster for being mad at my dad. He shook his head and looked away, his hands still flying. *I am mad at him though. He shouldn't have let this happen. It's selfish and we have enough kids at the Edge, heaven knows.*

It was hard to catch sarcasm and dryness in sign language, but Etta had interacted enough with Mitch to hear it in the silent movement of his hands. She tapped his knee and waited for him to look at her. "You help your mom by doing anything you can think of that she might need help with. It's five months, Mitch. Not forever. And when you're mad and overwhelmed and want to yell at her or your dad, you come to me, and I'll listen to you and feed you." She offered him a shaky smile. "Okay?"

He nodded and reached for her hand. Etta held it for a few moments, and then she reached for his phone. His mom and dad had both texted him in a group text between the three of them, and Etta responded to them by saying that she was with him and she was taking him to the homestead with her that night.

"Come on," she said, handing his phone back to him. She signed the next part so he could understand. "I didn't get many desserts and no food, so I'm still hungry. Can we go back to the party for just a little bit?" She stood up and looked at August and Mitch. "Just the three of us. You two can keep all the ranch wives from asking me questions about, well, everything, and we'll eat hot dogs and nachos and so many s'mores, we'll be sick all night."

She grinned at them while August chuckled and got to his feet. Mitch stood too, signing *okay*, and the three of them linked arms and started back toward the firepit and the party.

When Etta's phone rang in her pocket, she ignored it. Everyone needed a champion, and right now, she was going to be Mitch's.

Chapter Thirty-Six

Cactus mashed his fingers around the brim of his hat as he stood on the porch with Kyle. The doorbell sang through Bear's house, and surely the man hadn't gone to work yet. Cactus knew with every bone in his body how early the mornings had been coming lately, and Bear had a couple of years on him.

His brother opened the door, took one look at Cactus and Kyle, and sighed. "Everything is fine," he said.

Kyle said nothing, though he held his cowboy hat in his hands too. Cactus had taught him to be apologetic when going to ask for forgiveness. The boy remained silent, though his throat worked, and Cactus nudged him with his foot.

The children he and Willa had brought to the ranch last year had come with a steep set of challenges, most of which Willa and Cactus had been able to manage at home. They'd come up with the idea of having family lessons every

Monday night, and Cameron, Kyle, and Lynn had learned how to be polite, respectful, clean up after themselves, have a conversation, and ask for help with their homework.

The basic things of life that Cactus thought all children learned, he'd realized that Cam, Kyle, and Lynn hadn't. Willa had made chore charts for all of them, and Cactus had been teaching them about animals, fences, pastures, horses, and every other aspect of a cattle ranch. He adored summertime on the ranch, and he'd loved having his boys with him for the past several weeks since school had let out.

"Kyle," he prompted.

"I'm real sorry, sir," the boy said. "I don't know what I was thinking, and I hope y'all—and Smiles—can forgive me."

"We already talked about it last night," Bear said.

"The boy wasn't able to apologize properly last night," Cactus said, noticing movement behind Bear. Russ came toddling over to him, his face lighting up.

"Uckle Cacus."

"Hey, buddy." Cactus bent down and held out his hand for the boy to give him five, which he did. Cactus straightened and met his brother's eye. Bear grabbed onto him and gave him a hug.

"Things happen. They're boys, and it's probably not going to be the last time one of them gets hurt."

"This is different," Cactus whispered, and they both knew it. He stepped back and looked at Kyle, his eyebrows raised.

Kyle's bottom lip trembled, and he swiped at his eyes. "Is

Smiles here? Can I give him a hug?"

"Yeah, he's around somewhere." Bear stepped back and looked over his shoulder. "Smiles, there's someone at the door for you."

"Comin'!" the boy yelled, and Kyle pressed into Cactus's side.

He put his arm around the boy's slight shoulders and held him tight. "It's okay," he said. "Once, I punched Bear in the nose, and I had to do the very same thing you're doing now."

"How old were you?" Kyle asked, sniffling as little boy steps ran toward them.

"Oh, what? Forty-five?"

Kyle's eyes widened, and Cactus chuckled. "He'd done something that made me really mad, and I lost my temper."

"I did something really stupid," Bear said. "I deserved it."

"Smiles didn't deserve it," Kyle said. "I just...I honestly don't know what happened. I just got so mad." He'd given the same explanation last night as Cactus and Willa had sequestered him in their bedroom to question him and find out what had possessed him to slug another human being.

Smiles came around his dad's legs, a smile stuck to his face, of course. The slight bluish-purple bruise on his cheek testified of what Kyle had done, and Cactus closed his eyes against the sight of it.

"Smiles," Kyle said, dropping to his knees. "I'm so sorry for hitting you." He grabbed the boy in a hug, and Smiles embraced him right on back.

"It's okay, Kyle," Smiles said, still smiling.

"See? Fine," Bear said.

"I called a counselor for kids," Cactus said. "After I called our case worker. I guess if there's anything like this that happens, the child has to go see someone."

Kyle straightened, and Cactus drew him right back to his side. "Kyle doesn't want to go that badly, but I told him I've been seeing a counselor for about five years now, and there's no shame in it."

"None," Bear said, crouching down. "Kyle, we love you. I do, and Sammy does, and Smiles does. Don't even spend another minute thinking about this, okay?"

"Yes, sir," Kyle said, his voice tinny and filled with emotion. "I'm sorry, sir."

"You're a good boy." Bear drew the child into a hug too, and Cactus sure did love his brother in that moment.

"All right," Cactus said, clearing the emotion from his throat. "We've got work to do this morning. See you out there, Bear."

"Yep, I'll be out later." Bear lifted his hand in a wave, and Cactus and Kyle headed for the steps that went back to their truck. Once inside with the air conditioning blowing, Cactus looked at Kyle.

"You did real good, son. It's hard to admit you've done something wrong and apologize for it, but it feels so good afterward."

Kyle drew in a deep breath. "It does feel good." He looked at Cactus, fat tears still gathering in his eyes and then rolling down his face. "I'm sorry, Cactus. I'm sure you won't want to adopt me now."

"Nonsense." Cactus pulled the boy into another hug across the console. "As soon as we know anything—*anything*—about your dad, then we'll know. Willa and I would adopt all three of you tomorrow if Mister Millhouse would let us."

Kyle sniffled into his shirt and nodded, and Cactus stroked his hair. "I love you, boy. Not your actions. You're exactly what Bear just said—a good boy. You just did something stupid, like me taking a swing at my brother's nose."

Kyle pulled back and smiled. "What did he do that made you so mad?"

Cactus chuckled and put the truck in reverse. "He bought your momma a car and didn't tell me. See, Uncle Bear is a fantastic man, but he has a bit of a superhero complex...."

They trundled down the road, and Cactus sighed as this situation came to a close. Now he just had to figure out what to do about Mitch.

He hadn't come home last night, and Willa had cried until almost midnight. They knew he was safe and cared for with Etta, and neither of them had asked her to send Mitch home. Everyone needed a safe place to fall, and Cactus had thanked the Lord profusely for his cousin and that she'd been that place for Mitch.

With Willa's back and hip in a bad way right now, Cactus had said he'd take care of everything. So it was that he found himself pulling up to the homestead about ten minutes after leaving Bear's.

"You stay here," he said to Kyle. "I'll leave the AC running."

"Yes, sir."

Cactus got out of the truck, faced the homestead, and started praying.

* * *

Mitchell Knowlton couldn't hear the doorbell ringing. He didn't hear any noise coming from the kitchen, though the scent of maple syrup and sausage had woken him. He never heard his mother talking to him, and he'd never heard the sound of his father's voice.

Still, a well of regret lanced through him as he watched Cactus Glover walk toward the front of the homestead. He turned away from the window where he'd been sitting and signed to Etta.

He's here.

She wiped her hands on a dishtowel and nodded, determination and resolution entering her face. Mitch loved her fiercely, and he felt like he did everything in his life all or nothing. Everything was really good or really bad, and right now, he wasn't even sure how to talk to his mom and dad.

His biological father had raised him for a couple of years, and Mitch had hated it with everything inside him. His dad barely knew any sign language at all, and Mitch had often felt isolated and alone, existing with a person who wished he didn't exist at all.

His mother had never treated him like that. She loved

him and wanted him around and had done everything in her power to make his life easier and better. And once Cactus had come along, Mitch's life had improved drastically.

The man *had* loved him from the moment he met him, and when Etta turned toward the doorway that led into the foyer, Mitch assumed the doorbell had rung. Frost put his paw on Mitch's leg and trotted for the front door—another good indication that someone had arrived.

You stay right here, Etta signed. *I will deal with him.*

No, Mitch said quickly, reminding himself to sign slower than he normally did. *I want to talk to him.*

Etta reached for his face and ran her fingers down the side of his cheek. *Are you sure?* Her lips moved along with her hands, and Mitch nodded.

He stepped past the woman he stood taller than and followed his dog into the foyer. Frost sat right in front of the door, his tongue hanging out of his mouth. He backed up as Mitch opened the door inward and faced Cactus Glover, the man who'd been his father for the past few years.

His dad held his hat in his hands, and he wore a look of absolute nerves in his eyes. Part of Mitch wanted to rage at him, and the other part almost burst into tears.

I'm sorry, boy, his dad said, and Mitch lost the battle against being upset with Cactus. He didn't say anything as he stepped forward and hugged his father, Cactus's powerful arms coming around him instantly and easily. He held him tight, and while Mitch was much more wiry than Cactus, he tried to hug him back just as tightly.

They held one another for several long seconds, and then

Cactus stepped back. Mitch sniffed, his face feeling so hot. *I just needed a break*, he said. *I'll be home tonight. Etta said we get the whole day off today.*

That's fine, Cactus said. *Take your time. I just wanted you to know that you have every right to be angry with me. And with your mother. We should've told you.*

Mitch nodded, because they *should've* told him that his mom was pregnant. He couldn't be sure he'd have reacted any differently, but at least it wouldn't have been such a public argument. *She's in a lot of pain already.*

Cactus nodded and dropped his chin toward the ground. *I know*, his hands said. *She keeps telling me she's okay, but I'm going to get her down to the doctor.* He looked up at the end of the sentence.

Maybe they can do some of that physical therapy she did last time, with Chaz. He didn't have to sign slow with his dad, and Cactus said, *Maybe.*

Their eyes met again, and Cactus said, *I love you, Mitch. I'm going to need your help with your mom and the kids.*

I can help, he said. *I never complain about the ranch chores, do I?*

Cactus grinned and put his hat back on his head. *No, but that's because you're trying to bulk up to impress Melissa.* As he signed the last few letters of her name, Mitch grinned and shook his head, as if he could deny it.

Still, he said, *My body doesn't know how to bulk*, he said. *I just ate five pancakes and two pounds of sausage, and I'll probably lose weight.*

Cactus threw his head back and laughed, and Mitch

wondered what the sound of it would be like in his ears. He certainly looked joyful and carefree, and Mitch much preferred that over the timid, worried man who'd shown up a few minutes ago.

He felt vibrations move across his vocal cords, but he couldn't hear himself when he did make sounds. He wondered what his dad heard, what others thought of his voice that never got used. Sometimes he felt so trapped behind his ears and mouth, and other times, he knew exactly who he was and what he could do with his life.

He waited until his dad looked at him again, and then he said, *I love you, Dad.*

I love you too, son.

"All right," Mister said as he rubbed his hands together. "It's theme-deciding day." He looked at the desk in the barn office where Libby usually planned the Country Christmas with Mildred. Her sister wasn't there yet, and Libby forked up another bite of salad from a plastic container, seemingly nowhere near ready to get to work on the festival she ran every year.

He looked around like someone would jump out from behind one of the boxed Christmas trees and tell him he was being pranked. No one did.

"Are we talking about the theme for this year's show today?" he asked.

Libby looked up at him and nodded. "Yes, just waiting for Mildred. Sorry did I not say that out loud?"

"No, you did not." He grinned at his wife and went around the desk to kiss her. "You look tired, love." He dropped into a crouch, his hand going along her back to support her. She'd been getting up early this summer and heading out to work on her family ranch, and Mister worried about what life would be like for them once their house was finished at Shiloh Ridge.

She put in so much time and effort at Golden Hour, and it was twenty minutes from their new homesite.

She sighed into him, dropping her fork and abandoning her salad. "I am a little tired."

"All right," Mildred said, hurrying into the office. "I've got it, and you two are going to *love* this year's theme."

Mister stayed right where he was, though Mildred's enthusiasm entered the room on a tidal wave. He grinned at her and then Libby. "Let's hear it."

"You didn't map out the whole thing, did you?" Libby asked.

"Yes, but you'll see," Mildred said. She held a couple of whiteboards in her hands and she set them against the wall, where another board had been placed. Mister was used to that one being full of ideas, then checklists, until the day the Country Christmas opened.

They hadn't even erased it from last year yet.

"Are you ready?" Mildred turned around, pure excitement in her eyes.

"I suppose," Libby deadpanned, and Mister chuckled at

the two sisters. They got along really well, and Mister sure was glad he and Libby were able to get married soon after Mildred. Libby didn't like sleeping in the house alone, and Mister didn't like doing anything without her at his side.

"Okay." Mildred lifted the first whiteboard and flipped it around. She balanced it on the tray of the one mounted to the wall and stepped back. "Ta-da!"

It read, *Coming soon to a family ranch near you...*

"Oh, boy," Mister muttered.

"It could be a girl," Libby said, and his confusion pulled his eyebrows down as Mildred lifted the other whiteboard.

"What?" he asked.

"Christmas...babies!" Mildred yelled, drawing his attention again. The second whiteboard had cartoons drawn on it, all of them babies. A baby reindeer. A baby Christmas tree —complete with a diaper on it. Baby Santa Claus, which made Mister start to laugh and laugh.

Mildred pointed to a date on the whiteboard, and it read *February tenth*. Pieces started to click in his head, and he glanced down to Mildred's midsection. It was impossible to tell if she was pregnant or not. February was still six months away.

Then, Mildred moved over to the other side of the board and pointed to *April first*. She bounced on the balls of her feet, her mouth about to burst open with something.

Mister didn't know what was going on, but he got to his feet. Libby did too, saying, "Babies, Mildred? How will we do a show for babies?"

"We can dress the horses up like babies," she said.

Mister said nothing, because this was the worst idea for a Country Christmas Festival he'd ever heard. Especially compared to last year's *Rodeo Extravaganza*.

"We can have a baby petting zoo," Libby mused, approaching the whiteboard. Mildred went back to the other side of it.

"Baby monster trucks." She picked up a marker and circled the February date. "I'll be huge, and you won't be small."

"I'll still have three full months," Libby said.

Mister looked back and forth between them, landing on his wife's face when she finally faced him. "Liberty," he said slowly.

She opened her arms to him, tears filling her eyes. "We're going to have a baby, Mister," she said, and he simply stared at her.

He was going to be a father. Him. Have a baby. A tiny human that came from part of him. "Buckets," he said, rushing toward his wife. He gathered her into his arms and held her tight. "You're not kidding."

"Not even a little bit," she said. "I just found out a few days ago, and Mildred said we should surprise you." She pulled away. "Are you surprised?"

"Stunned," he said, happiness filling him from top to bottom and front to back. He looked down at her stomach too, but she had to be barely pregnant. Still, he put his hands on her belly and could feel the life pulsing there.

He met her eyes again and said, "I love you so much," just before kissing her.

* * *

Bear smelled the evidence of his wife's baking as he walked in the back door. "I'm home," he yelled, but no running feet, no baby shrieks of delight, and no Sammy responded. She and the children obviously weren't home.

He'd sent Link to Cactus's just now, as Willa needed some help with their garden, and Link was good for another hour of work.

Bear, however, was not. Exhaustion pulled through him, and he hoped the chocolate he could smell was for him. Knowing Sammy, she'd probably taken all of the brownies around to various people on the ranch.

He swiped up a note on the kitchen counter that said, *Went to see your mother and Aunt Dawna. The cake is for you.*

"Praise the Lord," he muttered, smiling at his wife's loopy handwriting. He moved toward the two-tiered cake on the other counter, the frosting a bright white that looked creamy and sugary from several steps away.

She'd decorated the top, and that was going the extra mile for their family cake. Most of the time, Sammy didn't have enough frosting to even finish icing the cake they ate for dinner. Not tonight.

A wad of balloons rose from the bottom of the cake toward the top, and some writing went over the strings.

"Surprise, surprise, how about five?" he read, and sure enough there were five balloons on the cake.

Bear wasn't the quickest cowboy in Texas, but he

thought he knew what this cake was celebrating. He tugged his phone free of his pocket and dialed his wife.

"Howdy, my husband," Sammy said.

"Tell me straight," he said. "We're going to have five kids, aren't we?"

She giggled, and that was all the *yes* he needed. He started to chuckle too, but Sammy sobered quickly and asked, "Are you happy, Bear?"

He thought about the turkeys he'd chased that afternoon. He thought about the heat raining down on Texas near the end of July.

He thought about his brothers and sister, his cousins, and all those who lived at and worked Shiloh Ridge Ranch alongside him.

He thought about the numbers on his last birthday cake. 51.

He thought back over the fifty-one years of his life, and nothing compared to the past six, since he'd finally gotten up his courage to ask Samantha Benton on a date.

"Yes," he said honestly. "I couldn't be happier."

"Are you sure?" she whispered. "It'll be the last baby, I swear."

"I'm blissfully sure," he said, opening the silverware drawer. "And now I'm going to eat this whole cake, in my air-conditioned house, by myself. You'll be lucky if I'm awake when you get home."

They laughed together, and Bear settled down to do exactly what he'd said he would. Later, when Sammy arrived with the children, she came to kneel beside him on the couch.

"I love you, Bartholomew."

He took her face in his hands and gazed at her. "You have completed me completely."

She grinned at him. "How...eloquent." She giggled. "We stopped by my parents' too. They say hello."

"How's your momma doing?" He sat up and grabbed onto Sammy, pulling her onto his lap. She giggled again, and Bear grinned at her.

He put one palm against her stomach and held it there. "Maybe I'm not the most eloquent man ever," he whispered. "But I sure do love you, sweetheart."

"It'll be the last one," she promised, pushing his hair off his forehead. "You look tired, Bear."

"I'm old, Sammy." He gave her a rueful smile. "I hate to think of you like my mother, dealing with all these kids alone."

"You're not going anywhere for a while," she said, leaning into him to kiss him. "Okay?" She pressed her forehead against his, and Bear simply nodded.

"Can we find out this time if it's a boy or a girl?" he asked.

"All right," Sammy said. "We'll find out this time."

"Get in here," Ward hissed, looking left and right as Ranger and Ace both hurried into Bull House. "She's going to see us."

"She's not even home," Ranger said.

"She has spies everywhere." Ward closed the door and twisted the lock. "August is already here. I smuggled him in through the garage."

"My word," Ace said under his breath. "What's the big deal? It's not like Etta doesn't know he's going to propose."

"She doesn't," Ward said at the same time August said it. He shook hands with Ranger and Ace, and the four of them looked at one another.

"Okay," August said. "So the best thing I have is that it's going to be August tomorrow, and my name is August, so I thought it would be the perfect time to celebrate...you know. Us." He shook his head, a hint of redness coming into his face. "That is the stupidest idea ever."

He looked at Ward, obviously crying for help. Ward grinned and said, "Think about Etta."

"She wants to get married outside," August said. "I went and talked to Jeremiah Walker, and he said we can absolutely get married at Seven Sons. Libby said we could use Golden Hour too. Any day, we just need to let them know as soon as we know—especially for Libby if Etta wants to get married before Christmas."

"She'll want to get married before Christmas," Ward said, putting down four glasses and returning to the fridge. He squinted inside it, needing his glasses to see better. He managed to pull out bottles of water, lemonade, or sweet tea and take them to the table.

"She will?"

"Etta is ready," Ranger said, popping the lid on a bottle of tea. He didn't bother pouring it into a glass first but went straight to drinking it from the bottle. "My guess is she'll need the longest to get a dress, and that's it. Two months, tops."

"That's October," Ace said. "If it's then, she'll want it to be way before the angel tree or halfway between that and Thanksgiving."

"I would think so," Ward said.

"What about your family, August?" Ranger asked.

"I don't know," he said. "They'll either make it work, or they won't." He poured his strawberry lemonade into his glass. "I just need a really good idea for how to ask her."

"What is going on here?" Dot demanded, and Ward jumped to his feet.

"You didn't lock the garage entrance?" Ace asked.

"Rookie mistake," Ranger mumbled as Holly Ann and June came inside Bull House behind Dot.

"Hey, baby," Ward said, taking his baby from his wife. "Nothing is happening here." He gave her a look that said, *Please, don't push this.*

"Oh, honey," Holly Ann said. "It sounded like August was asking for ideas for a proposal." She continued toward the table despite Ward's efforts to block her. "You came to the wrong Glovers." She sat right down next to August. "You should've come to the women."

She gestured the others closer. "Come on, ladies. Let's hear your ideas."

June held up her phone. "I'm calling Ida."

"Don't call Ida," Ward said, rolling his eyes. "*We* have good ideas."

"Let's hear them," Dot said.

"Etta loves cakes," Ward said. "And making posters. And he can include Hailey by making a poster and then baking a ring in a cake, and...." He trailed off, not really sure where this was going.

Dot looked at August. "Do you know how to make a cake, August?"

"Well, I—"

"Etta isn't fussy," Ranger said. "She just wants August on both knees, holding up a ring, and saying he's arranged the wedding at Seven Sons. That's romantic enough for her."

All of the women looked dubious, but Ward thought Ranger was pretty close to right.

"She loves the nieces and nephews," Ace said, "Maybe August could use each of them."

"Now we're getting somewhere," Holly Ann said, reaching for one of the bottles of water, as if she was getting ready to settle in for the long haul. "Cakes, children, and...."

"Bandages," August said, a smile spreading across his whole face.

"What?" Ward asked in tandem with several others. "What do bandages have to do with anything?"

Chapter Thirty-Seven

Etta returned to the homestead after her meeting with the school district office where she turned in all of her paperwork for the year. A sigh pulled through her body, because another school year was about to start.

More classes. More field trips. Another end to summer, and another start to autumn.

She couldn't help thinking about Mother as she crested the hill. She'd eaten lunch with her that day, and Mother had seemed so very lucid. She never slipped on a name, and she'd told Etta all about a bridge championship she'd played years ago.

She'd tired quickly, and Etta had taken her back to her room before making the drive to Shiloh Ridge.

She made the wide turn and pulled up to the homestead, where several other trucks had parked while she'd been gone. "Strange," she muttered, because she hadn't made lunch that day, and she hadn't received anything on the ranch text string about a party.

After collecting her purse, she dropped from the truck—and that was when she saw the first poster. Someone had drawn big, blocky letters that spelled out *Etta + August* and colored them in with bright markers.

She smiled at the sign nailed to the fence down a little bit from where she'd parked. She wasn't sure if she was supposed to take it in or not, as one year, Sammy had planted birthday cards all over the ranch for Bear to find.

"Auntie Etta," someone called, and she turned toward the voice. Smiles limped toward her. "Do you have a Band-aid? I tripped and hurt my knee."

"Of course I do," she said, rushing toward the boy, the sign all but forgotten. She reached him and dug in her purse, sure she had a little baggy of bandages in there.

But she didn't.

"Let's go inside," she said, scooping the boy into her arms. "I have some in the kitchen."

The front door bore a sign that read *August and Etta Forever*, and she grinned at it. "Did you make the signs?"

"No," Smiles said, all traces of his tears gone. "I can read it, Auntie. Can I read it to you? Momma's been teaching me to read."

"She has, has she?" Etta paused in front of the door. "Okay, then. Go on."

"August and Etta forever," Smiles said, not a stutter or hitch in sight. Etta knew then that something was amiss at the homestead—more than just a couple of signs and a boy all by himself.

She opened the door and heard giggles and shushing, and she set Smiles on his feet as she glanced around for more signs and more children.

She couldn't find either.

"Into the kitchen," she said loudly, and she went that way, finding a sign on the side of the fridge that read *August Winters loves Etta Glover.*

She wanted to frame that one, but she moved over to the skinny cabinet next to the stove. "I have bandages in here." She opened the cupboard—and it had been cleaned out. No Band-aids.

"Hmm," she said. "Maybe in my bathroom."

Before she could take a step in that direction, the back door opened, and Mitch limped through it. *Auntie Etta*, he signed. *I fell on the scooter. Do you have a Band-aid?*

"I'm mysteriously out," Etta said as she signed back to him. Plus, he wasn't bleeding.

"Auntie Etta," another teen said, and Link came into the kitchen through the arched doorway she'd just used. "I just kicked the doorway. My toe is bleeding. Do you have a Band-aid?"

Etta put her hands on her hips, grinning at the boys. "You've hidden them all."

"Auntie Etty," a tiny voice said, and Gun came crawling around the end of the couch. He wore a huge grin and started to giggle. That made several other little boys and girls giggle, and Etta looked over the back of the couch.

All of the littles had been gathered there, corralled by Ida and the ranch wives. Etta laughed and shook her head. "What are you guys doing here?"

"Excuse me, ma'am," a big, blustery voice said. "I heard there was a huge need for Band-aids here."

All of the nieces and nephews—including the teenagers —started to fake-cry, and Etta burst out laughing. She looked at August, and he set a couple of plastic grocery sacks on the counter. "Let's see. I've got pink ones. Blue ones. These regular ones, but I wouldn't recommend those. And a bunch with horses on them."

He unloaded box after box after box of Band-aids with horses on them.

Etta stilled, realizing something very important was happening here.

August looked at her, the brightest smile of happiness on his face. He picked up one of the boxes of bandages and came toward her. All of the children seemed to know it was time to be quiet, because a hush fell over the group of them.

"Etta," August said, more serious now, but still with that mega-watt smile on his face. "You changed my life with a simple Band-aid. You told Hailey that Band-aids do so much more than help with bleeding, and you were absolutely right."

He opened the box and pulled something out of it. Dropping to both knees, he held up a huge diamond ring. "With a single Band-aid, you have healed me completely. You took my withered, stony heart, and you made it beat again. You helped me learn how to love again. I love you." He swallowed, hope filling his eyes now. "I love you. I love you. Will you marry me?"

Etta's tears blurred the joy on his face, but she nodded. "Yes," she said through a terribly narrow throat. "Yes, I'll marry you."

He slid the ring on her finger while voices from six months to sixteen cheered, and then the door to her suite opened, the back door opened, and footsteps came thundering down the steps as everyone in the Glover family arrived.

Etta laughed through her tears, because this was about the most perfect proposal she could've hoped for.

"Let them go," someone said, and the next thing she knew, all the children were piling on her legs. She crouched down to hug all of them, and August came with her. Their eyes met, and Etta managed to say, "I love you," amidst the chaos of little voices and chubby fingers and big, bright eyes trying to get her attention.

"All right," Bishop boomed. "The cakes are here. She said yes, right?"

Etta picked up Robbie and stood, noting that August had Chaz in his arms. His daughter ran toward him, and he hugged her with his free hand. Hailey faced Etta, and she passed Robbie to Montana so she could hug the girl freely.

"I love you too, Hailey," she told the girl. "Are you happy?"

"Yes," Hailey said, beaming up at her. "I can't wait for you and Daddy to get married."

Etta looked at August, at the vibrant spirit he possessed and which radiated from him. "I can't either," she said.

She insisted all the children get their cake first, and then she took hers and went with August to the steps in the foyer. "Wow," she said, looking at her left ring finger. "That was incredible."

"You're incredible," he said. "I talked to Jeremiah. He said we can have Seven Sons for our wedding."

"Wow," Etta said, shocked again. "You know he doesn't let anyone get married there."

"Well," August said with one shoulder rising in a shrug. "You're a Glover, and I've heard they're pretty well-known around these parts."

Chapter Thirty-Eight

Dawna Glover appreciated the steadying bar mounted to the wall, and the way her daughters took the time to make sure her gown fell exactly right. She kept her eyes on her fingers— and what old fingers they were. What stories they could tell. What joy they'd been part of, and what heartaches they'd witnessed.

As she'd aged, Dawna had hated the deeper wrinkles and grooves that had come to her fingers. Hands did so much work, and they were always seen. After a few years of creams and treatments that didn't seem to slow aging at all, she'd decided to embrace the hands the Good Lord had given her.

They could still do good, even if they were slower. She could still play bridge, which she did twice a week at Nestled Oaks, the assisted living facility where she lived. She could still make bread, hang ornaments on a tree, and hold babies.

All the good things in life, Dawna could still enjoy.

Buttoning a gown was terribly difficult for her, but as

Ida helped her slow feet into her ruby slippers, Dawna looked up from her hands.

"Etta, I want to do the dress."

"It's all yours, Mother," Etta assured her, the kindest smile on her face. She'd come to sit with Dawna so often, and in the past couple of months since getting engaged to August Winters, she'd brought a binder with her. She'd talked about the plans she was making, and she'd shown Dawna dress after dress, all original designs from Aurora Walker.

The girl walked into the dressing room now, and she stopped in front of Dawna. "All the stars in Texas could not be brighter than you," she said, grinning at Dawna with all of her might. "Just wow. Can I get a picture for my portfolio?"

She'd made Dawna's mother's gown too, and the girl could really work magic behind a sewing machine.

"Of course," Dawna said, releasing the bar. She could steady herself enough to walk, but now, Etta stood beside Aurora and told her what to do.

"Put one hand on your hip, Mother. Push it out a little... yes, like that."

Dawna did, and Aurora tapped on her phone to get the picture.

"Your hair, Mother," Ida said. "Then your makeup, and then we'll dress Etta."

"I'm getting my hair done too," Etta said, linking her arm through Dawna's and taking her out of the master bathroom at one of the homesteads at Seven Sons Ranch and into the kitchen area.

All of the ladies were there, some doing their own hair and some working on others, with various mirrors set up like stations along the long countertop. Skyler Walker had generously donated his whole house as the preparation area for the wedding, and Dawna already had cards ready to mail to every single Walker at the ranch.

They'd been good friends to her sons, daughters, nieces, and nephews, and everyone loved getting a thank you card in the mail.

The whole room paused when Etta said, "Isn't Mother's gown stunning?" in a loud voice. Every eye turned to her, and Dawna felt the love and the power of good women rise through the air.

Oakley came toward her, and she wore a dark purple dress too. Hers didn't have sequins everywhere, nor did it have the dramatic, decorative strap that went sideways across her chest. She beamed at Dawna with tears in her eyes, reaching her and embracing her easily. Out of everyone, the only person who'd come to see Dawna more than Oakley had in the past year had been Ida.

Dawna had a terribly hard time getting down on her knees, and she had since her surgery years ago. But she knew the Lord heard prayers from any bodily position, and she'd been praying that her departure from the earth wouldn't be too terribly hard for Oakley. Ranger too, who'd made the drive down from the very busy ranch to see her often.

She felt like she had a few more good months in her, and she wanted to enjoy each day immensely. Being able to be so present for Etta's wedding was a blessing she'd been praying for as long as she could remember.

She sat and let Montana work on her hair. Holly Ann slicked on a very little makeup. Dot brought her a square of sandwich to eat, as they'd be serving a full dinner after the wedding in just a couple of hours.

Then Lois, her dearest friend for so many decades, took her in her arms and said, "It's time, my friend."

They went back into the master bedroom, where three full-length mirrors stood. Etta already waited in front of them, her undergarments on and ready. The wedding gown Aurora had sewn for her lay on the bed, and Etta looked up and into the mirror as Dawna arrived.

She smiled, and the seconds dazzled like diamonds between them.

"Okay," Ida said, striding into the room too. She wore her Maid of Honor dress, which was a blitzed-out version of the dress Oakley wore. Ida's shone with dark blue that looked like it had been frosted with gems. Etta had wanted deeper, darker fall colors for her wedding, but she hadn't dictated which ones.

Oakley had found a purple dress; Ida's was blue. Dot's could only be described as brick red, and it made her dark hair and olive skin shine like sunbeams. Holly Ann had chosen burnt orange, a color only a woman as talented, tall, and confident as she could pull off. They looked like a bouquet when they stood together, and Dawna loved them all so fiercely.

"Hold onto Holly Ann, Etta," Ida said. "I'll put the

dress down. Aurora will grab it over there." She gathered the yards and yards of fabric from the bed and moved to Etta's side. Holly Ann stepped in front of her and Etta lifted her hands to hold onto Holly Ann's shoulders.

Aurora went to the other side and pulled the dress around as Etta stepped one foot, then two, into it. She and Ida shimmied the fabric up Etta's legs and around her hips, then she threaded one arm through each of the straps.

Dawna stood with Lois, both of them watching as if they were witnessing the queen herself getting dressed. In a way, Dawna felt like she was. Etta had always been so regal. So sophisticated. So proper.

She'd loosened up a little bit, but she bore refined cheekbones and a pair of eyes that could see right into someone's soul. Those things couldn't be erased just because she'd experienced a hard handful of years.

Everyone dropped back, and it was Dot who said, "It's gorgeous."

The other women nodded and murmurs of assent moved through the group.

"Your turn," Lois said quietly, and she released Dawna to go work on the buttons that laced up the back of Etta's dress. Her hands would take some time to get them done, but she'd wanted to help Etta with this particular task so badly.

Aurora got her started and did about five buttons, then stretched up to kiss Dawna's cheek and said, "There you go, Aunt Dawna."

She busied herself with making sure every layer of the

dress lay the way she'd envisioned it would, and Dawna focused on her task.

Every button represented a memory for her, and she wanted to clothe Etta in the good times—and the bad—so she could take all of her experiences with her down the aisle. The first time she'd met August went into a button.

The first day of kindergarten for Ida and Etta, both of them with their hair cut short and huge backpacks on their tiny frames went into a button.

Dawna thought about the time Etta had come to her and proposed the idea of doing community outreach programs through Shiloh Ridge. That memory got poured into a particularly hard button for her to latch.

She thought of Noah Johnson, and how terribly upset Etta had been in the days, weeks, and even months leading up to that wedding. Another button held that memory for her.

The preparation and lead-in to this wedding had been completely different, and those smiles and all that laughter got stitched up in another button.

She pictured Hailey, the darling ten-year-old Etta would have the privilege of mothering, and she got secured in a button.

Dawna's eyes filled with tears as she remembered the numerous occasions Etta had stopped by her tiny apartment after a horrible date. The tears her daughter had shed. The times they'd prayed together for relief. For a solution. For the right man to come into her life at the right time.

She buttoned and buttoned and buttoned, her hands shaking with the effort as she neared Etta's shoulder blades.

"Mother." Ida put her hand over Dawna's, her voice almost a whisper. The quaking stopped, but Dawna could not see her daughter through her tears. "It's okay, Mother."

Etta turned, her full skirts brushing against Dawna as she did. She took her into a hug at the same time Ida did, and Dawna clung to them as she wept.

They were such good girls, and she only wanted the very best life had to give them. She knew there would be hard times. Ups and downs. Happiness and heartache. It was the way of the world. It was how the Lord taught His children the good from the bad.

"I love you girls," she said, opening her arms wider to include all of her daughters who had joined the family. Holly Ann, Oakley, and Dot joined the hug, and they clung to one another the way Dawna hoped they always would.

"You ladies rely on one another," Dawna said. "It's important that you stay close. It's hard to be a cowboy's wife or a police officer's wife, and you'll need each other." She hoped this would be the most emotional she got, and as the group broke up, she brushed at her tears.

Etta turned back to the mirror, and Dawna finished the last three buttons. One for Priscilla and Ranza Glover, who'd welcomed her so completely into the Glover family. One for her dear brother-in-law Stone, who'd loved his nieces and nephews the way Etta loved hers.

And one for Bull, Etta's father and the love of Dawna's

life. *Oh, how I wish you could be here*, she thought. *I miss you so very much.*

Then his presence filled the room, and Dawna knew he *was* there, if only in spirit.

What felt like a blink later, Dawna stood at the altar, her arm once again laced through Lois's. Etta and August were walking down the aisle together, with Hailey, and they'd wanted the whole family to parade down the aisle too.

The evening air held a crispness to it, just the way Dawna had prayed it would. The sun had started to set, but plenty of airy, golden light shone on the huge barn that acted as the backdrop for the wedding.

A huge American flag had been painted on the side of it, and rows and rows of chairs had been set up in front of it. The first four on each side were currently empty, and the Glovers would fill them after they'd come down the aisle.

The Walkers sat in the next few rows, and then a whole row of police officers and their families had come too. Every chair had an ivory covering concealing the back of the chair, and raffia had been tied around the chairs near the seat to make them look fallish and festive.

Street lamps edged the rows, with bright yellow, red, orange, purple, and blue flowers peeking through all the greenery. Etta hadn't wanted anything "too October" like pumpkins or straw bales, and Dawna thought she'd found the perfect balance between farm, fall, and October without going to Halloween.

"Here we go," Lois said, and her arm tightened in Dawna's. The crowd rose to their feet, and everyone turned to face the same direction which Dawna and Lois did.

Ranger appeared first, and Dawna's eyes teared up again. She blinked them back, because sometimes her mind wasn't as clear as she would like it to be. She wanted to see her children and family clearly today, and that meant the tears couldn't make everything blurry.

Her oldest son grinned down the aisle to his mother and lifted his fist to his heart. Then he looked right at his wife as she approached, and they linked arms. She shooed Wilder, their oldest, and Fawn, their youngest, in front of them, and together, the four of them walked down the aisle.

It took a few extra seconds with the toddlers, because they toddled so well but so slowly. Wilder ran the last few feet to Dawna, and she managed to bend enough to pick him up and give him a kiss.

"Gramma," he said, and she pressed her cheek to his.

"Go sit with your daddy," she whispered, passing the boy to Ranger. He gave her a quick kiss on the cheek before he left, and Dawna was reminded so much of Bull when she looked at him.

Her husband's real presence and looks had been given to Ward, and he came next down the aisle, his darling baby girl in his arms. Glory Rose was almost a year old now, but she couldn't walk—and she didn't need to when she had such a powerful, handsome father to carry her.

Dot rested her hand in the crook of Ward's elbow, and they made such a beautiful couple. Dawna had seen the way they took care of one another and she'd felt of their pure, simple love enough to know how lucky they both were that they'd found each other and made their relationship work.

They both paused to kiss her and Lois, and then they peeled off to their seats.

Ace and Holly Ann stepped toward them next, with Gunnison's hand in his mother's, and Pearl Jo on Ace's hip. He looked so healthy and so strong, and Dawna sent up a prayer of gratitude for her son's strength in spirit that had transferred to his body.

"Give Gramma a kiss," Holly Ann whispered to Gun, and she lifted him up to do just that. Then she did, and Ace kissed both of her cheeks before they moved to sit beside Ranger.

Ida and Brady had already started down the aisle, each one of them holding the hand of one of their twins. Judy and Johnny would be three just before Christmas, and they wore outfits that matched their same-sex parent.

Dawna's tears reared again, but she once again pressed against them, drew a deep, steadying breath, and kissed her beloved daughter, son-in-law, and grandchildren before they went to sit down.

She looked at Lois, who smiled back at her, and patted her arm. "Family is such a blessing."

"That it is," Lois murmured. "That it is."

Chapter Thirty-Nine

Lois Glover Parker stood at the head of the aisle, the altar supporting her back and giving her strength. Watching her nieces and nephews and their families walk down the aisle had touched her heart.

Her children and theirs would be coming next, and Lois's chest felt like a stampede of wild horses had somehow gotten inside and were frantic to get out.

She saw her children a lot; this was nothing new. She wasn't sure why this excited, nervous energy ran through her, only that it did.

Perhaps she didn't get to see her children all dressed up like royalty, their children combed and perfected the way she would in a moment.

"Can you believe this is where we are?" she asked Dawna as the parade paused. "Who'd have thought we'd see this day?"

"It's spectacular," Dawna said. "Oh, look at Bear."

Lois couldn't look away as her eldest son—the oldest Glover—came to the end of the aisle. He wore a huge, black cowboy hat, the exact same way his father had the day Lois had married Stone. He brought tears to her eyes, and a smile to her face, and all she could do was press her palm against her pulse.

Bear lifted his fist to his heart too, pressed it there, and then reached for his wife. Sammy came to his side, and Lois still thanked the Lord for the day Samantha Benton had come into her son's life.

Everything—positively everything—had changed in the family on that single day, in that isolated moment in time. She seemed to know the burden she carried, and she did so exceptionally well.

She took Heather from her mother and passed her to Bear, then reached for Lincoln's hand. They'd come to the ranch as a pair, and she still looked at her son with such fondness—the kind Lois felt streaming from her when she looked at her oldest son. Bear whispered to Smiles and Rock, got them in place, and then took the first step down the aisle.

The six of them came proudly, with another baby who would be born in the spring. They made a scene everywhere they went, and greeting the matriarchs at the altar was no exception.

"Look at my tie," Smiles said right out loud, holding it out. "And I have another loose tooth."

"That's so exciting," Lois whispered to him while Sammy tried to herd him away. Bear ended up picking up

Rock and carrying two children to their seats while Sammy tugged on Smiles's hand, her own smile cemented in place.

Lois loved them so completely, but she looked to her second son, who also had a large and growing family.

Cactus wore the same huge hat, his shoulders boxier than Bear's, and his presence just as powerful. He was quieter than Bear, but just as intense, and he stood immediately beside his wife, Willa, who leaned into him.

She was seven months pregnant now, and Lois hadn't seen her in the past few months without watching her cry at least a little bit. Her eyes were dry right now, and she hoped she wouldn't be too uncomfortable during the ceremony. Her son, Mitch, shored her up on her right side, and Cameron, their oldest foster child, held Chazzy on his hip. Kyle and Lynn completed the row in front of Cactus, and the children came toward her and Dawna first.

Lois kissed each one of them, holding them close and telling them she loved them, before she straightened to embrace Mitch.

She signed to him, *I'm so happy you're one of mine*, and kissed him too. She held Willa tightly, and then embraced her son. Cactus knew how to pour his emotions into an embrace; how to let others know how he felt without saying a single word.

Lois's eyes pricked with tears for her good son, and touched her fist to his heart before he stepped away to sit down with his family. He and Willa still didn't know if they could adopt Cam, Kyle, or Lynn, but they should know in a few months.

Judge and June had a much smaller family than Bear or Cactus, and they'd already lined up. Lucy Mae held her mother's hand, and Judge carried their son, Birch. Together, the four of them came down the aisle in measured steps, smiles on their faces, and Judge wearing that same cowboy hat as his brothers.

They must've found one together, because they literally were all the same. "Hello, Mother," Judge said, kissing her cheek, then Dawna's. He passed their son, who was growing up so fast, to June, and he cleared his throat as he moved to Lois's side. He'd officiate the wedding, and therefore, wouldn't be sitting with his family.

Preacher and Charlie stepped to the back of the aisle at the same time, immediately linking hands. She carried their darling daughter, Betty, who could've walked down the aisle, as she'd turned one at the beginning of the summer.

This son wouldn't want to be in the spotlight for as long as it would take his daughter to get down the aisle, and in fact, he and Charlie moved quicker than anyone else. He kissed Lois, and she whispered, "You're walking well."

"Thank you, Mother," he whispered back, and then they moved away. She watched him and Charlie for an extra moment, because while they were quiet and simply put their heads down and got the job done, Lois knew they hurt and healed the same way everyone else did. He caught her looking, and he pressed his fist over his heart as a way to say, *I'm okay. Thank you for checking.*

She did check too. She stopped by the farmhouse every single time she came to Shiloh Ridge, just to talk to Charlie for a few minutes alone. Just to find out how Preacher was truly doing. Her mother heart couldn't help worrying about and praying for the two of them, and standing at the altar, the Lord told her they were okay.

Arizona and Duke Rhinehart stood at the end of the aisle now. He carried their daughter Shiloh in his arms, and Zona rested one hand on her very pregnant belly. She wasn't due for another ten days, but everyone in the family had prayed she wouldn't deliver early. She certainly looked like she could, despite her warm smile as she moved down the aisle.

Lois pressed her eyes closed when she hugged her daughter, because she'd only gotten the one. Zona was having another girl, and Lois had told her how blessed she was to get two girls, something she'd never gotten.

Arizona had grown a lot in the past few years, and she let her husband help her into her chair.

Mister and Libby stood at the back of the aisle now, and they didn't have any children yet. He'd just announced his wife's pregnancy at the family dinner last night, and he'd said he and Libby would be parents come April first. Lois couldn't wait to see her wild son settle into his new role of father, as he'd come so far in the past two or three years as he'd discovered himself and accepted the kind of man he wanted to be.

She'd enjoyed watching him dote on his new wife, and he once again reminded her of Stone. They'd had children soon after marriage too, but for that first year, when it was just the two of them, he'd done the same types of things Mister did for Libby.

He'd pack her a lunch and take it to her without telling her he was coming. He'd change the wash without her asking him to. He'd order desserts and have them sent to her barn office.

Their house would be done in the next few months, and as she kissed them both, Lois couldn't help praying for relief for Bishop and Montana after that.

Of course, there was one more house to be built for Etta and August, but then, she really wanted Bishop and Montana to rest.

They stood at the end of the aisle now, and they looked at one another with pure joy and love. Robbie, who was almost three, stood in front of them, holding Aurora's hand. She gazed at her husband, Oliver Walker, the same way Montana looked at Bishop, and Lois's heart had never been happier.

The five of them walked down the aisle, and Montana had just announced they'd have a little girl at the end of February. The Glover family wasn't done growing, and that only made Lois even happier than she knew she could be.

"Love you, Mother," Bishop whispered, and she held her youngest tightly. Surprisingly, he wasn't the momma's boy— that honor went to Mister—but he'd been his daddy's shadow. Lois loved that about Bishop, and she loved that he'd created such beautiful places for everyone in the family to live together on the land they'd bought and developed.

She drew a deep breath, though the procession wasn't

over. The wedding hadn't even really started yet. There'd be dinner and dancing after the ceremony, and Lois shifted her feet, tired as they were already.

She threw a glance to her husband, Don, who sat on the second chair in on the front row, and his eyebrows went up. She gave him an encouraging smile, because her part was almost over.

Almost.

Shannon and Daniel Jones came together, their fingers easily linking, and they smiled their way down the aisle. Lois and Dawna had been entertaining them in Three Rivers for several days now, and Josie's parents were wonderful, kind people.

Lois had told them before, but as she hugged Shannon in front of the altar, she whispered, "Thank you for letting us borrow him and Hailey."

"They're yours," Shannon whispered back. "And they're ours." She pulled away, tears in her eyes, and Lois could not even imagine the pain of losing a child. She had not had to endure that path yet, and she honestly prayed she would not have to.

She'd experienced a taste of it when Mister had been badly injured in the rodeo. And another big bite of the heartache when Preacher had gotten in his car accident a few years ago. She knew fear, and she understood uncertainty, but she had not had to bury a child.

Her chest stormed, and she prayed for peace and comfort for her, and for Shannon and Daniel, as they watched their once-son-in-law become someone else's husband.

Finally, August appeared at the end of the aisle. He wore a suit as dark as night, with a lighter gray vest, his white shirt, and a tie made of plum-and-apple-colored flowers. His cowboy boots shone in the evening light, and he too bore the enormous cowboy hat.

Hailey, his daughter, put her hand in his, and she wore a white dress with thin straps over her shoulders and ruffle upon ruffle down to her ankles. Lois had been present when Aurora had presented the girl with the dress, and she looked absolutely angelic in it.

The crowd ahh'ed for a few moments before Lois saw Etta emerge from the right. August switched Hailey to his left side, and he brought Etta right into his side, his arm going immediately around her back.

His eyes drifted closed in love and bliss as he pressed his lips to her temple. Hers did too, her smile so complete that Lois was sure she'd never seen a couple more made for each other and more in love.

She stepped away from him and took his hand, holding her bouquet in the other. The three of them marched down the aisle in slow steps, and Lois didn't see a face without a smile on it.

"Mother," Etta said, her voice breaking as she embraced her mother and kissed her cheek. She did the same for Lois, as did August and Hailey.

Then, Lois's part was over. She helped Dawna to her seat right on the end of the row next to Ranger, and she took her place on the other side of the aisle next to Don. He slipped his arm over her shoulders, and she sighed as she leaned into his strength.

"Okay?" he asked, his mouth right at her ear.

"Okay."

Judge stood behind the altar now, and Etta and August faced him. Hailey went to sit beside Oakley, and Lois watched her son prepare himself to speak to the crowd. Judge had done several weddings—including hers—but it was still hard for him most of the time to draw the spotlight onto himself.

He also had a very special relationship with Etta, and Lois couldn't wait to hear what he'd say today.

Chapter Forty

August had already experienced an amazing time at the wedding. He turned as his oldest brother came down the aisle. Lawson also wore a cowboy hat, so he fit right in at this ranch wedding, and he escorted his wife, Paisley, down the aisle, their two kids leading the way.

August stooped and hugged his nieces, then his brother and sister-in-law. They did the same to Etta, who'd passed her bouquet to someone.

Christian came next, and his wife wore a dress that didn't feel entirely appropriate to August. He groaned inwardly, but Etta simply put her hand on his arm and whispered, "She's fine."

Laura was not fine; she was a special breed of human. But Christian loved her, and Laura apparently loved dresses that had a neckline that could show a person's belly button. Their three children held hands and came after them, and another round of hugging, laughing, and kissing ensued.

Finally, August's parents appeared at the end of the aisle, and his eyes welled with tears. He'd been so mad at them after the trip to San Antonio. His father had apologized many times, and despite him asking them not to say a single thing about Etta, they'd all texted to say how wonderful she was and how much they liked her.

"I'm so happy for you, baby," his mother drawled, and she had tears in her eyes when she looked at Etta. "He's so lucky to have found you. All of you."

"I told you there was a lot of us," Etta said as she embraced August's mother. "It'll be so loud later. You can escape to your hotel anytime."

"Nonsense," August's dad boomed. "We're thrilled to be here."

August waved at them to go sit beside Etta's aunt, and Lois made sure they knew where to go.

Finally, finally, finally, August faced the altar, Etta's hand tightly in his. Her cousin stood on the other side, looking proud and perfect and princely—if princes wore expensive cowboy hats.

"Welcome," Judge said. "I'm not sure what else there is to say after that procession. My cousin Etta told me I better give a good speech, because she's the last one of us to get married, and I made her read my vows at my wedding last year."

The two of them grinned at one another, and the special bond between them flowed easily into the atmosphere around them.

"I know a fair few of you have been to all of the

weddings in the Glover family. Many of you have heard me talk so much about family, faith, friends, and loved ones. I've given advice about putting your spouse first, and honoring the family name. I've assured some of you that your loved ones who are gone are not really gone. That they're here with us, and they're happy for us."

He paused, and August looked right into the man's eyes. He radiated such a spirit, and it was no wonder he and Etta were close. They were so similar, yet very different too.

"Today, I'm touched by seeing whole families come down the aisle. It's rare at a wedding to see that. We see groomsmen and bridesmaids. We see children, especially if one of the people getting married has them. We see fathers and daughters." He cleared his throat. "Well, we have no fathers in the Glover family, and Etta's brothers, sisters, and cousins mean the absolute world to her. Rather, the nieces and nephews mean the most to Etta. She's wanted to be a mother for as long as I can remember, and her road to this altar has been very long and very hard for her."

His voice broke on the last three words, and beside August, Etta sniffled. He looked at her, and she smiled at him and gave her head a little shake. She blinked and returned her attention to Judge.

"I think it's a real testament to a person's character," he said. "To watch them go through something hard. She didn't turn her back on the Lord. She didn't leave her faith and curse God. She didn't spend too many nights crying, though I'm sure there were some. She got up every day. She went on dozens of blind dates, courtesy of her sister."

A few people chuckled, but August wanted to hear where Judge was going with this.

"She kept working on the ranch. She kept her family close to her. She focused on what was important to her, and she prayed for an opportunity to come her way." He reached up and wiped his eyes. "I know, because I asked her, and then I copied her when it came to my own relationship."

He grinned at her, and when his attention came to August, he almost shrank back.

"August's road here has not been easy or short either. He lost his wife a few years ago, and that is something I cannot fathom. I'm sure there were many days and nights of turmoil, of feeling inadequate to be both mother and father, and a keen sense of longing to see Josie and speak with her."

He paused, and August took a moment to shuffle closer to Etta.

"He told me that he came to Three Rivers with about two hundred bucks in his pocket, a construction job he didn't want, and a one-bedroom apartment to look forward to. He needed a change. He needed a fresh start. Only four months later, he met Etta while on a field trip with his daughter."

Judge beamed out at the crowd. "I think that story is beautiful. It illustrates the goodness of God in our lives. Yes, hard things happen. Bad things might even happen. There are storms, darkness, indecision, uncertainty, and we often don't know the right thing to do, or the right way to go. But looking at Etta and August, two people who have prevailed over those things—who've kept moving toward the sunlight, praying it would come—I'm encouraged that whatever comes my way, I can handle it. I want y'all out there in the seats to know the same. You might be getting rained on right this very moment. Things in your life are not great. I would advise you, the same way I'm going to advise Etta and August, to keep going."

He drew in a breath. "Look up. Make your voice heard to the Lord. Turn to your spouse, or if you don't have one, a trusted friend. A sibling. A cousin." His voice broke again, and he added, "So many of my very best friends are my cousins, and I love them so much."

Etta reached out with her free hand, and Judge put his in hers. They gripped one another's fingers, and Judge said, "Don't give up. That's my wise advice for you today."

Another deep breath, wherein August reached to wipe his own eyes, and Judge said, "All right. It's time to get the I-do's done and dinner served."

He let go of Etta's hand while he chuckled, and the two of them turned to face one another.

"Etta Irene Glover," Judge said. "Knowing you love this man with your whole heart and soul, do you pledge yourself to him, to be his lawfully wedded wife, for as long as you both shall live?"

"I do," Etta said in a nice, loud voice.

"August Stephen Winters, knowing you love this woman with your whole heart and soul, do you pledge yourself to be her lawfully wedded husband, for as long as you both shall live?"

"I do," August said, his voice strong and clear, for which he was grateful.

"Then by the power vested in me by the great state of Texas, I now pronounce you husband and wife, legally and lawfully wedded for now and for all time."

The cheering started before Judge finished his sentence, but August waited to take Etta's face into his hands and kiss her. "I love you," he said, her smile radiant and glorious.

"I love you too."

He kissed her, and while it didn't last long because of the smiles on their faces, it sure did feel like the right step, the right thing, the fresh start he'd been craving when he moved to Three Rivers last year.

* * *

"Oh, it looks like I have to go, Mom." August got to his feet, his plate empty and his stomach full. His spirit soared somewhere above Seven Sons Ranch, and his love for Etta had reached the stars long ago. "Etta is coming."

His mother stood too, embracing Etta, who'd changed out of her wedding dress and into an equally spectacular party dress. The bright yellow fabric hugged all of her curves to her waist, where it then flared around her hips and fell to her knees. She wore a pair of flat, white sandals, as their post-ceremony dinner and dance was taking place in a huge barn here at Seven Sons.

"Etta, you are a wonder," August's mother said. "This is the best party I've ever been to."

"It's mostly because of Ida," she said, hugging his mom. "And Libby, who knows how to put on a great outdoor party."

"And Holly Ann," August said. "For all the food."

"And Bishop for the wedding cake," Etta added, stepping back. Her smile could charm entire nations, and when she looked at him, August wondered how he'd captured this gorgeous creature's attention. "I know you don't want to, but I want to go around to all of my teacher friends and show you off." She extended her hand toward him, and August would've gone anywhere with her.

"I want to," he assured her. "Mom, can you keep an eye on Hailey?" He found his daughter easily, as she wore the same dress as Etta, both of them having been designed by Aurora and constructed by Ida.

"Of course," Mom said. "Go." She grinned at the pair of them, and August moved with Etta as she led him to the next table over.

"Hey, hey." Peter Marshall rose to his feet and grabbed August in a hug. "Congratulations." He clapped him on the back and laughed. "I haven't seen you out at Courage Reins for a while."

"I've got a slot for when Etta and I get back from Niagara Falls." He stepped back, grinning at Pete. "Carly's got me set up for a monthly slot now."

"That's good news," Pete said. "I'll check the schedule and put myself in your group." He turned toward his oldest son, Paul, as he said, "Daddy."

"What's up?" Pete looked past him, toward the dance floor where adults and kids had taken their two-steps.

"Henry left with Thea." He frowned and folded his arms. "I hate that you asked me to spy on him."

"All right," Pete said, frowning too. "Chels."

"I heard," Chelsea, Pete's wife, said as she stood.

"Thea Olds?" Etta asked. "I did see her with her sister."

Pete sighed as Chelsea strode away, her step set on Mama-Bear. "Henry and Thea have been goin' out," he said. "That boy is going to be the death of me." He turned back to Paul and put his arm around him.

August looked around the table, and Squire Ackerman stood up. He wore gray in his sideburns, but August didn't think the man was any older than he was. "Howdy, August."

"Good to see you, Squire."

"Congratulations, Etta." Squire stepped into her and hugged her, and his wife, Kelly got up to do the same. "I was hopin' you'd wait for Finn to become an adult."

"Dad," Finn, his oldest son, said, plenty of disdain in his voice.

Etta burst out laughing, which broke the tension at the table. "Right," she said, giggling. "Like I would take Finn from Edith—which is a great name, by the way."

"Edith?" Kelly asked, her eyes narrowing at her son. "You said she moved."

"She did move," Finn said, his eyes flinging over to Etta with plenty of pleading in them. He blinked and looked at his mother again. "I haven't talked to her in forever."

"Mm hm." Kelly sat down and held out her hand.

Without another word, Finn hefted a huge sigh and dug his phone out of his pocket. He put it in her hand, and she started swiping and reading.

"Thanks a lot, Miss Etta," Finn grumbled.

"I'm so sorry," Etta said, her face growing redder by the moment. "Come on, August. I think we've done enough damage at this table."

"Not without a hug from me, dear." An older woman stood, and she hugged Etta and then August equally as joyously.

"This is Squire's mother," Etta said. "Heidi Ackerman."

"Oh, hello," he said. "You own the bakery."

"That I do," she said with a grin. "Still going strong, even with the newer dessert bars coming in."

"I'm glad," Etta said. "When are you going to open up your pie sign-ups?"

"November first," she said, dropping back to her seat with a sigh. "I'm tired about pie season already."

August had never heard the holidays called "pie season" before, but he smiled at Heidi and went with Etta toward the next table.

Another of Pete's sons sat there, and August could've been hallucinating, but he didn't think he was when he saw John pull his hand away from a pretty girl's under the table. "Cal," Etta said. "Have you met August?" She brought him forward and added, "Cal is a vet at Three Rivers. August wants to do some vet tech training."

"Oh, you should." Cal shook August's hand. "I know Boone is encouraging UT-Austin to set up an outreach program here in Three Rivers. Then you don't have to travel."

"He is?" August asked. "That would be awesome." He looked at Etta, his eyebrows raised. Yes, he was just a simple cowboy. Etta had already met with her brothers and cousins about building them a house at Shiloh Ridge. The spot had been chosen for it, and Bishop and Montana had started plans. They wouldn't be able to actually break ground until next year, but the house would sit between Bear's and the Ranch House, on the same road that led out to the Edge and led along the side of the cliff and then down to the highway.

When they'd gone to dinner with Cactus and Willa at the Edge Cabin just after they'd gotten engaged, all Cactus could talk about was how much work he had to do on their growing ranch. "We need another vet," he'd complained, and the seed had been planted in August's mind.

He couldn't take the time to attend eight years of college, especially as there wasn't one nearby he could reasonably get to. Veterinarian school wasn't exactly conducive to online learning either.

But becoming a veterinary technician...that was something August could do, and he'd been looking into programs all over the state, and even into Oklahoma, for the past few months.

August looked at Etta. "Who's Boone?"

"Boone Carver," Etta said. "He's Squire's cousin. I thought he was considering a move back to the Hill Country."

"Boone's always considering something." Cal semi-rose

from his seat. "He's right over there. See the woman with the red and blonde hair? That's his wife." He sat back down and picked up his fork.

"Let's go talk to him," Etta said, but she stopped to introduce August to two teachers at the high school, a Mr. Bays, who taught woodshop and coached the junior rodeo roping teams, and a Mrs. Lovesick, who taught home economics. She gushed and gushed about Etta's sweet and sour meatballs, and as August had eaten them before, he knew why.

"It's time for the first official dance," Ranger said into the microphone, and Etta paused in her journey toward Boone Carver. "Can I get the bride and groom out here, please?"

August led Etta onto the dance floor while Ranger cleared everyone else off of it, promising they could come back once August and Etta officially opened the dancing.

"The new Mister and Missus Winters want all of their siblings and cousins on the floor with them," Ranger said. "So stuff that last bite of cake into your mouth, Cactus, and get your wife up on her feet. Bring the babies if you have to. Come on now, Glovers and Winters. Don't be shy. Line up on the sides there."

August held Etta's hand while people did what he said, until they were ready. Finally, the first strains of *Bless the Broken Road* came on, and August grinned at his new wife. "You chose my song."

"It was better than mine," she said, falling easily into his arms. "Plus, you've done literally everything I've wanted for this wedding. I figured the one thing you actually had an opinion on, I should listen to."

"I would've danced to *Keeper of the Stars*," he murmured, bringing her nearer to him and positioning his mouth at her ear. He pressed his lips there, excited to be even closer to her later.

"I know," she said. "And we will. Later."

He moved with her, getting lost in the gentle strains of music of this song, which he loved. On the chorus, both he and Etta sang along.

This much I know is true
That God blessed the broken road
That led me straight to you

He kissed her right there on the dance floor, and Ranger said, "All right, folks. Let's join 'em out there, because as Judge said, we all have our problems, and God has blessed all of our broken roads."

August felt Etta's smile against his lips, and she pulled away and leaned her head against his shoulder. He met Judge's eyes, and the man pressed his fist to his heart.

August knew then, with that gesture, that he was truly a Glover, and he'd never experienced such comfort and happiness because of it.

10 months later

Etta Winters pulled up to what would be her house, smiling at all the cement and wood. "Wow," she said to herself. Well, and her unborn baby. She liked to sing to her baby boy inside, and he sure seemed to like it too, if the way he moved and kicked while she did it told her anything.

"Hey," August said, opening her door.

"It looks great," she said, turning sideways and putting both feet onto the ground before attempting to stand. August took her hand and steadied her, and Etta gave him a grateful smile. "Look, we have a chimney and a roof now."

"It's coming along," August said, his eyes trained on her. "Are you okay, Etta?"

"Just tired," she said, knowing she looked pale this morning too. She was nine months pregnant and due with her first baby any day now. She and August were only having one baby, and Etta was secretly glad she hadn't gotten twins with her first pregnancy the way Ida had.

"You didn't sleep well last night."

"Sorry if I kept you awake," Etta said, finally facing her husband. She'd finally gotten up around three-thirty, slipped out of the bedroom at the Top Cottage, and settled on the couch, where the flickering TV could entertain her while she dozed.

"I fell back asleep fast," he said. He'd been up early to study for his exam that week, and he'd finish another class in the vet tech program that he'd started in January by the end of August.

Etta stepped carefully with him as they picked their way toward the house. They came here about once a week just to see the progress on the house, and they sat on the front steps, which faced the town of Three Rivers. The view wasn't as good as that at the Ranch House, but Etta loved it all the same. This would be her house—hers with August and their family—and she couldn't wait to move in.

"Bishop is saying by Christmas," August said.

"Okay." Etta didn't mind waiting for the dream home, because she'd learned to take life slowly in the past year. August had asked her to marry him just over a year ago, and her life had drastically changed. She didn't want to live in waiting mode. She wanted to enjoy every day right where she was in her life.

She settled onto the top step, pain moving up her back and down her left leg. She groaned and adjusted her position while August waited for her to get comfortable. When she finally found a good spot, he sat next to her. "I don't want to have the baby on your birthday," she said, leaning into him.

"Mine's not for another week," he said.

"I could easily go another week."

"I hope not," August said.

"Me either." Etta sighed. "But it sure doesn't feel like he's going to come any time soon."

Etta had plenty of examples to look to for how to tell if she was in labor. Zona had given birth to another girl only three days after Etta and August had gotten married. They'd been in Upstate New York, and it had nearly killed Etta to meet her new niece via a picture over a text. They'd named her April Rivers Glover, and Etta did like the subtle nod to the town where Zona and Duke had both grown up.

Willa had survived her pregnancy, but she'd opted for a Cesarean section instead of having to endure labor. That had given her some relief for her anxiety, and it had allowed her to avoid having to push, which would've been very difficult for her physically.

She and Cactus had named their little girl Melissa Elly, and Etta could've died from the cuteness of the girl. She had Willa's lighter red hair, and she'd been born with a head full of it. And watching Cactus carry that pudgy baby around would melt the iciest of hearts, that was for certain.

Montana had gone into labor early, in Etta's presence, and she knew what labor pain looked like on another person's face. She hadn't taken even a moment to panic, and she had Montana in her truck before she could get Bishop in off the ranch. They'd taken her truck to the hospital, which was a good reason for Etta to be the first in their room to meet Georgia Everly Glover, yet another girl for the family.

Montana had wanted a state name for her daughter, and there was nothing cuter than Georgia, in Etta's opinion. She and August had been back and forth on their own baby's name, and they still hadn't decided on one definitively.

Her lower back ached, and Etta huffed out her breath. "I can't sit here. It hurts." She started to get up, and the tightness relieved slightly. August didn't let go of her hand, and Etta didn't dare take a step.

So much pressure bore down on her belly and then lower, and she forgot how to breathe.

"Etta?" August asked, but his voice echoed outside of her ears.

Her eyes closed, and Etta reached to wipe the sweat off her forehead. She needed a hat if she was going to stay out in the evening sun for much longer.

"Etta," August said, and when she opened her eyes, he stood in front of her now. "Talk to me." He held her under her arms, and Etta realized she wasn't holding herself up completely.

She blinked and straightened her knees, locking them and coming back to herself. "Oh," she said, but it might have been a groan.

"Come on," he said. "Let's go home. It's too hot out here."

She'd taken one step when the pressure released. Etta cried out as wetness ran down her legs, and she said, "August," in a gasping voice. She looked down, but there wasn't enough liquid to drip onto her sandals yet.

She looked up into her husband's eyes. "I think my water just broke."

"Let's go," he said. "It's a long way to the hospital."

Etta opened her mouth to argue with him, but a searing pain stole her voice. All she could do was nod in tight bursts, and she let him guide her to her truck and into the passenger seat. By the time she got there, the pain had gone, and she could breathe again.

"I was going to take dinner to Libby," Etta said, her mind scattering. "Maybe I can call Zona, and she can get it out of the fridge and take it to her."

"Etta," August said, a touch of impatience in his voice. "Libby has a husband who can get dinner."

"Bell's been teething," Etta said, naming Mister and Libby's baby boy. They'd given him the middle name Michael after Mister's real name, and Etta absolutely loved the odd first name that spoke to Libby's former surname.

"They'll handle it," August said, bumping too fast over the road. Etta reached up and grabbed the handle above the window, groaning. "Sorry," he said, throwing her a look and slowing down.

They continued on past the Ranch House, and when Etta didn't feel anything else, she started to doubt if they should go to the hospital at all. "August," she said when Bull House came into view. "Maybe it's nothing."

"Your water broke," he said. "You're supposed to go to the hospital when your water breaks, I know that much."

Etta leaned forward to get out a napkin, gasping at the slice of pain that went horizontally across her stomach.

"Yep, we're going," he said. He fumbled his phone and tapped as he reached the junction. The arch welcoming everyone to Shiloh Ridge stood to the right, with the highway down to the left. Mister's house had been finished several months ago, and he and Libby had been able to move in before Bell had been born.

Of course, Mister and Libby hadn't gotten pregnant within the first month of their marriage the way Etta and August had. She wasn't going to be upset that she'd have to take her baby boy back to the Top Cottage instead of her forever home.

Just the fact that she had a forever home was a ridiculous blessing for which she was so grateful.

"Oh, boy," Etta said. "Curses and cusses." Her fingers tightened on the handle, and she tried to push herself up with her feet, as if that would make the contraction easier to bear. It sure didn't, and Etta panted through the intense pain in her midsection.

August turned and got them moving again, his phone now ringing in his hand. "Howdy, August," Bear said. "Do not tell me the cattle didn't make it back today."

"They did," August said. "That's not why I'm calling. Hailey's at your house, right?"

"Sammy just sent her to Cactus's. Willa asked her if she wanted to come for movie night. They've got a big screen set up and their new trampoline has a sprinkler under it all the time." He chuckled as Etta's contraction subsided.

Hailey at Cactus's was a good thing. He and Willa had

gotten approval to adopt all three of their foster children after their father had been convicted several months ago.

The court system was slow, but they had a date in another few weeks to go before the judge to get the job done.

"Okay, well, could you call him?" August asked. "Etta's water broke, and we're on the way to the hospital. Maybe whoever comes down to the hospital first could bring Hailey?"

"Don't come right away," Etta called, pressing on her stomach as if that could keep the baby inside. "It's my first baby. I'll be in labor forever."

"I'll call Cactus," Bear said. "My guess is Ida will be there first, but I'll make sure Hailey gets down there lickety split."

"Not soon," Etta said. "Don't make her miss the movie."

August said something else, and the call ended. He turned onto the smoother highway, and then glanced at Etta. "Don't make her miss the movie? Etta, you're having her brother."

"She can come down in two or three hours," Etta said. "She doesn't need to miss the movie."

"What if she *wants* to miss the movie?"

"What do you want the middle name to be?" she asked, ignoring the question. "We need to decide."

"You're a Glover. I think that would be fun, like how Zona used Rivers." He shrugged. "I don't know."

"Joseph Glover Winters," Etta said, though they'd had this discussion before. "I don't know. I don't like it."

"We don't have to use Joseph," he said.

"I want to," she said. The name reminded her—and

him—of Josie, and Etta had no problem paying homage to the woman who'd come before her. She simply didn't want to be compared to her or be put up against her somehow. She couldn't compete with the dead, that much was certain.

"Joseph...." she mused. "I do like Jonathan, because of Judge, but Ida already used Jonathan."

"And Judge's name is just John."

"I don't like Joseph John," Etta said, shaking her head. "It's not syllabic enough."

August chuckled, the way he always had when Etta said naming had something to do with syllables. "All right."

"If it started with a different letter, maybe," Etta said.

"What about Ward?" August asked.

Etta nearly clawed her way through the roof as another contraction hit her, and her mind blanked on the topic of conversation. Everything turned black, in fact, and Etta sank into the blissful place where she didn't have to worry about what to name her son or how fast August could get them to the hospital.

Etta blinked, the darkness in her vision clearing. Her head floated, and her stomach hurt, and something smelled like rubbing alcohol.

"She's waking up," August said, and he appeared above her. "Etta, wake up, sweetheart."

"What happened?" she asked, trying to move.

"Don't move," he said. "They're taking you into the delivery room, and you're all hooked up to an IV."

"What?" Etta lifted her arm, and it was connected to an IV. "I don't want to do this."

"You have to have the baby," August said, moving above her. The ceiling moved too, and Etta looked to her right and found a woman walking there. She knew her, and sure enough, Kiley Hatch smiled down at her.

"Etta," she said calmly. "You passed out on the way here. We have to do a C-section."

"I don't want to do a C-section," she said. "I want to have the baby normally."

"I don't think it's an option, sweets," August said. "Every contraction drops the baby's oxygen level to zero. They're worried he won't make it through a normal delivery."

Etta didn't know how to argue with him. Frustration filled her, and then the bed bumped through double doors, and more voices joined the fray around her. Machines beeped, and a drape got put up between her face and everything else.

"You can stand here, Daddy," their doctor said, and he peered over the blue barrier, clearly smiling at her behind his medical mask. "How you doin', Mama?"

"Good," Etta said. "Is he okay, Doctor Flagstaff?"

"He's doin' fine right now," he said, looking over his shoulder. "We're going to get him out quick so he's not in any more distress."

"I just barely went into labor," she said, though she

didn't really know what time it was. "Has he been in a lot of stress for very long?"

"Not long," Dr. Flagstaff said. "But he needs oxygen, and every contraction robs him of it."

"They called a Code Blue," August said. "I told them to take him out as fast as possible."

Etta nodded and reached for her husband's hand. August laced his fingers through hers and got up on some sort of step so he could see past the drape. "Tell me everything," she said.

"They're just getting everything ready for the baby," he said. "A warming unit if they need it. There's three nurses here, Etta. You're going to be fine."

"All right," Dr. Flagstaff said, but she couldn't see him. "Tell me if you can feel this."

Etta could feel nothing, and she said so.

"They're getting ready," August said, and Etta closed her eyes.

"It's okay, baby," she said. "You don't have to tell me." She knew what a C-section entailed, and August wouldn't want to narrate the incision or what came after.

"Tell me if you feel anything," the doctor said. "Anything at all."

A nurse appeared at her shoulder. "You can just push this button to give yourself a bit more painkiller." She put a remote-like thing in her hand. "Okay?"

Etta nodded, her voice suddenly gone.

"Here we go," the doctor said, and Etta thought she'd experienced intense pressure during a contraction.

She'd been wrong.

She pushed the button to get more painkiller, not sure what type of pain the doctor had been speaking of.

"August," she whimpered. "What are they doing?"

"They're pushing him out, Etta," he said. "Since you can't."

For some reason, Etta thought they'd just reach in and pluck the baby out. Of course they'd have to push him out.

"She's contracting again," someone called out.

"Let's work with that," the doctor said, and the pressure came again. So much pressure. Funny how she couldn't feel any pain—sharp pain, slicing pain, white-hot pain—but the pressure.

Dear Lord, she thought. *The pressure.*

Her baby boy was worth it. She could do this for however long she needed to.

"Etta," August said.

"I'm here," she said.

"He's here."

Etta's eyes snapped open, and in the next moment, the wail of a newborn met her ears. She started to laugh and cry at the same time, and August stepped down from his perch. He pressed a kiss to her forehead and said, "I got a picture. He's so beautiful."

"Can I see him?" she asked, desperate to see her boy before they took him to clean him up.

"Right here," a nurse said, and she put the scrunched-up-faced baby on Etta's chest, on this side of the drape.

"Oh." Etta reached for him, pulling the blanket tighter

around his foldable shoulders. "Oh, he's amazing." He stopped crying, and Etta hummed to him, quieting him completely. His face relaxed, and the baby seemed to snuggle into Etta's chest.

She looked up at August. "We need a middle name for him."

"What about Ward?" August suggested. "Joseph Ward Winters."

Etta looked at her son, her tears thick. "I love that." She reached up to stroke his soft, light brown hair, which was still mostly slicked to his skull. "Hello, my son. It's your mama."

"Pick him up, Daddy," one of the nurses said. "Let's go give your son a bath while they finish up with your wife."

"I'll be back so fast, Etta," August said, and he cradled Joseph in his arms and went with the nurse. Etta stayed right where she was, her eyes closed as tears flowed from the corners of her eyes.

Only half an hour later, she sat partially up in a hospital bed, reaching for her freshly bathed son. "Can I feed him?" she asked the nurse who'd come in with August.

"Absolutely," she said. "Then, I'm not sure if you're aware, but the waiting room is full of people, and one of them said he'd be coming back in five minutes if he doesn't get an update."

Etta looked at August, and they said together, "Judge." She smiled at her husband, and August added, "I'll go talk to them."

"Tell them his name," Etta said. "And that I need thirty

minutes to try to feed him, and then you can take him to meet his family."

She gazed down at her son, every hope of her heart finally fulfilled with the man at her side and the infant in her arms. As August bent down to kiss her, Etta let her eyes drift closed as she prayed, *Thank You, Dear Lord. Thank You for not forgetting about me.*

Read on for a sneak peek at **TEX**, which takes you back to Coral Canyon for more amazing cowboy romance! You'll meet the Young family and see old favorites in the Hammonds and Whittakers!

Author's Note:

Well, we made it through another family! When I first wrote Seven Sons Ranch, I swore I would not do it again. It was a lot of people, with a lot of names, and a lot going on all the time. I needed everyone to tell that story, and some of the books grew to proportions I couldn't handle.

Then, when Shiloh Ridge started, I realized...I'd done it again.

Except with almost *twice* as many people! I honestly don't know what I was thinking. For those of you who've come on this journey with me, I am so grateful. I thank the Lord each day for you, the reader of this book, this series, and any of my books or series'.

Each of the Glovers and the people who've come into their lives have a little piece of my heart with them. I loved watching Cactus come back to his family. I enjoyed (probably too much!) the rift between him and Bear in his book, when he finds out Bear bought Willa a car.

I love the relationship between Sammy and some of her brothers-in-law, particularly Mister and Cactus. She emerged as a maternal figure for me about Book 3, and I wasn't able to truly give her that spotlight until these last couple of books.

I had a good time coming up with all the names for the people and children in this family, and I love the fun we've had in the reader group talking about them. I think my very favorite name is Ward, as he watches over the whole family. Or maybe Cactus, because upon first read, you think, *Really? Who would ever call their child that?*

But then, it fits so perfectly.

I do really love Georgia, the name of Montana and Bishop's baby at the very end here, and don't be surprised if you see that name as a heroine in a future book. I simply *love* that name, and I haven't written a Georgia yet.

I have to admit I love Glory Rose too. I gave that name to Ward and Dot's baby, and the name of Preacher and Charlie's girl—Betty—isn't far behind.

Come to think of it, Birch is a pretty spectacular name for a boy too...

I am going to need to write more books for all these fabulous people!

In all seriousness, I hope you've found a character you connect with in this family. I also want you to feel the very same way Etta does at the end of all of this. Her journey has been long and hard, but she didn't give up. She didn't stop hoping or praying.

I hope that wherever you are in your life, that you won't give up either. That you'll turn to loved ones, friends or family, and find the support and comfort you need with whatever you're struggling with. No matter what it is, I hope you'll remember that you are not forgotten either.

I love Three Rivers with my whole heart. I've written a lot of books and characters here, and I've always felt like the town and ranches surrounding it were touched with magic. I hope you've enjoyed seeing the Walkers as well as the cowboys at Three Rivers Ranch. Heidi at the bakery for a little cameo there at the end, and the town as it has grown over the past few years.

I'm sure we'll be back here at some point, and we'll get to see the Glovers as they continue their lives. I have ideas for Beau from Three Rivers, because that man needs to find someone to love him the way Etta loves August. And of course, when all of these Walker children and Glover children grow up, they're going to need to find their happily-ever-after as well...

No matter who you love best, this cast of people in Three Rivers has become part of my family, and I hope part of yours. They feel like real people, with real lives, real struggles, and real things to celebrate, and I'm glad you've been on this journey with them...and with me.

Until the next amazing ranch, with our next small town, as well as a stellar set of cowboys, cowgirls, and animals where we can all escape!

xoxo

Liz

PPS: Sammy and Bear named their last little girl Sunnie Charlotte. Etta went into labor before she could tell you that.

Sneak Peek! TEX Chapter One:

Tex Young drove past the sign welcoming him to Coral Canyon about the same time he realized another song hadn't come up on the radio. He glanced over to his son, who reminded him more of a man than a teenager.

Bryce was seventeen now, with only one more year of high school before he'd be unleashed on the world as an adult. His son met his eye and hastily reached for his phone. "Sorry. I was thinking about something."

Tex thought it was probably some*one*, but he didn't say anything. He didn't quite know how, and living in a permanent place wasn't going to be the only brand new thing Tex would have to learn how to do this summer.

He'd always had Bryce with him in the summers, and he'd loved taking his son around to various cities in the US as he traveled with Country Quad, the family band he'd founded and headed for the past fifteen years.

He smiled at his son and said, "Maybe something that isn't country."

"Are you insane?" Bryce asked with a chuckle. "There is no music other than country that's worth listening to." The twangs of guitar came through the speakers, and Tex did love a good guitar. He'd been playing since he was four years old, and he never felt quite as at-home as he did on a front porch with an instrument in his hands.

Even better was when Bryce sat next to him and sang the songs Tex had written over the years. Otis, one of his brothers in the band, wrote a lot of music and lyrics for the family band, and Tex admired his brother's gift.

Tex shifted in his seat, a question on his mind. He reached to turn down the radio, which also drew Bryce's attention. "You sure you want to stay here for senior year?" he asked.

Bryce looked away, out his passenger window. The boy had been growing facial hair for over a year, and he hadn't shaved since the last day of school, over a week now. Tex had landed in Boise to pick up his son, and they'd spent a handful of days there getting everything packed and loaded into the truck or the trailer currently attached to the hitch behind them.

"Yeah, Dad," he said.

"You never have told me why," Tex said as gently as he could. "Your mother's had you for years."

"Only because you traveled so much," Bryce said. "I came over to your place on every break when you were home."

"Yeah." Tex had traveled three hundred days a year, and while he maintained a residence in Boise, he'd sold that house and rented one in Coral Canyon, Wyoming. He glanced around at the town, noting all the changes. "Wow, look at this medical center."

He'd brought Bryce to his hometown before, when his father had announced he was going to sell the family ranch. Tex had seven brothers, but none of them had felt a deep love for Wyoming land, and no one had wanted the ranch a decade ago, Tex included.

They'd all converged to help Daddy pack, clean, and move out of the farmhouse and into a more sensible place in the middle of town. He lived with men and women his own age now, without any yardwork, animals to be fed three times a day, or howling winds and snowstorms to navigate to the barn.

Tex actually missed the cowboy life, and he wanted to get back to it. The house he'd rented sat on the other side of town from the ranch where he'd grown up, and he suddenly decided to drive by the farmhouse he'd known so well.

"How are you feeling? Need to use the bathroom? Can we drive by the farmhouse?"

"Sure," Bryce said. "I'm good."

Tex watched the new developments pass by the window, and he saw several new restaurants along this extension of Main Street. "Looks like some great new places to eat," he said.

"Let's try 'em all," Bryce said, referring to a summer he and Tex had spent together a few years ago, where they'd tried as many new restaurants as they could, in as many towns and cities as possible.

"Deal," Tex said with a smile. He passed the road that led back to the high school, then City Hall, then the library. Tex couldn't remember the last book he'd read, and he wondered if he should make a list of things he wanted to try this summer.

Reading would go on it. *Getting back to his cowboy roots* would too. *Writing a new song, getting and riding a new horse,* and *hiking* would definitely be on it.

"Maybe we should make a summer list," he said, glancing over to his son. "Things we haven't done it a while we want to do, or things around Coral Canyon we can't do anywhere else."

"Like the balloon festival,"

"Yeah," Tex said, grinning. "Like that."

"I heard there's a police dog academy here," Bryce said. "And they do tours."

"We'll look it up when we get to the house." Tex made another turn, and the road led past a couple of office buildings and then the residential part of Coral Canyon opened up. The houses along these streets sat fairly close together, and the farther they got from the historic Main Street, the more land surrounded the houses.

"Did you like growing up out here?" Bryce asked.

"Yeah," Tex said, sighing. "We had a pond right on the property. We could ride our bikes anywhere. Dad let us go fishing every Sunday after church." He grinned at his son. "It was an easy, slow life."

He had liked it, and the tender part of his heart longed for that life again. He'd stepped back from Country Quad to do exactly that, hadn't he? Relax more. Travel less. Find a community to belong to?

He had, and his chest swelled with another breath, which he blew out slowly. "It was a good life." He looked at his son again. "What happened in Boise to make you want to leave everything you've known and come do your senior year here?"

His dad had always shot straight with him, and Tex wasn't doing his son any favors by not making him talk. He'd stayed in touch with his son over the years, but Tex wouldn't label himself a good father.

He could talk to his son, and he'd given his advice over the years, but he hadn't been involved in the day-to-day parenting the way his ex-wife had. He knew that had been a major source of annoyance to Corrie, the woman he'd been married to for only two years before that marriage had dissolved.

He was actually looking forward to this summer and this year and all of this time off. He would finally be able to dedicate time and energy to Bryce, and they'd talked about this year a lot already on the drive here from Boise.

"Mom's...she's been saying some things."

Tex kept his gaze out the windshield. "What kind of things?"

"Lots of stuff," he said. "When she said she had put her whole life on hold to have me and she couldn't wait to do what she wanted, I got pretty mad at her. There was...sort of a...blow up."

Tex didn't know what to say. His chest stormed and his stomach turned inside out. "She loves you," he said.

"She told me she hated being a mom," Bryce said. "That's when I called you."

Tex whipped his attention to Bryce. "She did not say that."

"She said she wished she'd never had kids." Bryce kept his gaze out the window. "It's fine. I don't believe her, and I know she's been stressed."

"About what?" Tex demanded, trying to keep his grip on the steering wheel loose. "All the money I send her for the two of you? Her summers off from teaching? That perfect, two-story house that looks like it came out of a storybook?"

Bryce said nothing, and Tex stewed in his anger. Corrie had no right to make Bryce feel like he was unwanted.

"Bud," he said. "I'm sorry. I know she didn't mean any of those things."

"Yeah, I know too," he said. "But since you were coming already, and we always have the summers, I just figured, why not senior year too?"

"Jenny's why-not-senior-year-too," Tex said, sliding his man-son a look out of the corner of his eye. "You're still talking to her, right?"

"Yeah," Bryce said with a sigh. "We talk."

"You goin' with her?"

"I don't know what that means, Dad," he teased.

"It means she's your girlfriend." Tex gave him a full look.

"Your mother told me about the Sweethearts dance and the prom, and then the other prom...."

"Yeah, well, she lives in Boise, and I live here now."

Tex made another turn, this time not looking at his son. "Once we have a real chance, we'll look around and buy something. I'm going to stay here for a while." The right side of the road didn't have any houses, and the places out here were spaced far apart.

"Whenever," Bryce said. "We can put it on our summer list."

"I used to go with the girl who lived next door to me," Tex said, infusing a smile into his voice.

"You've told me, Dad," Bryce said dryly.

"See? You know what goin' with someone means."

Bryce scoffed—or maybe laughed—and shook his head. "All right, Pops."

Tex laughed too, saying, "It's right up here."

"You sure?" Bryce asked. "I've been here before, and it didn't look like this."

Tex frowned out the window too, because his son was right. The land sat in shades of yellow and brown. The fence that ran around the pasture that bordered the road looked like it could collapse if a two-ounce bird swooped down and landed on it.

"Maybe no one lives here," he mused. He didn't know who his father had sold the ranch to, and it had been ten years anyway. The property could've changed hands more than once by now.

The pasture gave way to the house and lawn, but it too

looked abandoned. No one lived here, that was for dang sure.

"Look," Bryce said. "There's a sign. Is the house for sale?"

Tex's heart jumped right up into his throat. If this house and ranch was up for sale, he wanted to buy it. "Is it?" He slowed the truck he'd owned for years and turned into the gravel driveway. Weeds and grass grew through the rocks, along with some pretty pink wildflowers Tex had long forgotten the name of.

He brought the vehicle to a stop long before the end of the driveway, which would take him all the way to the back steps. His mother would throw a fit if she saw the state of the front porch she'd once loved and tended to.

Tex could remember trimming this lawn behind a push mower, and he knew how to fix fences, tend to horses and cattle, and paint houses. His father had made his boys do all of it as they grew up, and he'd pitched in plenty.

He must be so disappointed in us, Tex thought as he looked at the house. Half of the brothers had passed on inheriting the ranch because of the band. The twins were still heavily entrenched in the rodeo and had barely been out of the house when Daddy had decided he was too old and too weak to keep up the two-hundred-acre ranch.

"Dad," Bryce said, and Tex blinked his eyes to get himself to stop looking at the peeling paint and the faded front door. He hadn't even noticed his son getting out of the truck. Bryce stood on the lawn—the crispy, brown grass—and waved at Tex to come over.

He heaved a sigh and got out of the truck, the heat of the day punching him in the lungs. It wasn't usually hot in the mountains, but the whole country was experiencing a heat wave this week.

"What is it?" he asked.

"There's an auction on this property," Bryce said. "Tomorrow."

"Tomorrow?" Tex arrived and looked at the sign, but the type was way too small to hold his attention for long. He'd always had such a short attention span, and he forced himself to read the big, blocky, black letters.

The property would be sold as-is to the highest bidder. The auction would be at the library at ten a.m. in the morning, and Tex's only thought was that he better be there.

"We should go," Bryce said. "You have some money, right, Dad?"

"A little," Tex said. Enough to buy a house with a loan. This was a cash auction, and Tex wondered how much it would go for. In Coral Canyon, Wyoming? A town of maybe twelve thousand? After a rush of growth? With other houses sitting empty?

"Let's look at the market," Tex said.

"I want to sit on the porch where you kissed Nina," Bryce said, chuckling as he jogged across the grass.

"That was eons ago," Tex called after his son. He returned his attention to his phone, and he started looking up the real estate market in Coral Canyon. The town had enjoyed a boom a few years ago, but the growth had stalled, and Tex didn't see anything out of his price range.

A broken-down, abandoned ranch further from town? No one would want this place, and Tex suddenly did. He could call Otis, Blaze, and Trace and find out if they'd like to go in on the ranch with him.

The band was taking a break this summer, as his brothers were trying to figure out if they wanted to rebrand Country Quad into Country Trio—or some other name—and continue making music, or if anyone else was ready to do something different with his life.

Tex knew Blaze didn't want to keep traveling. He'd been talking to a woman pretty seriously over a dating app, and he'd gone to Florida to meet her. Tex was expecting a text announcing his brother's engagement any moment now.

Otis and Trace had stayed in Nashville for now, but they were taking time off. Tex could text them both about chipping in for the ranch and get them out here to Wyoming by next weekend.

Cash only, streamed through his head. Country Quad had kept their calendar booked, but they weren't mega-stars. And they had to split the money four ways. Tex had always had enough for his needs, to send to Corrie and Bryce, and to enjoy himself without thinking too hard about how he'd pay for his next meal.

"You can't be on this property," a woman said, and Tex looked up from his phone. The sunlight glinted off his front windshield, momentarily blinding him. The woman's voice tickled something familiar inside him, but he couldn't quite place it.

"This is private property," she said. "We don't need any

land sharks coming into our town." She marched on toward him, her long legs clad in jeans despite the heat. She also wore a blue and white striped tank top and cowgirl boots on her feet. Her limbs were long, and she ate up the distance between them in a few last strides.

By then, Tex knew exactly who she was. Fireworks popped inside him, burning his lungs and rendering his voice mute.

Abigail Ingalls put one hand on her hip and gestured toward the porch. "Do you mind getting him off the porch?"

"Sure," Tex said, the word catching in his throat. He whistled through his teeth, something he'd always done to call his son and get him to come back to him. He'd been doing it since the boy could crawl, and it worked now too. Tex could barely look away from Abby, but in the brief moment he did, he saw Bryce coming down the steps and toward him.

"Sorry, Abby," he said, reaching up to tip his cowboy hat at her. He was suddenly so glad he'd bought it, because it hid his lack of hair, something he'd become more and more self-conscious about in the past couple of years.

The woman folded her arms now. "Do I know you?"

Bryce jogged up, and Tex indicated the truck. "We should go."

"Yeah, sure," he said, but he simply looked at Tex and then Abby. Abby looked back and forth between the two of them, her gaze finally landing on Tex, her eyebrows cocked high as she obviously waited for him to explain.

"You should know me," he said. "I took you to plenty of drive-in movies. A dance or two. I think I even told my son here about how I used to duck into your barn so we could sneak a kiss." He grinned at Abby, but a horrified expression filled her face instead of the fun, flirty vibe Tex had been trying for.

Sneak Peek! TEX Chapter Two:

Abigail Ingalls could not believe the man standing in front of her was Tex Young. He was the only one she'd ever shimmied into the barn to meet for a kiss, so it had to be. The young man with him looked like a mini-him—except he had the height. The head full of dark hair. The deep, penetrating eyes that seemed to see more than she wanted him to.

Tex still had that grin on his face, and Abby told herself to wait until it slipped. The man exuded confidence, he always had. But he wasn't infallible, and Abby knew if she waited long enough, he'd slip.

He blinked, and she saw it. The corners of his mouth drooped, and satisfaction dove through her. "Hello, Tex," she said coolly, arranging her face into something she hoped was passive and placid.

This man and his good looks did not influence her. Never mind that he hadn't lost an ounce of his charm or his handsomeness. He'd aged well, from what she could see, and she sure did like a man in a big, white cowboy hat, as much as she hated to admit that.

She would never tell him, that was for sure. Not again.

"This is my son, Bryce," he said, slinging his arm around his son's shoulders. "We're moving to Coral Canyon today."

Abby flicked her gaze toward the truck and trailer in the driveway. They weren't brand new, but she'd still expected to find a land shark scoping out the house and land, planning a way to raze everything and bring in steel, cement, and glass.

She still lived right next door, and she would not let that happen. She would not. She had no less than four alarms set for tomorrow morning just to make sure she showed up at the library on time. Lucky for her, she had a key, and the auction couldn't start without her to open the library. So she wouldn't miss the auction no matter what.

Her stomach still quaked with nerves, and she just wanted it over with already. Once she owned this property, she could hydrate it properly. She could move her horses onto it. She could think about renting out the farmhouse after she'd given it a thorough cleaning.

"Nice to meet you," she said to Bryce, because she did have some manners. "Where are you two staying?"

"We've got a rental over on the other side of town," Tex said. He pointed back to the house. "How long has it been like this?"

"A couple of years," Abby said. "The last couple who owned it left suddenly, and they couldn't sell it. He had a job that came up in intelligence, and they were here one day and gone the next. Neither of them came back, and a for-sale sign appeared a couple of months later. The bank eventually repossessed it, and they're doing an auction tomorrow."

"Yeah, that's what I was looking at," he said, his smile as brilliant as the summer sun shining down today. Abby tried not to find him attractive, but any woman would fail in that quest. Tex had the kind of face a woman longed to touch, if just to feel if that jaw was as strong as it looked.

He had large hands that knew how to coax the most beautiful melodies from a guitar, and Abby would only admit to herself in her quietest moments that she'd watched some of his videos online. He had a series of how-to's for kids to learn to play the guitar, and there were plenty of music videos to choose from.

His son stood as tall as Tex, and while he wasn't quite as filled out in the shoulders, they could both break a woman's heart.

Abby vowed it wasn't going to be hers. Not this time.

"Anyway," Tex said, a high note entering his voice. "We'll get out of your hair. It's too hot to stand out in the sun." He lifted his hat and moved his hand through his hair in such a familiar gesture that Abby blinked, and the world went black.

He and Bryce walked back to their truck, both of them talking in such similar voices, and she still stood on the fried grass. She shook her head and told herself to pull everything together. She'd been around plenty of good-looking cowboys over the years. Tex Young wasn't going to bring her to her knees.

"Oh, no, he is not," she vowed as she crossed the patch

of land that used to grow vegetables that separated this ranch from the farm she helped her brother run. Back in the house, she poured herself a big glass of lemonade as Wade wheeled himself into the kitchen.

"Who was it?" he asked. "I'll take some of that." He swiped off his hat and wiped the sweat from his forehead. "I got the pipes moved. We'll get the sprinklers on tonight."

"Okay," Abby said, handing the glass of lemonade to him. "I bet we can get the tomatoes and peas in this weekend. I don't think it'll freeze again."

"The weather is so weird right now," he said, shaking his head. He took a drink and set the glass on the counter. "But I bet you're right."

"So I'll go to the nursery after the auction tomorrow," she said. "We can do them tomorrow night." She'd already spent half a day putting in tomatoes that had then died in a late frost. Abby hated having to do work twice, and she had not been happy with Mother Nature that morning a few weeks ago.

"You're still sure about the auction?" Wade wore doubt in his eyes and wouldn't meet her gaze.

"Yes," Abby said. "We can take care of that land, and if we own it, then we control who lives right next door to us."

"Mm." Wade pushed himself over to the cupboard. "Don't spend more than eighty on it, or we'll be in trouble."

"I know." They'd discussed the budget for her auction habits, though she hadn't bid on any of the other properties around Coral Canyon. She just wanted to preserve the small town feel of the place where she'd grown up and still loved.

"Do we have any of that chicken noodle soup?" Wade asked.

"We're in the middle of a heat wave." Abby leaned against the counter and watched him pull out the packet anyway. How he ate that stuff, she'd never know. "I have homemade mac and cheese in the fridge."

"We've eaten that for three days." Her brother filled the electric kettle and set it on the element. After switching it on, he added, "We need to learn how to make smaller meals."

By "we," he meant her, as Wade hadn't actually cooked for years. Since returning from his military service, in fact.

"You're right," she said instead of arguing with him or suggesting he make something for dinner. Secretly, she liked making big pans of food, because then she didn't have to cook every evening. She always had something hot for lunch at the library, and she simply didn't have to use so much mental energy to keep herself and Wade fed.

Lord knew Abby had enough other things taking up the available space in her mind. An image of Tex's handsome, more mature face flashed across her brainwaves, and she pushed him right back out.

She definitely didn't have time for him. "I'll get the barn door done today," she said. "And I'll bring in the horses tonight. I want to work with Knitted Cotton."

"All right," Wade said, and Abby hadn't expected him to argue with her. Very few people did. She ran the library with firm fairness to the employees and the patrons, and she loved her job there. She loved gardening and prodding the land to produce a lot of what she and Wade needed to live. They had honeybees for honey, and a huge garden that produced plenty of vegetables. Abby had learned how to preserve them from her mother and grandmother, and they lived on spaghetti sauce, stewed tomatoes, bottled peaches, frozen corn and green beans, and more all winter long.

They grew all the hay their horses needed, and their two dozen chickens provided eggs. Abby loved her country life, even if the work was long and hard some days. The ranch next door had been neglected and overgrown since the Youngs had sold it a decade ago. She'd been worried about that, and she'd been right.

This was one time she hadn't wanted to be right, but that didn't change the fact that the two hundred acres next door was a severe eyesore for Mountain View Road, and Abby had always taken pride in where she lived.

She'd told Wade time and again that they didn't have to farm all of the acreage. She'd take care of the gardens and lawns. She'd work on the house over time, and they'd possibly rent it. Or, to prevent her from becoming a complete spinster who lived with her older brother forever, perhaps she'd move into the house next door and they'd each live alone.

After Wade's discharge from the service, he'd spent several months in a hospital in North Carolina, recovering from the loss of both of his legs. They'd been amputated from the knees down, and he had two prosthetics he could use. He said the wheelchair was simply easier in some instances, and Abby couldn't remember the last time he'd put on his prosthetics.

She'd been coming out of a failed engagement at the time and had been more than happy to help her brother transition back to regular life on the farm in Coral Canyon. Her parents had bought a smaller condo in town, and the four of them got along well.

Abby didn't need anything or anyone else.

Certainly not a former boyfriend to sail into town and buy his childhood ranch right out from under her nose. With horror, she realized that if Tex did manage to do that, he'd live right next door to her again. A hundred yards from the side door on her house to the back door on his.

That so wasn't happening.

Abby pulled out her phone and set a fifth alarm just to make sure she got up in time to put on just the right amount of makeup for the auction. After all, if Tex really was going to be there, she'd want to look as powerful as possible, and she knew just how to brush on bronzer to shape her face into its power pose.

The following morning, only a few people lingered in the multi-purpose room at the library. Abby wore a denim skirt and a blouse with running stallions on it, her cowgirl boots, and that powerful makeup. She couldn't help glancing around for Tex or Bryce, but she hadn't seen them yet.

Dale Flood had come, and she should've known he'd show his face here. The man came to every auction in Coral Canyon, and he'd bid if only to keep the outsiders out of town. Abby had to say she respected him for that. She didn't want more big corporations in Coral Canyon either.

Justin Wells sat in the front row, but Abby had seen him come to two or three auctions now and never raise his paddle. She wasn't sure what, if any, interest he held in the land out by her.

Zach Zuckerman had just walked in, and the man had a ton of money. He could easily outbid Abby for the ranch, though he lived further north on a pristine piece of property already. She narrowed her eyes at him and wished she could read minds. He simply gave her a friendly smile and asked, "My wife just checked out thirteen books. Isn't there some kind of limit?"

Abby gave him a tight smile. "Not for adults."

He chuckled and shook his head. "She'll probably get through 'em all this week anyway."

His wife worked as the chef up at Whiskey Mountain Lodge, but apparently she had plenty of time for reading. Abby wouldn't be able to name the last time she had leisure time. She did read a lot, but that was for her job. She had to know the latest bestsellers and be able to answer questions about a variety of books. People came into the library with the oddest questions sometimes, and they often mixed up author names and book titles, then relied on her to unjumble everything.

A couple walked in, and Abby smiled politely at them as they signed up and took their paddle. She knew Gill and Tricia Yardley, and again, she wondered why they were there. They already owned a big corner lot on the last true block before the farms and ranches took over the more rural parts of Coral Canyon. Not only that, but their property sat on the lake side, which was easily twenty minutes from Abby's east side of town.

The clock clicked closer to ten, and Abby glanced toward the stairs, imagining where the elevator would go if she could just get the funding for it. She'd been working on a grant for what felt like forever but had actually only been about a year. She'd made it quite far before realizing she had to bid out everything, and she'd had to start over.

She stepped over to the table and signed herself in, then moved halfway down a row about halfway back from the podium. The big screen had been pulled down for the auctioneer to show the property and go over the rules, but Abby knew both like the back of her hand.

Perhaps that was why she zoned out. She only looked over her shoulder once, and she didn't see Tex. She listened with half an ear as the man up front went over the acreage, the outbuildings, and that the property would be sold as-is.

"It's been appraised for two hundred and fifty thousand dollars, but you can see the land and home and buildings need a lot of work. We'll open the bidding at fifty thousand."

Abby waited, because she wanted to feel out who would really be bidding this morning. Dale lifted his paddle after glancing around at everyone.

"Fifty thousand," the auctioneer said, but he didn't increase in pitch or speed. He simply said it, and she'd learned that these land auctions weren't anything like cattle auctions. She'd worked in that industry for a few years right out of high school before deciding to go to school and get her degree in library science.

"Each bid has to be one thousand dollars more than the one lower," the man said, and Abby lifted her paddle.

"I have fifty-one," the auctioneer said. He wore an expensive suit, because he'd likely come from a bigger city like Cheyenne or even Denver to run this auction. He represented the bank, and they'd take whatever they could get for the property that had been in default for over a year.

"Fifty-two," he said.

Abby lifted her paddle, and he called out her bid.

When they reached sixty-one, Dale put his paddle down on the chair next to him. Abby's heart pounded. Getting that ranch for one-fourth of what it was worth would be a huge steal. A major win.

Excitement beat beneath her breastbone like hummingbird wings, and she swallowed to keep them down where they belonged.

"Sixty-two," the man said, and Abby surveyed the crowd to find who'd bid against her.

Tex.

Her hummingbird pulse turned into crow's wings. Big, huge flapping things that drove fury through her with every —single—beat.

Tex had some nerve, especially when he got up and moved closer, sitting right on the end of her aisle.

She threw her paddle into the air. So did he.

Back and forth they went until Abby was nearing her

ceiling. In fact, if she bid again, she'd be at eighty-one thousand for the ranch.

Tex looked at her, a glint in his eyes that issued a challenge in such a sexy way that she wanted to toss her paddle at his slightly crooked nose and make it even less straight. She gripped the handle of it as if seriously contemplating it.

"Eighty thousand," the auctioneer said again. "Do I have eighty-one?"

Slowly, she put her paddle in the air.

Tex frowned and turned back toward the front, his paddle up already.

Off they went again, and Abby's mind raced. She had no idea what she'd tell Wade. It was almost like she was operating outside of her body, and when she put her paddle up at ninety-three thousand, she called out, "One hundred thousand dollars."

Tex looked at her with wide eyes that didn't blink.

She stared straight back at him, trying to control how quickly her breath went in and out of her lungs. He would break; she'd seen him slip yesterday, and she could force him to do it again.

His shoulders slumped, and Abby could almost taste the victory.

"One hundred thousand," the auctioneer said. "Do I have one-oh-five?"

Tex didn't move.

"Sold, to 17, for one hundred thousand dollars."

The air rushed out of Abby's lungs, and she sagged back into her chair too. A smile touched her face, but it was just a façade. One she needed to keep in place as long as Tex's eyes weighed heavily on the side of her face, as they did now. And one she'd have to wear when she faced her brother and told him how much she'd overspent.

Ooh, more cowboys in Coral Canyon, and this land war is going to put hearts on the line... **TEX is available now in paperback!**

Get it here by scanning this QR code with the camera on your phone.

Books in the Coral Canyon Cowboys Romance series

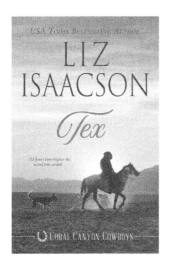

Tex (Book 1): He's back in town after a successful country music career. She owns a bordering farm to the family land he wants to buy...and she outbids him at the auction. Can Tex and Abigail rekindle their old flame, or will the issue of land ownership come between them?

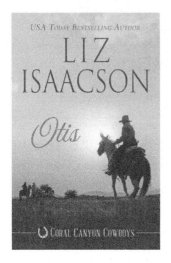

Otis (Book 2): He's finished with his last album and looking for a soft place to fall after a devastating break-up. She runs the small town bookshop in Coral Canyon and needs a new boyfriend to get her old one out of her life for good. Can Georgia convince Otis to take another shot at real love when their first kiss was fake?

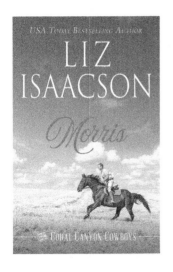

Morris (Book 3): Morris Young is just settling into his new life as the manager of Country Quad when he attends a wedding. He sees his ex-wife there—apparently Leighann is back in Coral Canyon—along with a little boy who can't be more or less than five years old... Could he be Morris's? And why is his heart hoping for that, and for a reconciliation with the woman who left him because he traveled too much?

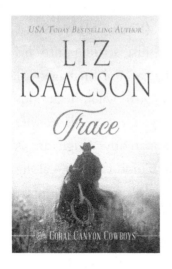

Trace (Book 4): He's been accused of only dating celebrities. She's a simple line dance instructor in small town Coral Canyon, with a soft spot for kids...and cowboys. Trace could use some dance lessons to go along with his love lessons... Can he and Everly fall in love with the beat, or will she dance her way right out of his arms?

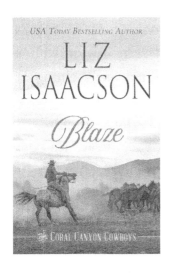

Blaze (Book 5): He's dark as night, a single dad, and a retired bull riding champion. With all his money, his rugged good looks, and his ability to say all the right things, Faith has no chance against Blaze Young's charms. But she's his complete opposite, and she just doesn't see how they can be together...

...so she ends things with him.

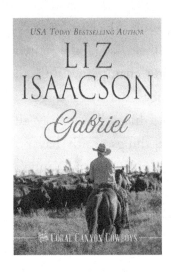

Gabe (Book 6): He's a father's rights advocate lawyer with a sweet little girl. She's fighting for her own daughter. Can Gabe and Hilde find happily-ever-after when they're at such odds with one another?

The Mechanics of Mistletoe (Book 1): Bear Glover can be a grizzly or a teddy, and he's always thought he'd be just fine working his generational family ranch and going back to the ancient homestead alone. But his crush on Samantha Benton won't go away. She's a genius with a wrench on Bear's tractors...and his heart. Can he tame his wild side and get the girl, or will he be left broken-hearted this Christmas season?

The Horsepower of the Holiday (Book 2): Ranger Glover has worked at Shiloh Ridge Ranch his entire life. The cowboys do everything from horseback there, but when he goes to town to trade in some trucks, somehow Oakley Hatch persuades him to take some ATVs back to the ranch. (Bear is NOT happy.)

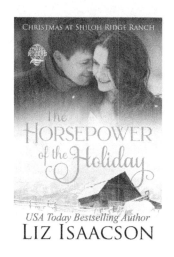

CHRISTMAS AT SHILOH RIDGE RANCH

The HORSEPOWER of the Holiday

USA Today Bestselling Author
LIZ ISAACSON

She's a former race car driver who's got Ranger all revved up... Can he remember who he is and get Oakley to slow down enough to fall in love, or will there simply be too much horsepower in the holiday this year for a real relationship?

The Construction of Cheer (Book 3): Bishop Glover is the youngest brother, and he usually keeps his head down and gets the job done. When Montana Martin shows up at Shiloh Ridge Ranch looking for work, he finds himself inventing construction projects that need doing just to keep her coming around. (Again, Bear is NOT happy.) She wants to build her own construction firm, but she ends up carving a place for herself inside Bishop's heart. Can he convince her *he's* all she needs this Christmas season, or will her cheer rest solely on the success of her business?

The Secret of Santa (Book 4): He's a fun-loving cowboy with a heart of gold. She's the woman who keeps putting him on hold. Can Ace and Holly Ann make a relationship work this Christmas?

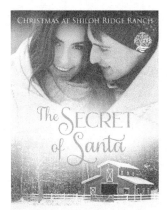

USA Today Bestselling Author
LIZ ISAACSON

The Gift of Gingerbread (Book 5): She's the only daughter in the Glover family. He's got a secret that drove him out of town years ago. Can Arizona and Duke find common ground and their happily-ever-after this Christmas?

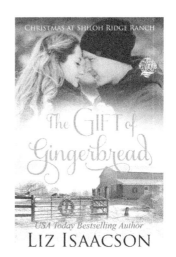

The Harmony of Holly (Book 6): He's as prickly as his name, but the new woman in town has caught his eye. Can Cactus shelve his temper and shed his cowboy hermit skin fast enough to make a relationship with Willa work?

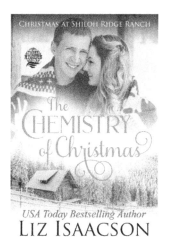

The **CHEMISTRY** of Christmas

USA Today Bestselling Author
LIZ ISAACSON

The Chemistry of Christmas (Book 7): He's the black sheep of the family, and she's a chemist who understands formulas, not emotions. Can Preacher and Charlie take their quirks and turn them into a strong relationship this Christmas?

The Delivery of Decor (Book 8): When he falls, he falls hard and deep. She literally drives away from every relationship she's ever had. Can Ward somehow get Dot to stay this Christmas?

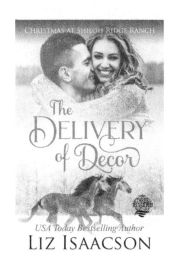

The Blessing of Babies (Book 9): Don't miss out on a single moment of the Glover family saga in this bridge story linking Ward and Judge's love stories!

The Glovers love God, country, dogs, horses, and family. Not necessarily in that order. ;)

Many of them are married now, with babies on the way, and there are lessons to be learned, forgiveness to be had and given, and new names coming to the family tree in southern Three Rivers!

The Networking of the Nativity (Book 10): He's had a crush on her for years. She doesn't want to date until her daughter is out of the house. Will June take a change on Judge when the success of his Christmas light display depends on her networking abilities?

The Wrangling of the Wreath (Book 11): He's been so busy trying to find Miss Right. She's been right in front of him the whole time. This Christmas, can Mister and Libby take their relationship out of the best friend zone?

The Hope of Her Heart (Book 12): She's the only Glover without a significant other. He's been searching for someone who can love him *and* his daughter. Can Etta and August make a meaningful connection this Christmas?

CHRISTMAS AT SHILOH RIDGE RANCH

The HOPE of Her Heart

USA *Today* Bestselling Author
LIZ ISAACSON

Seven Sons Ranch in Three Rivers Romance Series

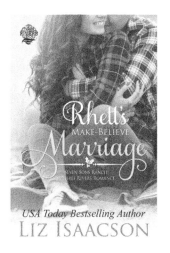

Rhett's Make-Believe Marriage (Book 1): To save her business, she'll have to risk her heart. She needs a husband to be credible as a matchmaker. He wants to help a neighbor. **Will their fake marriage take them out of the friend zone?**

USA Today Bestselling Author
LIZ ISAACSON

Tripp's Trivial Tie (Book 2):
She needs a husband to keep her
son. He's wanted to take their
relationship to the next level,
but she's always pushing him
away. Will their trivial tie take
them all the way to happily-ever-
after?

USA Today Bestselling Author
LIZ ISAACSON

Liam's Invented I-Do (Book 3): She's desperate to save her ranch. He wants to help her any way he can. Will their invented I-Do open doors that have previously been closed and lead to a happily-ever-after for both of them?

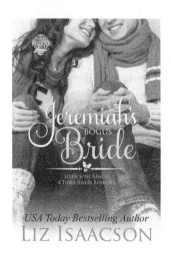

Jeremiah's Bogus Bride (Book 4): He wants to prove to his brothers that he's not broken. She just wants him. Will a fake marriage heal him or push her further away?

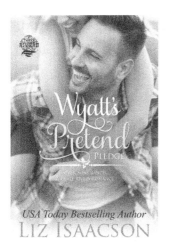

Wyatt's Pretend Pledge (Book 5): To get her inheritance, she needs a husband. He's wanted to fly with her for ages. Can their pretend pledge turn into something real?

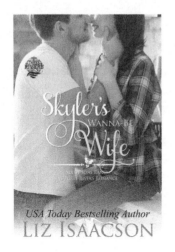

USA Today Bestselling Author
LIZ ISAACSON

Skyler's Wanna-Be Wife (Book 6): She needs a new last name to stay in school. He's willing to help a fellow student. Can this wanna-be wife show the playboy that some things should be taken seriously?

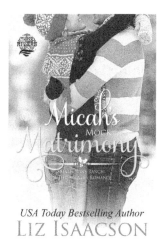

USA Today Bestselling Author

LIZ ISAACSON

Micah's Mock Matrimony (Book 7): They were just actors auditioning for a play. The marriage was just for the audition – until a clerical error results in a legal marriage. Can these two ex-lovers negotiate this new ground between them and achieve new roles in each other's lives?

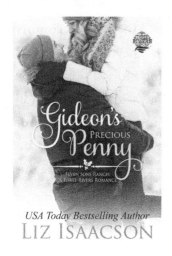

USA Today Bestselling Author
LIZ ISAACSON

Gideon's Precious Penny (Book 8): It's 1971, and Gideon Walker is on the cutting edge of all the technology coming out of Texas. He has big dreams and wants to make something of himself. Then he meets Penny Aarons, and everything changes. He only has eyes for her, but she's got plans and dreams of her own...

Read this origin romance for Momma and Daddy from the Seven Sons series today!

Books in the Christmas at Whiskey Mountain Lodge Romance series

Her Cowboy Billionaire Birthday Wish (Book 1): All the maid at Whiskey Mountain Lodge wants for her birthday is a handsome cowboy billionaire. And Colton can make that wish come true—if only he hadn't escaped to Coral Canyon after being left at the altar...

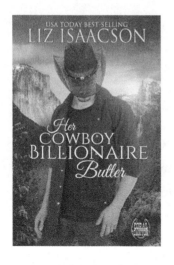

Her Cowboy Billionaire Butler (Book 2): She broke up with him to date another man...who broke her heart. He's a former CEO with nothing to do who can't get her out of his head. Can Wes and Bree find a way toward happily-ever-after at Whiskey Mountain Lodge?

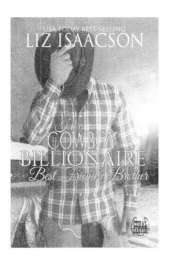

Her Cowboy Billionaire Best Friend's Brother (Book 3): She's best friends with the single dad cowboy's brother and has watched two friends find love with the sexy new cowboys in town. When Gray Hammond comes to Whiskey Mountain Lodge with his son, will Elise finally get her own happily-ever-after with one of the Hammond brothers?

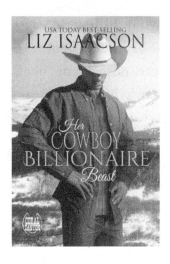

Her Cowboy Billionaire Beast (Book 4): A cowboy billionaire beast, his new manager, and the Christmas traditions that soften his heart and bring them together.

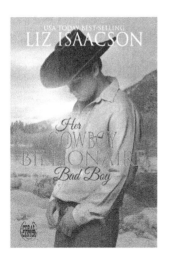

Her Cowboy Billionaire Bad Boy (Book 5): A cowboy billionaire cop who's a stickler for rules, the woman he pulls over when he's not even on duty, and the personal mandates he has to break to keep her in his life...

Books in the Christmas in Coral Canyon Romance series

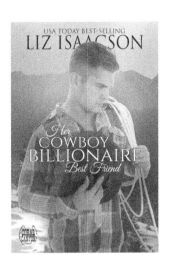

Her Cowboy Billionaire Best Friend (Book 1): Graham Whittaker returns to Coral Canyon a few days after Christmas—after the death of his father. He takes over the energy company his dad built from the ground up and buys a high-end lodge to live in—only a mile from the home of his once-best friend, Laney McAllister. They were best friends once, but Laney's always entertained feelings for him, and spending so much time with him while they make Christmas memories puts her heart in danger of getting broken again...

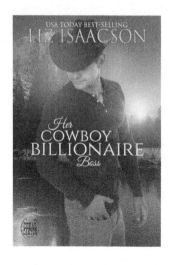

Her Cowboy Billionaire Boss (Book 2): Since the death of his wife a few years ago, Eli Whittaker has been running from one job to another, unable to find somewhere for him and his son to settle. Meg Palmer is Stockton's nanny, and she comes with her boss, Eli, to the lodge, her long-time crush on the man no different in Wyoming than it was on the beach. When she confesses her feelings for him and gets nothing in return, she's crushed, embarrassed, and unsure if she can stay in Coral Canyon for Christmas. Then Eli starts to show some feelings for her too...

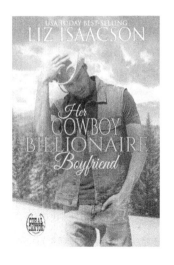

Her Cowboy Billionaire Boyfriend (Book 3): Andrew Whittaker is the public face for the Whittaker Brothers' family energy company, and with his older brother's robot about to be announced, he needs a press secretary to help him get everything ready and tour the state to make the announcements. When he's hit by a protest sign being carried by the company's biggest opponent, Rebecca Collings, he learns with a few clicks that she has the background they need. He offers her the job of press secretary when she thought she was going to be arrested, and not only because the spark between them in so hot Andrew can't see straight.

Can Becca and Andrew work together and keep their relationship a secret? Or will hearts break in this classic romance retelling reminiscent of _Two Weeks Notice_?

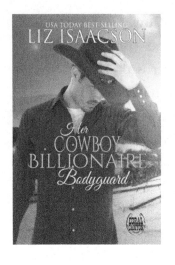

Her Cowboy Billionaire Bodyguard (Book 4): Beau Whittaker has watched his brothers find love one by one, but every attempt he's made has ended in disaster. Lily Everett has been in the spotlight since childhood and has half a dozen platinum records with her two sisters. She's taking a break from the brutal music industry and hiding out in Wyoming while her ex-husband continues to cause trouble for her. When she hears of Beau Whittaker and what he offers his clients, she wants to meet him. Beau is instantly attracted to Lily, but he tried a relationship with his last client that left a scar that still hasn't healed...

Can Lily use the spirit of Christmas to discover what matters most? Will Beau open his heart to the possibility of love with someone so different from him?

Her Cowboy Billionaire Bull Rider (Book 5): Todd Christopherson has just retired from the professional rodeo circuit and returned to his hometown of Coral Canyon. Problem is, he's got no family there anymore, no land, and no job. Not that he needs a job--he's got plenty of money from his illustrious career riding bulls.

Then Todd gets thrown during a routine horseback ride up the canyon, and his only support as he recovers physically is the beautiful Violet Everett. She's no nurse, but she does the best she can for the handsome cowboy. **Will she lose her heart to the billionaire bull rider? Can Todd trust that God led him to Coral Canyon...and Vi?**

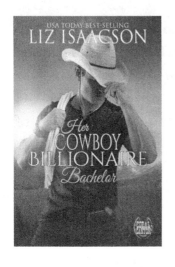

Her Cowboy Billionaire Bachelor (Book 6): Rose Everett isn't sure what to do with her life now that her country music career is on hold. After all, with both of her sisters in Coral Canyon, and one about to have a baby, they're not making albums anymore.

Liam Murphy has been working for Doctors Without Borders, but he's back in the US now, and looking to start a new clinic in Coral Canyon, where he spent his summers.

When Rose wins a date with Liam in a bachelor auction, their relationship blooms and grows quickly. **Can Liam and Rose find a solution to their problems that doesn't involve one of them leaving Coral Canyon with a broken heart?**

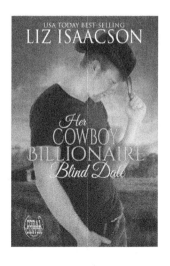

Her Cowboy Billionaire Blind Date (Book 7): Her sons want her to be happy, but she's too old to be set up on a blind date...isn't she?

Amanda Whittaker has been looking for a second chance at love since the death of her husband several years ago. Finley Barber is a cowboy in every sense of the word. Born and raised on a racehorse farm in Kentucky, he's since moved to Dog Valley and started his own breeding stable for champion horses. He hasn't dated in years, and everything about Amanda makes him nervous.

Will Amanda take the leap of faith required to be with Finn? Or will he become just another boyfriend who doesn't make the cut?

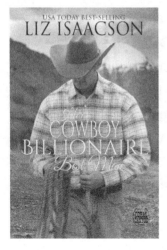

Her Cowboy Billionaire Best Man (Book 8): When Celia Abbott-Armstrong runs into a gorgeous cowboy at her best friend's wedding, she decides she's ready to start dating again.

But the cowboy is Zach Zuckerman, and the Zuckermans and Abbotts have been at war for generations.

Can Zach and Celia find a way to reconcile their family's differences so they can have a future together?

Books in the Three Rivers Ranch Romance series:

Second Chance Ranch: A Three Rivers Ranch Romance (Book 1): After his deployment, injured and discharged Major Squire Ackerman returns to Three Rivers Ranch, wanting to forgive Kelly for ignoring him a decade ago. He'd like to provide the stable life she needs, but with old wounds opening and a ranch on the brink of financial collapse, it will take patience and faith to make their second chance possible.

Third Time's the Charm: A Three Rivers Ranch Romance (Book 2): First Lieutenant Peter Marshall has a truckload of debt and no way to provide for a family, but Chelsea helps him see past all the obstacles, all the scars. With so many unknowns, can Pete and Chelsea develop the love, acceptance, and faith needed to find their happily ever after?

Fourth and Long: A Three Rivers Ranch Romance (Book 3): Commander Brett Murphy goes to Three Rivers Ranch to find some rest and relaxation with his Army buddies. Having his ex-wife show up with a seven-year-old she claims is his son is anything but the R&R he craves. Kate needs to make amends, and Brett needs to find forgiveness, but are they too late to find their happily ever after?

Fifth Generation Cowboy: A Three Rivers Ranch Romance (Book 4): Tom Lovell has watched his friends find their true happiness on Three Rivers Ranch, but everywhere he looks, he only sees friends. Rose Reyes has been bringing her daughter out to the ranch for equine therapy for months, but it doesn't seem to be working. Her challenges with Mari are just as frustrating as ever. Could Tom be exactly what Rose needs? Can he remove his friendship blinders and find love with someone who's been right in front of him all this time?

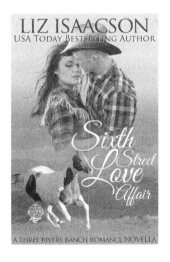

Sixth Street Love Affair: A Three Rivers Ranch Romance (Book 5): After losing his wife a few years back, Garth Ahlstrom thinks he's ready for a second chance at love. But Juliette Thompson has a secret that could destroy their budding relationship. Can they find the strength, patience, and faith to make things work?

The Seventh Sergeant: A Three Rivers Ranch Romance (Book 6): Life has finally started to settle down for Sergeant Reese Sanders after his devastating injury overseas. Discharged from the Army and now with a good job at Courage Reins, he's finally found happiness—until a horrific fall puts him right back where he was years ago: Injured and depressed. Carly Watters, Reese's new veteran care coordinator, dislikes small towns almost as much as she loathes cowboys. But she finds herself faced with both when she gets assigned to Reese's case. Do they have the humility and faith to make their relationship more than professional?

Eight Second Ride: A Three Rivers Ranch Romance (Book 7): Ethan Greene loves his work at Three Rivers Ranch, but he can't seem to find the right woman to settle down with. When sassy yet vulnerable Brynn Bowman shows up at the ranch to recruit him back to the rodeo circuit, he takes a different approach with the barrel racing champion. His patience and newfound faith pay off when a friendship--and more--starts with Brynn. But she wants out of the rodeo circuit right when Ethan wants to rejoin. Can they find the path God wants them to take and still stay together?

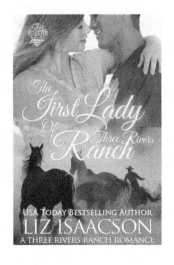

The First Lady of Three Rivers Ranch: A Three Rivers Ranch Romance (Book 8): Heidi Duffin has been dreaming about opening her own bakery since she was thirteen years old. She scrimped and saved for years to afford baking and pastry school in San Francisco. And now she only has one year left before she's a certified pastry chef. Frank Ackerman's father has recently retired, and he's taken over the largest cattle ranch in the Texas Panhandle. A horseman through and through, he's also nearing thirty-one and looking for someone to bring love and joy to a homestead that's been dominated by men for a decade. But when he convinces Heidi to come clean the cowboy cabins, she changes all that. But the siren's call of a bakery is still loud in Heidi's ears, even if she's also seeing a future with Frank. Can she rely on her faith in ways she's never had to before or will their relationship end when summer does?

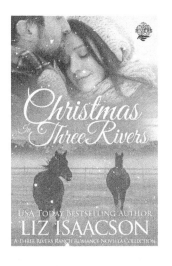

Christmas in Three Rivers: A Three Rivers Ranch Romance (Book 9): Isn't Christmas the best time to fall in love? The cowboys of Three Rivers Ranch think so. Join four of them as they journey toward their path to happily ever after in four, all-new novellas in the Amazon #1 Bestselling Three Rivers Ranch Romance series.

THE NINTH INNING: The Christmas season has never felt like such a burden to boutique owner Andrea Larsen. But with Mama gone and the holidays upon her, Andy finds herself wishing she hadn't been so quick to judge her former boyfriend, cowboy Lawrence Collins. Well, Lawrence hasn't forgotten about Andy either, and he devises a plan to get her out to the ranch so they can reconnect. Do they have the faith and humility to patch things up and start a new relationship?

TEN DAYS IN TOWN: Sandy Keller is tired of the dating scene in Three Rivers. Though she owns the pancake house, she's looking for a fresh start, which means an escape from the town where she grew up. When her older brother's best friend, Tad Jorgensen, comes to town for the holidays, it is a balm to his weary soul. A helicopter tour guide who experienced a near-death experience, he's looking to start over too--

but in Three Rivers. Can Sandy and Tad navigate their troubles to find the path God wants them to take--and discover true love--in only ten days?

ELEVEN YEAR REUNION: Pastry chef extraordinaire, Grace Lewis has moved to Three Rivers to help Heidi Ackerman open a bakery in Three Rivers. Grace relishes the idea of starting over in a town where no one knows about her failed cupcakery. She doesn't expect to run into her old high school boyfriend, Jonathan Carver. A carpenter working at Three Rivers Ranch, Jon's in town against his will. But with Grace now on the scene, Jon's thinking life in Three Rivers is suddenly looking up. But with her focus on baking and his disdain for small towns, can they make their eleven year reunion stick?

THE TWELFTH TOWN: Newscaster Taryn Tucker has had enough of life on-screen. She's bounced from town to town before arriving in Three Rivers, completely alone and completely anonymous--just the way she now likes it. She takes a job cleaning at Three Rivers Ranch, hoping for a chance to figure out who she is and where God wants her. When she meets happy-go-lucky cowhand Kenny Stockton, she doesn't expect sparks to fly. Kenny's always been "the best friend" for his female friends, but the pull between him and Taryn can't be denied. Will they have the courage and faith necessary to make their opposite worlds mesh?

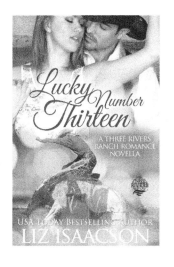

Lucky Number Thirteen: A Three Rivers Ranch Romance (Book 10): Tanner Wolf, a rodeo champion ten times over, is excited to be riding in Three Rivers for the first time since he left his philandering ways and found religion. Seeing his old friends Ethan and Brynn is therapuetic--until a terrible accident lands him in the hospital. With his rodeo career over, Tanner thinks maybe he'll stay in town--and it's not just because his nurse, Summer Hamblin, is the prettiest woman he's ever met. But Summer's the queen of first dates, and as she looks for a way to make a relationship with the transient rodeo star work Summer's not sure she has the fortitude to go on a second date. Can they find love among the tragedy?

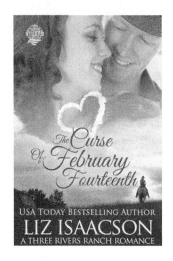

The Curse of February Fourteenth: A Three Rivers Ranch Romance (Book 11): Cal Hodgkins, cowboy veterinarian at Bowman's Breeds, isn't planning to meet anyone at the masked dance in small-town Three Rivers. He just wants to get his bachelor friends off his back and sit on the sidelines to drink his punch. But when he sees a woman dressed in gorgeous butterfly wings and cowgirl boots with blue stitching, he's smitten. Too bad she runs away from the dance before he can get her name, leaving only her boot behind...

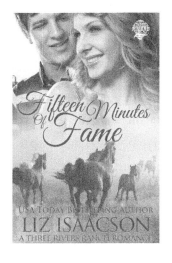

Fifteen Minutes of Fame: A Three Rivers Ranch Romance (Book 12): Navy Richards is thirty-five years of tired—tired of dating the same men, working a demanding job, and getting her heart broken over and over again. Her aunt has always spoken highly of the matchmaker in Three Rivers, Texas, so she takes a six-month sabbatical from her high-stress job as a pediatric nurse, hops on a bus, and meets with the matchmaker. Then she meets Gavin Redd. He's handsome, he's hardworking, and he's a cowboy. But is he an Aquarius too? Navy's not making a move until she knows for sure...

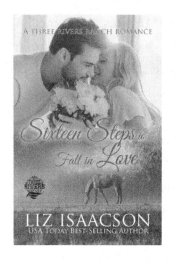

Sixteen Steps to Fall in Love: A Three Rivers Ranch Romance (Book 13): A chance encounter at a dog park sheds new light on the tall, talented Boone that Nicole can't ignore. As they get to know each other better and start to dig into each other's past, Nicole is the one who wants to run. This time from her growing admiration and attachment to Boone. From her aging parents. From herself.

But Boone feels the attraction between them too, and he decides he's tired of running and ready to make Three Rivers his permanent home. **Can Boone and Nicole use their faith to overcome their differences and find a happily-ever-after together?**

The Sleigh on Seventeenth Street: A Three Rivers Ranch Romance (Book 14): A cowboy with skills as an electrician tries a relationship with a down-on-her luck plumber. Can Dylan and Camila make water and electricity play nicely together this Christmas season? Or will they get shocked as they try to make their relationship work?

Books in the Last Chance Ranch Romance series

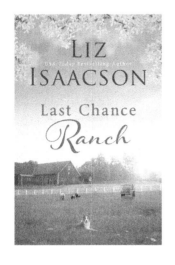

Last Chance Ranch (Book 1): A cowgirl down on her luck hires a man who's good with horses and under the hood of a car. Can Hudson fine tune Scarlett's heart as they work together? Or will things backfire and make everything worse at Last Chance Ranch?

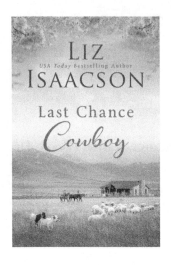

Last Chance Cowboy (Book 2): A billionaire cowboy without a home meets a woman who secretly makes food videos to pay her debts...Can Carson and Adele do more than fight in the kitchens at Last Chance Ranch?

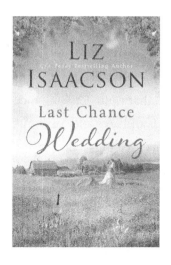

Last Chance Wedding (Book 3): A female carpenter needs a husband just for a few days... Can Jeri and Sawyer navigate the minefield of a pretend marriage before their feelings become real?

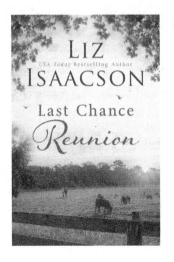

Last Chance Reunion (Book 4): An Army cowboy, the woman he dated years ago, and their last chance at Last Chance Ranch... Can Dave and Sissy put aside hurt feelings and make their second chance romance work?

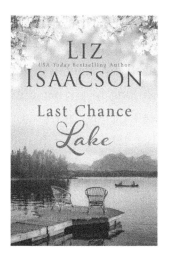

Last Chance Lake (Book 5): A former dairy farmer and the marketing director on the ranch have to work together to make the cow cuddling program a success. But can Karla let Cache into her life? Or will she keep all her secrets from him - and keep *him* a secret too?

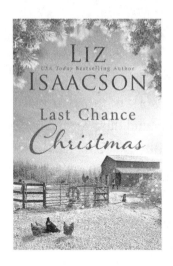

Last Chance Christmas (Book 6): She's tired of having her heart broken by cowboys. He waited too long to ask her out. Can Lance fix things quickly, or will Amber leave Last Chance Ranch before he can tell her how he feels?

Books in the Steeple Ridge Romance Series:

Her Billionaire Cowboy (Book 1): Tucker Jenkins has had enough of tall buildings, traffic, and has traded in his technology firm in New York City for Steeple Ridge Horse Farm in rural Vermont. Missy Marino has worked at the farm since she was a teen, and she's always dreamed of owning it. But her ex-husband left her with a truckload of debt, making her fantasies of owning the farm unfulfilled. Tucker didn't come to the country to find a new wife, but he supposes a woman could help him start over in Steeple Ridge. Will Tucker and Missy be able to navigate the shaky ground between them to find a new beginning?

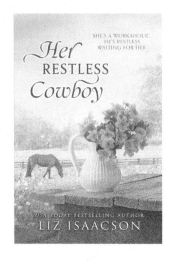

Her Restless Cowboy: A Butters Brothers Novel, Steeple Ridge Romance (Book 2): Ben Buttars is the youngest of the four Buttars brothers who come to Steeple Ridge Farm, and he finally feels like he's landed somewhere he can make a life for himself. Reagan Cantwell is a decade older than Ben and the recreational direction for the town of Island Park. Though Ben is young, he knows what he wants—and that's Rae. Can she figure out how to put what matters most in her life—family and faith—above her job before she loses Ben?

Her Faithful Cowboy: A Butters Brothers Novel, Steeple Ridge Romance (Book 3): Sam Buttars has spent the last decade making sure he and his brothers stay together. They've been at Steeple Ridge for a while now, but with the youngest married and happy, the siren's call to return to his parents' farm in Wyoming is loud in Sam's ears. He'd just go if it weren't for beautiful Bonnie Sherman, who roped his heart the first time he saw her. Do Sam and Bonnie have the faith to find comfort in each other instead of in the people who've already passed?

Her Mistletoe Cowboy: A Butters Brothers Novel, Steeple Ridge Romance (Book 4): Logan Buttars has always been good-natured and happy-go-lucky. After watching two of his brothers settle down, he recognizes a void in his life he didn't know about. Veterinarian Layla Guyman has appreciated Logan's friendship and easy way with animals when he comes into the clinic to get the service dogs. But with his future at Steeple Ridge in the balance, she's not sure a relationship with him is worth the risk. Can she rely on her faith and employ patience to tame Logan's wild heart?

Her Patient Cowboy: A Butters Brothers Novel, Steeple Ridge Romance (Book 5): Darren Buttars is cool, collected, and quiet—and utterly devastated when his girlfriend of nine months, Farrah Irvine, breaks up with him because he wanted her to ride her horse in a parade. But Farrah doesn't ride anymore, a fact she made very clear to Darren. She returned to her childhood home with so much baggage, she doesn't know where to start with the unpacking. Darren's the only Buttars brother who isn't married, and he wants to make Island Park his permanent home—with Farrah. Can they find their way through the heartache to achieve a happily-ever-after together?

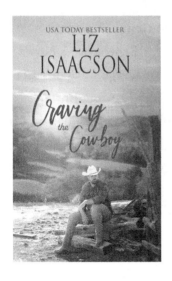

Craving the Cowboy (Book 1): Dwayne Carver is set to inherit his family's ranch in the heart of Texas Hill Country, and in order to keep up with his ranch duties and fulfill his dreams of owning a horse farm, he hires top trainer Felicity Lightburne. They get along great, and she can envision herself on this new farm—at least until her mother falls ill and she has to return to help her. Can Dwayne and Felicity work through their differences to find their happily-ever-after?

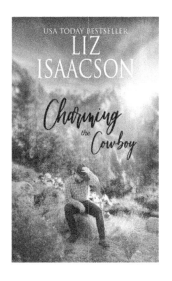

Charming the Cowboy (Book 2): Third grade teacher Heather Carver has had her eye on Levi Rhodes for a couple of years now, but he seems to be blind to her attempts to charm him. When she breaks her arm while on his horse ranch, Heather infiltrates Levi's life in ways he's never thought of, and his strict anti-female stance slips. Will Heather heal his emotional scars and he care for her physical ones so they can have a real relationship?

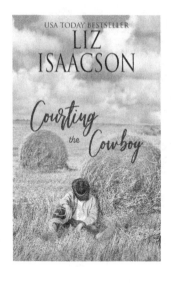

Courting the Cowboy (Book 3): Frustrated with the cowboy-only dating scene in Grape Seed Falls, May Sotheby joins Texas-Faithful.com, hoping to find her soul mate without having to relocate--or deal with cowboy hats and boots. She has no idea that Kurt Pemberton, foreman at Grape Seed Ranch, is the man she starts communicating with... Will May be able to follow her heart and get Kurt to forgive her so they can be together?

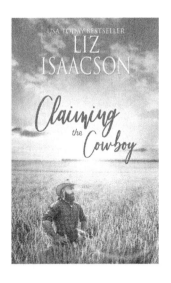

Claiming the Cowboy, Royal Brothers Book 1 (Grape Seed Falls Romance Book 4): Unwilling to be tied down, farrier Robin Cook has managed to pack her entire life into a two-hundred-and-eighty square-foot house, and that includes her Yorkie. Cowboy and co-foreman, Shane Royal has had his heart set on Robin for three years, even though she flat-out turned him down the last time he asked her to dinner. But she's back at Grape Seed Ranch for five weeks as she works her horseshoeing magic, and he's still interested, despite a bitter life lesson that left a bad taste for marriage in his mouth.

Robin's interested in him too. But can she find room for Shane in her tiny house--and can he take a chance on her with his tired heart?

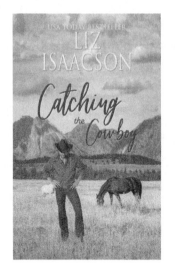

Catching the Cowboy, Royal Brothers Book 2 (Grape Seed Falls Romance Book 5): Dylan Royal is good at two things: whistling and caring for cattle. When his cows are being attacked by an unknown wild animal, he calls Texas Parks & Wildlife for help. He wasn't expecting a beautiful mammologist to show up, all flirty and fun and everything Dylan didn't know he wanted in his life.

Hazel Brewster has gone on more first dates than anyone in Grape Seed Falls, and she thinks maybe Dylan deserves a second... Can they find their way through wild animals, huge life changes, and their emotional pasts to find their forever future?

Cheering the Cowboy, Royal Brothers Book 3 (Grape Seed Falls Romance Book 6): Austin Royal loves his life on his new ranch with his brothers. But he doesn't love that Shayleigh Hatch came with the property, nor that he has to take the blame for the fact that he now owns her childhood ranch. They rarely have a conversation that doesn't leave him furious and frustrated--and yet he's still attracted to Shay in a strange, new way.

Shay inexplicably likes him too, which utterly confuses and angers her. As they work to make this Christmas the best the Triple Towers Ranch has ever seen, can they also navigate through their rocky relationship to smoother waters?

Praise for Liz Isaacson

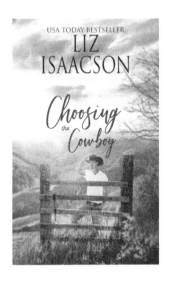

Choosing the Cowboy (Book 7): With financial trouble and personal issues around every corner, can Maggie Duffin and Chase Carver rely on their faith to find their happily-ever-after?

A spinoff from the #1 bestselling Three Rivers Ranch Romance novels, also by USA Today bestselling author Liz Isaacson.

Books in the Horseshoe Home Ranch Romance Series:

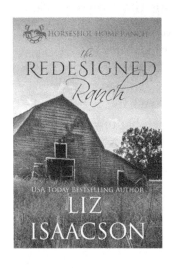

The Redesigned Ranch (Book 1): Jace Lovell only has one thing left after his fiancé abandons him at the altar: his job at Horseshoe Home Ranch. Belle Edmunds is back in Gold Valley and she's desperate to build a portfolio that she can use to start her own firm in Montana. Jace isn't anywhere near forgiving his fiancé, and he's not sure he's ready for a new relationship with someone as fiery and beautiful as Belle. Can she employ her patience while he figures out how to forgive so they can find their own brand of happily-ever-after?

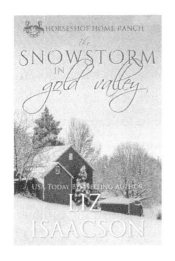

The Snowstorm in Gold Valley (Book 2): Professional snowboarder Sterling Maughan has sequestered himself in his family's cabin in the exclusive mountain community above Gold Valley, Montana after a devastating fall that ended his career. Norah Watson cleans Sterling's cabin and the more time they spend together, the more Sterling is interested in all things Norah. As his body heals, so does his faith. Will Norah be able to trust Sterling so they can have a chance at true love?

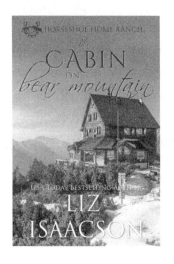

The Cabin on Bear Mountain (Book 3): Landon Edmunds has been a cowboy his whole life. An accident five years ago ended his successful rodeo career, and now he's looking to start a horse ranch--and he's looking outside of Montana. Which would be great if God hadn't brought Megan Palmer back to Gold Valley right when Landon is looking to leave. Megan and Landon work together well, and as sparks fly, she's sure God brought her back to Gold Valley so she could find her happily ever after. Through serious discussion and prayer, can Landon and Megan find their future together?

Be sure to check out the spinoff series, the Brush Creek Brides romances after you read FALLING FOR HIS BEST FRIEND. Start with A WEDDING FOR THE WIDOWER.

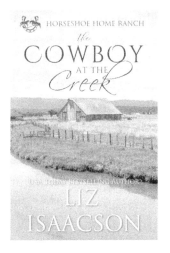

The Cowboy at the Creek (Book 4): Twelve years ago, Owen Carr left Gold Valley—and his long-time girlfriend—in favor of a country music career in Nashville. Married and divorced, Natalie teaches ballet at the dance studio in Gold Valley, but she never auditioned for the professional company the way she dreamed of doing. With Owen back, she realizes all the opportunities she missed out on when he left all those years ago—including a future with him. Can they mend broken bridges in order to have a second chance at love?

The Wedding in the Winter (Book 5): Caleb Chamberlain has spent the last five years recovering from a horrible breakup, his alcoholism that stemmed from it, and the car accident that left him hospitalized. He's finally on the right track in his life—until Holly Gray, his twin brother's ex-fiance mistakes him for Nathan.

Holly's back in Gold Valley to get the required veterinarian hours to apply for her graduate program. When the herd at Horseshoe Home comes down with pneumonia, Caleb and Holly are forced to work together in close quarters. Holly's over Nathan, but she hasn't forgiven him—or the woman she believes broke up their relationship. Can Caleb and Holly navigate such a rough past to find their happily-ever-after?

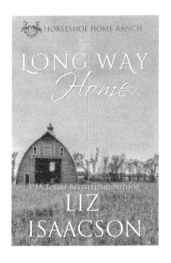

The Long Way Home (Book 6): Ty Barker has been dancing through the last thirty years of his life--and he's suddenly realized he's alone. River Lee Whitely is back in Gold Valley with her two little girls after a divorce that's left deep scars. She has a job at Silver Creek that requires her to be able to ride a horse, and she nearly tramples Ty at her first lesson. That's just fine by him, because River Lee is the girl Ty has never gotten over. Ty realizes River Lee needs time to settle into her new job, her new home, her new life as a single parent, but going slow has never been his style. But for River Lee, can Ty take the necessary steps to keep her in his life?

Christmas at the Ranch (Book 7): Archer Bailey has already lost one job to Emersyn Enders, so he deliberately doesn't tell her about the cowhand job up at Horseshoe Home Ranch. Emery's temporary job is ending, but her obligations to her physically disabled sister aren't. As Archer and Emery work together, its clear that the sparks flying between them aren't all from their friendly competition over a job. Will Emery and Archer be able to navigate the ranch, their close quarters, and their individual circumstances to find love this holiday season?

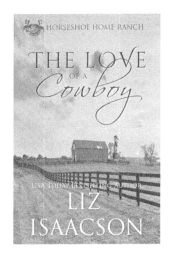

The Love of a Cowboy (Book 8): Cowboy Elliott Hawthorne has just lost his best friend and cabin mate to the worst thing imaginable—marriage. When his brother calls about an accident with their father, Elliott rushes down to Gold Valley from the ranch only to be met with the most beautiful woman he's ever seen. His father's new physical therapist, London Marsh, likes the handsome face and gentle spirit she sees in Elliott too. Can Elliott and London navigate difficult family situations to find a happily-ever-after?

Books in the Brush Creek Cowboy Romance Series:

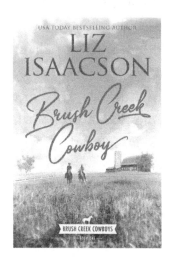

Brush Creek Cowboy (Book 1): Former rodeo champion and cowboy Walker Thompson trains horses at Brush Creek Horse Ranch, where he lives a simple life in his cabin with his ten-year-old son. A widower of six years, he's worked with Tess Wagner, a widow who came to Brush Creek to escape the turmoil of her life to give her seven-year-old son a slower pace of life. But Tess's breast cancer is back...

Walker will have to decide if he'd rather spend even a short time with Tess than not have her in his life at all. Tess wants to feel God's love and power, but can she discover and accept God's will in order to find her happy ending?

The Cowboy's Challenge (Book 2): Cowboy and professional roper Justin Jackman has found solitude at Brush Creek Horse Ranch, preferring his time with the animals he trains over dating. With two failed engagements in his past, he's not really interested in getting his heart stomped on again. But when flirty and fun Renee Martin picks him up at a church ice cream bar--on a bet, no less--he finds himself more than just a little interested. His Gen-X attitudes are attractive to her; her Millennial behaviors drive him nuts. Can Justin look past their differences and take a chance on another engagement?

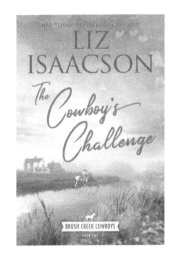

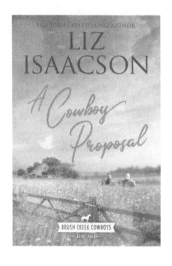

A Cowboy Proposal (Book 3): Ted Caldwell has been a retired bronc rider for years, and he thought he was perfectly happy training horses to buck at Brush Creek Ranch. He was wrong. When he meets April Nox, who comes to the ranch to hide her pregnancy from all her friends back in Jackson Hole, Ted realizes he has a huge family-shaped hole in his life. April is embarrassed, heartbroken, and trying to find her extinguished faith. She's never ridden a horse and wants nothing to do with a cowboy ever again. Can Ted and April create a family of happiness and love from a tragedy?

A New Family for the Cowboy (Book 4): Blake Gibbons oversees all the agriculture at Brush Creek Horse Ranch, sometimes moonlighting as a general contractor. When he meets Erin Shields, new in town, at her aunt's bakery, he's instantly smitten. Erin moved to Brush Creek after a divorce that left her penniless, 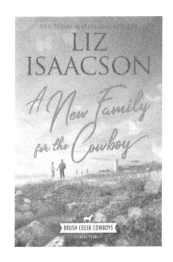 homeless, and a single mother of three children under age eight. She's nowhere near ready to start dating again, but the longer Blake hangs around the bakery, the more she starts to like him. Can Blake and Erin find a way to blend their lifestyles and become a family?

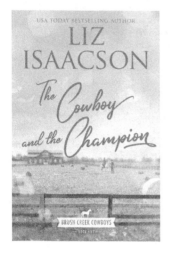

The Cowboy and the Champion (Book 5): Emmett Graves has always had a positive outlook on life. He adores training horses to become barrel racing champions during the day and cuddling with his cat at night. Fresh off her professional rodeo retirement, Molly Brady comes to Brush Creek Horse Ranch as Emmett's protege. He's not thrilled, and she's allergic to cats. Oh, and she'd like to stay cowboy-free, thank you very much. But Emmett's about as cowboy as they come.... Can Emmett and Molly work together without falling in love?

Schooled by the Cowboy (Book 6): Grant Ford spends his days training cattle—when he's not camped out at the elementary school hoping to catch a glimpse of his ex-girlfriend. When principal Shannon Sharpe confronts him and asks him to stay away from the school, the spark between them is instant and hot. Shannon's

expecting a transfer very soon, but she also needs a summer outdoor coordinator—and Grant fits the bill. Just because he's handsome and everything Shannon's ever wanted in a cowboy husband means nothing. Will Grant and Shannon be able to survive the summer or will the Utah heat be too much for them to handle?

Books in the Fuller Family Romance Series:

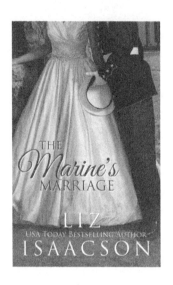

The Marine's Marriage: A Fuller Family Novel - Brush Creek Brides Romance (Book 1): Tate Benson can't believe he's come to Nowhere, Utah, to fix up a house that hasn't been inhabited in years. But he has. Because he's retired from the Marines and looking to start a life as a police officer in small-town Brush Creek. Wren Fuller has her hands full most days running her family's company. When Tate calls and demands a maid for that morning, she decides to have the calls forwarded to her cell and go help him out. She didn't know he was moving in next door, and she's completely unprepared for his handsomeness, his kind heart, and his wounded soul.Can Tate and Wren weather a relationship when they're also next-door neighbors?

The Firefighter's Fiancé: A Fuller Family Novel - Brush Creek Brides Romance (Book 2): Cora Wesley comes to Brush Creek, hoping to get some in-the-wild firefighting training as she prepares to put in her application to be a hotshot. When she meets Brennan Fuller, the spark between them is hot and instant. As they get to know each other, her deadline is 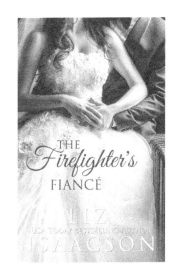 constantly looming over them, and Brennan starts to wonder if he can break ranks in the family business. He's okay mowing lawns and hanging out with his brothers, but he dreams of being able to go to college and become a landscape architect, but he's just not sure it can be done. Will Cora and Brennan be able to endure their trials to find true love?

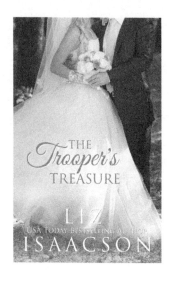

The Trooper's Treasure: A Fuller Family Novel - Brush Creek Brides Romance (Book 3): Dawn Fuller has made some mistakes in her life, and she's not proud of the way McDermott Boyd found her off the road one day last year. She's spent a hard year wrestling with her choices and trying to fix them, glad for McDermott's acceptance and friendship. He lost his wife years ago, done his best with his daughter, and now he's ready to move on. Can McDermott help Dawn find a way past her former mistakes and down a path that leads to love, family, and happiness?

The Detective's Date: A Fuller Family Novel - Brush Creek Brides Romance (Book 4): Dahlia Reid is one of the best detectives Brush Creek and the surrounding towns has ever had. She's given up on the idea of marriage—and pleasing her mother—and has dedicated herself fully to her job. Which is great, since one of the most perplexing cases of her career has 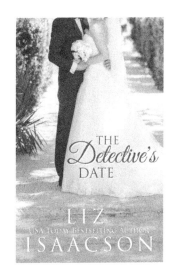 come to town. Kyler Fuller thinks he's finally ready to move past the woman who ghosted him years ago. He's cut his hair, and he's ready to start dating. Too bad every woman he's been out with is about as interesting as a lamppost—until Dahlia. He finds her beautiful, her quick wit a breath of fresh air, and her intelligence sexy. Can Kyler and Dahlia use their faith to find a way through the obstacles threatening to keep them apart?

THE
Paramedic's
PARTNER

LIZ
USA TODAY BESTSELLING AUTHOR
ISAACSON

The Paramedic's Partner: A Fuller Family Novel - Brush Creek Brides Romance (Book 5): Jazzy Fuller has always been overshadowed by her prettier, more popular twin, Fabiana. Fabi meets paramedic Max Robinson at the park and sets a date with him only to come down with the flu. So she convinces Jazzy to cut her hair and take her place on the date. And the spark between Jazzy and Max is hot and instant...if only he knew she wasn't her sister, Fabi.

Max drives the ambulance for the town of Brush Creek with is partner Ed Moon, and neither of them have been all that lucky in love. Until Max suggests to who he thinks is Fabi that they should double with Ed and Jazzy. They do, and Fabi is smitten with the steady, strong Ed Moon. As each twin falls further and further in love with their respective paramedic, it becomes obvious they'll need to come clean about the switcheroo sooner rather than later...or risk losing their hearts.

The Chief's Catch: A Fuller Family Novel - Brush Creek Brides Romance (Book 6): Berlin Fuller has struck out with the dating scene in Brush Creek more times than she cares to admit. When she makes a deal with her friends that they can choose the next man she goes out with, she didn't dream they'd pick surly Cole Fairbanks, the new Chief of Police.

His friends call him the Beast and challenge him to complete ten dates that summer or give up his bonus check. When Berlin approaches him, stuttering about the deal with her friends and claiming they don't actually have to go out, he's intrigued. As the summer passes, Cole finds himself burning both ends of the candle to keep up with his job and his new relationship. When he unleashes the Beast one time too many, Berlin will have to decide if she can tame him or if she should walk away.

About Liz

Liz Isaacson writes inspirational romance, usually set in Texas, or Wyoming, or anywhere else horses and cowboys exist. She lives in Utah, where she writes full-time, takes her two dogs to the park everyday, and eats a lot of veggies while writing. Find her on her website at feelgoodfiction-books.com

Made in United States
Orlando, FL
28 July 2024

49642891R00382